JILLIAN HUNTER

FAIRY TALE

POCKET BOOKS
New York   London   Toronto   Sydney

This book is a work of fiction. Names, characters, places and incidents are products of the author's imagination or are used fictitiously. Any resemblance to actual events or locales or persons living or dead is entirely coincidental.

An *Original* Publication of POCKET BOOKS

POCKET BOOKS, a division of Simon & Schuster, Inc.
1230 Avenue of the Americas, New York, NY 10020

ISBN-13: 978-0-671-00157-5
ISBN-10:   0-671-00157-4

First Pocket Books printing April 1997

10   9   8   7   6   5   4   3

POCKET and colophon are registered trademarks of
Simon & Schuster, Inc.

Front cover: Lettering by David Gatti. Illustration by Jon Paul.

Manufactured in the United States of America

For information regarding special discounts for bulk purchases,
please contact Simon & Schuster Special Sales at 1-800-456-6798
or business@simonandschuster.com.

Chapter

1

The Scottish Highlands
1723

It was the first time in his life that Duncan MacElgin had been ambushed and undressed by a female—as a hostile act.

One minute he could hear the thin wailing of pipes and the bloodthirsty MacElgin war cry rising from the hills, the next he was flat on his back with his breeches pulled down around his ankles.

The shock of it had stopped his reflexes cold.

He had expected any number of things from his homecoming. Rowan crosses nailed hastily to the cottage doors he passed. Hounds baying from the hilltops to warn of his approach. Children and old women running hysterically at the sight of him, Bibles clutched to their chests. Still, he hadn't expected to be dragged off his horse and stripped mother-naked by the unruly Highlanders who by Celtic law owed him their respect, if not their worthless lives.

Above all, he had not expected a girl to be supervising his ambush like a damned French field marshal on the front lines. The hellion had stirred his men into a frenzy. Glaring hard at the dainty hooded figure bellowing out orders on horseback, he vowed he would deal with her the moment he had finished fighting.

The incredible half-wits tried to tar and feather him next.

With no less a degrading substance than chicken feathers and smelly peat sludge. He kicked one man in the groin and hurled another over his shoulders before lunging to his feet to examine the damage done to his person. Pungent black sludge dripped down his forearms, into his leather gloves. Plucked hen's pinfeathers protruded limply from the crook of one elbow.

Self-contempt darkened his fiercely sculpted face. Naked, humiliated, fighting for his life—why had he nurtured the pathetic hope that anything had changed?

A husky gnome of a man with a long grizzled red beard and bandy legs tossed Duncan's boots into the stagnant water of a tarn. Chuckles of approval arose from the scruffy band of clansmen planted at strategic angles on the crag that overshadowed the pass. The dulcet tones of sweet feminine laughter rang incongruously in the robust gales of male amusement.

Duncan's temper erupted in earnest then, a horrible thing to behold; his pride and dignity had been stripped as bare as his body. The boots were expensive Russian leather, his other clothes wouldn't arrive for days, and the damned woman thought it was a joke. Oblivious to his nakedness, he leaped over a line of low boulders and shoved away the two Highlanders who charged at him as a giant would a pair of gnats.

"Who," he roared into the sudden quiet that had fallen at his show of brute strength, "*who* is responsible for this outrage?"

Something in the thunderous range of voice he usually reserved for the battlefield obviously communicated authority to his ambushers. The seven Highlanders on horseback gaped at him in varying degrees of awestruck curiosity and the beginnings of a healthy fear. The two men at his feet wisely scrambled around him to take refuge on higher ground.

Fury dilated every blood vessel of Duncan's body, numbing him to the caress of the pleasant June breeze on his skin, to the fact that he stood stark naked (except for his black leather gloves) before this band of his pathetic clansmen. There. He took a breath of savage satisfaction. That had gotten their attention. It was what Duncan did best: Giving orders. Frightening the hell out of people.

"Lachlan MacElgin," he shouted at the stocky man perched like a careworn buzzard directly above him on the crag, "do you have any notion in that hollow turnip of a head who you have just assaulted?"

The man named Lachlan swallowed uneasily at being singled out, while the mounted men who flanked him broke into a flurry of speculative muttering. "How do ye know me?" Lachlan demanded when he could squeeze the words through his constricted vocal cords. "Who are ye then?"

"Who am I?" Duncan repeated the question with a nasty smirk that promised vengeance. He grabbed one of the two men trying to sneak past him by the scruff of his unwashed neck, shaking him like a hare he'd extracted from a hole. "You, Owen, who do *you* think I am?"

Owen blinked his lashless lids, frozen with sheer terror in his tracks. "T-the King of England?" he said, with an ingratiating buck-toothed smile at Duncan in the unlikely event his outlandish guess proved right.

"The King of England?" Duncan gave a low dark laugh that sent chilling prickles of apprehension down the spine of more than one man present. "Do I *look* like the blessed King of England?"

"I dinna ken," Owen ventured timidly, squinting up at Duncan. "'Tis possible, aye, 'tis likely. Ye've the face for it, now that ye ask."

Duncan smiled grimly and released the man, his shoulder-length blue-black hair, loose from its queue, tangling in the breeze. "And was His Majesty expected to come riding into the northern wilds of Scotland this very afternoon as you incredible dunderheads sat waiting to ambush him?"

"We wasn't expectin' to ambush the king," Owen went on, a little more confidently now, since it looked like the naked giant wasn't going to kill him after all. "Ye're the one who brought his name into the conversation."

His lean brown face disgusted, Duncan whipped off the man's faded plaid and attempted to wrap it around his own body. But the threadbare length of tartan had not been woven for his towering frame—he'd as well wrap himself in fig leaves—and in the wretched end he had to make do with covering his important parts. Although he had yet to see her face, he'd sensed that blasted girl's presence while he'd been prancing about like a denuded Hercules dodging thunderbolts. A lesser man would have blushed.

He snatched his sword from the clansmen who'd confiscated it and was holding it in a clumsy grip across the neck of a piebald pony. "Do any of you have the vaguest idea *who* I am?" he demanded of his enrapt audience.

"The Earl o' Hell?" someone suggested half-seriously.

"And if I were the Devil," Duncan said with dangerous softness, "what do you suppose the punishment would be for attacking me?"

A wave of uneasy whispering rippled through the unsightly band, men in tattered trews and coarse worsted plaids slumped on weary-looking ponies. At Duncan's unwavering stare, at the hint of hellfire and damnation he had planted in their minds, they began to edge backward into the mountain pass. Everyone in the Highlands knew that the Earl o'Hell—or Old Hornie, as he was sometimes called—frequently appeared in the guise of a well-endowed and naked young man. The fact that they were the ones who had rendered him naked could be reasonably attributed to his Satanic sense of humor.

Duncan stabbed his sword into the rich red loam at his feet, his voice coldly enraged. "Well, I'm still waiting for an answer. Since not one of you appears to have a clue as to my identity, may I inquire whose crackbrained idea it was to attack an incomer without the least provocation?"

The men had all but faded into the gloomy protection of the overhanging crag. High overhead, in the violet-gold shadows of the summer sky, Duncan caught the lazy circling of a hawk. It did not occur to him then, in his anger, to connect the bird's languid flight with what happened next.

A petite rider on an exquisite Spanish mare picked a path through the Highlanders to confront him. The girl who had shouted the order to ambush him. With her arisaid, an ankle-length blue-purple plaid, pulled up over her head like a hood, Duncan found to his monumental frustration that he could not make out a single feature of her face, which lent her a ludicrous air of mystery. But there was mischief in her demeanor, and she carried herself with a dignified aplomb that belied her fragile appearance.

Duncan narrowed his eyes, his defenses on the alert.

"You're not the king," she announced, so composed he wanted to shake her delicate shoulders. "Everyone kens he has a fat arse and sausage of a nose. You're probably not the Earl of Hell, though I admit one could make the association. Who are you then, to be riding your fancy Sassenach uniform onto MacElgin land?"

Who was he?

Duncan drew another breath, considering how to answer her blessed impertinence. In most of Europe his name had become legend, dubbed the merciless Marquess of Minorca, protégé of the Duke of Marlborough, personal advisor to the Russian czar and Dutch war minister. In the civilized world he was a celebrated military general of the *corps d'elite* Scots Greys horsemen, who had captured Europe's imagination with his brilliant calvary war campaigns and daring rescue of his captured countrymen from a High German citadel only six short months before.

Hell, last month in Holland, hordes of nubile young women had thrown themselves at his carriage and hidden themselves in his apartments, popping out of his wardrobe at all hours like jacks-in-the-boxes.

And now here he stood explaining himself to a girl as hopelessly uncivilized as the savage land that had spawned her.

Here, in this unholy wart on Scotland's rugged northern coast, in a forgotten village squashed between mountain, moor, and sea, he was merely Duncan MacElgin, *Duncan Dubh* as the villagers had once whispered behind his back; Black Duncan, the tall skinny boy believed to have murdered his mother and her husband, the boy whose unofficial banishment by his natural father almost fifteen years before had been met with wholesale relief by the people of MacElgin.

He was also reluctant heir to the chieftainship of Clan MacElgin, and a sorrier excuse for a group of humanity he had never seen in his life.

He strode up to the girl's horse, catching only the gleam of amused gray-green eyes like Scottish mist on the sea before she drew back into the shadows of her hood. A soft laugh escaped her. Self-consciously he glanced downward to make certain his important parts were still covered by the scratchy plaid. The hawk circled lower, a flash of graceful power in Duncan's peripheral vision. Tension gathered in the air like storm clouds. He felt like an utter ass.

"Unfortunately, I am not the Earl of Hell," he drawled, annoyed that he was reduced to explaining himself to this anonymous slip of a thing. "However, the whole miserable lot of you might have been better off if I were. I don't suppose the name *Duncan MacElgin* is going to be met with a chorus of rousing cheers."

He heard the girl's startled intake of breath and wondered vaguely if she were even old enough to remember his black history or had been merely threatened into obedience by a well-meaning parent with tales of Duncan's violent youth. His face tightened as the old taunts resounded in his head. Remembered humiliation burned in his chest.

Dinna walk down the lane after dark, lass, or Duncan Dubh will sneak out and steal ye away. Dinna leave yer horse out at night or Duncan Dubh will sell it to the gypsies. Dinna play with Duncan. Dinna let his shadow cross yer path. Hold yer breath when he passes by.

"Duncan . . . Duncan MacElgin," Lachlan said, dismounting slowly and coming toward him. "But it canna be. We'd heard that ye were dead like yer dad, that you died in one of yer wars on the Continent."

They'd *hoped* he was dead, Duncan amended silently, feeling the hostility toward him rising in waves with a personal intensity that was palpable. Aye, his clansmen had hated him; and after the grief he'd caused, who could blame them? Still, after fifteen years even Duncan was surprised that the memories of his youthful sins could arouse such a potent surge of resentment.

He suppressed his unexpected reaction of disappointment as if it had not penetrated any deeper than a wasp sting. They could despise the ground he walked on, but he would bloody well command their respect. From the look of things, however, he had a damn long way to go in gaining it.

And the girl. He threw her a castigating look, debating

how to handle her, wishing he could simply toss her over his knee and whack the disobedience out of her; the handling of unruly ragamuffins was beyond his considerable expertise. How dare she question him with that absurd sense of hauteur? Why did she keep staring at him like he was the first man she'd ever seen? Didn't she realize what he was entitled to do to her?

He grabbed his long cavalry sword and reflexively started to resheathe it before remembering his scabbard and knee breeches had sunk to the bottom of the tarn. His black cocked hat floated on its algae-rimmed surface. At his ferocious scowl of displeasure, a clansman vaulted off his pony and attempted to fish Duncan's apparel from the murky shallows of the pool.

"Ain't too bad, my lord," he announced, scurrying back to wave Duncan's shirt by its dripping lace cuffs. "Just give it a few good shakes to get the scum off, and 'twill be like new."

"Get this disgusting mess off my arm," Duncan snapped. And while two other clansmen hastened to rub the feathery sludge from his forearm with their own filthy plaids, Duncan glanced up again unwillingly at the girl, aware that, unlike the others, she hadn't given any sign of remorse for her outrageous conduct. He squared his shoulders in irritation. Well, let her smirk in silence. When he confronted her family, he suspected she wouldn't be so blasted self-possessed.

"What's wrong with her anyway?" he snapped at the pair of Highlanders who were scrubbing a bare patch on his elbow in their effort to remove the sludge. "Is she disfigured by pockmarks or some physical infirmity that she has to hide beneath that infernal hood?"

He regretted the insensitive remark the moment it left his mouth, but neither the girl—who gave a loud, unladylike chortle of amusement—or the two men seemed to take offense.

"The hood is for protection," she explained calmly.

He frowned, intrigued by the beguilingly pale wine-red curl he could pick out against the dark wool of her plaid. "Protection from what?" he asked, scowling.

She waved her fine-boned hand toward the crag, where

the hawk sat staring down directly at Duncan. "Protection from Eun."

Eun, the hawk. Duncan studied the bird in thoughtful silence. "That hawk shows more intelligence in its eyes than the entire lot of you combined." His face impatient, he snatched his elbow away from his startled clansmen. "Which brings me back to the original question: You never did tell me who it was you intended to ambush today. I assume this pathetic attack was planned and that you don't habitually lie in wait with your tar barrel and chicken feathers, hoping for some unsuspecting sod to pass."

The girl tilted her head back toward him, and he felt the strange, fey warmth of her eyes searching his face again, probing deeper than anyone else would have dared. A prickle of curiosity tinged with anticipation crawled up his spine. Who the hell was she? What uncanny influence did she wield over the clan? Did he know her?

"Of course it was planned," she said patiently. "We saw your fancy clothes and thought you were the captain of the damned Sassenach dragoons come to carve up our fields for another road."

Duncan snorted in disdain. "I suppose it never occurred to any of you that assaulting a king's officer could get you hanged?"

"Didn't assault no king's officer," a clansman behind the girl murmured. "We assaulted you, my lord."

"It was an honest mistake," she added, a hint of temper edging her voice. "I don't see why you're making such a fuss."

Duncan's dark blue eyes darkened to slate. "Oh, you don't?" he said softly. "I suppose you think I should just go about my business and pretend I don't have feathers stuck on my—"

"You could jump in the sea and wash," she suggested, unperturbed by his outburst. "The water's almost bearable this time of year. Besides, you've not broken anything that I noticed."

"And you noticed everything," he retorted in annoyance.

"'Twas difficult not to," she agreed, grinning.

For a moment Duncan nearly surrendered to an overwhelming impulse to turn tail and run all the way back to

England, pretending he bore no relation to or responsibility for this clan. But his entire future hinged on the success he met here. In view of what he had seen already, it was a daunting thought. Yet he was under the explicit orders of the Crown. The responsibility for his clan had been dumped at his feet by the War Office itself.

Over the course of time, reports of his clansmen's mildly violent yet persistent attacks on the Crown's officers had trickled all the way back to London. As luck would have it, Castle MacElgin sat right in the middle of an ancient road that led to a British garrison on the remote, rock-strewn coast that had been used for years as a port of entry for French spies and Jacobite rebels.

Because of Duncan's late father's notorious subversive activities against the English king, Castle MacElgin had been confiscated by the Crown the winter before. Duncan would have wished them the joy of it, but he hadn't been given that appealing option.

The Crown, as it turned out, didn't really want another crumbling castle to maintain. In fact, if Duncan could restore order to his unruly clansmen long enough for the English soldiers to complete work on their military roads, Duncan would be rewarded with a handsome Border dukedom.

Hell, he'd whipped the most miserable troops in Europe into shape. He had turned foreign mercenaries into fighting machines. How difficult could it be to rekindle the self-respect of his own clansmen?

Discipline. That was the first order of the day. And Lord knew this lot hardly looked like it possessed the self-motivation to scratch their own behinds in the morning.

He'd started off on the wrong foot with them too, let them make him look like a fool. He'd have to deal them a double measure of discipline to shift the balance in his favor. And he would start by making a public example of their ringleader. Right or wrong, they had to learn their disorganized attacks didn't have a chance in hell against the British army.

He glared down his nose at his distant cousin Lachlan, a plumpish young man with thinning brown hair and a perpetually worried frown. "Enough of this bloody nonsense. Who is responsible here?"

Lachlan looked up in alarm, having obviously realized that life as Clan MacElgin knew it was about to change, and most likely not for the better. "Why, you are, my lord," he said cautiously.

"Yes, but who was responsible before I came? Who, precisely, masterminded the attack on your lord and chieftain?"

"It was me," the girl said in an unapologetic voice, pretending to examine her ragged fingernails. "And now that we've got that settled, there's no need to go on making such a bother about the whole thing, is there?"

"You?" Duncan's voice rose into a shout as he swept a scathing gaze over the men watching him. "Do you mean to tell me that Clan MacElgin follows the foolish directives of a mere woman?"

"Most of the time your clan follows no directives but those motivated by its most basic urges," she continued with a touch of resentment in her tone. "But, yes, since you seem to need someone to vent your temper upon, then I shall shoulder the blame. I'm the one responsible for the attack today."

"You? A girl?"

She inclined her head as if she were a princess receiving a compliment from a peasant.

The man who had brought great European generals to their knees in surrender found himself at an utter loss. How could he make an example of a stubborn *girl?* How could these men be so incredibly stupid as to obey this rebellious female's whimsical orders? "Explain this to me, Lachlan," he said, shaking his head in bemusement. "Why on earth would you allow a little woman like this to mislead you?"

Lachlan snagged Duncan's elbow, covertly plucking away a pinfeather to draw the bigger man aside to warn him. "Her uncle is possessed of mystical powers, my lord. He saw a vision in the Samhain bonfire that told him Marsali should try to stop the next Sassenach who rides through the pass."

"A pity her uncle's mystical powers couldn't differentiate between a Scotsman and a Sassenach," Duncan said dryly. "Where are her parents?"

"Dead."

"And her living relatives—that is, is there a husband or relative responsible for the troublesome creature?"

Lachlan frowned; everyone in the clan regarded Marsali with fond affection. "Marsali is responsible for herself, unless ye count old Colum, the uncle I just mentioned. He's a wizard, ye ken," he added slyly, in such a tone of voice that hinted Duncan should expect great cosmic repercussions from mistreating the wizard's niece.

"Colum, the wizard," Duncan said sarcastically. In the shadows of long-forgotten memories stirred the image of a rather nasty, white-haired old fellow who used to prance around the moor talking to rocks and peering up the shepherdesses' skirts while casting spells that never availed much.

"Witchery runs in her family," Lachlan said in an undertone. " 'Tis said Marsali has the power but is hesitant to use it."

Marsali. Had he heard that name before? He had suppressed so many memories. Perhaps she was a newcomer to the village, the daughter of a rival Highlander who had broken with his own clan to join Clan MacElgin. Either way, whoever she was, she was a disgrace.

"You're afraid of the girl?" Duncan asked, suppressing a scornful smile.

"Och, no."

Duncan glanced back appraisingly at Marsali, reminding himself he was back in the Highlands, where witches, fairies, and ghosts were daily fare. "Remove your hood," he ordered her imperiously. "I would see your face when I address you."

"No," she said.

"No?" he repeated in disbelief, his voice climbing. "You dare outright defiance to your laird?"

"You're forcing me to defy you, my lord."

He studied her in grudging amusement, aware of the clansmen waiting to see how he would surmount the hurdle of her obstinancy. She was pushing him to the limit, this mysterious young woman, and he wasn't going to have it. This was as good a time as any to prove his power.

"Do not force me to make a scene, Marsali," he said, low-voiced and leaning toward her. "I shall remove the hood myself if you refuse."

"I cannot remove the cloak, my lord." She sounded perplexed, as if only an idiot would make such a request. "Furthermore, you'll be very sorry if you lay a hand on me."

A muscle ticked in Duncan's broad jaw. She had done it now—forced his hand, even if he had been inclined to show her mercy. He spared Lachlan a glance. "She is not disfigured, you say?"

Lachlan quailed at the cold anger on his chieftain's face. "Er, no, my lord, she isna, but if I may be permitted to warn ye—"

"Permission denied," Duncan said, frowning as he turned back to Marsali. "You're making this so much worse for yourself, Marsali. Take off that blasted hood."

"The hell I will." She raised her chin, adding with a resentful little sniff, "my lord."

Duncan proceeded to physically hoist her off her horse, realizing the time had come for a show of his power. She resisted for only a moment, stronger than he expected, but she was as light as a sack of feathers as he swung her down between his legs. Her fist flew up to clip his jaw. He caught it easily, an angry chuckle escaping him.

"Put me down!" she cried, jabbing her elbow into his side.

"With pleasure."

His face smug with satisfaction, he plunked her down on her feet and reached up to shove the hood back on her shoulders. She flinched, throwing up her hands to stop him. The movement deterred Duncan as much as a pair of butterflies would stop an ogre. Still, for a moment he hesitated, hearing a collective groan of apprehension from the clansmen hovering around them.

Was she in fact a monster? It would not bode well for him to humiliate one of life's mistreated in front of the clansmen who obviously cared for her. But there was a principle to consider here. Compassion for whatever deformity that may mark her did not matter.

He forced her backward until she stood trapped between

him and the horse. "You're going to be sorry, my lord," she warned him again, a split second before he wrenched off the hood.

He stared at her, his eyes narrowing in confusion. He forgot what he was supposed to be doing. He had not expected the little outlaw's heart-shaped face to reflect such an incongruously poignant combination of sweet vulnerability and indomitable will.

Gray-green eyes that looked more resigned than resentful. Well-defined cheekbones. He noted strength in her jawline, more than a hint of sensuality and humor in her soft, mobile mouth. He wouldn't call her beautiful, not with that tangled mop of glossy auburn hair and tip-tilted nose, but she was unique, a child-woman who could have passed for a fairy princess. If he had believed in such fanciful creatures.

"You should not have disobeyed me," he said as he recovered, injecting a note of sternness into his voice. "Now I'll have to make an example of you."

She sighed quietly. The powerful beating of wings filled the air. A shadow darkened the enchanting brightness of Marsali's face, obscuring her expression of alarm.

And then the hawk came at Duncan.

Chapter

2

Well, the MacElgin could only blame himself for his troubles. If he had surrendered immediately upon being ambushed, if he had identified himself and worn Highland clothing instead of that garish red jacket with all those boastful gold epaulets, then the mistake would never have been made. Marsali supposed she could make him suffer. She could order Eun to peck off the chieftain's proud aquiline nose, not to mention other parts barely covered by Owen's plaid.

Still, he was too fine a specimen of maleness to let Eun attack. From the privacy of her hood, Marsali had caught an unwilling glimpse of the chieftain's physical strength in action. Actually, it had been impossible *not* to be impressed by his prowess, the way he fought and tossed the men about, like a Greek god dropped to earth to play ninepins with the mortals.

Marsali had never seen anything like it in her life. She had almost applauded his aggression, forgetting he was supposed to be the enemy, the oppressor. Good Lord, it had taken seven men just to pull down his breeches.

Even watching him now as he swung his thick-muscled arms above his head to deflect the hawk's swift descent, Duncan was a masterpiece of male beauty in action. What a pity he was the most hated Highlander in anyone's memory. Still, everyone deserved a second chance, and excitement coursed through Marsali's veins as she wondered if he might prove the answer to her prayers. Was he the one she had been waiting for?

"Stop it, Eun!" she cried in a sharp voice, coming to her senses. "That's our chieftain you're attacking."

At her scolding tone, the hawk wheeled abruptly and circled to settle down on her shoulder, digging its talons into the softest flesh of her collarbone. She closed her eyes, cringing at the discomfort. After a moment the bird hopped up upon her head, tucked in its great wings, and fixed Duncan with an unblinking stare.

Tears of pain welled in Marsali's eyes. Duncan slowly lowered his sword, his black hair disheveled as he stared in disbelief at the predator perched on the delicate woman's head, her neck wobbling like the stem of a flower too fragile to bear its blossom. Marsali looked accusingly at Duncan, temporarily forgetting herself. "You've frightened the life out of him."

"*I* frightened *him,* did I?" Duncan glanced down in astonishment at the long angry scratches crisscrossing his shoulders.

"Well, honestly, my lord, I did try to warn you. You can't think I wear this hood on a warm summer day to appear the height of fashion."

Duncan's mouth thinned in an ironic smile. "No, Marsali. It's much more likely that you're wearing the hood to conceal your identity. If you are in the habit of robbing hapless incomers, then there is probably a well-deserved price on your head."

"Not to mention a hawk," Lachlan said, chuckling, only to subside into silence at the quelling look Duncan gave him.

"Most hawks are trained to land on a man's fist," Duncan said dryly.

"Eun isn't trained at all," Marsali retorted. "He was a fledging in a cliff that the soldiers blasted through for their roads. My uncle nursed him back to health, and the wee birdie's been a bundle of nerves ever since."

Duncan did not reply, suddenly distracted by a movement behind her. One of the clansmen had retrieved Duncan's waterlogged velvet jacket, hat, his knee breeches, sword belt, and jackboots from the tarn. Darting Duncan a sheepish grin, he deposited the soggy articles at Duncan's feet before sidling back toward his kinsmen.

Duncan stared down at the tadpoles swimming in the watery depths of tarn water that filled his boots. His blue eyes like ice, he raised his head and scanned the slack faces of the men he had the length of the summer to turn into a semblance of human dignity. Surely there was one man among them he could select as his successor. Pray God, let there be at least one.

His gaze swept back to Marsali, wincing audibly at Eun's agitated movements on her head. There were welts and nasty scratches on the skin of her shoulders too. Ridiculous girl.

"I could have beheaded that creature, Marsali," he said, indicating the long Toledo-steel sword he had lowered to his side, "if I were a man of less restraint."

She arched her delicately winged brow. "I do not doubt it, my lord." She shifted her hand slightly to bring it up against her mount's mane, revealing the flintlock pistol she was holding. "And I could have blasted you to kingdom come—if I were a woman of less restraint."

Rude sniggers of amusement erupted behind Duncan. He allowed a smile to touch his own lips. "I'm very afraid you're going to wish you had done away with me, lass," he said, then added softly, "after I'm through with you."

Someone behind Marsali gave a whistle of mock apprehension. Marsali's face reflected only the tiniest flicker of concern. Then suddenly Eun, spying a fox racing toward its den, leaned forward and launched from her forehead into the blue June sky.

She rubbed irritably at the red talon tracks on her scalp. "Do you mind explaining what you mean by the nature of that veiled threat, my lord?"

"It is no veiled threat, lass," he said. "As incredibly asinine as it appears, these men are acting on your orders, and as their leader, you shall be held responsible for their crimes."

"Is it to be the bastinado or banishment?" she asked in

mock alarm. "Or may I choose between public flaying and a firing squad?"

"Dinna forget the finger pillory, lass," one of the clansmen suggested in a jovial voice.

Duncan's blue eyes narrowed in warning that Marsali had stretched the limits of his patience. He raised his voice. "As the laird and chieftain of Clan MacElgin, I order you to sacrifice your summer as my maidservant in Castle MacElgin. You are to polish my boots, see that my wardrobe is in repair—"

Marsali blinked, her composure almost cracking at this unexpected turn of events. *Her,* a maidservant? Of all the cheek. "I'm to *what?*"

"Answer my correspondences, assuming you can read and write, and in general perform any other menial errand that it pleases me to request."

"This is rather presumptuous, my lord. You have yet to be officially sworn in as chieftain of the clan to be ordering me about. By ancient law, you have to stand on the white stone by the sea to take the oath."

"It is no less presumptuous, Marsali, than to have a wild young woman assaulting innocents on the moor."

He straightened his shoulders; against her will Marsali watched the subtle interplay of powerful muscle and sinew beneath his weather-browned skin. His face reminded her of one of the medieval knights carved into the cold stone of the castle crypts. Beautiful but impassive. Angular, aristocratic . . . unfeeling. Only the intense blue of his eyes and the laugh lines etched around his mouth hinted he ever allowed any emotion to show. She wondered what it would take to crack the iron bands of his self-control.

"As to the matter of my chieftainship," Duncan continued, focusing a level look around him, "is there a man here who would challenge me, or assume the responsibility?

The utter silence almost made him smile.

"Hell's bells," Marsali said in astonishment, craning her neck to glance around. "Isn't *anyone* going to stop him?"

Lachlan gave her a somber if sympathetic look. "No, lass, we are not. He might be dressed like a jackanapes Sassenach—well, he *might* have been dressed like one, I should say. And he might have left a load of ill feelin's behind when his dad sent him off to war, but it appears he is our laird and chieftain, and we'll obey him, until he's proven otherwise."

"Well," Duncan said with a self-assured nod, "that appears to be the end of it, doesn't it?"

"It appears to be," Marsali said crisply. And she couldn't entirely fault her companions. To her annoyance, some primitive instinct deep inside her was also responding to the raw power that characterized Duncan's every movement, the spell he had cast over his ragged clan.

Duncan allowed himself to relax, having expected anything but this pleasant acquiescence. "I could have made it much worse for you, you realize. I could have turned you over to the authorities."

He thought he saw the shadow of a smile flit across her bewitching face. "I'm very afraid you're going to wish you had turned me over, my lord," she said, adding softly, "after I'm through with you."

Marsali Hay had lived on MacElgin land all her life. She was four years old when the late laird and chieftain, the sixteenth marquess of Portmuir, Kenneth MacElgin, had bought his incorrigible only son, Duncan, a commission in the British army. It had been an act of desperation. Kenneth had hoped that fighting wars would provide a safe channel for the anger and hostility that had characterized Duncan's tempestuous youth. The lad was beyond his control.

She remembered her father telling Mama more than once that Duncan probably could not help his wildness; it had been beaten into him by the cruel fisherman who had raised him. But Marsali could recall little beyond that, except Mama retorting that even if Duncan could not help his wildness, someone still had to stop him from terrorizing the village with his drunken, wenching ways.

And then there had been a scandal, a hushed-up affair involving a doctor's young wife and a baby, and Duncan had disappeared like a puff of smoke, banished by the laird for his misconduct.

Occasionally, over the years, the old laird would read from a tattered newspaper at a clan meeting or local gathering, recounting his son's military exploits in the cavalry. By then, of course, the reports were several months old, and Duncan had scored another military victory, or received another promotion or charmed another foreign princess. His talent for warring and winning hearts apparently knew no bounds.

Everyone pretended to be pleased. But in reality, Duncan had left behind too many raw wounds and unresolved accusations for anyone to view him as the hero he was to the rest of the world.

To this day, Marsali had never cared to trace the truth of those accusations. Duncan MacElgin had played no more importance in her life than the man in the moon. He was no more real to her than the water horses that supposedly lived at the bottom of the loch.

He was important, and real, albeit reluctantly, to her now.

As if she did not have enough problems.

Two years before, her father and her fiancé had been killed supporting Duncan's father in a plot to bring James III to the throne. Duncan's father had been killed too, but that hadn't stopped Marsali's two brothers from taking over where Kenneth MacElgin had left off, hatching their own half-cocked Jacobite revolt last winter. Her older brothers, Adam and Dougall had not returned at all, and young Gavin had come back a cripple.

Marsali could not bear to lose another loved one in these petty plots that were only doomed to failure. She wanted the British soldiers to go away forever. She wanted her nieces and nephews to grow up planning weddings, not funerals. She ached for the quiet pattern of their lives to resume. There was nothing that meant more to her than family. Grief upon grief had destroyed her future.

Could this man who fought like a devil and looked like an archangel be the answer? Her heart hammered wildly with anticipation at the thought.

For months her uncle had been predicting the dramatic arrival of the man who would restore power and dignity to the clan. Of course, Uncle Colum's predictions were typically more wrong than right, but Marsali had a powerful feeling about this one; she *needed* to believe it.

Desperation compelled her to give Duncan MacElgin a

chance. Hope enabled her to sacrifice a little pride and physical labor to save lives. The fact that he was gorgeous didn't hurt either. That everyone had believed him dead only enhanced his dark mystique.

"Here." Duncan's deep voice broke her train of thought; she glanced up just in time to catch the sodden ball of his clothing he hurled at her, the action anything but heroic. "Carry those back to the castle, Marsali, and launder them before nightfall. My belongings should arrive in another few days."

"I can't possibly carry all this on my horse, my lord," she complained, striving not to stagger under the dripping load.

He chuckled, sun-lines deepening at the corners of his eyes. Despite herself, Marsali had to admit that when he relaxed his guard, he looked a little boyish and far less threatening, an illusion that he proved could not be trusted by his next callously spoken words.

"No, Marsali, you cannot carry that load on horseback. Which is why I intend to ride *your* mare while Lachlan tries to find my horse on the moor. He was frightened away by the boulders you rolled into our path."

"Speaking of boulders, these things weigh as much as a standing stone, my lord."

Duncan marched past her, his face unconcerned. "You'll probably discover you have many hidden strengths as well as weaknesses under my guardianship, Marsali." He almost added, out of habit, that he'd make a soldier of her yet, but he caught himself in time.

She struggled to keep pace with his enormous strides, glaring at her grinning clansmen over the top of her wet bundle. Sniveling traitors who didn't appreciate the noble sacrifice she was making for their sakes. "Excuse me, my lord, did you say 'guardianship'?"

"Like it or not—and I don't—I am your chieftain, responsible for your behavior. Your actions reflect upon my leadership." He vaulted onto her horse, smiling down into her small disgruntled face as if he savored the challenge of turning her into a drudge. "You'd better move, lass. It's a long walk to the castle, and you've a full day's work ahead."

"Nobody has ever ordered me around before," Marsali

said slowly, the shining image she had built of him in her heart already beginning to tarnish.

His smile widened. "Ah, well, there's a first time for everything, isn't there?"

Marsali did not move, watching him manipulate the horse with the same elegant conceit as he had her. And damn if the mare didn't respond to his expert handling, prancing around the fragrant tufts of heather and bracken fern and carrying the gorgeous giant as if it were an honor. Resentment gripped her.

She wondered suddenly if she ought to save herself from the situation by blaming one of her dimwitted cousins for masterminding the ambush. But what a sight Duncan had been, bare as a boiled egg, and fighting singlehandedly with that casual grace that had made his clansmen look like the unskilled buffoons they were. She couldn't evict the elemental splendor of him from her mind. She had been entranced. Not only by his strength and physical magnificence, his sharply chiseled face and muscular horseman's body, but by the aura of mastery around him, the raw energy of will that struck a spark in her own passionate soul. This was a man equal to any enemy.

Still, an undeniable conflict had begun to rage inside her, pitting emotion against intellect. As proud and beautiful as Duncan MacElgin appeared, he conducted himself with a cold inflexibility that did not bode well for the clan. He might have learned self-control since his youth, but had he learned compassion?

True, the clan needed a cool head to stop its decline into chaos. But that cool head also demanded the tempering balance of a warm heart. And if Duncan's history gave any hint to his present emotional state, he would be a ruthless leader. Physically strong but empty within. She shivered, imagining how he could misuse such power, how easily it could ensnare the unwary.

The danger lay in his personal magnetism. A man like that could persuade his followers to do anything. Look at her, trudging about with his damned laundry, following him like a lost kitten.

She couldn't decide what to do. Her instincts had never misled her before, but then she had never been tested like this. Was it not said that indecision was the Devil's own dance?

"Hell," she said, and she tossed the heavy bundle back into the tarn.

No sooner had she enjoyed the deep satisfaction of watching his lace-edged lawn shirt sink to the bottom of the tarn again than Duncan wheeled the mare around and cantered back toward her.

She bit her lip, a shiver of hot-cold apprehension raising gooseflesh on her skin as he reined in before her. She'd done it now.

"Not an act of insubordination already, Marsali?" he asked, allowing the horse to press forward until Marsali balanced herself with her heels tottering over the tarn.

"I slipped on the moss and dropped your things," she lied baldly, defiantly crossing her slender brown arms over her chest.

He raised his eyebrows and tried to judge her age, staring involuntarily at the faint outline of her figure revealed by the wet patches of water that marred her pale blue muslin gown. She was a small sprite of a thing, fine-boned, with curves in the right places, and she seemed far too delicate to be leading Highland ruffians on ambushes. The strange thought came to Duncan that he could crush her in his palm like a butterfly, if she ever allowed herself to be caught. She possessed an ethereal quality that he couldn't reconcile with her outrageous behavior and boldness of character.

Her character was in fact what his betrothed, Lady Sarah Grayson, would undoubtedly call common. But in the depths of this young woman's sea-mist eyes, in that low impertinent voice, Duncan had detected a disturbingly "uncommon" intelligence and refinement that defied bloodlines. Marsali had managed his maneuvers with the instincts of a rival general. Even now he sensed she held the upper hand.

If he hadn't known better, he'd have sworn he was about to walk into another ambush, something infinitely more complex and dangerous than what he had just escaped.

He scoffed inwardly at the notion. "I'm waiting," he said, with an aristocratic dip of his head. "Let's see how fast those little feet of yours can march across the moor."

She spun from him, muttering under her breath, and bent to retrieve his clothes from the tarn. Then, just as she had restacked the wet bundle back into her arms, she felt something flat and cold prod against her behind.

She pivoted, outraged, this personal insult more than even she could bear, considering herself an unusually tolerant person. But it was not his big hand fondling her backside, as she had imagined. Instead he was holding his heavy sword, hilt down, toward her. Against her will she raised her gaze, absorbing a stunning view of powerfully muscled thigh and torso, before she reached his austere face.

"You'll need to carry my sword too, lass," he said, sounding hugely unapologetic. "I'm afraid it's frightening the horse."

"I don't give a—"

"Careful, lass. I don't tolerate swearing from my servants."

He wheeled the mare back toward the moor before Marsali could set him straight on her position in the castle. She blew out a sigh and glanced back up at the crag. Her cowardly clansmen had retreated like rats into the shadowy crevices of the mountain pass where many of them lived. Most of the clan, herself included, preferred the bleak elements to the gloom of Castle MacElgin, which seemed to have fallen under a dark enchantment of anarchy and abandon.

Eun alone remained to protect her. Eun, who belonged to her uncle the wizard and who obeyed only Colum's wishes, and then only half the time at that.

The hawk swooped down to trail above her slow awkward march toward the castle. Its overshadowing presence reminded Marsali that she could turn to Uncle Colum's magic in handling the MacElgin. In the event her own plan to handle him failed.

As Duncan rode ahead to the castle, ignoring the wild beauty of the moor, he cursed himself for allowing a handful of savage, undereducated Highlanders to arouse insecurities he had spent years struggling to overcome. Blast them. He shouldn't give a damn. Except that they were his people, linked to him by bloodlines and tradition too ancient to trace or to disentangle. He belonged to them as they belonged to him, the ties that not only bound but strangled.

He cursed himself for coming back, for reopening the old wounds, for reawakening the old ghosts.

He cursed that wrathful angel of a girl for standing up to him on the moor, challenging the years of rank and authority he had earned.

In a corner of his heart, he'd hoped that, despite all the trouble he'd caused, he would be welcomed home a hero. A clap on the back to acknowledge his accomplishments. A tentative smile to signal his sins had been forgiven. His father opening his arms in forgiveness, inviting him back to the hearth. His half-sister, Judith, ruffling his hair in affectionate exasperation.

What fantasy. What a fool.

His father was dead. Judith had long ago escaped from this village to the peaceful seclusion of her island convent. His clan loathed him.

He reined in the mare and glanced over his shoulder at the girl, a reluctant smile softening the harshly sculptured contours of his face. Her progress appeared painful. The sword slid every few steps into the masses of purple heather that edged the hilly track. To lighten her burden, she had donned Duncan's boots over her own and was clumping along like an ill-tempered Puss-in-Boots. Every so often she would pause to curse Duncan to the heavens, the phrases pungent and inventive.

Where had a girl like that cultivated the strength of will to stand up to a man of his experience? How had she learned the art of surrender without losing a shred of her ridiculous dignity?

Duncan shrugged off the unwelcome sense of concern that threatened to cloud his clear judgment. He couldn't afford to care or soften his stance with his future at stake. Neither forgotten nor forgiven, he had no reason to tarry longer here than he had to.

Still, like it or not—and he didn't—the chieftain had come home.

Chapter

3

At first Duncan did not believe his eyes as he beheld the unsightly hulk of the thirteenth-century castle on the hill overlooking the sea. He told himself he was fatigued to the point of hallucinations. That couldn't be a skull and crossbones pirates' flag flapping from the parapets in place of the MacElgin standard. Those weren't chickens scratching in the dry dusty moat, the same ditch that had once been fed from fierce tidal channels to repel Danish invaders.

He rode up the hill and through the barbican, dread creeping over him. A pair of hens fluttered around the mare's hooves. He could hear a rhythmic thudding from behind the castle walls and the echoing refrain of raucous, off-key singing.

He dismounted and threw a stone at the drawbridge. A few moments later a scullery maid in a shift and dirty apron appeared above him on the watch turret. Without warning, she hoisted a hunting horn to her mouth and gave it a deafening blow before proceeding to bellow down into the barbican at the top of her considerable lungs.

"HALT!" she began, squinting down nearsightedly. "Be ye friend or be ye foe? For if ye're foe, then away ye go, but if ye're friend then ye're bloody out of luck anyway because

Archie is piss-pot drunk in the gatehouse, and I'm no lowerin' that damned drawbridge again today by myself!"

Duncan blinked, her strident voice ringing in his ears, and looked around him. From the corner of his eye he could see Marsali trudging up the winding road to the castle, and even though he could barely see her face, he suspected it reflected a wicked enjoyment at his predicament.

"Abercrombie!" he shouted, banging at the drawbridge for the Lowland Scot steward the Crown had appointed to keep peace in the castle until a permanent owner could be installed. "Archie, or whatever your name is! Someone had better lower this damned drawbridge, and they had better do it now!"

A surly-looking guard poked his head through the gatehouse window. "I'm no deaf. State yer business and be gone."

"My business, Archie, you drunken old coot, is to get into my castle and throttle every last one of you."

Archie leaned precariously out the arched window. "Who the Devil are ye?" he whispered, his voice rasping.

"He's Duncan MacElgin, your laird and chieftain," Marsali announced, limping through the barbican and dumping her bundle against the wall to sit upon it, her head cradled in her hand. "And he's not the most reasonable person I've ever met, Archie, so you'd best do exactly as he said. He made mincemeat of the others on the moor less than an hour ago."

Duncan turned to look down at her. "Thank you so much for the glowing introduction."

"Well, I—Oh dear, save your hide, my lord!"

She broke off to leap at Duncan like a frog, snatching the reins from his gloved hands and yanking the mare back frantically toward the barbican gate, the horse's hooves flattening his hat into the dust.

Save his hide from what? Duncan wondered a fraction of a second before a horrible, grinding burst sounded from behind the castle wall and the drawbridge came crashing down straight for his head.

He dove instinctively for cover, flinging himself up against Marsali and knocking them both to the ground. She groaned and went very still under his weight, a soft moan of pain from the impact breaking in her throat. Duncan had never felt like such an oaf. She was a fragile little thing, for all her fire. Concern that he had crushed her delicate bones with his clumsy weight stopped his heart until she dug her elbow into his stomach, grunting.

"Get off me, my lord. You're breaking my—"

The thundering fall of the drawbridge to the ground absorbed the rest of her complaint. Clouds of choking dust sprayed them. Duncan was dimly aware of the agitated squawking rising from the ditch, acutely so of the rumpled girl who was giving him a knee in the groin and swearing like one of his soldiers. No sooner had he hauled her to her feet than a crowd of scrawny, frightened chickens descended on them, Marsali shooing them away by snapping the corner of her plaid at them with practiced ease.

He brushed the dust off his arms, his voice furious. "I suppose this is where you get your supply of feathers for your nasty little assaults. What colossal idiot ordered the moat dammed off?"

"Your own cousin Johnnie MacElgin," Marsali replied with a grin, her hair and chin powdered with dust, her cheeks pink from the hike across the moor. "He said it was for the clan's protection, as I recall."

Duncan arched his brow. "How ingenious. A handful of underfed chickens are meant to protect the castle?"

Marsali blinked. For an intelligent man, he could be rather dense. "No, my lord, the chickens are happenstance. The ditch was dammed up to protect your clansmen from falling drunk off the walkways into the moat while they were on watch."

Duncan closed his eyes for a moment, drawing a breath that sounded as it came from the depths of his soul. Marsali almost felt sorry for him. As bad as this appeared, he had no idea what horrors were hidden inside the castle. She hoped he was as powerful as he looked.

Archie, the gatehouse guard, poked his shiny bald head through the window again like a tortoise. "The drawbridge is down," he announced unnecessarily.

Duncan slowly turned from Marsali to stare straight

ahead through a veil of settling dust. The castle's laundry—
hose, trousers, tunics, plaids—hung from the portcullis's
iron grating to dry in the feeble sunlight. A slow flush crept
upward from Duncan's neck to stain his sharply chiseled
face. Marsali suppressed a smile at his reaction. Aye, he was
in for a big surprise, and she was bubbling with gleeful
expectancy to witness the moment.

"Raise the damned portcullis, Archie," he shouted up at
the gatehouse window.

"Can't. I have me orders! 'Tis laundry day."

"Orders?" Duncan repeated sarcastically. "You mean
someone is actually responsible for this bedlam?"

"Cook's the only one who can give the order to raise the
portcullis on laundry day," Archie stated, about to pull
back inside.

Duncan's flush deepened. "And what bloody good is it to
lower the drawbridge if the portcullis remains closed, you
moron?"

"Look," Archie said, his own tone getting nasty again,
"ye're the one who insisted I lower it, and I can't see that it
makes a bit of difference whether the damn thing is up or
down, this being laundry day and Cook being a besom
about such affairs."

That said, he retreated back into the gloom of the
gatehouse. Duncan glanced down at Marsali, his face unfathomable in the shadows. "Give me your gun," he said
quietly.

"Why?" she asked, drawing away from him with a delicious shiver of dramatic anticipation going through her.

"You will not question my actions, Marsali. Just give me
your gun."

"Oh, all right." She knelt, bracing one small hand against
his arm for support while reaching under her skirts for the
gun tucked inside her scuffed riding boot.

Duncan swallowed and stared up at the castle, pretending
the trusting pressure of her fingers on his wrist did not
arouse a certain pleasurable stirring inside him. "It's dangerous to carry a gun in your boot like that," he said, his
throat suddenly dry and tasting of dust. "You might have
fallen off your horse and shot yourself in the foot."

She lifted her face to his. "Actually, I couldn't have, my lord, because you took my horse and forced me to walk. But it's nice to know you're considering my welfare."

Duncan made a face but could not bring himself to correct the ragamuffin's absurd statement. "Hurry up," he said gruffly, wanting to have the ordeal over and done with.

It was dark in the barbican, secluded, warm, and intimately shadowed. He felt the pressure of her disturbingly soft breasts against his hip as she straightened, the transient sting of regret mingled with relief when she moved away. For a moment he fought an impulse to draw her back against him, enjoying the warmth of her. Fortunately he had more self-control than that.

"Here." She slapped the gun into his hand with an utter disregard for safety that made him cringe. "Do you intend to discipline Archie because he refused to raise the portcullis?"

Duncan stared down at his hand. There had been something profoundly unsettling about the sight of such delicate fingers wrapped around the cold barrel of a gun, fingers that should be plying a needle or stroking a bairn's hair. He wondered if she would really have shot him coldbloodedly on the moor a little while before. Had she shot men before? He glanced up into her face, searching the composed gray-green eyes for a clue to her character and coming up against a wall. Of all the responsibilities he'd anticipated, keeping a wild girl like this under control had not been one of them.

"Why are you not married?" he asked bluntly.

Her gaze remained level with his. "I would have been wed two years ago, but my betrothed followed your father into his rebellion and was killed."

He shook his head, sensing a grief beneath the calm explanation that she refused to show. "I'm sorry," he said, feeling the words inadequate. "What an unfortunate waste of a life."

"There have been too many senseless deaths, my lord, although I realize that making wars is your world."

"*Winning* wars is my world, Marsali. Under the ideal circumstances, killing is completely unnecessary."

She smiled at him, a glint of what he imagined could be

approval in her haunting eyes. The disconcerting thought came to him that if he had never left the castle he might have known this girl intimately. He might even have courted her, or her older sister. There was something achingly familiar about her face. Yet he could swear he had never met her.

"Do you intend to shoot Archie?" she repeated, her innocent voice breaking into his thoughts.

He sighed loudly. "No. Not unless he provokes me into it. Now stand back. Take the horse with you, please. And do not question me further."

"But—"

"Not another word."

He raised the gun to the portcullis. Marsali watched him intently for several moments before obeying his order to remove herself and the horse to the barbican entryway. She supposed he knew what he was doing, being the renowned general that he was.

"By the way, the gun is not loaded, my lord," she called back over her shoulder.

"What?" He swiveled around, annoyance tightening his austerely handsome face. "Why the blazes didn't you tell me this before?"

"Because I thought you might have another purpose in mind for it which I am too slow-witted to perceive." Her face looked guileless in the shadows. "And you did warn me not to question you again."

He lowered his arm and strode up before her, swallowing the urge to laugh at the absurdity of it all. But a show of humor at this point would deflect from the discipline so desperately needed here. He raised his hand to give her back the gun, then stopped abruptly, glancing up at the shadow of the hawk settling on the barbican wall.

"It's all right, Eun," Marsali said in a soothing voice. "This man does not mean me harm, do you, my lord?"

"I suppose that depends on your point of view." Disgruntled, Duncan brought his arm back to his side. "But whether I decide to punish you or not—and I admit the probability exists—that bird cannot follow you into the castle. I forbid it."

"Then you shall have to find a way to make him go, my

lord. Eun is under my uncle's spell and does only his bidding."

Duncan's heavy black eyebrows drew together. "Apparently, I'm going to have to put this uncle of yours in his place."

Marsali pursed her lips. In her opinion it was more likely to be the other way around. "As you say, my lord."

Duncan nodded, wondering vaguely why every victory he scored with her ended with a hollow ring. "I know my father had the secret gates sealed off before I left. How does one get into the castle now when the portcullis is not raised?"

"Well." She folded her arms across her chest, appearing to give the matter great thought. "In the olden days, I believe a battering ram would have been used. Some soldiers apparently tried to scale the walls with ladders, but I understand this method frequently met with failure. Pots of boiling oil and such. All that mess and bother."

"A battering ram. A ladder."

"When invaders were really desperate to get in, they would dig tunnels under the castle walls. This, however, took time and determination, not to mention strength. Oh!" She brightened in a flash of inspiration. "The really, really desperate ones attempted to climb up the latrines." She wrinkled her retroussé nose. "But can you imagine the smell?"

She was playing a game with him, he saw that now. Oddly enough, he was actually starting to enjoy it. "If *you* wanted to get into the castle, Marsali, how would you go about it?"

"Ah." She smiled smugly. "Well, if I were chieftain, I'd have the portcullis raised."

"A brilliant concept. And how would you go about doing this?"

"I'd ask Effie, of course."

"Effie?"

Marsali waved enthusiastically to the scullery maid who was grinning down at them from the watchtower. The scullery maid waved back.

A reluctant smile relaxed Duncan's face. "Ask Effie to raise the portcullis, Marsali. I am not accustomed to standing around in a piece of wool with my private parts exposed."

"Very well." She brushed around him, cupping her hands, pistol and all, to her face to shout, "Raise the portcullis, Effie!"

"It's laundry day, Marsali!" the thin-faced woman yelled down with an apologetic shrug.

"Aye, I realize that, but this man is not accustomed to standing around in a piece of wool with his privy parts exposed, and he's demanding to be let in!"

Effie dropped her hunting horn to fish a pair of cracked spectacles from her apron pocket. Leaning precariously over the watch turret, she looked Duncan up and down for several critical moments. "I canna see anything exposed, Marsali, but the man is built like a war horse! My God, he has a chest on him. Where did ye find him then?"

"On the moor," Marsali shouted back. "He's claiming to be our new chieftain, but we tossed his clothes into the tarn, and he had to borrow a plaid."

"Ye dinna say. Well then, I'll fetch my sister from the barrelhouse and have her give me a hand. 'Twill take a few minutes, ye ken, to raise the damned thing up. Ooh, look at his hindquarters, Marsali. All that lovely muscular haunch."

"You should have seen him running about for his life on the moor, Effie, bare as a boiled egg right down to his—"

"Excuse me." Duncan clamped his hand down, hard, on Marsali's shoulder. "There is a crowd gathering on the battlements, and I would appreciate it if you did not discuss my various body parts as you would a stallion's for sale at a fair."

Marsali stood unmoving, immobilized not so much by his painful grasp as by her reaction to it. Wonderful flurries of sensation washed through her, warm and thoroughly wicked; her reeling senses still hadn't recovered from the pleasant shock of lying beneath him in the dirt. She turned woodenly to face him. "I'm sorry, my lord," she said with a sheepish grin. "I didn't hear a word you said."

"I'm not surprised, with all the shouting about my anatomy going on."

He lifted his hand from her shoulder, frowning at the imprint on his fingers underlaid with the talon marks of the hawk. The pretty young pagan spoke in a cultured voice at odds with her station in life. The embroidered girdle around her waist where she had casually stuck the pistol had cost a pretty penny. Obviously someone had taken the trouble to educate and arm her. But why, and who? The mystery of her deepened.

The portcullis began its creaking ascent, the muffled sound of women swearing from behind the double doors breaking Duncan's concentration. He backed away from Marsali, mounting the mare with a satisfied nod. He'd gotten his way; that was what counted.

Marsali stood in silence, watching as he passed beneath the portcullis, laundry dropping onto his elegant head. He looked proud of himself, as if he had scored a major coup by having the portcullis raised. Actually, considering the fact that today was laundry day, he *had* done quite well for himself.

But Marsali knew that the self-satisfied look he wore would shortly erode into horror. She knew that the worst was yet to come. For her own part she usually avoided the castle and its environs except in an extreme emergency. Clansmen had been known to enter and never be seen again.

She hefted the chieftain's clothes back against her chest and hurried after him. He was probably going to need her protection. There was no telling what he might encounter. After all, he had countermanded Cook's orders, and nobody in Marsali's memory had dared such an offense and lived to tell of it.

Chapter

4

Cook slowly lowered the spyglass, her oblong face going ash-gray with the shock of what she had just witnessed. "Dear God in Heaven, it's that wee bastard Duncan Mac-Elgin, and his horse is trampling all over my clean laundry."

The three people standing beside her on the battlements—her spinster daughter, Suisan, the ancient head groom, Angus, and Johnnie, Kenneth MacElgin's former lieutenant-at-arms—all reached to wrest the spyglass from her plump, age-speckled hands at the same time.

Johnnie snared it first. He was a middle-aged man with a leonine mane of grizzled brown hair that came to his shoulders. Narrowing his eye, he peered down at the horseman entering the middle bailey. "By damn," he said, a whistle escaping his cracked front teeth. "The prodigal son's come home."

"But I thought he was dead," Suisan exclaimed, wrenching the spyglass from Johnnie's hands to see for herself. "Why do ye suppose—Oooh, he's wearin' naught but a plaid like one of the old Highlanders. The laddie is all grown up, Ma. He's no a wee bastard anymore."

She scowled in disappointment as Angus confiscated the glass, giving a deep throaty chuckle at the sight of the laird draped in the castle's laundry. "Duncan MacElgin. Aye, there'll be trouble in spades now. About time too."

"What do you suppose it means?" Cook asked worriedly, wringing her hands.

"No tellin'." Johnnie's pleasant face puckered into a frown. "Someone should have warned us to expect him, though."

Suisan giggled softly. "He doesna look dead, does he?"

"He'll find out about Abercrombie now," Angus said, with another ominous chuckle at the prospect.

"Abercrombie," the three others whispered in horrified unison.

Cook heaved an enormous sigh. "And here I was set to enjoy a long peaceful summer. Look at the man, the size of him, letting his horse stomp my clean laundry into the ground. Laird or no, I willna have it."

Johnnie snatched the spyglass back from the old groom's hand and leveled it on the middle bailey. "Aye, and ye can give up yer hope of a peaceful summer, old woman. The MacElgin's brought Marsali Hay along wi' him."

"Our Marsali?" Cook said, her features lighting up in relief. "Aye, weel. That's a good sign then."

"She's carryin' the MacElgin's clothes and his sword, by the look of it," Johnnie murmured. "She's no exactly laughing with pleasure either."

Cook's face fell like one of her egg soufflés. "That's a bad sign then."

"He's ridin' her horse too," Johnnie added, clucking his tongue.

"That's the worst sign," Cook said grimly. "It can only mean the wee bastard is every bit as wicked as the day his puir papa sent him off to the wars. A lion canna change his stripes, I always say."

"He doesna look at all like a good-natured man," Johnnie was forced to agree, handing the spyglass back to Suisan, who was fairly dancing with impatience for another look at the MacElgin. "To think he hasn't seen the worst of it yet. He'll no be pleased."

A knife-throwing contest was well under way by the time Duncan penetrated the middle bailey. In the confusion—

the drinking, the cheering, the furious betting—no one paid much attention to the lone horseman who approached, his face a dark mask of displeasure at the evidence of total disorder.

A buxom blonde serving wench, blindfolded and with an apple on her head, stood flattened against the dog-kennel door, knives whizzing toward her with a careless accuracy that chilled Duncan's blood. Before he could interrupt the sport, a band of scruffy-looking boys and girls came charging at him from the direction of the dovecote.

He grinned unwillingly at the innocence of their play, the toy crossbows and arrows they aimed straight at his heart. Then from the corner of his eye, he saw Marsali streak past him as if running for her life, his clothes and sword clutched like a shield to her chest. An arrow sailed over his head. That was when he realized that the little buggers charging at him with Indian war whoops were armed to the teeth with real weapons. He spurred the horse into a canter toward the safety of the stables, reaching Marsali's side and swooping her up across his lap. She landed rump first on his massive thighs. He caught her in a crushing grip and rode with his arm clamped around her ribcage as if their lives depended on it. Which they possibly did.

"Thank you," she said breathlessly, wriggling to wedge a position for herself between his legs. Duncan's body stiffened at the not unpleasant intrusion of her bottom squashed against his groin. "Children will play their games, won't they?"

"Those aren't children, Marsali," he said tersely. "They're undersized monsters with murder in their ugly wee hearts."

She dared to lean back against his chest, feeling protected by his strength as another arrow whizzed over their heads. "Everything is going to change now that you're here, isn't it?" she called up in a hopeful voice.

"Yes," he said, and he frowned at the flicker of doubt that entered his mind.

He slowed the mare to enter the stables, surprised that it at least appeared to receive regular attention. A startled undergroom tumbled out of his bed loft to take the horse.

Duncan nudged Marsali off his lap, watching her drop to the ground as agile as a cat.

"How did the ambush go, Marsali?" the young boy asked excitedly, rubbing sleep from his eyes. "Did ye humiliate the bastard?"

Marsali cleared her throat, trying to avoid Duncan's sharp gaze as he dismounted. "Well, we tried our best, Martin. But sometimes the best of plans go awry. The worst ones apparently do too."

His red hair sticking up in tufts at various angles from his head, Martin looked over shrewdly at Duncan. "So I see," he said, his voice low and curious. "Is this the bas—is *he* the captain, Marsali?"

"This is Duncan MacElgin, Martin," she explained solemnly, lowering her awkward bundle to the floor. "He is our new laird and chieftain. I humiliated him on the moor, and now he's going to make an example of me."

The raw-boned boy, a few years younger than Marsali, stared at Duncan in suspicious silence as if she had just introduced him to the Devil. It was clear he'd made the association in his mind, probably long ago. Apparently Duncan had become a legend in his own time, and not a nice one either.

He frowned, curbing his irritation. "See to the horse, would you, lad, while I walk ahead to the castle. I can only hope it's as well kept as your barns."

The boy said nothing, refusing to acknowledge the compliment. Duncan shrugged and finally turned away, his face more reflective than angry as he walked back outside. For all he knew the lad had reason to fear him. For all he knew he had roughed up the boy's siblings in his own hell-raising youth.

"Do they still hate me that much?" he asked quietly, sensing Marsali walking up behind him.

She hesitated. She could not see his face, but she could hear the pain and confusion in the deep timbre of his voice. He would probably be furious with her if he realized he'd revealed such emotional weakness, being the famous warrior to the rest of the world that he was. But Marsali took this as a good sign. There was some feeling in him after all. Part of him could be hurt by a lowly stableboy's opinion.

"Why do you care what they think, my lord?" she replied. "You are their chieftain. They need only obey you. What they feel for you in their hearts is insignificant."

He turned to stare down into her piquant face, expecting mockery, finding instead an understanding beyond her years. Perhaps he had grown too accustomed to sophisticated females. Perhaps he had grown disenchanted with the painted, perfumed noblewomen who had enticed him into their anonymous beds, who had satisfied his body and left his soul aching for something more.

His betrothed would be on her way to Scotland at the end of the month. And yet to his surprise he felt an unwilling kinship with this strange moppet who saw more deeply into his character than he would like. Even his intimate friends were not privy to his past. And this girl seemed to know too much. Was there more substance to her than he'd realized?

He forced a smile. "And what grim tales have *you* heard about me, Marsali? Did they tell you I tortured the servants in the castle dungeon for sport?"

She met his gaze, honest and unflinching. "No, they didn't. They told me you had gotten drunk and blown up the clan's barley mill out of spite."

His throat tightened. Her words sickened him more than he could show. "Go on."

"Well." Her voice faltered a little as she recounted the ugly snippets of gossip. "They said that a man died as a result of your wickedness and that another was disfigured. They said that the cottars went hungry that summer from the loss of income. But we both know how they exaggerate such things."

"Is that all they say?"

Marsali gazed past him, her voice almost inaudible. "No, there are the rumors about your mother and her husband . . . and something about a doctor's wife."

A cold chill passed through Duncan. What an ass he'd been, to hope he would convince these people that he was no longer that hell-bent youth. Or was he really all that different? Had the old demons within ever died or only gone dormant, dozing until the right opportunity to ruin him came along? This girl, he was sure, would not stare so guilelessly into his eyes if she guessed he was entertaining the idea of luring her to his bed to show her he could master her in more ways than one. That dark thought alone proved he hadn't changed. He had traded reckless destruction for selfish desire and cold ambition.

"You are right, Marsali," he said at last, his voice weary. "No one has to like me, but I will be obeyed. Now take me to the keep. I intend to know why Abercrombie has allowed the castle to fall into such disgrace."

Within twenty minutes of entering the keep, Duncan had tripped over the pair of piglets running down the stairwell; fended off the advances of a well-endowed woman who'd popped out of an empty herring barrel, mistaking him for a clansman named Georgie; and had come face to face with an old portrait of himself as a child that hung in the gallery above the great hall.

He was amazed at first, considering his history and subsequent banishment, that the portrait had remained all these years alongside the other honorable MacElgins. Warriors and chieftains who had not shamed their ancestors with tales of adolescent evils.

Only on closer inspection did he see the Devil's horns and pitchfork penned over the original portrait, the cloven hoofs protruding from his best knee breeches. Even now he could feel the anger and resentment that blazed from the eyes of the wild boy he had been, the bewilderment of being dragged from the scene of a double murder and discovering his true identity in an unforgettable night with the Beltane bonfires blazing in the background.

He remembered the morning that the portrait had been painted. Only three days had passed since he'd learned that the abusive drunk named Fergus who had raised him was not his natural father, that the clan's laird and chieftain, the Marquess of Portmuir, Kenneth MacElgin, had waited until the man's death to claim Duncan as his heir and only child. On the day of the portrait-painting, Kenneth had stood guard at the door with a broadsword to make sure Duncan did not escape. If Kenneth was determined that the world would pay homage to his precious son, Duncan was just as determined to prove he was not worthy of such homage if it killed them both.

Duncan smiled grimly. No, Fortune had not been at all kind to the old MacElgin. For thirteen years Kenneth had kept his long-ago association with Duncan's mother, Janet, a secret. He had pretended ignorance of the son that had come as a result of their brief illicit union, a trophy of Kenneth's manhood that he had not dared acknowledge for Janet's sake, out of respect for her deep religious conviction and the shame of an adulterous affair that had borne fruit.

But when Janet and her cruel common-law husband had been found mysteriously murdered in their cot one Beltane night, Kenneth MacElgin and his tacksman had swooped down like avenging angels to save Janet's two orphans— Duncan and his older half-sister, Judith. For if Kenneth had appeared to turn a blind eye to Duncan's existence, he had coveted him in his heart and had waited for the day he could claim him.

At last Kenneth could announce to the clan that he had produced an heir, a feat of virility he had not accomplished with the two legitimate wives he had outlived. Duncan, sullen and belligerent, immediately tried to escape the parade of tutors and tailors, of fencing lessons and servants that now shadowed his every move. He rebelled against the love his natural father tried to shower on him, not trusting it. He rebelled against his heritage, seething inwardly that his father had not intervened before, when Janet was alive.

Fergus may not have sired Duncan from his own seed, but he had left his mark all the same. The constant beatings, the verbal belittlement, had shaped Duncan's character in devious channels as powerful as the laws of heredity.

And when the inevitable whisperings began that Duncan had murdered his own parents, he had not bothered to deny them. He had behaved like an impostor in his father's castle, fueling the suspicions. His clansmen gossiped behind his back, recalling the small cruelties he'd inflicted on them in his youth.

"God." He drew a breath, staring at the portrait. "God. Somebody take that thing off the wall and have it burned."

"It doesn't look a thing like you," Marsali said quietly behind him.

He turned on her, startled from his thoughts and enraged

at having been caught in a moment of unguarded vulnerability, the pain of the boy in that painting as raw as if it had
been only yesterday. For an instant he was tempted to shove
her aside and run, as he would have done years ago, shame
threatening to overshadow the man he'd become.

"Look harder, then." He grasped the crook of her elbow
and drew her over to the dim light filtering through the
window, his voice deliberately cruel. "Why, I could sprout
horns at any second. I could abduct you to my underground
kingdom and devour you, little girl. I'll wager you could find
any number of men in the courtyard below who will swear
I've been seen prowling the halls with smoke pouring out of
my nostrils."

She eased her elbow free of his bruising hold, more sorry
for his pain than afraid of his anger, which she sensed was
not directed at her. "Isn't that what you wanted them to
think?"

"I don't give a damn what they think."

"Yes you do," Marsali said with infuriating certainty,
remembering the stricken look in his eyes when the stableboy had rebuffed him. "You owe them your help."

"No, I—" He smiled reluctantly, realizing in amazement
that he was arguing his personal affairs with a maidservant.
Who was she to remind him of his guilt, his need for
atonement? "Ah, we're forgetting your place in this castle,
aren't we, Marsali? You are to serve me and see to my
comfort. You are *not* to give me advice."

She shook her head in chagrin. "But you need advice, my
lord. In fact, I have never seen a man in more dire need of
advising than you."

"Marsali, hear me well." He walked her back against the
window embrasure, his face pressed to hers. Her eyes
widened. She lifted her hand to the black cord at her throat,
but she held her ground. Duncan gave her credit for that.

"I can hear you quite well, my lord, as probably can the
rest of the castle."

"Good. Because I want you to know that I have *paid*
advisors to advise me. Men who are mathematical geniuses,
historians, military strategists, former soldiers, and minis-
ters of state."

"You see," she said with a knowing smile, "that's the problem right there. All your advisors are men, and all *men* can think about is fighting wars."

He had to laugh at her irrational reasoning. "That is what they are *paid* to think about."

"Wars and money," she said with a sigh.

Suddenly Duncan could not decide if he wanted to throttle her or take her in his arms. Now that she had finally stopped lecturing him, he could enjoy staring at her up close, smelling the elusive honey sweetness of heather in her hair. For the first time he noticed the tiny mole at the corner of her mouth. The pulsebeat at the hollow of her throat drew his gaze downward to a black silken cord that disappeared into the cleft of her breasts. One way or another, either with her convoluted arguing or her beguiling presence, she was going to drive him up the wall. Hungry, travel-weary, disgusted at his homecoming, he had allowed the girl to penetrate his guard.

Marsali moistened her lips, fascinated by the conflicting emotions that crossed his face. The angrier he became, the more she realized she had to be patient with him because her father had taught her that great outward displays of anger usually came from deep internal pain. Men like Duncan did not reveal themselves easily. It behooved her to help him become the great chieftain the clan needed, even if it appeared an impossible task. She would have to call upon all her courage.

"Why are you looking at me in that way?" he asked in a suspicious voice.

A blur of movement in the courtyard below caught his attention before she could answer. His clansmen were playing golf with broadswords and a basket of hard-boiled eggs. The sight wrenched him back to the restrictions of reality. He had an objective, a promise to the Crown, and only a limited time to achieve it. Seducing a bedraggled little baggage who did not know her place was not part of his plans. Perhaps she would even run away during the night. It might be easier for him if she did in the end.

He drew back from the window, noticing the involuntary shudder, most probably of relief, that passed over Marsali.

All the better. He frightened her. That showed the beginning of respect, although he doubted she understood what the word meant, obviously having been allowed to run unsupervised for too many years.

"I've wasted enough time," he said, moving past her but deliberately not glancing at the portrait. "What am I going to do with this place?"

She touched the pendant around her neck. "When *I* didn't know what to do about a problem, my mother always read to me from the Bible."

He almost laughed at her incredible naiveté. "I suspect this castle is beyond even the Almighty's help."

Marsali stared at his broad, sun-burnished shoulders in annoyance. She had her work cut out for her, all right, turning this hard man into a wise and compassionate ruler. She couldn't decide if she should question her uncle's vision on the matter. After all, Uncle Colum had gotten the timing wrong for the ambush on the captain of the dragoons. Her own intuition on the matter had apparently become muddled by her embarrassing preoccupation with Duncan's physical presence.

"Take me to Abercrombie, Marsali," Duncan said, sounding impatient.

Marsali didn't move, dreading what was about to happen. *She* wasn't responsible for what had happened to Abercrombie, whose fate no one in the castle either knew or cared to admit. But Duncan would probably find a way to blame her all the same.

He glanced around, studying her worried face.

"Dear God." He took an involuntary step toward her. "The blasted fools have murdered him, haven't they? They've actually murdered an appointee of the Crown."

Marsali opened her mouth but no sound came out, leaving her in condemning silence.

"Answer me, Marsali." His face became a study in darkness, unyielding angles, shadowed planes. The devil-boy in the portrait full grown, in the flesh. "When was the last time you saw Abercrombie?"

"Well." Her voice finally emerged as a nervous croak. "Well, that would have been on Hogmanay."

"January." He frowned. "Six months ago. Was he alive?"

She stared down at the tips of her scuffed boots. "You have to understand that he was a horrible little man."

He came forward, forcing Marsali to stumble back until she stood directly under the portrait of him with all its insulting graffiti. Yes, he *was* that boy. Urges of a definitely demoniac nature were rearing inside him.

"He was walking the edges of the battlements blind-folded," she said in a small choked voice.

"What? Was the man trying to commit suicide?"

Marsali put her hand to her heart again. It gave her palpitations when his voice dropped to that ominous baritone. "I was delivering some herbs to Cook at the time, so I never really knew the details. However, from what I could gather, Mr. Abercrombie wasn't exactly walking the battlements blindfolded of his own free will."

"Where is he now?" Duncan asked, his face grim.

Marsali dared draw a breath. "To be honest, the last I heard he was hiding out in the chapel."

"In a coffin?"

"I don't know," she whispered.

He caught hold of her hand, crushing the feeling from her fingers. "The chapel. God help me. Heads are going to roll if they've killed a government agent."

Chapter

5

Duncan plucked loose a handful of the arrows embedded in the exterior of the chapel's heavy oaken door and threw them to his feet. "It's Duncan MacElgin, Abercrombie," he shouted, kneeling at the keyhole. "If you're in there, man, answer me."

Silence. Then a shuffling so faint Duncan couldn't tell if he was conversing with a man or a family of mice inside the chapel. "I'm a friend, Abercrombie. Open this damned door now!"

"Savages," a muffled voice responded. "MacElgin is naught but another word for savages, and this castle the Devil's playing field."

Duncan glanced back at Marsali, catching her broad grin before she could wipe it off her face. "You find this amusing, Marsali?" he asked softly.

"Of course not, my lord," she murmured, her lips twitching in a traitorous smile. "It's a disgrace."

Duncan banged his fist again, dislodging another spray of arrows. "This is General Duncan MacElgin, Abercrombie, and I will protect you. However, I cannot do so if you continue to cower behind that door."

Silence again.

Duncan swung around, prepared to take his frustration out on Marsali. This time, however, she was ready for him, shaking her head in sympathetic agreement.

"A shocking disgrace, my lord."

He got to his feet. "This is your last chance, Abercrombie. I swear to God if you do not let me in right now, I am going to get a ladder and order all those nasty children in the courtyard to climb up after you with their crossbows."

The threat apparently worked.

The crossbar creaked from within. Duncan managed to jump back a fraction of a moment before the door flew open to reveal the diminutive figure cowering in the chapel.

Disbelieving, he stared down at the Lowland Scot administrator who hid behind a MacElgin medieval shield and whose head of unkempt white hair and suspicious face were overshadowed by the holy basin he wore as a helmet on his head. "You—*you're* Abercrombie? The Crown sent you to manage my castle?"

"I am. They did." The suspicion in the man's hazel eyes hardened into fearful hostility as he in turn noticed Duncan's half-nakedness and the dingy MacElgin plaid. "But you're no distinguished marquess and general—you're one of *them.*"

Panic in eyes, he extended all his puny strength to slam the door in Duncan's face. On reflex Duncan threw up his arm and sent the door crashing up against the wall, rattling the row of plucked chickens strung from the chapel rafters. Stepping over the threshold, he stared around him in amazement: papers, books, blankets, eating utensils. The chapel was a regular encampment.

"What the hell has been going on here?" he demanded, his voice booming in the confined space.

Abercrombie dropped his shield and grabbed the broadsword that lay across the pew behind him. "One more step and you're a dead man," he said in a menacing squeak, a mouse assaulting a lion.

"Put the sword down before you hurt yourself, Abercrombie," Duncan said calmly, struggling not to laugh. "I am not one of them."

"You're dressed—or undressed—like one of them."

Abercrombie poked his finger at Marsali as she sneaked in behind Duncan. "She's one of them, to be sure. A wild thing, she is, with that bird of prey that follows her like a shadow and her uncle in league with the Devil. And—"

Abercrombie broke off, glancing from Duncan to Marsali, as if suddenly wondering if she were the Devil's handmaiden and this dark man her master.

"I am as much a victim of the clan's anarchy as you are, Abercrombie," Duncan tried to explain again. "They assaulted me on the moor and took my clothes. How long have you been locked in here, man?"

Abercrombie lowered the sword, tears of self-pity filling his eyes. "Two months, my lord. Two long months of fending off the wicked bastards."

"You should not have ordered my cousin flogged your first day here," Marsali interrupted, her eyes flashing. "It made a very bad impression on the others."

"Hold your tongue, Marsali," Duncan said, not looking at her. "Obviously this man has been mistreated, and I will see justice served."

"Liam was only twelve years old," she continued, her voice rising at the memory. "Twelve years old and flogged unconscious for a minor transgression."

"What did the lad do?" Duncan asked Abercrombie.

"Threw a glass of goat's milk in my face, my lord." Abercrombie glared at Marsali. "An act of sheer defiance if ever I saw it, and this woman should have been whipped alongside him. Stripping grown men and forcing them to wander about that cold desolate moor. It's an outrage, an insult to manhood, an—"

"Yes, I have my own opinions of her conduct," Duncan said in an ironic tone. "But where are the soldiers the Crown sent to remain here and see your orders executed? Don't tell me they're holed up in the dungeon?"

"They disappeared their first night in the castle, my lord," Abercrombie answered, blinking furiously beneath the basin. "I suspect they were chased off by your clansmen. Possibly even murdered."

"Untrue." Marsali pushed between Duncan and the other man, no longer able to control her anger in the face of the blatant lie. "The big cowards ran off during the night and no one has seen them since. And they stole a month's supply of provisions."

Duncan gently nudged her aside and wrested the sword from Abercrombie's trembling hands, his voice revealing none of his deep contempt. "Whatever has passed before is past, and Mr. Abercrombie and I will be putting our heads together to make a great many changes."

"I am not staying, not another day." Abercrombie's voice quavered at the prospect. "No, now that you are here, my lord, I shall collect my things and . . ."

His protest died away into a whimper as Duncan lifted the sword a little higher, his face set like flint. "You are going to stay here and help me, Abercrombie, as you have been ordered to do."

"Please, my lord." Abercrombie looked pathetic, his holy-basin helmet sliding down over his forehead. "Cleave me in half wi' that sword if you will, but don't make me stay. I cannot face these heathens again."

"Compose yourself, Mr. Abercrombie. You're an embarrassment, begging like a dog for a bone, and in front of a woman, to boot. Where's your pride, your dignity to behave like this?"

Abercrombie answered with a loud sniff, sinking back down onto the pew in abysmal dejection at the prospect of remaining inside the castle. "Please, my lord," he whispered again, only to jump to his feet as Duncan took a menacing step toward him.

"Pull yourself together, Mr. Abercrombie. Remove that ridiculous bowl—it makes you look like a toadstool—and take me on a tour of the castle."

"A t-tour, my lord? We'll be taking our lives into our hands."

"Yes, a tour." Duncan started to lay down the weapon, then decided it couldn't hurt his image to be seen walking his domain adequately armed. Besides, Abercrombie had a point: He might damn well need the protection.

He strode to the door, stopping briefly to consider Marsali, the fading afternoon light picking out wine-red glints in the tumult of her long curly hair. Again he was struck by her fey loveliness, the illusion of fragility that hid a quick mind and feral heart. Again he felt that tug of haunting familiarity as he stared into her face. *Did* he know her?

She gave him an impudent grin. He glanced away before he could grin back.

"Make yourself useful there, lass," he said gruffly. "You can start by working on washing my clothes. Come on, Abercrombie. Help me find something decent to wear." He paused, staring above his head. "By the way, is there a reason why you have five plucked chickens strung up from the rafters?"

Abercrombie squared his stooped shoulders and followed Duncan to the door. "They were my sustenance, my lord. I fished them out of the moat when the guards were drinking and playing cards, which fortunately for me is the majority of the time."

Duncan managed to keep a straight face, hearing Marsali succumb to muffled laughter behind them. "Ingenious, Abercrombie. But you don't expect me to believe you've survived on raw chickens for two entire months?"

"Och, no, sir." Abercrombie gave Duncan a smug look. "I roasted them late at night in the sanctuary lamp wi' a bit of holy oil."

Marsali snorted. "And here everyone was wondering where all those delicious smells were coming from in the wee small hours."

Duncan shook his head in mock admiration. "My, my, Abercrombie, aren't you the resourceful one? But what did you drink, man, those two long months?"

Abercrombie puffed his chest out like a pigeon. "Eucharist wine, my lord. What else?"

"Why, you crafty old fox. I'll not turn my back on you."

Duncan chuckled dryly and clapped the little man on the shoulder, practically driving him to his knees as a hammer would a nail. Abercrombie staggered but pretended to laugh too, and the pair of them headed toward the door, the sound of their shared amusement grating in Marsali's ears, excluding her.

She trailed slowly after them, a troubled frown creasing her forehead. Had she misjudged the MacElgin then? For certain he had failed a crucial test: He should have tossed the miserable little traitor out the window when she'd told him about the flogging of a child. As chieftain, Duncan should have displayed deep anger toward Abercrombie, compassion for his victim, and then at the very least he should have put the pompous Scot into the finger pillory for a fortnight to be pelted with rotten produce.

She stared down the shadows of the spiral tower stairs at Duncan's big receding figure, disappointment weighing like a stone in her chest. Perhaps she was too impressed by the man's air of authority to perceive his deeper flaws. Perhaps she was blinded by the beauty of a man who looked like a medieval knight commissioned by the saints to save his people. She wanted to believe he had been sent as an answer to her prayers because she was heartsick with burying brothers and cousins, not to mention a father.

Someone had to take the clan under control. But was the cost of salvation a pact with the Devil? Someone had to show the chieftain fealty. Why did it have to be her? She sighed, shaking her head as she hurried to catch up with them, not wanting to miss one moment of this exciting day.

She would give Duncan one more chance, although it concerned her that he had failed a very critical test of his character. It concerned her almost as much as the fact that she wanted to believe in him for reasons she suspected had nothing whatsoever to do with the clan.

By nightfall the news of Duncan's arrival had penetrated every nook and cranny of the castle. His presence had cast a somber pall over the usual nightly activities. The much-enjoyed running naked in and out of the great hall had been canceled, as had the dropping of young frogs into drunken clansmen's trews at dinner.

Duncan had not exactly won friends with the curt demands he had barked out during his "tour." His most dramatic run-in had come when he and Cook had butted heads during supper. They had never shared a warm relationship, even in their earlier years, and Duncan had not further endeared himself to the woman by summoning her to the hall to criticize her supper as he handed her a list of suggested French menus with a purse of coins to buy more palatable supplies.

"I do not *ever* want to lay eyes upon, let alone eat, another one of your stringy overcooked chickens again," he announced over the woman's spluttering protests.

Cook's face empurpled like an eggplant. No one had ever dared to complain about her cooking within her earshot. Several clansmen even ducked under the massive table for fear a violent battle would ensue.

Marsali was aghast at Duncan's tactless tyranny, challenging the heretofore most important woman, if not person, in the entire castle. And he'd done it publicly. At the table. Reduced to acting as serving maid as part of *her* punishment, Marsali had been severely tempted to empty a flagon of wine over his insensitive head. In fact, the force of her anger had driven her to storm out of the hall, defying him to stop her.

Which he did.

She had just reached the door when he'd half-risen from his massive Jacobean chair on its bulbous lion's-claw feet to summon her back.

"I do not remember giving you permission to leave, Marsali."

Hell's bells, the man had eyes like Eun, she thought in resentment, pivoting slowly as total silence blanketed the hall. Her clansmen regarded her with varying degrees of embarrassed amusement, trepidation, and relief that their chieftain was temporarily, at least, overlooking them.

Word had spread through the castle like wildfire that the MacElgin was capable of *anything*. Only that afternoon he had ordered the men to rewash all their sweaty plaids, another grave insult to Cook, who had already supervised this month's washing. He had forbidden women to pop bare-breasted out of herring barrels, and he had banished Effie's pet piglets to the castle yard.

But the penultimate insult was the punishment he'd inflicted on brave wee Marsali Hay, making her his personal servant—Marsali, a blue-blooded descendant of Olaf the Black himself, King of Man and the Isles. Marsali, who had lost a father, lover, and two brothers in the space of three years. Marsali, with her easy laughter and unwavering loyalty. It was an affront to what piddling little the clan held dear.

"I am waiting, Marsali."

Her hackles rose at his tone of voice. She anticipated trouble, that somehow she was about to become the brunt of his black sense of humor. She reminded herself that she was submitting to him for a reason, that her patience would bear the fruit of peace for the clan.

As she approached his chair, she screwed up the courage to look him straight in the eye. The midnight-blue intensity of his gaze took her off guard. Heat suffused her face, but she held her head high, struggling to subdue the impact of his stare, which warned he had something horrible in store.

Duncan subsided back into his chair as Marsali returned in reluctant steps to the table, her small face set in a scowl of irritation.

"You have dropped your serviette again, my lord?" she inquired in a tone that suggested she'd like to strangle him with it.

Duncan waved the white linen napkin limply in her direction. "No, it's right here."

"Your wine goblet is too heavy to lift?" she asked, the dangerous glint in her eye growing brighter.

He leaned back in his chair, long muscular legs out-sprawled like an indolent conqueror's, studying her in cold unblinking silence. Marsali stared back, positive now that she and Colum had made a severe metaphysical miscalculation. This man could not possibly be the link to bringing peace and prosperity to the clan, born to the position or not.

Aye, he reveled in the role of chieftain tonight, his tall handsome frame emphasized to advantage in a costume he'd evidently found in his father's wardrobe: white ruffled shirt of fine lawn and black velvet knee breeches, white linen hose encasing his muscular calves, the MacElgin plaid pinned to his broad shoulder with a silver brooch encircled by Chinese amethysts. His long black hair fell loosely, framing his handsome face. It struck Marsali as a cruel irony that someone graced with such devastating physical appeal had been cursed with an utter absence of emotional depth. But there it was. The sad truth.

"There is another draft on your neck, my lord?" she asked in a falsely solicitous voice.

Duncan raised his goblet to his lips to conceal a wolfish

grin. He was enjoying himself immensely. The woman's spirit added incredible spice to his efforts. Spice. Ah, that was the word for her with that warm sun-kissed skin and that small lithe body, its sensuality ill-concealed by her drab gown. He would have dearly loved under other circumstances to take advantage of her subservient role.

He cast a casual glance around the hall, struck anew by the overt hostility that engulfed him. Hate him or not, he'd be willing to wager this was the first night since his father's death that his clansmen were behaving like human beings. Hope, albeit dim, rose inside him.

"Marsali, you will fetch the ladder and remove the tapestries from the wall. I find the smell of mold offensive while I'm eating."

Marsali nodded weakly, suppressing the urge to roll her eyes. "I'll have it done after supper."

"Not after supper." He drummed his long tapered fingers on the chair's lion-paw arms. "Now."

She took a deep fortifying breath. She would find a way to sneak out of the castle and confront Colum tonight if it killed her because another day of pretending servitude to this selfish wretch would kill her. She could not bear the way he played her like a puppet on a string, and he liked it too.

"Yes, my lord." She edged away from the table, digging her nails into her palms. "I'll find a couple of lads to take care of the offensive smell."

"I want *you* to take care of it, Marsali." He folded his arms across his chest, his face as arrogant as an emperor's. "This instant, before the dessert course is served, and my appetite is spoiled."

From the corner of her eye she caught the sly grins of her clansmen. Stung by their amusement, she lowered her voice. "You want *me* to climb on a ladder and pull down the tapestries?"

He tossed his napkin onto his plate, his blue eyes reflecting the flame of the candles flickering on the table. "Unless you know of a better way to remove them."

She sauntered up to the side of his chair, pretending to brush a few crumbs from his shirt as she whispered with cold fury, "And shall I trim your toenails with my teeth when I'm finished?"

"If you like," he said calmly. "But not too closely, mind."

Marsali gazed down, infuriated, into his dark chiseled face, wondering if she could overturn the soup tureen in his lap and make it to the door alive.

He reached for his goblet, a lazy smile touching his lips. "Have you suddenly turned to stone, lass? I'm expecting guests at any day, my dessert any moment, and I cannot abide the reek of mildew. I have a delicate nose."

Marsali gritted her teeth. "Yes, my lord." *But this is the last bloody time. Tomorrow I'll put as much energy into humiliating you as you have me.*

She whirled, her pale blue muslin skirts swishing behind her like an angry cat's tail. Duncan chuckled to himself, savoring the victory. Poor Marsali. She had no idea of the little humiliations he had planned for her tomorrow. He had restrained himself this evening. He had been kind to her while he assessed the situation. In the morning she would learn the true meaning of respect, and he would have fun while she did. Nothing too cruel, though. Just the proper dose of domestic discipline to put her in her place.

Chapter

6

Duncan's glow of satisfaction had already begun to fade before midnight, replaced by the unwelcome barrage of memories that assaulted him as he began to prowl the twisting torchlit corridors of the castle.

As if it had been only a week ago and not fifteen years, he remembered his poor stunned father dragging him through these very passageways, the clan's tacksman, Andrew, following with concern on his gentle face, trying to reassure the young terrified boy that all would be well.

And how had Duncan repaid the man?

He had spat in Andrew's face, rejecting, mocking the kindness he had never known even as his lonely heart craved it. He had cursed and swung with all his might; he had broken loose from his father and Andrew to run shrieking through the kitchens, breaking bottles and chairs, shoving a much younger Cook against the stove with such uncontrolled rage he dislocated her shoulder.

"Young demon," she had whispered, cowering tearfully in the corner. "Dirty murderer . . ."

Demon. Murderer. But no one had ordered *him,* at only eleven years old, to be flogged when God only knew he'd done far more than Marsali's cousin to deserve it. Abercrombie would have to pay for that cruelty, after Duncan had gotten his use out of the stupid man.

Eager to escape the oppressive atmosphere of the castle, he left the deserted great hall by a side passage and walked to the stables, his order to be let outside obeyed with comical swiftness. His stallion had been found at the moor by a shepherd and curried (by Marsali) only hours ago, the last demand he had made of the exhausted woman before dismissing her for the night. No doubt she would sleep like the dead until dawn, when he intended to awaken her with a fresh list of demanding chores. He chuckled softly at the prospect.

He rode without thought to his destination, contempt hardening his face at the black piles of rubble littering the roadside where English soldiers had begun to clear cottages to build their military road. He was not insensitive to the Highlanders' feelings nor unmoved by the sight of this destruction. But he could see little point in men sacrificing their lives for the inevitable thrust of progress into even these remote wilds. And he had more than enough experience in the British army to predict the Jacobite cause would die a violent death.

He swore it was not intentional, but suddenly he found himself staring down at the thatched stone cottage in the tangled beech copse where he had been born, where his mother and the vicious bastard she had married had died, violently, on a Beltane night over two decades ago. He slowed his horse, unprepared for the dark emotions that swept over him, the painful lure of the past.

He had lived an incredible life since then, he had been fêted in foreign courts; he had won the hand of a gently bred English lady and the sponsorship of her politically influential father. He had risen from the tomb of personal tragedy.

But when he dismounted and walked inside the forlorn abandoned cottage, he became an angry and abused eleven-year-old boy again, and all the glory he had achieved dissipated like mist.

The door behind him gaped open, its broken crossbar hanging at the exact angle from when Kenneth MacElgin and his retainers had kicked it, drawn by the sound of Duncan's aunt sobbing hysterically for help. Even the breath of the nearby sea could not cleanse the remembered stench of blood, ale, and peat smoke from Duncan's nostrils. He closed his eyes, assailed by repressed grief and unspent anger.

Aye, for all the honor bestowed on him, for all the years that had passed, as he stood in that dark cottage, he was a child again, caught in a nightmare of deadly violence, and escape was no easier now than it had been then.

Duncan lifted his head, the dark circle of his thoughts broken by the vibrations of a rider galloping across the ridge that overhung the cottage. Deliberately not looking down at the floor where he had last seen his mother lying, lifeless, he hurried outside to the sunken yard and looked up in amazement at the figure that seemed to fly like an otherworldly being across the tree-shadowed path.

Marsali. Damnation, it was that girl again, flagrantly disobeying his orders to remain inside the castle until he gave her permission to leave. Anger welled inside him, a welcome distraction from the torment of his memories. Was she running away, fed up with her punishment and suspecting he had even grimmer chores planned? Had she followed him here to flaunt her defiance?

He strode toward his own horse, smiling unwillingly at the absurd memory of her sliding down the ladder in the great hall to fall on her rump, unbalanced by the weight of the enormous tapestry she had singlehandedly hauled down.

The look of fury she had shot him.

He mounted and cantered around the cottage, remembering the private ways of childhood, the hidden paths he had discovered years ago to avoid Fergus's drunken rages. She had to be heading for the cove, with its honeycombed caves and rock archways, a place of secrets and shadows. His smile faded. In the old days the cove had provided an ideal trysting spot for lovers. He'd met more than one village maid there at midnight himself. He had no reason to believe human nature had changed that much in twenty years.

A sultry summer night. A young clansman waiting eagerly for her in the moonlight. A backdrop of crashing ocean waves to serenade the two lovers. For a moment Duncan was tempted to turn around and pretend he hadn't seen her. He could deal with her disobedience tomorrow. But after the unpleasant visit to the wretched cottage, he was too soul-weary to interrupt an intimate moment.

As he reached the rocky knoll path that led down to the beach, he started to urge his horse back onto the castle path. Then he saw her again, her bright hair like a beacon in the gray shadows of glooming, her bare brown legs exposed and clutching the mare's sides as she rode toward the dark cluster of caves at the end of the cove.

The sight of her sparked something indefinable inside him.

He wanted to chase her down. He could outrun her horse and lead her himself into one of the damp private caves where he had hidden for hours, hearing Fergus call him from the cliffs. He wanted her vibrancy to counteract the coldness of his spirit. He wanted to tumble her to the sand. But what was the point? He couldn't impress her with his legendary skill at seduction. If he tried to charm her with the clever badinage he had learned from the intellectual courtesans of the Parisian salons, she would laugh in his face, confused by words and customs she had never learned.

She would look at him, as the other Highlanders had looked at him all day, and he would become the outcast again, Duncan the Black Demon, the boy whose beautiful mother had bewitched the laird into believing he had fathered her son.

Marsali wouldn't give a damn that grateful hordes had strewn flowers at his feet in the streets of Holland. Cook in her sublime ignorance would not care that he had given her the identical menu, and the purse to buy it, for a month's meals worthy to grace the table of Czar Peter the Great.

He rubbed his hand across his unshaven face. Christ, why should *he* care? Peasants, women, drunks, Jacobite sympathizers, who would all end up getting themselves killed like his father.

He lowered his hand, a chill of suspicion cutting through his depression. He *assumed* out of his own irrational imaginings that Marsali was meeting a lover when in fact she might have a more dangerous objective in mind.

Intelligent, sharp-witted, strong-willed, a woman with

good cause to hate the English for the loss of the men she'd loved. God only knew the wee hellion could be hatching another rebellion right under Duncan's nose, and when it failed, he would be the one to shoulder the blame. The world-famous military general who could not control a mere girl.

The hotheaded little fool would destroy everything, including herself, just as his gentle misguided father had done. Duncan's head pounded with visions of being stripped of his rank and court-martialed, of losing the plump Border prize the prime minister had dangled before him like a carrot. He saw himself dishonored and impoverished, his hopes crumbled to dust, his achievements in ashes.

Hell, for all he knew, he could expect a knife in the back on the lonely ride home, courtesy of the clan welcoming party. He would end his life as he'd begun it, in violence and despised.

Everything destroyed by a fairy brat's defiance. A serving wench who barely came to his waist. A girl he had allowed himself the dangerous indulgence of pitying, of desiring. An urchin with the arrogance of a princess.

He leaned forward and spurred his stallion after her, his long black hair coming loose from its leather thong to lash his coldly determined face. Even if he had to chain her to his damned bedpost at night, she would not disobey him again. He would break her spirit before she ruined them both.

Marsali vented a sigh of frustration and slid to the sand. As she marched toward the caves, her mare stood resting at the shore. Uncle Colum thought himself very clever and elusive, never staying in the same location for more than a few months at a time. But Marsali was fed up with all this mystery.

First, he had lived on the moor to better communicate with the old gods. Then he had installed himself in the castle dungeon as resident wizard because he was reading a book about alchemy and thought he'd give turning base metal into gold a try. The previous summer he had wandered willy-nilly in the woods to contact the spirits of his Druid ancestors.

But ever since last autumn he had set up housekeeping in a wrecked old ship to study the ebb and flow of the waves. The ship was almost to the end of the cove, the tide was rising as a storm brewed offshore, and earlier in the day he had mentioned something about casting a solstice spell in a cave at midnight.

Well, hell. There had to be at least two dozen caves, and one looked about the same as the other to Marsali, her perception dulled by a day of grueling physical labor and public humiliation.

Furthermore, she had a knot on her head from that smelly tapestry falling off the wall and a throbbing bruise on her behind from where she had landed.

"Find the old codger for me, Eun," she called to the bird perched on the hooded lip of yet another cave before her. "Magic or not, he and I are having a straight talk about the chieftain."

She had just stepped inside the mouth of the cave when she felt the thunderous resonance through the soles of her feet of a rider approaching. Her mare whickered in warning and moved swiftly down the cove out of sight, as if sensing danger in the air. It crossed Marsali's mind to make a similar escape. But there was no time. Besides, she was more curious than afraid.

Tightening her shawl around her shoulders, she edged back to the mouth of the cave, her eyes widening in anticipation as the horseman drew his lathered horse to a halt. Duncan, of all people. Dear Lord, the man was magnificent, long muscular legs gripping the horse's lathered flesh before he vaulted to the sand, his black hair framing a face that an artist might have chiseled in a fit of inspiration.

Marsali frowned, not certain if he had seen her or if she could continue to admire him in secret. He was heading straight for the cave, the length of stride portending trouble. Before she could duck back inside, she was pinned against the wall like a butterfly by his large frame. She wriggled helplessly. The scent of camphor and lavender from his father's old clothes mingled with his own male musk to make her aching head swim. The tips of her breasts tingled, flattened against the wall of his chest. Her heart racing, she stared up at the underside of his clenched jaw, trying not to remember what he looked like naked. The harder she tried, the clearer the image became.

His gaze raked her briefly before darting to the end of the cave. "Where is he?"

"Where is who?" Intrigued, she glanced back herself in the direction of his scrutiny, grateful to be distracted from her own thoughts.

His gaze swung back to her face. "The lover you planned a tryst with," he said grimly.

"The who I planned a what with?" she asked, blinking in bewilderment from behind her wind-blown tangle of hair.

"The spy then," Duncan said impatiently.

She lifted her hand in a tentative caress to his lean cheek. "You are unwell, my lord?" she inquired gently. "I should have warned you about Cook's potage. She tends to use the nastiest ingredients, and you did insult her cooking in front of everyone. Perhaps she poisoned—"

He jerked his hand from her hand, liking her delicate touch too much. "I know all about your Jacobite associations, Marsali."

"You do?"

"Yes. All about the rebellion you're planning."

She frowned, trying to remember if madness ran in the MacElgin family. Surely the man wasn't referring to her harmless little ambushes as rebellions? "You didn't drink any of the mead Johnnie uses to clean the dirks, did you?" she asked guardedly.

Something in her voice, the almost maternal concern and absurd innocence, penetrated the dark mood that had ensnared him earlier. She was making him feel like a fool again; he was suddenly embarrassed by his frenzy to follow her here, unsure of what he'd hoped to prove. He might have conquered great armies, but apparently not his own deepest insecurities. The girl reduced him to raw emotion. She brought out a side of him he'd never confronted before.

"I thought I gave you orders to remain inside the castle."

She clenched the dangling corners of her shawl, curling

her bare toes into the crunchy white sand. His voice was doing strange things to her system again, and his large body blocked any hope of escape. What had angered him so? "I couldn't sleep, my lord."

Duncan forced her back even farther, not caring that he left her little room to breathe. The point of their conversation eluded him. Minuscule droplets of fine summer mist spangled her hair, reflecting the moonlight. He felt like a dragon snorting fire on a fairy princess. He also felt like an idiot for longing to believe the innocence in her eyes when logic warned him she had to be lying.

"You were meeting someone, weren't you?"

"Yes," she replied, seeing no reason to lie.

He covered an unexpected jolt of disappointment with a cynical smile. "Lover or spy?"

"Neither, actually." She shrugged blithely, her conscience clear. "I was looking for my uncle, but I don't know which cave he calls a covenstead these days."

A peculiar alchemy of feelings clashed inside Duncan: relief, amused contempt at his own suspicious nature, and some other deeper emotion he didn't care to explore. "Your uncle—"

"The wizard," Marsali said, fascinated by the sudden medley of strange emotions that transformed his face, hinting at roiling depths below the calm surface.

A droplet of mist ran down the curl that caressed her cheek and etched a silvery track to the base of her throat. Duncan slowly lifted his hand and smudged it with his thumb, his touch amazingly tender. "You defied me," he said in a subdued voice. "I'm afraid I'll have to discipline you."

His voice was low with undercurrents as powerful as the sea outside, and no doubt just as treacherous if a woman let herself wander out too far. Unfortunately, Marsali's spirit had always loved a bit of adventure. "I couldn't sleep," she said again, a shudder of anticipation shooting all the way down to the soles of her feet.

He smiled slowly, his eyes taunting her. "Then I'll give you more work tomorrow."

A spurt of anger broke through the spell of sensual

lassitude that immobilized her. "You're a bastard," she said. "You enjoyed humiliating me."

"Aye," he admitted, chuckling. "There were moments."

"The . . . the tide is rising, my lord."

He tugged lightly at the curl that touched her cheek, twining his forefinger around the auburn threads of her hair. "Let it rise."

She lowered her eyes, studying the ruffles of his finely embroidered shirt until her vision blurred. "My heart is pounding like the surf outside," she said softly. "I'm not sure my legs will continue to support me. My head is swimming, partially because the tapestry fell upon it but mostly due to you, and—" She drew a breath, her gaze flying to his as he hooked his thumb into her gown and drew her by the rough muslin against him. The warm abrasion of his callused skin against the swell of her breast sent tendrils of heat curling deep down into her belly. Marsali had never experienced such delightful confusion. She had never known a man like him in her life.

She shivered, whispering, "What are you doing?"

He was silent for a moment, his blue eyes unfathomable.

"God only knows, Marsali, and He's probably too afraid to watch."

Before she could decide how to handle this, he had drawn her into his arms and lowered his mouth to hers, kissing her with an erotic tenderness that electrified her. Her entire body jerked as if seared by lightning at the contact. His mouth tasted cool and redolent of wine, possessive, gently demanding an answer. When he gripped her tighter, she felt her resistance melting into a strange anticipation. The power of his kiss stole her breath. She trembled violently.

"Marsali."

His deep voice resounded in the distance. She was falling down a bottomless hole, floating on a current of endless enjoyment—until he brought his hands to her shoulders to give her a rousing shake.

"You're shivering like a larch in a spring gale," he said in amusement. "Do I frighten you that much, lass?"

She blinked, resenting the return to reality. "Sometimes you do," she admitted with a deep sigh, snuggling into him.

"But I'm probably shivering more because the water is coming up to my toes, and it's damned cold at the cove even in summer."

Duncan stood perfectly still as she rubbed her feet against his ankles. Uninhibited, unaware of how she affected him, she had no inkling of the black urges he was battling. Very carefully, he lifted his hands from her shoulders. Her innocence flayed him to the core. Only a minute ago his anger at her had threatened to rage out of control. And now here he stood, spellbound, forgetting time and place, intrigued by a girl who had never trod one dainty toe beyond his wild land. A girl who had watched her clansmen smear his naked body with sludge and chicken feathers only hours ago.

A girl whose fey power he was just beginning to understand. The power of a pure heart and unbroken spirit, of loyalty and the ability to laugh in the face of adversity. A girl who trusted even him, and who tempted him beyond reason.

"You're a strange wee thing." He caught her chin in his fingers, examining her face as if it held an answer to her puzzling allure. "Most women wouldn't notice the cold when I was kissing them. "Didn't I do a proper job of it then?"

"I have nothing to compare it to," she said honestly, then leaned into him with a gasp as another wavelet broke around their feet.

"Your betrothed never kissed you?" Duncan asked in astonishment.

"Aye, but not like that," she confessed, grinning mischievously. "My father would have killed him."

Duncan fought the reaction that rose inside him, the stirrings of conscience and uncomplicated lust. This woman had no protector, he tried to remember, unless he counted himself, as a surrogate, as her laird and chieftain, and the impulses racing through him were anything but paternal. In fact, they were unspeakably wicked.

"Let go of me, Marsali," he said, taking a breath and praying the cool sea air would quelch the fire building in his loins.

"Why, my lord?" She sighed, pressing closer, confused by

the resurgence of anger she detected in his tone. Had she done something again to offend him? It seemed he was angry because he'd kissed her, but for her it had ended far too soon. "You're keeping me warm, and I like the feel of you."

"Wear a plaid," he said curtly, bringing his hands to her shoulders to push her away. The fire inside him wasn't dying out, after all. It was raging into a bloody bonfire, and if the damned girl didn't have the sense or experience to understand he was a heartless bastard who would take advantage of her innocence, then she could only blame herself.

"What about this uncle of yours?" he asked harshly, suddenly wishing someone else would assume responsibility for her. "And don't ever tell a man you like the feel of him again."

Marsali stiffened, remembering where she was with a horrible jolt of conscience. Whatever had she been thinking? What would happen if Uncle Colum were to suddenly materialize behind them? After all, a wizard possessed certain powers that even a chieftain could not claim.

What if her uncle were to catch her in Duncan's arms and change Duncan into a lobster, a power Colum allegedly owned but that Marsali had never witnessed? What if he hit Duncan over the head with his yew staff in his temper and knocked him out? Dear heaven, what if Colum took a very dim human view of the situation and demanded that Duncan marry his niece? Marsali snorted softly at the ridiculous image, picturing herself standing at the altar pledging her troth to an unconscious lobster.

Duncan arched his brow. "Most women don't snort the first time I kiss them either."

"Well—"

She broke off with a gasp of alarm, grabbing Duncan's arm to tug him toward the mouth of the cave as a large wave rolled toward them and thundered against his knees. The impact barely budged him, but it did bring his head around in surprise.

"We're going to drown, my lord! The cave fills within minutes."

Even as she spoke, the next wave gathered force and crashed against them, its unleashed power propelling them deeper into the cave. Marsali staggered backward as if drawn by an invisible hand, so slight it took little to unbalance her.

She fell backward, throwing her hands out behind her, only to feel icy sand envelop her up to her elbows. As the wave broke against the wall, saltwater stinging her eyes, she realized she had stumbled into one of the hidden sinkholes Uncle Colum had warned her about more times than she could count. She wasn't really worried, though. She knew the chieftain would save her.

Chapter

7

Duncan swung around to grab her, belatedly remembering the deadly riptides that had borne more than one of his relatives to an early and unexpected death. What in God's name had he been doing? Dallying with a dirty-faced hoyden. Misusing his power to intimidate a maidservant. He was worse than one of his raw teenage recruits, letting himself be charmed by a girl who had more audacity than his entire regiment.

How the hell had it happened? He had set out intending to punish her. Instead, he had trapped her like a lion in his lair. He had taken advantage of her inexperience, and in the end it was the sweet innocence of her response that had punished him.

Cursing his unawareness, or rather his irrational absorption with Marsali, Duncan dragged the sputtering girl into his arms and ran, carrying her outside in a wild race against the next wave. With an agility that he had sharpened on foreign battlefields, he splashed around a bank of submerged rocks and tumbled her down to a secluded inlet overshadowed by a cliff. To his amazement, she was grinning impishly at his efforts to save her, amused by a misadventure that could have swept them both out to sea.

He grunted and stretched out flat on his stomach, grateful at least that the cold sea water had dampened his absurd desire for the brat.

"It's very nice to be appreciated," he said wryly.

She burrowed up next to him; he tried to elbow her away and rolled onto his back. "Stop doing that. It's annoying."

"I can't help it," she said. "I'm wet and cold."

"Do you often ride alone at night?" he asked, scowling up at the sky.

"I do in summer." She sat bolt upright, flinging sand in his chest. "The horses—"

"—had the sense to seek higher ground." Damn if she didn't roll against him again, the position all the more arousing because she'd initiated it. "You're going to have to obey a curfew like everyone else," he said, wiping off his shirt. "No more riding alone."

"Hmmm."

Duncan cursed softly as he felt her wet little body relaxing against his, soft curves seeking a haven in the hard contours of his flank, tempting him all over again to take advantage of her drowsy vulnerability. "Look, I'm sorry you lost the man you loved," he said in a desperate bid to break the dangerous intimacy between them. "When Abercrombie finishes the accounts, I'll see if I can manage to dower you. God knows I'll probably only be able to scrape up a chicken or two."

She twisted around slowly, her dark tangled hair falling against Duncan's arm. "But I don't need you to dower me," she said in confusion. "I just need you to stay here and make sure there's no more killing. As soon as my brother's back is a little better, we're all going to Virginia to raise tobacco. I expect I'll find a husband there."

"You're what?" Duncan stared at her, the statement so patently absurd and yet sincere he couldn't help bursting into loud insulting laughter. "Virginia, Marsali. You've heard too many fairy tales, the romance of the red Indian, the wealthy planter's wife. Didn't anyone ever warn you of the dangers you'll face?"

She dribbled a handful of sand through her fingers, pursing her lips in annoyance that she'd revealed her private hopes, only to have him laugh in her face.

"There are dangers enough here," she said steadily.

He raised up on his elbows to look at her, his face sardonic. "You didn't exactly strike me as a woman who avoided danger this morning on the moor. You're courting it, Marsali. Someone is going to get killed."

Marsali's delicate features tightened in resentment. "The idea is to humiliate and discourage the English, not to kill them. You know there will be bloodshed enough once they finish that road on the coast and install their troops in the old fort."

"You ought to be at home raising babies, not chasing soldiers around the moor."

"Perhaps I could raise babies if there were any decent men left to have them with," she said heatedly, the subject a sore spot. "But I won't have to run around the moor now that you're here to keep the English under control, will I?"

Duncan lapsed into noncommittal silence, studying the sea to avoid her hopeful gaze, which pricked his conscience. He ought to tell her he'd been sent to do exactly the opposite, but he wasn't in the mood to shatter her naive faith. Let her believe in her silly dreams. He'd be gone before disillusionment dimmed the stars in her eyes.

"Talk to me," he said restlessly, aware that those eyes were riveted to his face. "Silence can be a dangerous thing."

Talk? Marsali flexed her fingers, suddenly wide awake. What a strange man he was. "What shall we talk about, my lord?"

"I don't care. Anything." Anything to distract him from the raw ache she had raked alive in him, a craving that had nothing to do with seduction, but a need to let the brightness of her unblemished spirit into the dark, cobwebbed corners of his own. Anything to delay returning to that castle where memories of grief and rejection mocked every success he had struggled to achieve since his banishment.

"Will you make the English go away?" Marsali asked, her voice so earnest that he could not bear to look at her.

"I don't want to talk about politics, lass," he murmured, flicking a bit of sand onto her knuckles with a self-mocking smile.

Marsali stared down in perplexity at his compelling profile. "Your clansmen won't respect you if you don't take a strong stand against the Sassenachs. You should know that."

Duncan lifted his broad shoulders in a nonchalant shrug, pretending indifference. "They only have to respect me the length of the summer. After that, the chieftain who replaces me can worry about how to handle them. Johnnie shows possibilities, don't you think?"

An unpleasant chill of apprehension darted up from the base of Marsali's spine. For a moment she'd tricked herself into believing in him again. Now she couldn't believe how cold, how uncaring he'd become. "Johnnie? Standing an oath on the white stone? He'd be laughed right into the sea. Johnnie would never make a chieftain. He doesn't own a single sheep."

"Hell, that doesn't matter," Duncan said, warming to the idea. "I'll deed him the castle. It's not as if it holds fond memories for me." He eased up higher on his elbow, lifting his free hand to tug at the black silken cord that disappeared into the cleft of her breasts. Yes. Anything to divert the conversation from the painful topic of his past.

"What's at the end of this thing then?" he asked in amusement, oblivious to the confusion that gripped her. "No, let me guess. It's a peat-bag crystal you wear for luck. Or a chicken bone blessed by your mystical uncle."

Marsali held her breath, her emotions churning, as he slowly drew the cord from between her breasts. The nerve of him. The slow glide of silk began to tickle her skin. The length of the summer. The words surfaced through the fog that had invaded her mind, cold spears prodding her into tense expectancy. That was what he had said. He had no intention of staying at all. His beauty had betrayed her. The corrosion that had eaten away at his soul years ago had destroyed every last bit of decency in him. Clearly she could not count on him to save the clan.

He sat up, unaware of the emotional battle she had fought in the space of a few seconds, his face intent on the silver object that hung on the end of the cord.

"Ah, it's a Celtic cross. My God, these are real rubies." Incredulous, he practically yanked her neck off trying to get a closer look. "I've seen this before, haven't I?" he said slowly, sounding puzzled.

"How should I know?" she said through her teeth, annoyed at his stupid preoccupation with a piece of jewelry.

He raised his head, suspicion burning in his eyes. "Where did you get it?" he said coldly.

Marsali refused to answer him, too enmeshed in her own misery to bother. She couldn't understand the fuss he was making over a family heirloom, and at the moment, her personal disappointment in him overrode the urge to care. Let him think she had stolen it during a raid. He didn't give a damn about the castle or his clansmen, which he treated as unwanted possessions. The years had only hardened him. She did hate him, after all. She hated everything he represented.

"This necklace belonged to very dear friend of mine, Marsali." His eyes bored into her like strands of blue ice. "In fact, he was the only man I left behind whom I could call friend. He carried this cross with him everywhere because it had belonged to his young wife."

Marsali looked up slowly, his words penetrating her anger. "The wife he mourned," she said, intrigued by the depth of emotion in Duncan's voice when only a moment earlier he had been so detached she could scream. Aye, there were feelings in him, all right, but he guarded them behind a thorny wall of indifference, which a person might never pierce. She could not understand why he had spoken of her father with an astonishing affection, even reverence.

"How do you know about his wife?" He nudged her face into the moonlight with his knuckles, the cross pressing into her chin. "How did you come to be wearing this?" he asked gruffly.

Again she was tempted to let him believe her a common thief, but the bruised anguish in his gaze stopped the impulse. "It . . . it was my mother's."

"It wasn't." He swallowed, his eyes searching her face in stark denial, almost a plea. "Tell me you're lying. You *are* lying."

"Papa asked me to wear it always when he went off that last time with your father," she whispered dryly.

Duncan slowly drew his hand away from her face, stricken by the truth he saw in her defiant loveliness, unprepared for the joke that Fate had executed at his expense again. To

71

seduce the orphaned daughter of the one person who had helped him salvage what scrap of human dignity his step-father had not thrashed out of him. He took a breath, the self-contempt that rose in his throat thick enough to suffocate him. Why had he come back? Even a damned dukedom wasn't worth the price of this emotional torture.

His embittered laughter broke the silence that had fallen. "Now I know why you seemed so familiar, Marsali. Now I know who I saw every time I looked in your face. Sweet wee Marsali. Dear Jesus, Andrew Hay would be rolling over in his grave if he could see what you'd become."

"What have I become?" Marsali asked in guarded fascination, realizing that by an accident of birth she had suddenly been elevated to a position of mysterious importance in Duncan's eyes, wondering what it would mean to her, her cunning mind plotting how to make the most of it.

"A criminal. An outlaw. A . . ." He frowned down into her enrapt face, alarmed to discover he had slipped his other arm around her waist while they were talking. "Respect for your father prevents me from saying the word aloud," he finished grimly.

"What word?" Marsali asked, curiosity more compelling than propriety.

He wrenched his hand away, afraid to imagine what might have happened in another moment. "Never mind. It doesn't bear saying."

"How dare you," Marsali said, her back stiffening at the insult, which had taken on graver proportions for being unspoken.

"How dare *you*, Marsali Hay." His heavy black eyebrows drew together into a reproachful scowl. "How dare you ambush and undress men on the moor, only to let them take advantage of you on the beach like a—Well, it's that word again. God, when I think about what we almost did."

"What *you* almost did," she said indignantly. "I didn't do a damn thing. I was only trying to get warm."

His smile was merciless. "In another minute I would have had you lying beneath me with your skirts pulled up, and you would have liked it too."

"You hypocrite," Marsali exclaimed, her temper flaring. She sprang to her feet, wanting only to escape him before she could give him the pleasure of watching her break down like a bairn, accusing her of something she barely understood. He gripped her wrist and drew her back down onto the sand. But this time stark distrust replaced the mood of playful seduction that had built between them.

"I gave you a chance, my lord," she said, breathless with anger. "But you *are* a black demon."

"Yes." He stuck his forefinger under her nose, his face unrepentant. "Hypocrite, bastard, demon, murderer, I've been called every dirty name under the sun, but let me tell you one thing, Marsali: You were the apple of your papa's eye. Yes, I remember the day you were born. Andrew was already planning to marry you off to a Danish prince. 'My daughter is descended from Olaf the Black,' he told any poor idiot who would stop to listen after your birth."

An unwilling smile eased the taut line of her mouth; she missed her father so much. "Really?" she whispered distrustfully.

"Yes, really. And no one was allowed to so much as breathe on his precious little princess. That old wizard uncle of yours drew a charmed circle around your cradle and stood vigil until your christening to prevent an evil fairy from claiming your soul. I should have made the connection. Damn it."

Moisture glistened in Marsali's eyes. "Papa always protected me," she said, her heart aching with a pain she rarely allowed herself to acknowledge, a pain she avoided by filling her life with dangerous distractions.

"He protected me too." Duncan ran his hand through his long disheveled hair, his mind still reeling from the shock. "Of course I never appreciated him at the time, but you, well, it would break his heart to see you now."

Guilt crept into the hurt and anger building inside her. "I wouldn't be whatever it is you claim I've become if the heir to the chieftainship had not been off fighting wars for other countries."

"Banished, lass," Duncan said, his own voice rising in self-defense. "And don't fault me for the life you've chosen. But all right, Marsali. All bloody right. I'll accept some of the blame because your loved ones were blown up accompanying my father on his fool's mission." He gave her a chilling smile. "I'll atone for my past sins and repay my debt to Andrew by assuming responsibility for you."

Marsali subsided into a brief resentful silence, unconvinced she wanted this dark volatile warrior dictating her future, good motives notwithstanding. "I'm going to have to decline your kind offer," she said, tossing back her mop of tangled hair to glare at him.

Duncan shook his head, his voice mocking. "But you weren't given the choice, my dear. We're going back to the castle together. I'll have you installed in the turret bedchamber. From now on, I'm going to shadow your every move."

"The turret is haunted, my lord," she said in genuine alarm, "by the ghosts of your ancestors."

"Well, then at least they're family ghosts, aren't they?" Duncan looked her over with a cold appraising criticism that made Marsali shiver. "My God, you're a mess. Your father wouldn't know you." He paused, his face reflective. "My betrothed is due to arrive at the end of the month. I didn't want her to come, but now I think I'm glad of it. She can decide how to manage you. I'm certainly not up to the chore."

Marsali blinked, incredulous, her brain struggling to absorb the unexpected blow. "Your . . . betrothed?"

"Lady Sarah Grayson. Well, we're not officially engaged yet, but we will be at the end of summer. The woman is a walking treasure trove of social trivia. If anyone can turn a sow's ear into silk, it's—"

Marsali slapped him then, not the light stinging palm across the cheek of a woman insulted, but a forceful crack against the jaw that jerked his head back several inches.

"What the hell was that for?" he asked in astonishment, his hand lifting to his face.

"Your betrothed, my lord," she retorted self-righteously. "And for calling me a pig's ear."

He scowled. "My betrothed is perfectly capable of slapping me herself."

"And you've given her plenty of reason to practice, I'm sure."

He gripped her hands in his, dragging her toward him, but Marsali refused to budge, digging her heels into the sand and reasoning that Duncan as a friend might turn out worse for her than as an enemy. A merciless task maker who would shadow her every move. A man in love with another woman—a prissy English noblewoman at that. Marsali cringed in horror at the prospect of being bound up in a corset and shipped off to a boarding school, her speech mocked, her heritage sneered at. Wasn't she gentry in her own right?

"Get up, Marsali." He pulled her to her knees. "My patience is wearing out, and there's a storm moving inland. I'll be damned if I'm riding back in the rain because of you."

She fought a sense of panic, a black terror that if she did not fight to retain her freedom she would never own herself again. She needed help. This man's power would imprison her. In the course of a day he had forced her through a dizzying gamut of feelings, leaving her wrung out and bewildered. The wild hope of wishing him a hero. Humiliation. The bittersweet stirrings of desire. And now the fear of losing her freedom, the nebulous future he had planned for herself. She needed Uncle Colum more than she'd ever needed him in her life.

"I can't go back to the castle yet," she said desperately. "I have something important to do first."

"Not in the middle of the night." His face unyielding, he knelt and tightened his hold on her wrists. "From now on you don't ride anywhere without a bodyguard, and then only on my approval. Now get up. We—"

He heard the faint crunch of a footstep in sand a second before Marsali's face whitened in startled recognition. He glanced around at the same moment she made a frantic effort to rise, wrenching her hands from his. And something inside Duncan, the same infallible sense of intuition that told him when to charge and when to retreat on a military campaign, told him that his fate had just been irrevocably sealed.

Chapter

8

The regally tall figure of a white-haired man in a blue robe stood behind them in the surf. The hawk Eun sat on the man's shoulder, its hooded yellow eyes fixed keenly on Duncan.

"Oh, dear," Marsali murmured, going very still. "Now there's going to be trouble. I do hope you can swim, my lord."

Duncan ignored her, jumping halfway to his feet, only to freeze with an involuntary yelp of pain. "Damn it," he said under his breath, sinking back down beside her, "let go of my hair, Marsali."

"I haven't touched your blessed hair," she retorted in an indignant voice, giving it another hurtful yank.

Duncan spared her a glance, aware that the peculiar robed man was rapidly striding through the surf toward them. He got to his knees. "Stop pulling my—"

He saw the problem in an instant; Marsali was trying desperately to stand, unaware that several strands of Duncan's hair had become entangled in the silver claws of her cross.

"Get my hair loose, Marsali. And hurry."

"Do it yourself," she whispered. But when she gave the necklace a sharp tug to free herself, she discovered that her own hair had also gotten tangled with Duncan's, that they were virtually joined at the neck like some sort of mythological Hydra.

"It's my uncle." Panicking, she fell back onto her knees to grab a fistful of Duncan's hair, twisting it this way and that.

"I gathered that, Marsali. Hell, woman, you're ripping my hair out by the roots."

A long shadow fell across them. Ominous silence swelled in the night.

Duncan couldn't remember when he had been caught in such an absurd position. Dangerous ones, yes. Compromising ones—well, there had been more than a few before he'd met Sarah. And it seemed there was nothing he and Marsali could do to gain their freedom besides tearing into each other like a pair of tomcats. Every effort to extricate himself only made him appear more guilty, as if they had been caught in the act instead of an accident of incomparable stupidity.

The man behind them spoke then, his voice cultured and cool with irony.

"I am quite sure there is a perfectly innocent reason for this midnight tryst. I suspect there is even a hidden metaphysical significance to the disturbing juxtaposition of your carnal bodies. However, at the moment, an acceptable explanation for either escapes the workings of my brain."

"Good evening, Uncle Colum," Marsali said meekly, leaning as far away from Duncan as possible, a move that only succeeded in dragging his head closer to her chest and making him wince aloud.

"It is morning now, Marsali," Colum pointed out. "We are in the wee small hours."

"Yes, well, be that as it may, Uncle Colum"—she gestured to Duncan's downbent head—"this is our new laird and chieftain, Duncan MacElgin. I gave him a rather rude welcome earlier today, and now I'm—"

"She's decapitating me," Duncan said in a muffled voice.

Colum stared down his sharp beak of a nose at Duncan, his expression duplicating the regal hauteur of the hawk on his shoulder. "I'd heard his arrival at the castle this afternoon caused something of a stir. Had I not been in the middle of an important ritual I would have welcomed him myself. Unfortunately, his rank is not what presently concerns me."

"It doesn't concern me much either," Duncan retorted. "At least not in comparison to the enormous pain in the neck your niece is giving me."

Colum's expression did not change. "What exactly are the pair of you doing in such a strange position, Marsali?"

She averted her gaze, mumbling, "Trying to get his damn hair untangled from my cross."

"Should I ask how his hair became entangled in your cross?" Colum inquired wryly.

"I was admiring her rubies, sir," Duncan answered, his head forced into a perpendicular angle by Marsali's attempt to distance herself from him.

"Admiring her rubies." A humorless smile flitted across Colum's gauntly elegant face. "May I suggest, my lord, that henceforth you admire my niece's assets from afar?"

Duncan gave him a dark look. "May I suggest that you discourage your niece from her midnight escapades, not to mention the illicit ways she passes her afternoon hours?"

"I cannot control her, my lord. Obviously you're not much better at it yourself."

"Obviously," Duncan snapped. "And I've got the cramp in my neck to prove it."

Marsali sighed loudly. "Could you please just get us free, Uncle Colum, and leave off discussing my sinful nature until a more convenient time?"

Shaking his head in chagrin, the wizard unsheathed a bone-handled knife from his belt and knelt in the sand. His hazel eyes unfathomable, he raised the long curved blade to Duncan's neck, then hesitated.

"I've always known you would return, my lord."

Duncan grunted, pretending to be unaffected by the keen perception in Colum's eyes. "Then you must be a true mystic because I had no intention of setting a single foot on this godforsaken land again until the Crown ordered it two months ago. Now, are you going to cut me loose or not?"

Colum positioned the knife between Duncan and Marsali, severing the unwelcome bond that held them with one skillful slash.

"There. It's done."

"Well, thank God," Marsali said, springing to her feet in a shower of flying sand.

Duncan straightened, his face dark with embarrassment, and brushed off his tight black trousers. "Thank God is right. What a bloody absurd day this has been from beginning to end. You, Marsali, are to ride directly back to the castle and await my orders."

"Too late, my lord."

"What?" Duncan said, looking up with a frown.

"I said you're too late." Colum scratched his sparse white beard, his gaze moving beyond Duncan. "My niece is already gone. I'm afraid it will take more than a few harshly spoken words to control her."

Disbelieving, Duncan glanced up at the black scowling cliffs, toward the sea, then back into the shadowed orifices of the caves. As impossible as it appeared, Marsali had vanished. Frustration pounded at him like the waves at his feet.

He was horrified at the way he had treated her, shamed her, desired her. In his mind he had always pictured Andrew's daughter growing up to marry the foreign prince her father had coveted for his only child. But this. Barefoot, bedraggled, incorrigible, and so inexperienced she'd not only let Duncan steal a kiss, but had invited others with her guileless response. He could have taken her with ease; the thought unsettled him.

"Where the blazes did she go?" he demanded of the wizard who stood calmly observing him and who, now that Duncan had risen to his full height of six feet two inches, seemed rather frail and far less threatening than a few moments earlier.

"I cannot say, my lord," Colum said with a weary shake of his head. "Marsali comes and goes like a cat, at all hours, to unknown destinations. The girl exhausts me."

Duncan walked farther down into the water, his heart accelerating with anger that she'd slipped away from him again. "You're her flesh and blood," he said over his shoulder. "Why have you allowed her to run wild?"

Colum joined him at the shoreline, apparently unconcerned by the waves lapping at his legs. "Am I a shining example of the conventional life, my lord?"

"She's liable to get herself arrested, or killed," Duncan said, his voice sharp with accusation.

"I don't think she cares."

"That's ridiculous." The thought of a young mischievous spirit like Marsali's headed down a path of self-destruction pierced Duncan's usual cynical view of the world. "It doesn't make sense for her to take such risks with most of her life still ahead of her."

"She has lost so much," Colum said reflectively. "Her parents, two brothers, her first love. Why should she believe her future holds anything more than heartache?"

Duncan was silent, finally catching sight of Marsali farther down the beach, walking her horse with heartbreaking loneliness through the lacy silver surf, no one caring enough to stop her. He knew what it was to suffer loss and lash out in pain. Perhaps, because he was male, his reaction to life's assaults had been violent and aggressive; he had struck out blindly in his hurting, and he had hurt others on his way.

For the first eleven years of his life, he had been raised in an atmosphere of ignorance, violence, and neglect. His mother's love, when she had dared defy her husband to show it to him, had probably saved Duncan from complete emotional annihilation. His older sister, Judith, a victim of her father's abuse herself, had tried to protect her little brother and save them both with her constant prayers to a God Duncan thought either could not hear them or did not care.

But Marsali Hay had been raised by a gentle loving father, a man who would despair of his daughter's sad destiny. She was not cursed with the darkness, the wild violence in her soul, that Duncan battled against nearly every day of his life. No, Marsali's way of denying her grief was to plunge headlong into danger herself while helping others.

"If not for Andrew, I would long ago be dead," he said aloud, staring at her receding figure until he lost sight of her. "Someone has to help his daughter."

"Aye," Colum quietly agreed, his face shuttered.

"You've given up on her," Duncan said, surprised at the anger and dismay he felt.

"She's almost a woman grown. Saving Marsali would take more time and dedication than I have left on earth, my lord."

Duncan shrugged his massive shoulders. "Time and dedication are two things I do not have myself."

"But you have power, my lord."

"Yes," Duncan said reluctantly, lifting his face to the eerie blood-red sky. "I have power, for what little it's worth. The question is how best to use it."

Less than an hour later, Marsali sneaked into her uncle's cabin in the bowels of the wrecked ship that listed at permanent anchor in a bed of submerged rocks. The smoke of sandalwood incense stung her eyes, and she blinked, her vision readjusting to the candlelit gloom.

Waves battered the ship's hull at periodic intervals and brought showers of surf through the porthole, only partially protected by the leather targe her uncle had nailed to the wall.

As she ducked to avoid the next saltwater assault, she stumbled over the wooden bucket set in the middle of the floor; she assumed its function was to catch the water leaking through the splintered deck above. To regain her balance she lunged for the desk bolted to the warped floor.

A ship's bell went clanging over the edge.

"God of all creation!" Half-asleep, Colum exploded from the bunk where he had lain under a pile of quilts with a flannel-wrapped brick between his feet. "Could you possibly make a little more noise when you enter a man's home, Marsali?"

She giggled, swinging around to face him. "You might consider not placing a bucket of water in the direct path of persons paying you a visit."

A young woman's irritated voice cut into the conversation from the doorway behind them, the door itself hanging on the threads of a rusty hinge.

"Och, you've gone and knocked over my sacred well water, Marsali, you clumsy thing! I almost broke my back lugging up that bucket."

Marsali glanced back at her older cousin Fiona, her eyes widening at the woman's unkempt appearance: a lopsided crown of woodbine on her forehead, wet sand and foxtail burrs plastered to her linsey-woolsey gown, her glossy black hair a bird's nest of mist-lacquered curls.

Curiosity overrode Marsali's own urgent reason for visiting. "Whatever have you been doing, Fiona?"

Fiona swept into the cabin like a gust of sea wind and tossed a handful of pebbles onto the desk. "Well, for the past seven evenings I've been at the high cairn studying how to get into the Otherworld. In fact, last night I managed to project my ethereal body into the strangest place, but nothing I do so far can budge my physical form."

"What's it like in the Otherworld anyway?" Marsali asked casually, helping herself to the silver chalice of water sitting on the desk.

Fiona gasped and bolted across the cabin to knock the chalice from Marsali's mouth. *"Dhé Mhor!* You almost drank the potion I brewed to arouse Hughie the shepherd's lust."

"I did drink it. Ugh." Marsali shuddered and swiped her wrist across her mouth. "What a disgusting thought, arousing an old married man with a wen on his nose and whiskers in his ears."

"It's for his wife to use on him, hinny." Fiona sniffed the contents of the chalice. "You of all people know I'll die a spinster before finding a man worth the energy of casting a love spell. Who, I ask you, is worth arousing for a hundred miles?"

Marsali nodded in wholehearted agreement, more than a little disconcerted when Duncan MacElgin's dark face sprung fully detailed into her mind. Now, there was a man unlike any other she or Fiona were likely to meet in their isolated Highland life. In fact, the MacElgin was larger than life, but Marsali had decided he was a sham, a fortress so tightly guarded against human emotion that a woman would receive more satisfaction from loving a pile of rocks.

And he had shattered her trust using only the truth as a weapon. His betrothed. The length of the summer, he had said. It was clear his sense of commitment lay on loftier goals than a forgotten Scottish castle. To think she had kissed him, and liked it. Aye, her lips still felt pleasantly bruised with the memory. Worse, she had done his damn laundry, scrubbing his clothes in the cold water of a wooden trough until her knuckles bled.

Her laird.

Her chieftain.

Her self-appointed guardian.

Fiona glared down in concern at the chalice she'd placed back on the desk. "You're going pale, Marsali. You're looking very unwell, indeed. How much of that potion did you drink, anyway?"

"It's not the potion," Marsali muttered, turning away in agitation.

"It's the MacElgin." Colum swung his legs over the bunk, bony knees protruding from his nightshirt. "That's what has the lass all undone, isn't it, Marsali?"

A large wave crashed against the ship. Fiona grabbed Marsali's arm and guided her over to the bunk, the candles in the brass sconces on the bulkheads guttering in their wake.

"Come on, Dad, move over a moment." Fiona crowded into the bunk beside Colum, dragging a reluctant Marsali down between them.

"Go to your own bed, Fiona," Colum said with a disgruntled sigh. "I'm resting to work late tonight."

"My cabin is leaking again," Fiona complained, "and you've stolen all the warm quilts. We were better off living in the woods. And you, Marsali, you're the one in the family who's supposed to have all the common sense. Why are you not home snug in Bride's cottage? Who is this MacElgin anyway, to be brewing such a tempest?"

Marsali curled up under the threadbare quilts Fiona had confiscated from her father. Bride was Marsali's sister-in-law, always pregnant, always tired, always needing a hand with her brood of children. The cottage, with its reek of peat smoke and genteel poverty, depressed Marsali beyond words.

As much as she adored her boisterous nieces and nephews, even her own dimwitted brother Gavin, Marsali felt unbearably lonely in the crowded home, restless with needs of her own that she was half afraid to analyze, reminded of the future she had lost. Aye, she had her dreams, dreams of a snug home to call her own, bairns snuggled on her lap by the fire, a fine man . . .

"When my back gets better, lass," Gavin would console her, "I'll find work again, and we'll set sail for Virginia. We'll grow rich raising tobacco and carriage horses. There'll be no rebellions and raids in the middle of the night. You'll sip tea and wear satin."

Duncan MacElgin had laughed at that dream, and suddenly, damn him, it did seem stupid, if not impossible.

She sat forward, her small face intense. "I need your help, Uncle Colum." She untied the silken cord from her neck and laid it carefully on the quilt. "I want you to take the MacElgin's hairs from this necklace and work your most powerful spell on him tonight."

Colum did not respond, staring down at the quilt with a frown of concern. She had never asked him to work magic for herself before.

Fiona ran her forefinger over the cross, her eyes misty. "A love spell. Oh, my poor desperate cousin. The man is no here a full day, and you, who scorn the ancient arts, who deny the Wiccan blood in your own veins, are imploring me to use my powers to win the man's heart. I'm so happy for you, Marsali, I think I'm going to cry."

"Well, don't take out your handkerchief yet, Fiona," Marsali said waspishly. "And not to offend your awesome talent for spellcasting, Cousin, but it's Uncle Colum's help I really need. He has a wee bit more experience with this sort of—"

"It didn't look to me like you and the laird needed the help of a love spell on the beach," Colum said gruffly, not touching the cross.

Fiona's leaf-green eyes widened. "Why? What were they doing then?"

"Nothing at all," Marsali said, her face warming at the embarrassing memory. "We were stuck together by accident. And I don't want to win his damned heart either because he probably doesn't have one."

"Then what exactly am I to do with his hair?" Colum asked, a frown carving deep grooves in his forehead.

Marsali's voice dropped to a whisper. "Send him into the

Otherworld. Or make his man-thing wilt for a month. Cut his pride down a notch or two. Make him feel powerless."

"Was he misusing his man-thing?" Colum inquired sharply.

Marsali squirmed under the quilt. "Well, no, but one can assume he had it in mind. Eventually, I mean."

"How 'eventually'?" Colum demanded.

"Did he show it to you?" Fiona whispered. "Was it very big?"

Marsali gave a loud sigh. "Look, Uncle Colum, I know you've been predicting for months that the man destined to be our chieftain would magically appear out of the mountains like some sort of ancient god, but I'm afraid Duncan MacElgin is not the man in your vision."

Colum's hazel eyes glittered in the gloom. "How would you know that, Marsali, you who has refused to cultivate your own talents for prophecy?"

"Well, at first I thought you were right, and I was happy to let him order me around in front of the others—for the sake of the clan, you understand. But I'm afraid we've made a serious mistake. He has no intention of staying here longer than the summer, and he's not going to punish that ass Abercrombie for having Liam flogged."

"I saw the vision in the Samhain bonfire as clearly as I am looking at you now," Colum said after a long silence.

"Well, Dad, it isn't as if you've never made a mistake before," Fiona said gently. "Remember when you predicted that flood, and we had the whole clan and all their smelly goats crowded onto this ship? It was the driest winter in anyone's memory."

Marsali leaned her head on her uncle's shoulder, her voice sweetly cajoling. "Are you going to help me with the MacElgin, or do I have to get the others to do it?"

"I love you like one of my own, Marsali." Colum's voice grew reflective. "But heaven knows I have failed your father in watching over you. I should never have let things go this far. I taught you the academics, but nothing of life. Yes, I will help you with this man."

Marsali swung her feet to the floor, restraining herself from releasing a whoop of victory. "Then it's settled. What a relief."

"Fiona, accompany your cousin halfway to the castle," Colum said crossly, pushing off his warm quilts with a deep sigh at the night's work that lay ahead. He had planned to concentrate on improving the oat crops, but that would have to wait.

"Do you think that the MacElgin might be lying in wait for her along the way, Dad?" Fiona asked, a gleam of hope in her big green eyes.

"I doubt it." Colum looked preoccupied, waving his blue-veined hand in the direction of the door. "But I need peace to work. Get out, the pair of you. Your babbling drains my energy."

The two young women crept like mice from the cabin and crossed the deck to the ship's gangplank, a warped length of wormy oaken board that extended into the cliffside path to provide passage to dry land during high tide.

Without warning Fiona whirled around, grabbing Marsali by the arm with a wicked grin just as she stepped onto the wobbly planking.

"Are you in a hurry to return to the castle, Marsali?" she called over the wild music of the waves hitting the ship's hull.

Marsali hesitated, shoving her bright curls from her face. Something inside her ached to see the MacElgin again before Colum turned him into a lobster, just to convince herself his voice was not as deep as she imagined, his magnetism not as overpowering. Something inside her wanted to give him another chance at redemption to prove his integral goodness. Hope did not die easily in her stubborn heart.

But then she remembered that he belonged to another woman, that he'd promised to "take control" of Marsali's life—with all its chilling implications. And he'd fought for the English, given them the loyalty he owed his own people. Away from him, she could begin to untangle her thoughts.

Indecision tore at her. She thought of the various facets of his character that he'd revealed during the day: authority and anger, the talent for tactical organization that had served him so well as a military leader. The grudging respect he'd commanded from his reprobate clansmen.

But it was the vulnerability beneath the mask of defiance worn by the boy in the portrait that haunted her. Aye, it had touched her, made him a little more human. That and the horrible black humor he'd displayed when he humiliated her a few hours ago.

Duncan the man, matured with all his dark emotions channeled if not conquered. No longer just the boy in the portrait but the fierce ancestor who hung above it. A Celtic warrior born into a position of privilege.

A sad unpredictable warrior with the power to decide the destiny of a common girl such as she.

"No, I'm not in any hurry," she said, shrugging off the day's anxiety and exhaustion. "What are we going to do?"

Fiona gave her a sly look. "Won't the laird be angry if you disobey him?"

"I don't know." Marsali shivered as a smattering of spindrift hit her face, remembering Duncan's unbridled anger when he'd confronted her in the cave. "I don't care, either."

"It's still light, Marsali. I was going to sneak back to the cairn and give the Otherworld another chance. But let's try and raise a storm instead. I'll just run back to the cabin to fetch my things."

"Oh, all right," Marsali said without a great deal of enthusiasm. From her perspective, however, the day had begun and ended stormily enough, with no lull on the horizon either. Everyone said her uncle worked genuine magic, and she'd never really taken advantage of his occult abilities until now, except to help a sick bairn or animal.

All she knew was that he'd have to work quite a spell to help her out of this coil. The MacElgin obviously possessed his own potent brand of power, a power that had proved to Marsali her precious freedom could not only be threatened but taken away by a snap of his long elegant fingers.

Fiona slipped soundlessly back into the cabin. Easing the door shut, she paused to breathe in her favorite scents in the world: melted wax, herbs, burnt wine. Eun did a shifting dance on his driftwood perch, recognizing her through the little red velvet hood he wore.

Her father did not acknowledge her at all. Mumbling to

himself, hunched over the assortment of Wiccan's tools arranged on his desk, he was already too deep in concentration to notice his daughter's return.

She picked up her pouch of sacred stones, wolves' teeth, and flowers plucked under a full moon at midnight, padding up behind him. "No one's ever asked me to make a man-thing wilt before. Do you mind if I watch?"

He spun around, clearly startled by her voice, if not the question. At the strange intensity of his face, his gaze so oblique in the candlelight he appeared not to know her, Fiona stumbled back a step.

"Dad," she whispered, a quiver in her voice, "are you all right?"

He scowled at her from beneath his thick white brows, his voice a rasp of sound. "Get out of here, Fiona. Now."

She stared past him in fascination toward the desk. An altar strewn with dried rosebuds and a red silk cloth; a mortar and pestle; salt, oil; a thurible burning cloying incense. Gasping softly, she lowered her gaze to the strands of hair woven into nine thin knots, black tightly entwined with auburn.

Lovers' knots.

The chieftain and her cousin.

Swallowing, she noticed the triangle drawn in chalk on the dull wooden floor. "Dad," she said again, backing into the bucket Marsali had overturned earlier. "The Irrevocable Spell. Why are you doing this?"

"She needs a protector, Fiona. I have failed at the task, and the man who loved her is dead. No one else in the clan is good enough."

Fiona shook her head in bewilderment. "But everyone said Duncan MacElgin is a devil. He caused a clansmen's death and disfigured another. He—he murdered his own parents."

"Andrew said the lad had been mistreated and had a good heart beneath all the drunken deviltry."

"Then it must have been buried very deep," Fiona said in a tremulous voice. "And he must have terrified the life out of Marsali to bring her here for help against him in the middle of the night." She darted forward to stay his arm. "You can't do this."

He shook her hand away, his fine white hair falling into his face. "I'm only helping along the attraction I saw with my own eyes tonight. If it's not meant to be, then all my magic will not matter anyway. Now leave me to do my work. See your cousin back to the castle and mind you behave yourselves."

"Papa—"

His voice rose into a fearful roar. "You will not learn the secret of penetrating the Otherworld if you interfere with me tonight. Go!"

Throwing him a final desperate look, Fiona found her pouch in the wall cupboard and hurried from the cabin. As she met Marsali pacing on deck, she squelched a surge of guilt at the enormity of what her father had undertaken.

The chieftain and her cousin.

Duncan and Marsali.

Bound together for all eternity in earthly passion and spiritual partnership in a spell that linked soul to soul. Fiona was sick with fear and envy.

She lowered her troubled gaze, marching past Marsali to the gangplank. She had no power, mortal or magical, to countermand her father's spell. "Come on," she muttered. "We'll work our own magic from the cliffs so the waves won't wash over us when I start to raise the storm."

Marsali glanced back skeptically at the sea, the waves already lashed into angry whitecaps by a strong northwest breeze. In her opinion, there was a good chance of a summer storm before dawn, magic or not.

"I hope this won't take long," she grumbled as she followed Fiona down the unsteady gangplank, her skirts blowing up to her knees.

Fiona waited on the crooked path carved into the cliff, her face averted, her hand outstretched to Marsali. "It might take longer than usual since you knocked over my bucket of sacred well water. That was part of my offering to Taranis, God of Thunder, and the mermaids."

God of Thunder. Mermaids.

Marsali rolled her eyes at this nonsense and allowed Fiona to pull her up onto the path. In silence they climbed to the clifftop, a raw breeze buffeting them. When they reached the summit, Marsali was reassured by the sight of her horse standing patiently behind a grove of wind-blasted brush.

Duncan, however, was nowhere to be seen.

She shrugged, turning back to Fiona, who had deftly assembled a little altar at the edge of the cliff. With her thin brown arms thrown up to the sky, the would-be witch was chanting at the top of her lungs to a hodgepodge of Celtic gods.

"Hurry up, Fiona," Marsali shouted irritably. "I'd almost rather be back at the castle waiting on his miserable lordship than standing here watching you making a fool of yourself."

Fiona pivoted slowly, studying Marsali in concern. "It's working already, isn't it?" she whispered, biting her lip. "My poor Marsali."

"'Poor Marsali' what?"

"Nothing. You could throw me into a den of lions and I'd never tell." Fiona whirled back to the sea and hurled a handful of polished stones into the water. "Dance around the altar three times, Marsali."

They danced. They blew their warm breath onto Fiona's sacred stones. They took turns waving Fiona's rowan wand over the ocean. If anything, the waves calmed, the breeze lessened. Finally, overcome with delayed fatigue, Marsali lurched to her feet and yawned.

"I'm going back to the castle and see if his lordship has been changed into a lobster. This is damned silly."

Fiona looked up from her forlorn little altar, murmuring sadly, "Poor brave wee cousin. I should have done something to stop him. It's probably too late now."

Marsali was too worn out to try to understand what her cousin meant by her cryptic remarks. Marching to the verge of the cliff, she tossed over the stones and wolves' teeth she'd been clutching in her hand.

"Those were for you, Taranis, God of Thunder, and the mermaids, though what the hell you'll do with them is beyond me." Her voice climbed into a mischievous shout. "Rise up and storm on Duncan MacElgin! Rain on his handsome head, strike him down where he . . ."

She hesitated, not hating him quite enough to wish him

actual physical harm, although he undoubtedly deserved it. "Strike the ground he walks on!" she concluded with a satisfied nod. "There, Fiona. I've said my piece. Good luck raising your storm."

She whirled and threw the rowan wand back into Fiona's lap. She had not taken two steps past the altar before thunder rumbled over the mainland. Fiona rose to her feet and stared, disbelieving, at the lightning that zigzagged directly over Castle MacElgin, illuminating the stark parapets in a flash of silver.

Fiona jumped to her feet. "You did it!" she shrieked, squeezing Marsali's shoulder. "You raised the storm. For all we know, he might have been standing on the battlements, watching for you, and your lightning struck him dead."

Marsali swallowed, reaching around her throat for the familiar comfort of her cross before remembering she had left it with her uncle. "I didn't raise the storm, Fiona. It was going to happen anyway. All I did was give it a little helping hand, if even that."

Fiona looked unconvinced, torn between professional jealousy and admiration. "But the lightning—right over the castle, Marsali."

"Look, Fiona, if it struck him dead, then that was meant to be too. I won't lose any sleep over it. And now it's starting to rain, which means I'll be soaked before I reach the castle."

As Marsali strode off toward her horse, Fiona turned and stared down at the ghostly silhouette of the wrecked ship wedged between the cliffs of the cove. Yellow candlelight glowed behind the heavily curtained porthole of her father's cabin.

It was going to happen anyway.

She glanced up appraisingly at Marsali, her rain-blurred figure already receding as she cantered her horse toward the castle in the gloaming light. Strange how Marsali's words had practically echoed Colum's. Fiona didn't know what conclusions she ought to draw from this, but she did know that Marsali had more talent for witchery than she'd ever admit. Or use. What a terrible waste. Fiona had to work so hard for her spells.

* * *

Duncan stared down in astonishment at the crumbling mortar of the turret that had landed at his feet from the lightning blast. Another few inches and he might have been cleaved in two. Even the weather in this accursed castle was conspiring against him.

Andrew's daughter. What a cruel joke.

He gripped the wet stone of the battlements, heedless of the storm that had erupted without warning. Soft summer rain splashed down his face and soaked his shirt front. He didn't fight it. Aye, he needed to stand in a cold downpour after tussling with that imp in the sand. The irony of discovering her identity mocked his well-constructed plans.

To think he had even considered seducing her like a common serving girl.

Andrew Hay's *daughter,* for the love of God. It made sense now. Hay's had been the only voice of wisdom in his disordered clan, and it was with his death, and not the old chieftain's, that the castle had begun to fall into chaos. No wonder everyone loved Marsali. They had loved the loyal-hearted Andrew too.

He lifted his brooding gaze back toward the sea. The first night he had encountered Andrew was still emblazoned on his mind like a burn that had healed into a deep painful scar.

Panic. Fear. Grief. Rage. Memory after memory cascaded over him, a waterfall of human emotions. His chest tightened even now with the shocked disbelief of dragging his older sister away from the sight of their mother and Fergus's unmoving body. He held his hands out to the rain unthinkingly as if to wash the viscous warmth of the blood from his fingers.

His older sister Judith's voice, stark with horror, echoed in his mind. "What have you done, Duncan? Dear God, what has that violent temper made you do now?"

He pushed around her and stumbled outside, heaving in the thistle-choked yard until his stomach emptied. Judith followed, recoiling when he straightened and she saw his battered face in the moonlight. High on the hills behind them, the bonfires of the Beltane celebration burst into the night, a fitting backdrop of hell. The muted laughter of revelers rose into the silence, punctuated by the hysterical screaming for help of Fergus's elderly sister, who had awakened to see her brother and his wife dead on the floor.

Duncan grabbed his sister's hand and dragged her into the woods that surrounded the stone cottage. She was the only person he had left; even though she was five years his senior, he towered over her, tall for his age. They had always protected each other.

"We have to run away, Judith," he said in desperation. "We'll take one of the fishing boats from the cove and row to France."

"France? *France?* We've no siller, Duncan. No relatives over there. Who would take us in?"

There were shouts coming closer to them, hoofbeats, dogs barking. Judith worked her hand free, giving a quiet sob as she wiped the blood off her gown.

"Mama," she whispered, clutching her midsection as she stared back at the cottage. "We can't leave her there like that."

The sound of wood splintering, an ax biting through the door, filled Duncan with a fresh surge of panic. He knew what his punishment would be. Never mind the reason. The chieftain wouldn't let the crime go unpaid.

"Go, Duncan," Judith cried softly, pushing at his shoulder.

"I'm not leavin' you here to—"

Before he could finish, a gruff but gentle voice broke into the darkness of the tall beech trees that protected them. A short cloaked man stood staring down the incline. "The bairns could not have gone far, my lord. Pray God they were not hurt in the violence tonight. With any—"

A startled cry from inside the cottage interrupted him.

They'd found both bodies now, Duncan's mother, the obscenity of her death, concealed beneath the plaid he had laid over her. He heard one of the chieftain's retainers murmur, "Double murder," and at that Judith panicked anew, shoving Duncan deeper into the wood.

"Go. I'll be all right. *Go.*"

He wavered before he started to run, but he did not get far. Andrew Hay, the chieftain's tacksman and closest friend, caught him even before he reached the top of the hill. Two great slavering hounds pounced on his back and pushed him face down into the soggy grass. When Hay stuck his booted toe into Duncan's ribs to turn him over like a snail, Duncan was cursing and crying, raising his fists to defend himself against the punishment he anticipated from experience.

The unexpected compassion in Hay's eyes struck him even more deeply than any physical assault. Duncan was an admitted thief, always in some sort of trouble. No one knew, or cared, that he was beaten into stealing for Fergus.

"Someone's killed your parents, laddie," Hay said quietly, lifting his foot away. "Do you know who it was?"

He leaped up and tried to run around Hay, only to find the castle dogs and the tall intimidating figure of the chieftain barring his way. Even then, staring into his natural father's rugged face, he did not recognize the similarities between them. He spat instead at his feet, wild in his fear and grief, resenting the nobleman who represented everything Duncan would never be.

"Take the boy back to the castle," Kenneth MacElgin said after appraising Duncan in endless silence. "See that he's well treated as befits my only son and heir."

Duncan sneered, ducking the hand Andrew extended to help him. Well treated. My only son and heir. Had the old man lost his mind? Was this a demented Beltane prank?

The memories faded. He forced himself to breathe. His lungs burned as if he had been running for miles.

The rain had stopped.

Brought back to his present dilemma, Duncan turned his head and stared out across the castle battlements. From the start, Andrew Hay had treated him with an understanding and a respect he had never deserved. Not even now, two decades later. He swallowed dryly. He wished that he hadn't come back here at all, that Marsali Hay did not exist as a reminder of past sins and future temptations. He didn't need to worry about a wild little waif.

He also wished that his fiancée, Sarah, and her brother were not due to arrive in a fortnight's time. It would take an act of God to restore order to the clan before then, and God hadn't bestowed any favors on the desolate castle for more years than Duncan could count. It didn't take a crystal ball to foresee the disaster looming on the horizon.

"There ye are, my lord."

Duncan glanced around at the vaguely familiar voice, recognizing the lumpy figure of Lachlan standing at the top of the stairs that led into the keep. The clansman stared down in awestruck silence at the pile of mortar at Duncan's feet, clearly convinced the chieftain had torn the tower apart with his bare hands, perhaps even his teeth, in a fit of black temper.

"What do you want, Lachlan?"

"Er, never mind, my lord." He crept back a step, a nervous grin pasted on his face. "Perhaps 'tisna a good time to disturb ye."

"What do you want?" Duncan repeated.

"Well, there's been another sighting in the guardroom. The men thought I should tell ye."

"A sighting?"

"Aye, Effie—that's the girl wi' the piglets—was preparing a room for Marsali next to the guardroom, as ye asked, when the ghostie appeared, swearin' her head off because Effie had moved the chamberpot."

"Am I imagining this conversation?"

"I dinna know, my lord, but Effie said she heard Giorsal knock over a suit of armor and shout that 'that damned chieftain will be the death of me yet,' which of course wasna a reference to you, my lord, but to her already dead husband, Bhaltair, who was the chieftain two hundred years ago."

Duncan's smile faded. "Then it was probably some drunk in a nightshirt looking for the privy. Don't waste my time with such nonsense again."

He broke off as the crash of the drawbridge and subsequent resentful squawk of chickens in the moat heralded a late-night arrival to the castle. Duncan returned to the parapets and stared down in unwilling fascination, Lachlan completely forgotten.

Marsali had dismounted in the outer bailey, her tiny figure drawing a crowd of clansmen and castle servants from the darkened outbuildings. Even from the distance Duncan could sense their concern for her, conspiracy humming in the air as they gathered to discuss their common enemy.

Him.

He straightened almost in self-defense as Marsali lifted her face in defiance to the turret, where he stood as if to assert her independence. For now she held the upper hand, but not for long. She had no idea what she was up against.

"There will be a clan meeting the day after tomorrow in the hall," he said curtly, moving past Lachlan to the dark hole of the stairs. "See that everyone is in attendance. And sober."

"Aye, my lord." Lachlan screwed up the last of his nerve to pluck shyly at Duncan's shirt sleeve. "And the ghosties?"

Marsali's soft laughter rose like a silver bell in the breeze, taunting, a challenge to the night. Duncan paused, his face caught half in darkness, half in moonlight. A chill of foreboding crept down his spine.

"Let the ghosts alone," he said as he turned away. "They belong here more than I ever will."

Chapter

9

He had been dreaming about Marsali when an unearthly shriek penetrated the layers of his sleep. They were lying in the sand, bodies locked together, the surf rushing toward them. He'd brought his mouth to hers, and she tasted like spun sugar; he pressed her deeper into the sand, the soft curves of her body yielded to his, and then he heard the shriek.

The bedchamber door banged open. Cold musty air washed over him, an insult to his senses. An impatient voice called his name. From reflexes instilled in him during his soldier days, he rolled out of bed and grabbed his cavalry sword from the nightstand to face the unidentified intruder.

Marsali stood in the dimness of the doorway, demanding he awaken. The candle she held cast undulating shadows over the room. "What is it?" he asked in alarm, throwing his bare legs over the bed. He strapped his swordbelt on over his long shirt, the only garment he hadn't bothered to remove for sleep. He couldn't imagine the problem. There was no cattle for a rival clan to steal. It was probably a drunken squabble in the hall.

"Hurry up, my lord."

He peered under the bed for his trews. "I'm not breaking up a fight half dressed, Marsali."

"Well, you broke up a fight on the moor wearing a lot less today, my lord."

"I had little choice," he said wryly. "Why were you shrieking to raise the dead?"

"It wasn't me. It *was* the dead. It was Giorsal chasing Bhaltair."

He looked up slowly as she stepped closer to the bed. She was wearing nothing more substantial than a white dimity shift that emphasized her fragile bone structure, the feminine curves and hollows. Desire stirred in his blood like a beast too long lain dormant. He lowered his sword, a sigh of weariness escaping him.

Clansmen had begun to run up the stairs. Hope apparently still ran high that Marsali would manage to get rid of the chieftain before another day passed.

"I don't believe this," he said. "I'm going back to bed."

And he did. Or at least he tried to, but how could a man sleep with that sweet face hovering over him? Not to mention the hot wax she was dripping from her candle onto his sheets.

"Good night, Marsali."

She didn't move. He closed his eyes, only to force them open as the patter of big noisy feet fell around the bedstead.

"Dear God," he said, looking around him.

One by one his clansmen crept into the room, four of them actually brash enough to sit down beside him on his bed. Indignation rendered him speechless.

"We heard ye shriek, my lord," Owen said, patting Duncan's hand. "Dinna be embarrassed. Ye must have been havin' a nightmare."

Duncan pulled the sheet up to his head. "And I'm not having one now?"

Marsali chuckled and sat down at the foot of the bed, the candlelight framing her face. "That's a good one, my lord. Now stir yourself and make the ghosts stop fighting so we can all get some sleep."

He laid his head back against the damasked pillow board of the enormous Elizabethan four-poster. His body still felt uncomfortably aroused from the dream. He could see the silhouette of her breasts and softly rounded hips through her shift, and if he could see her that much, then the others could see her too. Unbelievable that only a few blissfully ignorant hours ago he had envisioned luring her to his bed. "Cover yourself," he said in a terse voice. "Johnnie, Lachlan, one of you cover Marsali with your plaid."

The two men, squashed together next to Duncan's torso, exchanged baffled looks. "Why do we need to cover her up, my lord?" Johnnie inquired after a moment.

"Because she is not decent, damn it, that's why. Owen, get off my feet."

"She looks decent enough to me," Lachlan commented bravely.

Marsali gave him a little smile of appreciation. "Thank you, Lachlan. It's good to know everyone doesn't think I'm indecent."

A small crowd had moved into the bedchamber, clansmen making themselves right at home with the others on the bed, maidservants vying for space between the wardrobe and windows. Donovan, the clan's harpist, lugged in his harp. Suisan, Cook's daughter, spread a plaid on the floor and passed out biscuits and cheese.

"What's the matter?" Effie asked, fishing her spectacles out of her sleeve. "What has the chieftain done now?"

"He's insulted Marsali," Donovan answered. "He said she wasna a decent woman."

Duncan leaned forward, his voice like frost. "I did not. Damn it, get out of here."

"Yes, ye did, my lord," Johnnie said. "I'm afraid I heard it myself."

Marsali nodded in agreement. "So did I, my lord."

"What I meant," he said, a muscle ticking in his jaw, "was that she should not parade around the castle in her shift. It does things to a man's imagination."

A short silence passed. Then Owen timidly cleared his throat.

"It doesna do anything to my imagination," he said.

"Nor mine," a dozen or so male voices echoed around the room.

"What does he mean?" Lachlan dared to ask.

Duncan set his jaw. "What I mean is that when she is dressed like that a man sees things he is not meant to see."

"I dinna see anything," Johnnie said, shaking his head.

Owen frowned. "I see her feet. Perhaps that is what the chieftain means."

"I see your feet too," Lachlan whispered to Johnnie. "We'd best start wearin' our brogues to bed if it's going to upset the laird so."

"She swims naked in the loch summer evenings along wi' the rest of us," Effie offered as further evidence.

"Only last week," Marsali added in her own defense.

"Not anymore." Scowling, Duncan raised his long legs to dislodge his unwanted guests from the bed, irritated by the thought of her frolicking naked for the world to see. As he reached up to pull the curtains closed, he glimpsed Marsali darting across the room.

"She *swam* naked," he said, turning around to emphasize this point to Marsali, only to notice her disappearing out the doorway and back down the hall.

He got up from the bed, everyone watching him in distrustful silence. He felt like the damned court jester. "Where do you think you're going, Marsali?" he shouted.

"One of us has to confront the ghosts," she called back over her shoulder.

He hesitated, then strode down the hallway after her. She had vanished down a narrow corridor, her candle flame flickering like a will-o'-the-wisp. From memory he delved down a secret passageway to intercept her outside the iron-hinged door of the chapel. She looked surprised when he appeared, but almost immediately she recovered her aplomb.

"Are you going to help me or not?" she asked in a cool voice.

"It's the middle of the night."

"I realize that, my lord, but ghosts don't usually appear during the day."

He tried to soften his tone as the image of her lonely figure walking in the surf returned to him, reminding him to show her the tolerance her father had shown him. "Why did you come back to the castle, lass?"

"Because you told me I had to," she said in surprise.

"And you're going to obey me from now on?"

She studied his face, the sharp planes and shadowed contours. "Only if it will help the clan to obey you."

"I see," he said slowly. "You're a very strange girl, Marsali."

"Thank you." She turned away. "And now that we've got that established, I'm going to find the ghosts. As usual, it's the women in this castle who end up doing all the work."

He caught her arm, and she pivoted slowly to face him. He was so handsome, so masterful, his eyes moving over her with the arrogance of a man fully aware of his sexual power. She suppressed a shiver of unadulterated pleasure as his strong body brushed against hers. He smelled faintly of musk and woodruff soap. The candle shook in her hand, spilling scalding wax onto his bare foot. He swore under his breath and reached down to rub his burning instep.

She bent, wincing in sympathy, and said, "I'm so sorry, my lord," as a few more drops of wax plopped onto the back of his neck.

Duncan went very still before he straightened, the movement creating a draft of air. The castle flame expired, throwing the passageway into complete darkness. Marsali caught her breath. He was an unpredictable man, a dangerous man, and she regretted that she'd had to resort to magic to make him go away. Something inside her refused to relinquish her faith in him.

Her heart gave a disturbing flutter. It was an exciting moment, her imagination heightened all the more by her utter inability to see him. Anything could happen.

"Are you still there, my lord?" she whispered, which was unnecessary because she could certainly sense his presence, and the silence was almost too suspenseful to bear.

"No, Marsali, I'm in the courtyard." With a sigh of resignation, he rescued the dripping candle from her hand and propped it in a wall niche above them.

"Why are we standing in this passageway in our night-wear, Marsali?"

"Because Giorsal is a very unhappy spirit. She throws things at her husband's ghost—his name is Bhaltair—in her temper, and sometimes she misses and hits the men by mistake. She was looking for a chamberpot tonight. It's her favorite missile."

He wanted to touch her. He ached to press her sweet little body against the wall and stop the preposterous discussion with a wild desperate kiss. The soft brush of her unbound hair teased his arm. The low melodic tones of her voice tempted him to take advantage of the darkness.

"Ghosts don't use chamberpots," he said, wondering what the prime minister would think if he could hear this conversation.

"But Giorsal does because she doesn't want Bhaltair to go to battle. Don't you remember the pair of them fighting in the guardroom when you lived here? They've been at each other's throats every summer evening for almost two centuries."

Duncan considered it imprudent to tell her exactly what had occupied the summer nights he'd spend prowling these dark passageways, the young women he'd cornered, seduced, forgotten. Conflicting urges stirred in his blood, primitive and protective. He tightened his grip on her arm and, without warning, began guiding her through a corridor she hadn't previously noticed.

"Where are we going?" she asked in curiosity, her voice echoing against the cold stones that enclosed them.

He didn't answer. Cobwebs brushed her face as he pulled her through a maze of unlit passageways. They ducked into an alcove. Duncan shoved his shoulder against a wall stone until a secret door swung open and they were standing in the cavernous fireplace of the old guardroom.

He stepped off the hearth and into the room. Marsali followed, stumbling over the hideskin shield that Duncan had dragged into the center of the floor while investigating a suspicious-looking coat of armor.

"There are no ghosts here," he announced with an air of authority.

She tiptoed up behind him. "I never said there were. Giorsal was in that awful room you put me in, and she was looking under my bed. When I woke up, she started to shriek that she had lost something."

"Probably her mind." Duncan strode past her to the door. "I have a feeling I'll be making the same quest myself. Stay here until I check your room."

Of course there weren't any ghosts. What did he expect? Duncan couldn't believe she had convinced him to peer under her bed in the middle of the night. The clansmen, suspicious of Duncan's motives, observed his every move from the doorway of Marsali's room. They shadowed him as he sneaked back to the guardroom until he finally lost them in the confusing maze of corridors that he remembered by instinct.

He found Marsali asleep on the floor, her face resting against the hideskin shield. With a perplexed sigh, he knelt and stared at her. The urge to touch her tangled hair stole over him, to lay beside her and listen to the rhythm of her relaxed breathing. She looked so defenseless that his own strength seemed obscene in comparison.

In the years that had followed Duncan's arrival at the castle, it was only Andrew Hay's compassion for a young boy's anguish that had made the adjustment bearable. Strangely, in Marsali's wildness, Duncan viewed as if in a distant mirror an image of his own earlier rebellion.

How well he knew the secret pain that motivated such behavior, the seeking to obliterate a life that had become intolerable, the burden of grief too heavy to bear. He had taken his quest to deaden his emotions and made it a career.

"I have a plan for you, lass," he said quietly.

She stirred, giving him a drowsy grin. "I have a plan for you too, my lord."

Her honesty, her humor, disarmed him. He hoisted her relaxed body into his arms and stood, swallowing hard as the soft warmth of her seeped into his taut muscles.

"Where are we going now?" she asked with a yawn.

He looked down at her, his lids narrowed. She was as light as a sprig of heather in his arms. She tilted her head back, arching her neck, so trusting he could not stand it. He hated himself for the thoughts that crossed his mind, the urge to subdue, dominate, possess.

"Why aren't you wearing your cross?" he said to distract himself as he carried her down the hall.

She put her hand to her throat. "I'm having a spell put on you," she whispered, hiding her abashed face in the folds of his shirt. "I hope you don't mind, but I was desperate."

He seemed to hesitate. His chest felt as cold and impenetrable as the castle wall against the warmth of her cheek. She resisted the urge to snuggle closer, to prove to herself that deep beneath those bands of corded muscle beat a genuine human heart and not the detached emptiness of a warlord cast in stone.

Which she doubted only a few seconds later.

The moment he reached her room, he carried her to the bed and spilled her from the strong haven of his arms like a sack of oats.

"Ghost or no, you are sleeping in this room tonight," he said and then he left, slamming the door on the lonely shadows that engulfed her. "I want a lock put on this damned door in the morning," he shouted as an afterthought, loud enough so that not only she but the entire castle could hear him.

Chapter

10

Duncan sat with his head resting against the scrolled chair, his eyes half closed in contemplation as his clansmen filed in from the great hall. Grumbling amongst themselves. Casting him resentful glances over their shoulders. If they hadn't hated him before, they did now. Aye, they could thank their arrogant laird for the mountain of dirty chores he'd assigned each and every one.

Sweeping out the mews. Scrubbing the latrines. Chasing the chickens out of the moat. Weeding the moat. Unstopping the moat. Combing their hair.

It was Marsali's turn for judgment next. She sat slumped at the opposite end of the table, face buried in her folded arms, the emotional turmoil of the past two days having taken its toll on even her irrepressible wellspring of exuberance. Bringing out the best in the chieftain wasn't proving as easy as she'd hoped.

The man derived diabolical glee from spoiling everyone's fun.

The first thing this morning he had called a "drill" in the courtyard, assembling his ragged clan for a pitiless inspection. When Marsali failed to appear, he marched straight to the scullery, where, in defiance of his orders, she had ensconced herself, and dragged her out of her cozy pallet by the fire. Then he preceded to soak her head under the pump while everyone watched in horror.

"You were a very bad girl last night," he whispered in her ear. "Don't think I'm unaware of what you and Effie were doing down in the root cellar into the wee hours."

Marsali could only sputter in indignation and shake herself off like a wet cat. She was too woozy from sampling the strawberry wine she and Effie had made months ago in the cellar to defend herself.

Twenty minutes after the drill, Duncan and Cook had faced off in the kitchen. Cook openly defied the chieftain by tearing up his suggested menus and tossing them in the fire. Duncan retaliated by confiscating her rolling pin for the day.

No one had breakfast. No one was happy.

"The matter of Marsali Hay is to be decided next," he said in a low, precise voice.

She cranked up her chin an inch and shot him a suspicious look across the ale tankards littering the table. His deep baritone voice reverberated in her groggy head like a drum roll.

"I've been giving the matter of your future great thought," he said with a malevolent smile.

Which actually was an understatement. He had barely slept a blessed wink in two whole days, what with worrying about ghosts, Jacobite spies, Sarah's imminent arrival. And Marsali Hay.

She rubbed her nose. "Go on. The suspense is killing me."

"I considered a convent—"

She pretended to gasp. "Oh, no. Anything but that."

"But out of pity for the nuns, I decided against it."

"A damned good thing too," she said with such vehemence that she set off a fresh wave of pounding agony in her skull.

"A wee drop too much last night," Duncan said in a dry voice. "It will be your last binge, then. You'll remember we discussed finding a husband for you? Apparently the search is more urgent than I suspected."

Marsali cradled her head in her hands as gingerly as if it

were a cracked egg. "Oh, fine, my lord. Whatever you say. Who is it going to be?"

"I don't know yet. But it will be a man important enough to honor your father's position and loyalty to the clan." He leaned forward on his elbows, struck by a bolt of inspiration. "It will be whomever I choose as my successor: I think your father would be pleased to see you the chieftain's bride."

Marsali stared at him in shocked disbelief. "You're going to marry me to someone in the castle?"

Almost in unison, they glanced around at the few men loitering in the hall. At Angus, the ancient groom, snoring with his chin tucked into his flowing beard. At Lachlan, playing tiddlywinks with a stale crust of bread and a fossilized pea. At Johnnie, studying a spider crawling across the table as if it were the most fascinating sight in the world.

Duncan's gaze met hers, conceding the point. "All right. The search might take a little effort."

Marsali sighed, her head sinking back onto the pillow of her arms. "I appreciate your concern, but it's useless. Robert was the best in the bunch, and my father didn't really care for him. There's no one else."

"Within the castle boundaries, perhaps," Duncan was forced to agree, rising from the table. "But take heart, lass. There has to be a suitable husband for you somewhere in Scotland."

Marsali stiffened, watching him pace behind her chair like a caged lion. She did not like the steely resolve in his eyes at all. "I doubt it, my lord."

"Stand up, lass," Duncan said briskly, beckoning her from the chair.

She cast an uneasy look at Johnnie. "What for?"

"Just do as I ask."

As she reluctantly obeyed, he subjected her to a long silent scrutiny, his face impassive as marble. At first Marsali was amused; she even liked the attention, putting one hand on her hip and performing an impudent pirouette around her chair.

"Hold still," Duncan snapped.

Her grin faded. The piercing blue of his gaze as it bored

into hers was potent enough to start her poor head pounding all over again. Suddenly she was aware of her still-damp hair, the straw on her skirts, the sheer size of the man intimidating her with his unspoken criticism.

He motioned in distaste to the pink blotches on her bodice. "Pray God, what are *those* from?"

"Probably strawberries," she answered, unconcerned. "They'll fade in time."

Duncan's upper lip curled at one corner. "'Probably strawberries. They'll fade in time.' Marsali, it is not acceptable behavior to pass your evenings getting drunk in the root cellar."

She frowned. "I wasn't getting drunk on purpose. I was sampling the wine for Effie to sell at the fair, and if I got drunk it was only because we couldn't get the flavor right the first few times. There's a world of difference between getting drunk on purpose and by accident, as I see it."

"I see it that way too, lass," Lachlan said, interrupting his game of tiddlywinks to offer his support.

"Well, I don't," Duncan said in a voice that put an end to the debate. "And along with the midnight rides and the ambushes on the moor, it has to stop. A man hardly wants to marry a woman who can drink him under the table. Now hold out your chest, Marsali."

She flushed indignantly, holding her chin in the air. No one had criticized the state of her bosom before. Come to think of it, no one had noticed she even had one. The chieftain was the only man in the castle aware of her femininity, and he'd made her aware of it too.

"I *am* holding it out, my lord."

"Aye," Johnnie agreed somberly. "'Tis as far as I've ever seen it go."

Lachlan directed an admonishing frown at Duncan. "'Tisn't fair to expect it to go any farther, my lord. There are some things decided by nature that even a chieftain canna change."

"If I want anyone else's opinion, I will ask for it," Duncan said. His face devoid of expression, he lowered his gaze from Marsali's bright pink face to the pistol she wore in an embroidered girdle at her waist. Amazing that the girl could look so appealing and bedraggled at the same time. She was like the castle kitten: fey, adorable, protected by all, yet owned by none despite the affection she garnered.

"Trade the gun for a fan," he said flatly.

"A fan?" Her eyes flashed with temper; this was becoming a personal attack. "And how am I supposed to shoot game with a fan? Or crack open a hazelnut?"

"Not to mention defendin' herself," Johnnie said in concern.

Duncan raised his eyebrows. "Her husband will defend her. That is, after all, the whole point."

Angus, waking up to all the fuss, gave a dry chuckle. "Aye, but will he spear her fish and crack her hazelnuts, my lord?"

"I don't really care," Duncan said in exasperation. "If he could summon the energy, perhaps he will."

Marsali crossed her arms over her chest, her expression volatile and forbidding. "Papa bought me this pistol."

"I thought ye said it belonged to yer brother," Lachlan began, only to stammer to a halt at the warning gleam in her eye.

"Papa gave it to me," she insisted, nudging the chair between herself and Duncan with her toe.

Duncan leaned down to look into her face. "It makes you look like a little brigand," he said with intimidating softness. "Get rid of it. The damn thing isn't even loaded."

"Yes, it is."

"No, it isn't." He was getting angry now. "I tried to shoot the portcullis open, don't you remember? The damn gun wasn't loaded."

"Well, I loaded it myself last night in the root cellar."

Duncan shuddered at the thought of her drunk and loading a pistol. "Give me the gun, Marsali."

"But . . ."

Her voice died off as the heavy door behind them banged open, the wooden planks shuddering in their iron braces: Effie had returned, her thin face flushed with excitement, her mop cap askew. Drawing a deep breath, she marched over to the table and bobbed Duncan such a deep curtsy that her spectacles slid to the end of her nose. Before she had straightened, a pair of pink and white piglets trotted up to the table, whiskery snouts quivering in the ever-hopeful search of a snack.

"I thought I banished those damned porkers to the castle yard," Duncan said, looking around in irritation. "Johnnie, have Cook pen them up and find a recipe for—"

"Ye canna put the twins on the menu," Effie said in horror, grabbing Marsali's hand as if the very possibility made her feel faint.

"The twins?" Duncan said.

"Alan and Ailis," Marsali explained, kneeling to scratch the pair's bristly ears.

"Pigs belong outside," Duncan said. "And you, Effie, are supposed to be milking the cows."

"Yes, my lord," Effie said breathlessly. "I just wanted to ask if Marsali could help me. There's no one who can milk a cow like Marsali. It's a special talent she has."

Marsali rose, frowning in confusion. "I hate milking cows, Effie. What are you talking about?"

Effie gave her a meaningful little nudge. "Don't be modest. Everyone in the clan is always marveling how good you are at things like milking cows . . . riding horses . . . catching lobsters."

The blank look fled Marsali's face, replaced by a flicker of comprehension that Duncan caught but did not immediately understand. In fact, there wasn't much he seemed to understand these days.

"Cook says it's time to milk the cows, Marsali," Effie said emphatically.

And then, without waiting for permission, Marsali swept around Duncan and walked with Effie to the door, the piglets following. "You're not to sample any more strawberry wine, Marsali," he called to her receding figure. "And I will expect you to get rid of that gun before supper."

He stared at the door, ignoring the niggle of unease in the back of his mind that told him something devious was brewing in the furtive looks between the two girls, their conversation hiding a secret code. But after the scene at the water pump with Marsali that morning, he thought it unlikely she would cause him grief again. He'd frightened her. Aye, the girl was finally coming to respect him. He decided she wouldn't cause him half as much trouble as he'd feared.

He returned slowly to his chair, distracted by the swags of cobwebs that festooned the MacElgin coat of arms hanging crookedly above the massive fireplace. Talk about trouble. How in God's name was he to make the castle presentable for Sarah's arrival in less than a fortnight? He'd done everything to discourage her from coming except tell her the truth.

They said that the truth hurt. In this case it was going to kill.

He hadn't exactly lied to Sarah, but he hadn't been open about the details of his dubious beginnings either. He cringed now at the white lies he'd allowed her to believe, never dreaming he would have to confront his past again at the Crown's bequest. Never dreaming that Sarah would actually make the daunting trek across the Highlands and invite herself to his familial home.

To Sarah he had been a military hero from the hour of his birth, the beloved heir of a revered Highland chieftain. No hint of scandal, murder, abuse to taint his sainted name. Why would he destroy himself by confessing sins he had spent years trying to forget? Why would he acknowledge the past when he'd hoped it was long buried? God above, why hadn't he told the whole ugly truth when he'd had the chance?

Sarah, the daughter of an English earl, was in for a shock.

She expected a fairy-tale medieval castle in the clouds with graceful turrets rising against gentle hills of eternally blooming heather. She expected bonny red-cheeked village children to hand her bouquets of wildflowers in shy welcome, as befitting the wife of the duke he would soon become.

She would expect to dine nightly on fresh succulent venison his clansmen caught in her honor, the tasty trout from the sparkling waters of his loch.

She would expect a staff of loyal servants to fight for the privilege of serving her.

And what would she find instead?

A crumbling pile of rocks encircled by a chicken-infested moat, which, if she survived being flattened by the drawbridge, she would cross only to dodge a fatal barrage of arrows shot courtesy of the clan's children.

She would then choke down a supper of stringy poultry plunked down before her by a handful of belligerent Highlanders. A well-meaning clansman might whack her on the back if she turned blue at the table, or he might not, depending on how drunk he was.

If she was lucky, no one would drop a frog down her dress at the table, or roll her around the courtyard in a herring barrel. If she made it that far and did not run shrieking from the castle, she would probably be awakened during the night by the resident ghost looking for the chamberpot.

And she would realize that her betrothed was detested by the clan he had led her to believe revered him.

"I'm doomed." He spoke the thought aloud, his attention returning to the two men still seated at the table.

They were watching him closely. Too closely. He sat forward, the skin of his nape crawling. Trouble was brewing. They knew something.

"What is it?" he demanded, glancing from one to the other.

Angus gave him an evil grin.

"What is what, my lord?" Johnnie asked innocently.

Duncan's face darkened as he scanned the suddenly deserted hall. "Where did Lachlan go? I wasn't finished assigning him his duties on the watch."

"He's gone off, my lord," Johnnie said.

"Gone off? To do what? Milk a—"

Milk a cow. Ride a horse. Catch lobsters.

Duncan rose slowly from his chair, hovering over the two men like a hammer about to fall. Lobsters: lobsterbacks. It was ludicrously obvious. While he sat on his behind bemoaning his fate, the fairy princess was leading her band of misfits on another ambush. Only this time her victim would be a genuine, Highland-hating English captain of dragoons who would jump at the chance to retaliate.

"That's it." He pushed his chair aside, his voice clipped and furious. "I can't believe I felt sorry for her. I'm marrying her off to the first unlucky bastard who'll take her. Angus, have the horses saddled. Johnnie, off your duff. You're helping me."

He strode from the table, his spurred boots ringing on the sunken flagstones. Johnnie hoisted up his trews and hurried after him. In the aftermath of Duncan's outburst there was a stretch of absolute silence until Angus's muffled chuckling erupted into full-fledged laughter that echoed to the smoke-blackened beams of the empty hall.

He rode his Flanders stallion like a fury to intercept the ambush but arrived too late. In helpless frustration, he watched the denouement of the scene unfold from the same knoll where only two days earlier he had laughed at Marsali clumping about in his boots.

Two days, he raged inwardly. Only two days and his life had already begun to unravel like the threads of the ancient tapestries that had hung in the great hall. He tugged the spyglass from Johnnie's hand, his jaw taut with anger as the disheartening details of the ambush came into focus.

His clansmen had not only ambushed the captain of dragoons and his small command of soldiers, but also the coach that the captain had presumably been escorting to safety. Duncan's mind raced. What idiot would commission a coach to carry him into these wild Highland hills? A foreign dignitary who wished to hunt deer on a whim? What bloody stupid . . .

He looked up at the dainty figure on horseback a few yards from the scene. She was bellowing out orders to Effie, who strode back and forth like a sergeant, with the piglets wallowing in the muddy water of the tarn.

He leaned over the pommel, a vein pulsing in his temple as a tall cloaked figure emerged from the coach waving a white handkerchief in surrender. Lachlan followed, prodding the mercifully dressed victim toward the band of soldiers, who were huddled together in humiliation at the base of the crag.

"Well, they've done it now," Johnnie murmured, shaking his head in what might have been admiration or apprehension—Duncan was too upset to tell.

He lowered the spyglass, his fingers flexing inside his gloves. What should he do? March back to the castle and pretend ignorance of the hellion's activities? There would be a price on her head after this. A captain wouldn't easily forget the humiliation of being paraded bare-bottomed in front of his men.

Unnerved by Duncan's silence, Johnnie cleared his throat. "What do we do now, my lord?"

"God help me if I know. I'm damned if I come to the captain's rescue, and damned if I don't. And that idiot in the coach—"

The idiot in question chose that precise moment to raise the lace hanky to give its nose a resounding blow. It was a gesture so annoyingly familiar that Duncan's heart plunged in recognition. He'd know that honk anywhere.

He forced his horse down the hillside and raised the spyglass again, praying he was wrong. He wasn't.

The cloaked figure was a woman. He groaned in despair.

"What about that idiot, my lord?" Johnnie prompted softly, intrigued by the play of emotions that crossed his chieftain's face.

Duncan swallowed over a knot in his throat the size of a crab apple. "The idiot is Lady Edwina Grayson, my future bride's aunt and chaperone, although I use the term advisedly. If Sarah and her father are in that coach, there isn't going to be a wedding. Only a funeral. Mine."

Chapter

11

Duncan advanced on Marsali like a panther, forcing her back toward the heavy Jacobean four-poster that dominated the castle bedchamber. "I can't quite decide what to do with you," he said with deadly calm. "The thumb screws come to mind. And there are other ways . . ." He rubbed his chin thoughtfully. "Your father used to leave me alone down in the dungeon for days at a time himself."

She wrapped her thin arms around the carved bedpost, her heart pounding in her ears. "Everyone in the castle will come running to my rescue if you hurt me."

His smile chilled her. "The damage will be done by then, won't it? Let them come. I'm in the mood for a fight."

He began to peel off his gloves, tossing them down upon the bed with cold deliberation. Marsali closed her eyes, pressing her spine against the post. Where was Uncle Colum when she needed him? What good did it do to have a damned wizard in the family if he had no sense of timing?

"Help," she whispered weakly, feeling the angry heat of Duncan's body against hers. And then in a louder, frantic voice, "Help! He's going to kill me!"

Nothing happened.

Eun did not slam against the shutter and burst into the bedchamber to peck off Duncan's nose.

Her clansmen did not batter the door down to save her. Nothing.

His warm breath brushed her cheek. His low voice sent chills of anxiety arrowing down her spine. "Do you have any idea whose coach you ambushed today, Marsali?"

She gave a stiff shake of her head, then gasped in terror when he cupped her jaw, forcing her face toward his. She squeezed her eyes shut in anticipation.

Duncan stared down at her scrunched-up face, resisting an absurd impulse to laugh. "Stop cringing like that, for God's sake. I am not going to hurt you."

She cracked one eye partially open to take a peep at him. "You're not?"

"No."

She opened her other eye, regarding him with suspicion. "What about the thumb screws?"

"I don't think they'd fit."

She swallowed, searching his face for a sign of forgiveness. "I did what I had to do," she said loudly.

"That was my future aunt-in-law's coach you ambushed."

"*What?* Oh, hell." She released her breath, guilt and embarrassment deflating her fear. "Well, how was I supposed to know?"

"You're a reckless, impulsive creature."

"You should have warned us, my lord," she said, with an injured sniff at the insult.

He studied her face in silence. "What do I have to do to put an end to the ambushes?" he asked unexpectedly.

"Make them stop building the road."

"I can't. You're asking the impossible."

She lowered her arms, her throat aching. The repercussions of his calm resignation frightened her more than his temper. "But if you can't stop them, then no one can and the killing will go on."

"Not necessarily. However, I'll handle it in my own way, and you are *not* to get involved."

"How are you going to handle it?"

"Leave the matters of war to men, little girl," he said quietly. "Your interference will only make things worse."

They stared at each other, anger and antagonism preventing any attempts at understanding. He wondered how such a fragile slip of femininity could harbor such a fierce soul. She wondered what it would take to make him care.

"What good is a warrior who refuses to fight?" she asked aloud, her face challenging.

The door burst open before Duncan could reply, and he felt a stab of resentment at the interruption, not only because he'd had no chance to defend himself but because she had actually managed to engage his emotions at a deeper level than anyone else had ever dared.

She froze in her flight to escape halfway across the room, realizing in shock that the figure in the doorway was not a clansman who'd come to her rescue but a stately older woman in a Chinese silk dressing robe. The woman with the English army officers whose carriage she had ambushed on the moor.

Marsali backed away from her until she bumped up against Duncan, who stood unmoving, his face exasperated at the interruption. She felt trapped, caught between the Devil and the deep blue sea.

The Englishwoman grinned, recognizing her, her heavily painted features warm and friendly. "You're the girl on the moor," she said, studying Marsali's disgruntled face in amusement. "That was a wonderful joke you played on us, by the way. I haven't enjoyed myself so much in ages."

Marsali looked at her in suspicious silence, taking in her powdered silver-blond hair, the pearl necklace and dangling earrings, the broad, almost masculine shoulders, and expressive gray eyes. Why was she not furious for being humiliated like the others? Why did she wear that silly green gown with butterflies embroidered along the billowing sleeves? And what was the old fool blathering about? Was she a mental case?

She jumped, startled out of her thoughts, as Duncan bent his head to hers. "I explained to Edwina about our little 'prank' this morning. About the Highland sense of humor, the ambush you staged to welcome her."

"And she believed you?" Marsali asked in an incredulous voice.

"Duncan and I have always played jokes on each other." Edwina sauntered into the room, eyeing the heavy Jacobean furnishings with a delicate shudder of distaste.

"Yes." Duncan smiled wryly. "I remember the Christmas

Eve that you and Sarah brought all the barnyard animals into the drawing room."

"That wasn't a joke," Edwina murmured. "The poor darlings were freezing."

"Sarah cut up my favorite cloak to make dresses for them, and she thought it was funny."

At the mention of Sarah, Edwina's pleasant expression took on an edge of tension. She made a great pretense of examining an ivory casket on the dressing table. "Sarah had her moments," she said after a pause, as if she were speaking of someone who no longer existed.

Marsali gave her a sidelong glance. Sarah. This frivolous old Sassenach's niece was the woman the chieftain loved. Marsali felt her first pang of possessive jealousy of all the people outside the castle who had laid claim to Duncan's loyalty. The world had kept him long enough.

Duncan moved around her, his demeanor unruffled. "This is Marsali Hay, Edwina, the daughter of the clan's late tacksman."

Edwina gave her a friendly smile; she almost seemed relieved to turn her attention away from Duncan. "You're a very lovely young lady, Marsali."

Marsali plopped down on the bed, refusing to be moved. "You're a silly old thing."

Duncan swung around, his eyes boring into hers. "You will apologize to her ladyship for that rude remark."

She scowled up at him, her toes twitching with a tension that gripped her entire body. Apologize? She set her jaw, stubbornly silent. The day she apologized to a grinning Sassenach with pearl earrings was the day she died.

Duncan leaned down until his face was level with hers. His low voice vibrated with warning. His hand pressed down on her backside. "There are rats in the dungeon, lass."

She pushed herself up onto her elbows and glared at Edwina. "Oh, all right. I'm sorry that you're a silly old thing."

Edwina began to laugh. "How refreshing! The girl is as straightforward as a pin."

Duncan squared his shoulders, forcing a smile. "She could take a few lessons in decorum from Sarah, couldn't she?"

Edwina met his eyes in the mirror. "I'm not sure about that," she said in an undertone.

Duncan gave her a puzzled look. "It's that Highland sense of humor," he said again, a little uneasily. "She and my clansmen take getting used to."

"Well, I suppose I can't blame her for resenting me." Edwina stooped before the pier glass to smooth her powdered ringlets. "After all, I am considered the enemy in these parts. Believe it or not, though, Marsali, I do have sympathy for the Scottish cause. I've read all about your plight in the papers."

Marsali flipped onto her stomach, hiding her face in the pillow. She refused to let the silly creature charm her. Bad enough that she herself was so enamored of the chieftain, who hadn't done a damn thing to earn her trust. She refused to be disloyal to those she had loved and lost by liking the enemy. If not for the English, Marsali's family and many others would still be alive.

"We will expect you downstairs for supper, Marsali," Duncan said in a cool voice. "You will please wash your face before coming to the table. And you will change into another dress."

She bounced over onto her back. "I don't have another one. I'm poor. The chieftain of my clan prefers gallivanting around the world to taking care of his people. What does he care that he left us in rags?"

Duncan's blue eyes held hers in a long intense stare until she began to squirm. "I'm not through with you, *Cinderella,*" he said with a heartless smile, and then he turned away, quickly ushering Edwina to the door as if afraid of what Marsali would say to embarrass him next.

She lay unmoving where he'd left her on the bed, glowering at his back and listening intently to the conversation between him and that damned Englishwoman in the robe.

"When did you say Sarah was arriving?" she heard Duncan ask in an anxious voice. Then, "God, I wish you'd told me you were coming. . . . Come on, let's go to the chapel. It's the last place in the castle where we're likely to be interrupted."

Chapter

12

Duncan sank down onto the pew, unable to absorb the emotional blow Edwina had just dealt him. "If this is one of your jokes," he said after a moment, "I don't find it any more amusing than what happened to you on the moor this morning."

Edwina glanced up uneasily at the strands of rope dangling from the rafters. "I know the Highlands are rather primitive, but don't tell me they *hang* people in here," she murmured, unconsciously fingering the pearls at her throat.

"I wouldn't be surprised," Duncan said tersely, irritated by the woman's lapse in attention. "You *were* joking, weren't you?"

Edwina sighed, her gaze drifting back down to Duncan's troubled face. "I only wish it were a joke. Her father and I reacted just like you at first. It was so out of character for Sarah." She patted his hand. "The cowards sent me all this way to tell you. I was the only one with the guts for it."

"I can't believe she would do this to me."

"Those aren't chicken feathers on the floor, are they, Duncan?"

"It's been, what?—only three months or so since she came to me with a list of people to invite to our wedding.

You were there, Edwina. Did you notice anything wrong between us? Did I miss something?"

Edwina glanced away, distressed by Duncan's uncharacteristic show of emotion. "Duncan," she said quietly, "that is the problem in a nutshell. It's been *thirteen* months since you and my niece had that conversation."

"What? Thirteen months? No." Duncan lifted his head, disbelief and shame spreading across his face. "You're wrong. You have to be."

"It's been over a year, Duncan. Yes, on my honor it has, and so much can happen in that time. You really can't blame Sarah for doubting there was ever going to be a wedding. I doubted it myself."

Duncan got to his feet, his voice wounded and indignant. "I'll bring her back home. No, I won't. To hell with her. Where did they go? How long ago did they leave? My God, didn't your family try to stop them? It can't be too late for an annulment."

"It is," Edwina said, cringing at the look of black fury that overshadowed Duncan's face. She swallowed, her voice faltering. "The last I heard she was pregnant."

And then Duncan lost his temper.

Marsali pulled away from the keyhole where she crouched, evesdropping, shocked from head to toe at the swearing and yelling that profaned the chapel. Not that the MacElgins had ever had much use for religion to begin with, except when they were dying or marrying a woman they'd abducted, and then it was only to haul the poor old priest across the moor to administer the last rites or wedding Mass to a clansman.

But the language Duncan used, the creativity of his curses, blistered her poor ear. He used words she'd never used but wished to remember: Wouldn't the clan be impressed if she could swear like that? She grinned at the thought, wondering how best to use the weapon of her secret knowledge to her advantage.

His English lady love had jilted him, thrown him over for an elderly viscount—which only proved the woman hadn't been worthy of him in the first place, the way Marsali saw it.

She rose to her feet and stretched, shaking her head at this fortuitous turn of events. He was all the clan's now, as the good Lord obviously intended it to be. Things were going as planned.

She paused and crept toward the stairwell, then held her breath as the chapel door banged open and Duncan, emerged, to stomp over the very spot where she'd sat eavesdropping not seconds before.

Dhé! The hurt anger on his face actually moved her to pity him, to forgive him for heartlessly ordering her to make friends with a foolish Englishwoman, while Marsali's beloved, her brothers and father, lay buried forever under a cairn of cold lonely stones.

She pressed herself against the wall as he swept past. To her surprise, he didn't even glance her way, too self-absorbed in the anger of betrayal to even notice her.

He strode beyond her sight, his profile so forbidding it looked as if it were etched in stone. Releasing her breath, Marsali turned and darted down the stairs, her throat strangely dry, her sense of victory suddenly hollow at the image of the proud man's pain.

Duncan stood outside the door to the stone kitchen, struggling to control the foul mood that possessed him. He had sat alone in his chamber for two hours, wallowing in bad wine and self-pity, and then he had sat in a drunken stupor at the head of the banqueting table for another hour in the great hall, staring at Edwina's guilt-stricken face, Sarah's betrayal standing like a barricade of stones between them.

Supper had been delayed.

Not a single clansman had appeared. Not so much as a bite of stringy poultry had been served. In fact, a ghostly air of abandonment hung over the castle. The very walls whispered sly accusations and seemed to mock him.

And the reason?

Ah, yes, the reason. Well, the reason herself was perched on the oak chopping block in the cavernous kitchen, holding court to a spellbound audience of MacElgin clansmen. With a dramatic flair worthy of Drury Lane, Marsali Hay performed her passionate little heart out to a captive audience.

Duncan could almost admire her theatrical talent. Her voice caught just the right inflection; her small face portrayed an astonishing range of emotion; her supple body played out the pantomime with brilliant skill.

And the subject of her performance: Was it a Shakespearean comedy? A Highland folk tale?

No. Duncan's mouth tightened into an unpleasant smile. The girl was acting out Sarah's betrayal, while in the background Cook and her enrapt scullions allowed the salmon supper to go up in smoke. Chopped vegetables cooked to mush in the forgotten broth. Never mind that Marsali portrayed *him* with embarrassing empathy as the wronged party and Sarah as a heartless, haughty Jezebel. Never mind that a few of his hardened clansmen sniffed back a tear or two in sympathy for their chieftain. Duncan's humiliation was not only complete, it was also the evening's entertainment.

Footsteps sounded in the dirt behind him. He glanced around to see Edwina tramping across the unlit yard in a red taffeta evening gown, looking hopelessly lost.

"Finally, Duncan," Edwina said loudly, her aristocratic face annoyed. "It was bad enough to leave me sitting alone at the table without so much as a crust of bread. But to just get up and—"

"Be quiet, Edwina. Listen to this."

Edwina listened, her earnest gray eyes widening in amazement as an astonishingly accurate imitation of Sarah's cultured voice wafted across the yard from the kitchen door.

"It's been over a year, and is Duncan planning our wedding? Is Duncan sending me tender love notes, consulting a jeweler about my betrothal ring?" Marsali's voice rose into an indignant squeak. "No. Duncan is in *Scotland.*"

This she pronounced with a shudder of contempt, pinching her nose as if she had stepped in a cesspool. "In a castle with some medieval clan of traitorous men who wear skirts. To think that I was prepared to make the ultimate sacrifice and actually *travel* there . . ."

"What a nasty woman," Owen interrupted, never once questioning that Marsali's version of the story might be a little biased.

"Aye, holdin' her nose at us."

"And makin' fun of our clothes."

"She called us traitors too," Cook chimed in from the fireplace.

"Even the chieftain doesna deserve such a faithless creature," Lachlan said.

Marsali nodded in agreement. "He's a hard man, but she's no cause to treat him like that."

"Does this mean we have to be nice to him now?" someone asked.

Marsali shrugged. "Well, it wouldn't hurt. My father always said that even the fiercest beast responds to kindness."

"The chieftain is well rid of her," Johnnie shouted from the corner.

Effie pushed to the forefront of the crowd gathered around the chopping block, a piglet squealing under each arm. "Ye're breaking our hearts, Marsali," she said with a deep sigh. "What did the chieftain say when he heard the news?"

"I was just getting to that part before everyone interrupted me," Marsali said in annoyance. "Give me a moment. I've got to get back into the mood. Ahem."

Duncan glanced back at Edwina, realizing by the woman's enrapt face that she was actually enjoying the brat's performance herself.

"I'm going to kill her, Edwina," he said quietly.

"Hush," Edwina whispered, peering around Duncan's shoulder for a better view. "She's doing my part now. Damn, do I really sound like that?"

She did. Sitting on the block, hanging her head in abject shame, Marsali let a long dramatic silence ensue. "The last I heard she was pregnant."

"And then what happened?" Lachlan prompted, literally on the edge of the seat he had taken with the others on the stone sinkboard.

Marsali narrowed her eyes. "Then he lost his temper, and it was so sad and frightening to see the great man brought low by the faithless Sassenach. Aye, it was the saddest and most frightening thing I've ever heard."

"How frightening was it, lass?" Cook asked bravely, her voice quivering in anticipation. "What did he say?"

Marsali slowly rose back to her full height. She cleared her throat, closing her eyes in concentration.

"He said . . . he said, 'Those dirty God damned little f—'"

The door banged against the wall with enough force to fan the flames under the chickens roasting to blackened embers on the spit. Marsali's eyes popped open, pinned to the dark figure who thrust his way through her audience toward the chopping block. Nobody breathed a word.

Marsali stared down at him in terrified silence.

"That was quite a performance," Duncan said wryly. "Your talent for mimicry is surpassed only by your total lack of indiscretion and soaring imagination."

Marsali swallowed, her self-confidence slipping a notch. His voice had dropped to that baritone again, portending bad things. What had she done wrong? Only spoken the truth. Not a lie had passed her lips. She'd stirred up sympathy and understanding for him, was all.

She crossed her arms over her chest, aware of her heart hammering in triple time. "They had to know," she said passionately. "They need you, and *she* obviously doesn't."

He glanced around the smoky candlelit kitchen, at the unfriendly but familiar faces turned expectantly to his. His clan. Dear God, he had lost Sarah, and look what life had left him in return. What a joke. On him.

"I expect supper on my table within the hour." His lips curled as he surveyed the black smoke wafting from the ovens. "Or what can be salvaged of it."

Without warning, he headed straight for the chopping block to catch Marsali around the legs and sling her over his shoulders like a haunch of venison. "You're going to regret this, lass," he promised softly, his arms tightening around her like a vise until he heard her gasp for breath.

"Dear God," she grunted, pressing her palms into his shoulder blades for leverage. "Isn't anyone going to stop him?"

"Apparently not," Duncan answered calmly, maneuvering his way undeterred through the shocked but unhelpful clansmen, who parted to let him pass.

Marsali threw Cook a desperate look. "What about you, Aggie?" she wailed. "Will you let him treat me like this?"

Cook elbowed into Duncan's path; pressed to her stout bosom lay a long thin French rolling pin, which had whacked more than one complaining clansman over the head. Even Duncan was not wholly unaffected by the sight. He remembered quite well that same cruel weapon cracked across his kneecap years ago when he had refused to finish his soggy haggis one Hogmanay. His knee joint still ached occasionally on a cold night.

They faced off like gladiators. Cook was herself built not unlike a Celtic warlord. A tall imposing figure with long straight steel-gray hair, she intimidated everyone who crossed her path. Her broad shoulders might have hefted a claymore in her salad days. It was the clan's collective opinion, however, that she inflicted enough damage with an ordinary kitchen utensil.

In his younger years Duncan had stood in stark terror of the woman. "Step out of the way, Agnes," he said, unconsciously tightening his grip around Marsali's wriggling rump.

"Ye've no changed at all," the woman said, her face flushed with anger. "The fancy titles, the medals, the honor—they're naught but a disguise for the darkness within ye. You always used force to get yer way. 'Tis cruel to take yer pain out on this innocent lassie."

Duncan despised the emotional chink in his character that allowed her words to penetrate. "Your personal feelings do not change the fact that I am your chieftain, and it is not your place to gainsay me. Now step aside, Agnes. I refuse to argue with a servant."

The cold authority in his eyes gave Cook pause, forcing her to acknowledge that the wild youth had grown into a formidable man. "What are ye going to do with the girl?" she asked, her gaze flickering to Marsali, who had somehow managed to drape herself around Duncan's neck like a fox collar come to life.

"None of your business. The only thing that should concern you is that supper is to be on the table within the hour. I expect claret, lots of it. Donovan, you are not to play the harp drunk again tonight. We have a guest. Effie, get those damn pigs out of here or they'll be sizzling rashers of bacon in the morning."

With that he hoisted Marsali higher and walked from the kitchen to the door where Edwina waited, grinning in shameless enjoyment. Duncan considered it a major triumph that he made it to the yard without Cook's rolling pin descending on the back of his head. But it was a bitter victory.

He swung Marsali to her feet, catching her hand when she made to bolt. "Oh no, not so fast. You embarrassed us both in there, lass. I'm not forgiving you that easily."

She tugged her hand free, surprise brightening her eyes. "But I only spoke the truth about what that awful woman did to you. 'Twasn't your fault."

"You've humiliated me for the last time, Marsali Hay. That convent is sounding better by the minute."

"There's no convent within a hundred miles of here," Marsali said, unperturbed. "Now try to calm down. I'm not going to take your behavior personally."

He scowled. "Why not?"

"Because I realize you've been hurt by what that woman did to you, and you only *think* you're angry at me."

"I am angry at you." His voice rose an octave as if to prove the point.

"Calm down, Duncan," Edwina said.

"I have a right to be angry." He was practically shouting now. "I *am* angry."

Marsali smiled at him in sympathy. "No, you're not. You're just a poor wounded beast lashing out in its pain."

"You have to feel sorry for him," Edwina said.

Duncan snorted. "All right, I'm not angry. I am a beast lashing out. But my sister, Judith, is still the mother superior of a convent school on a small island off the coast. She's built her order on the dowries of troublesome young women just like you who were sent to her by concerned families."

Marsali frowned. "Sometimes I wonder why I bother. You don't appreciate anything I do."

"You can say that again."

"You treat me like I'm a child."

"Exactly."

"Now *I'm* getting angry," Marsali said. "In fact, if you're so anxious to take care of a child, perhaps you should look for the one you left behind."

"What the hell is that supposed to mean?"

"Oh, never mind, my lord. It was just kitchen gossip. You made me lose my temper. 'Twas just something I heard when I was little. You made me angry, and I misspoke."

"That's why people shouldn't get angry, Duncan," Edwina said.

"Is there any truth to the gossip?" he demanded.

"Not as far as I know," Marsali said honestly.

"Then do not repeat it again."

"Excuse me." Edwina gave Duncan an admonishing stare. "Marsali might have embarrassed you, but her heart was in the right place."

"Stay out of this," Duncan said.

Marsali shook her head again. "Now he's lashing out at you, Edwina."

The older woman sighed. "It was bound to happen."

Duncan resented the empathetic look the two of them were exchanging. "I will not have Marsali humiliating me and risking her damned neck. I will restore order to this damned castle, and that's the end of it."

"What can Duncan do to stop the problems between you, Marsali?" Edwina asked gently.

"All I ask of him is that he stay and take care of us—"

"She expects me to behave like some medieval chieftain who sacrifices life and limb for his moldering castle," Duncan broke in, his patience snapping.

Edwina frowned. "Well, traditional obligations are important, Duncan. Imagine what would happen to the world if we all just decided to abdicate our responsibilities. Surely a man with a dukedom in his future understands the weight of stewardship."

Marsali was really starting to like Edwina. "That's exactly what I tried to tell him."

Duncan threw up his hands in defeat. "There's no arguing with women."

"Control yourself," Edwina said.

"All right, Edwina. You think you're so blasted clever,

then you take care of her. Take care of the whole castle if you like. It's yours. She's yours. Have fun. I'm finished."

His face set like flint, he strode from the yard toward the keep. For a moment there was stunned silence behind him. Then he heard Edwina's voice.

"I've never seen him behave like this. It must be the shock of losing Sarah."

Duncan scowled, resisting the urge to turn around. Yes, it was bad enough to lose the woman you intended to marry, and thanks to that wretched girl he hadn't even been allowed the luxury of mourning the loss in private. But what was almost as disturbing was the sneaky alliance he could sense brewing between Edwina and Marsali. As incredible as he found it, even his former fiancée's aunt appeared to be moving to the enemy camp, and the thought unsettled him. It unsettled him almost as much as Marsali's taunting allusion to a child he had left behind.

Chapter

13

Edwina fed a few morsels of raw rabbit meat to the hawk on the driftwood perch inside the ship's cabin. "What a nice birdie you are. Colum, I do believe Eun is coming to like me a little more every day."

The wizard glanced at Edwina's warm face and robust figure in admiration. "My lady, you would charm the most wild of creatures. How could he resist?"

Edwina tittered, lowering her eyelashes in pleasure as she turned from the hawk's perch, her taffeta skirts rustling.

Fiona, sitting ignored on the bunk with her face hidden behind her Book of Shadows, rolled her eyes heavenward. Sickening, that's what it was, the way these two old people had struck up a friendship only two short weeks ago on the moor.

Colum had been collecting elf-bolts by the cairns. Edwina had been taking her exercise. One look and they were meeting almost every day since like soul mates. A merging of the minds, her father said. Fiona couldn't stand it.

Colum handed Edwina a goblet of mulled wine. "Some libation for your ladyship?"

Edwina clasped the goblet in her beringed hands. "I shouldn't. Marsali and I are going to row out across the loch this afternoon."

"How goes the battle between her and the chieftain?" Colum asked casually.

"Unchanged. Duncan is still intent on marrying her off, and she is determined he will stay." Edwina shook her head. "I have been working on her deportment. She's far too lovely to end her days as an outlaw."

Colum frowned. "The best spells take time. Perhaps when you're finished with Marsali, you could work on my daughter."

He and Edwina glanced simultaneously at the petite barefoot figure pretending to be invisible on the bunk.

"Yes," Edwina said, sipping her wine with a pensive air. "Possibly on my next visit. In the meantime, it is all I can manage to help Cook keep peace in the castle."

Colum touched her forearm, smiling into her eyes. "Patience, my lady. Magic cannot be rushed." He lowered his voice, leading her across the cabin to where Fiona could not hear. "Are we still to meet at midnight on the cliffs so I may draw down the moon in your honor?"

Edwina sighed in anticipation. "I wouldn't miss it for the world."

A month had not exactly wrought any miracles. Sometimes Duncan had nightmares of trudging back to London with his tail between his legs, admitting defeat, explaining that a handful of Highlanders had broken his spirit. He could have trained the castle chickens easier than his clan. The hope of his Border dukedom grew dimmer by the day.

He bit back a scathing remark as he entered the great hall. A piglet barreled past him. Ailis or Alan, he still couldn't tell the "twins" apart and was all but resigned to their presence. He stumbled over Lachlan asleep on the floor, the mug of beer on his chest rising and falling with the sonorous rhythm of his snores.

"Lachlan." He nudged the unconscious figure with his foot.

"It's time to rise, my lord?" Lachlan called up groggily.

"Oh no, Lachlan, why do you ask? It's just past noon. You were only to relieve the sentry on the tower four hours ago. Don't bestir yourself. I wouldn't want you to lose a wink of your beauty sleep."

Lachlan scratched his unruly eyebrows, the sarcasm lost on him as he gave his chieftain a grin and promptly fell back asleep.

Yes indeed, what miracles a month had wrought, Duncan thought, sinking into his ceremonial chair with a ponderous sigh.

He blamed it partially on Edwina's influence, Edwina's passion for playing "jokes" and having fun. Whereas Duncan's hereditary title commanded only a modicum of grudging respect, Edwina had won the stubborn Highland hearts of everyone in the castle, from Cook to stableboy, with her flamboyant charm. Everyone avoided Duncan. Everyone sought Edwina's opinion and colorful company. Including Marsali. Duncan had never felt more like an outcast.

Edwina had taken the wild girl under her wing like a mother hen, promising to transform her into a prize no man could resist. At first Duncan had been amused by the project. After all, despite her uncivilized behavior, Marsali had been born and bred a lady. It wasn't as if Edwina were re-creating the original woman. All Marsali needed were a few finishing touches here and there. A bit of polish.

Still, it wasn't yet July, and Edwina had already commissioned a pair of dressmakers from Inverness to costume her, a parfumier originally from Paris to create an original scent to match her character, and a cobbler to sheathe her dainty feet in dancing slippers. Duncan had been kept in the dark about the details of the transformation. He had been spending his time trying to find the girl a husband.

He glanced up irritably as an ominous shadow fell upon the table. "Yes, Cook. What is it?"

She hesitated, her expression stern. "Actually, my lord, I was looking for Lady Edwina. I canna find her anywhere."

"Perhaps I will do instead. What is it you wish to ask her?"

"Nothing to worry yerself about, my lord," she replied, giving him a perfunctory curtsy before turning away. "A small domestic matter, 'tis all."

"Perhaps I can help you," Duncan said loudly. "After all, this is supposed to be my castle, and I am supposed to be the chieftain."

Cook turned stiffly, raising her eyebrows at his reaction.

Damn Edwina anyway, Duncan thought moodily. She meant well, but she'd become a pain in the neck by playing fairy godmother to Marsali's Cinderella. Which, Duncan reflected sourly, probably made him the equivalent of her wicked stepmother.

"What is the problem, Cook?" he asked in an impatient voice.

She inched toward his chair. They had come to an uneasy truce over the summer, at Edwina's encouragement, but Cook clearly didn't trust Duncan, and Duncan still refused to taste the first spoonful of her potage when it was served.

"I dinna like to bother ye, my lord, with the little things."

Duncan frowned. "I am concerned with the running of the castle. If there is a problem, even a minor one, I would like to be informed. That is why I am here."

"Well, my lord, I canna decide if we should serve the fish croquettes or the truffles before the ball on Friday. And I had a question about the Rhenish wine Lady Edwina ordered. Then there was the matter of the strawberry tortes, and the rosemary for the rack of lamb."

"Ball on Friday?" Duncan repeated, the nerve endings on his nape stirring. "Is there to be a ball on Friday?"

"I'll just check with Lady Edwina," Cook said, edging away from the chair at the tension vibrating in his voice. "I'll—"

Duncan rose to his feet, feeling his power slipping through his fingers like grains of sand. "Where is Abercrombie?" he asked. "I haven't seen the man in over a week."

"He's hidin' in the chapel again," Cook said. "The children were chasing him all over the castle, and he couldna take it."

Duncan glanced around, distracted by the sight of Johnnie and Effie rolling a pair of empty herring barrels into the hall. Owen followed with an armload of pink satin ribbons, which he proceeded to drape over the antlers of the ancient deer mounted above the fireplace. "What the hell are those barrels for?" he demanded.

Johnnie glanced up morosely. "They're for the ball on Friday, what else? Lady Edwina said they'd have to do in place of urns for the potted plants. Pots of lupines and sweet peas, she wants. Don't see what use they'll be, though, seeing as all the damned plants in the garden are dead."

"Lady Edwina said that, did she?" Duncan smiled unpleasantly as he pushed his chair back from the table. "And where precisely has Lady Edwina enthroned herself this morning?"

Effie righted the barrel she'd rolled up against the wall. "She's in the solar with Marsali, but ye're not allowed to interrupt them. We've all been banished until they're through."

Duncan shoved his chair back so hard it bumped into Lachlan, who awoke with a violent start and upset his mug of beer onto the floor. "I am not allowed to interrupt them?"

Effie blinked, moving behind Johnnie for protection. "Th-that was what Lady Edwina told us."

He hovered outside the solar door, a muscle twitching in his cheek. To judge by the air of secrecy that shrouded the castle, by Edwina's excited whisperings and Marsali's accompanying gasps of pain, Duncan might have concluded that something very peculiar was going on inside that room.

He could hear other voices, a pair of females chattering in the background; and if it hadn't been so ludicrous, Duncan would have suspected Marsali of convincing English-to-the-core Edwina to join the Jacobite cause. Whatever their conspiracy, he had been excluded. He resented it. Being forbidden to use his private sanctuary, women taking over the castle, his life.

He pushed the door open. And nearly fainted. Bolts of every fabric under the sun from watered silk to Valenciennes lace, from taffeta to tartan, smothered the fastidious order of his desk. Frills and furbelows, fans and strands of faux pearls squashed his priceless maps, his military memoirs, battle plans, and notes.

Standing unnoticed in the doorway, he listened to the conversation within. Marsali was bouncing around a long cheval glass while Edwina scolded her to hold still, and a pair of seamstresses sewed furiously at the hemline of a gold tulle gown that billowed from her slender waist like petals from a rose stem. A feathered headdress sat atop her untidy mop of hair.

"There is a language to wielding a fan, my dear," Edwina was in the process of explaining. "For example, what would you do if you'd like to let a gentleman know you are interested in him?"

"I'd tell him straight to his face," Marsali said. "I'd walk right up to him—"

"No, you would not," Edwina interrupted, rolling her eyes. "You would position the fan against the side of your cheek like this. It's far more subtle. No, darling, don't scratch your nose with it. That's very crass."

"But my nose itches," Marsali said. "It's from all of these horrid feathers stuck in this ridiculous thing on my head."

"It's called a *tiara,*" Edwina continued, unperturbed. "By lowering the fan to your throat you're issuing an invitation to a private meeting."

Duncan entered the room. Sneaking up behind Edwina, he grabbed a sandalwood fan from the clutter on his desk and bopped the other woman on the head. "And this means you're an extravagant ninny, Edwina. Do you mind telling me what you're doing?"

Edwina glanced around, batting the fan away in annoyance. "I am helping this dear young woman in her quest to attract a mate."

"Edwina, I have arranged to interview every prospective suitor within a hundred miles on Friday afternoon. The dowry I am offering is hefty enough to lure MacDuff from the grave. Do you really need to impoverish me and undermine my influence with your well-meaning inanity?"

Edwina plucked a loose thread from Marsali's hair. "I suppose you were going to get her out in rags and parade her like a guttersnipe?"

Duncan gently shouldered Edwina aside and stared out through the window, deliberately not glancing at Marsali. The seamstresses at her feet fell silent, watching the renowned warlord in awe. Rarely did they glimpse the man in such a personal moment.

"I'll take the dress off if you don't like it," Marsali said with a self-martyring shrug, breaking the silence that had fallen. "I look like a baby duck that's been tortured in it anyway."

Duncan turned slowly, assessing her with a long, heavy-lidded look.

To tell the truth, she despised the fussy dress, her small white breasts forced into full view by the bindings of her gusseted bodice. She lowered her gaze to the floor, frowning as the silence lengthened.

He swallowed with effort, struggling not to smile. "You do not look like a baby duck at all, lass."

She glanced up, hope replacing her uncertainty. "No?"

He shook his head. "No. Not at all." A slow grin broke across his face. "You look . . . like a baby turkey a fox dragged across the farmyard."

She gasped. Then she stepped over the two seamstresses sitting in wide-eyed interest on the floor and punched him in the shoulder, pretending outrage. Duncan backed into his desk with a helpless grin, making little gobbling noises behind his hand.

"Stop it," Edwina said, giving Duncan a cold glare. "Marsali, you're going to ruin that dress. Both of you, stop acting like infants."

Marsali ignored her to pull off her feathered headdress and throw it at Duncan. He caught it in one hand and put it on his head, mimicking a turkey strutting around the room. Marsali laughed until she couldn't breathe, until she was bent over at the waist and leaning against the desk for support.

Edwina braced her arms on the desk and watched them in disapproval. The seamstresses straightened, sharing amused smiles. The chieftain never behaved in such a manner.

"Look at this, my lord," Marsali gasped between giggles, pulling her gown down over her shoulders. "Edwina put powder on me *here*. As if anyone would care. Have you ever seen such a thing in your life?"

Edwina yanked the gown practically back up to her nose. "He's seen more scented shoulders than anyone I know, darling. Save such an intimate view for your husband."

Duncan lowered his gaze and pulled off the headdress, his light mood broken by the reminder of the reason behind all the fuss: to make Marsali attract another man. What had come over him? He shot the seamstresses a stern look to silence their delighted whispering. He should have let Edwina do as she wished.

"Who's supposed to be paying for all this nonsense anyway?" he asked, his curt voice chilling the air.

Marsali's amusement faded, confusion flooding her as she watched him clear the clothes from his desk onto a chair. Distant again. The curtain of stony reserve was pulled back down between them. It was almost as if he resented her for making him laugh. What had she done wrong?

"You're paying for it, Duncan," Edwina said in a hard voice. "Don't you think Marsali is worth it?"

Duncan rifled through the papers on his desk, his heavy black brows drawn together in a frown. "You might have asked my permission first before you turned the solar into a sewing room. It took me weeks to organize these entries. Yes, I think she's worth it. Damn it. Those feathers are everywhere." He glanced up, his gaze dark with an emotion Marsali could not fathom. "Isn't there another room you could use besides the solar?"

Edwina studied Duncan's face. "The light is better here than anywhere else in this gloomy castle. I take it you're not going to deny us permission to hold the ball in the great hall?"

"It's a foolish idea." Duncan looked down at his desk again, flicking a lacy garter off a biography of Julius Caesar. "I had planned to interview suitors in a civilized manner. I don't see the point in turning it into a public spectacle."

"The plain fact, Duncan, is that you're putting her on the auction block," Edwina said, her voice growing in volume.

Duncan pushed back his chair, his knuckles white as he gripped the desk. The two seamstresses crept around the table, then fled into the hall without a word. Marsali covertly grabbed her half-eaten oatcake from the desk and ensconced herself in the window embrasure to enjoy the argument. She loved to watch the chieftain lose his temper, especially over her.

"The auction block," Duncan repeated. "I resent what you're inferring."

Edwina shrugged her broad shoulders. "You could at least

cloak the arrangement in a milieu of refinement. You're the one who said that she couldn't be expected to impress anyone of consequence looking the way she did."

"I never said anything of the sort," Duncan retorted.

Marsali's hand stopped halfway with the oatcake to her mouth. This was getting good. "You made fun of the strawberry stains on my skirt," she reminded him.

"There are five men who answered my summons and whom I judged worthy of granting an interview," Duncan continued, ignoring Marsali. "Providing them with hospitality for a night or two hardly calls for a ball. This is not London, Edwina. We are not doting parents hoping to unburden ourselves of a spinster daughter."

"Only five?" Edwina looked personally affronted that all her efforts for Marsali would draw such a scant audience. *"Five,* Duncan? There must be a mistake. Without a decent means of communication, it could take months to hear from everyone."

"All I need is one," Marsali said pragmatically, but in her heart, she was convinced that although Duncan might be a master tactician, he was a terrible matchmaker. He hadn't even asked her what sort of man she wanted to marry.

She chewed the oatcake in thoughtful silence. It wouldn't have mattered anyway. Duncan could have hand-picked five hundred Highlanders and she'd have remained emotionally unmoved. The man of *her* dreams would have to have a heart as deep as the sea and the courage of a lion. He would have to love children, and—

"I hope you aren't going to sit like that when you're introduced to your future husband," Duncan said in a rude voice, motioning to the feet she had casually planted on the wall. "There's no need to give the entire world a view of your underthings, even if they did come all the way from France."

That said, he sat down at his desk.

Amused, Marsali sneaked a look at Edwina, who was standing over Duncan with her forefinger pressed to her lips as if to warn her this was not the time to cross the chieftain. She scooted her bottom up against the worn cushions and covertly tugged down her gown. This past week Duncan's outbursts of temper had everyone in the castle practically treading on eggs to avoid setting him off. He made no secret of how eager he was to get her off his hands. He'd told her over and over that it had taken a feat of diplomatic genius to convince the captain of dragoons not to have her arrested for treason.

Uncle Colum's spell clearly hadn't done a damn bit of good. The chieftain's emotions were more elusive than ever.

A dangerous impulse came over Marsali to touch him. Aye, just to smooth the frown from his forehead, or to brush back the strands of black hair that waved around his broad shoulder. She could stare at him for hours.

"Your feet, Marsali." He scowled at her over the sheaf of letters in his hand, his voice rich with sarcasm. "Do you think you could manage to keep them on the floor? In fact, if you and Edwina are finished with the royal fitting, might I be allowed an hour in privacy to repair the damage done to my desk? I'm accustomed to outfitting men with bayonets. Your wardrobe is outside my realm of interest."

Edwina snatched up an armload of petticoats with an injured expression. "Come along, Marsali. We'll set up shop in my bedchamber, and I don't want to hear *anyone* complain about the high cost of candles either."

Marsali darted an uncertain look at Duncan as she swung her feet to the floor. "Let's leave it till later, Edwina. I thought I'd go fishing this afternoon."

"Fishing?" Edwina cried, collapsing in horror against the door. "Tell me that you're going to change out of that gold tulle gown first."

Duncan glanced up, narrowing his eyes. "You are not going fishing, Marsali. Not in a gold tulle gown, nor in a sackcloth. Not with only four days left before you're to be presented as a . . . a prize."

"A prize?" she repeated, a pleased grin lighting her face. "Are you going to hold an archery contest for the honor of my hand?"

Duncan lowered his gaze, his voice muffled. "No."

"I should certainly hope not," Edwina said from the door. "A contest. How plebeian."

Marsali danced around Duncan's desk, her eyes bright with excitement. "A boxing contest, my lord?"

"No. Leave me alone, lass."

"A sword fight?" she whispered in delight, draping herself around the back of his chair with her cheek brushing Duncan's chin.

An imperceptible shudder went through him. He leaned forward, breaking the spark of electricity between them. "No, you bloodthirsty wee pagan. There won't be any lives lost on your account if I can help it."

Her small face sagged in disappointment. "Well, if I'm to be dangled as a prize, how am I to be won then?"

Duncan turned stiffly in his chair, a little alarmed to find her practically falling into his lap. "You are to be won with honesty and the ability to control you. You are not to be 'dangled' like a worm before trout."

"Oh," she said with a deep sigh, and she reached around him for the velvet ribbon hanging from the hourglass on his desk. "'Honesty and the ability to control me?' What a thrilling prospect. Perhaps I'll end up with a sheep herder, or the village bell ringer. I can hardly wait."

Duncan sat back in his chair to watch her tramp to the door; her dainty body was rigid with resentment. "You'll thank me one day. When you're a little older and settled down, you'll come to realize I had only your best interests at heart."

She turned at the door, delivering her own parting shot before she ducked under Edwina's arm to escape. "And perhaps when *you're* older, you'll realize you'd have done better to wear a hairshirt to pay for your sins than to sacrifice my life in order to save yours."

Duncan stared at the door as she disappeared behind it. Startled, Edwina hastened after Marsali to escape Duncan's reaction to her all-too-honest assessment of the situation. No one had ever dared speak so freely to Duncan's face.

Silence fell over the solar, but, to Duncan's chagrin, Marsali's presence lingered like a sprinkling of fairy dust in the sunlight.

He exhaled quietly and tried to bury his disquietude beneath the pretense of reorganizing his desk. Rude ungrateful girl. Incorrigible, irreverent creature. Not a word of thanks for the effort it had taken to weed out the dozens of horrible suitors who had been lured by the handsome dowry that accompanied her hand in marriage. The letters he'd handwritten to noblemen near and far, the discreet inquiries into the personal backgrounds of the hopeful petitioners who had presented their names for Duncan's consideration.

And only five names had emerged unscathed from Duncan's harsh scrutiny from the list of fifty. Five men who had no history of sexual perversions, physical deformities, drunkenness, or profligate ways. Five men who would petition him to prove themselves worthy of his old friend's daughter.

He pushed aside the clutter on his desk and paced to the window, noting her old discarded gown on the cushions where Marsali had tossed it. He had grown fond of her. But how could he guarantee that the man he chose would treat her well? How—

"What the hell?" he said aloud.

He stared down through the window as a figure running from the kitchen yard in a gold tulle gown caught his eye. A fishing pole protruded from the wooden bucket slung over her arm. Sunlight glinted in her hair as she darted across the yard like a dainty damselfly.

He opened the window, sighing in exasperation, and stuck his head outside. "Put down that pole before the hook catches in your gown! I am not made out of money."

She grinned at him and thrust the bucket behind her back. Unfortunately, the fishing pole stood a good two inches taller than she, and it protruded from the side of her head. "What pole, my lord?"

He fought a smile at her impertinence. "Put this on," he said, waving her old blue muslin out the window. "I'll leave it outside the door. Edwina would have a fit if you got fish scales on her creation."

"But everyone is already on their way to the loch. There'll be no fish left if I change."

"Do as I tell you, lass."

He ducked back inside, his throat tightening with an unfamiliar emotion at the sight of her small ridiculous figure trudging back toward the keep. The wrong man could so easily destroy her innocence. Yes, she was a strong young woman in many ways. She had lived among his crusty clansmen too long to have remained untouched by some of life's harsher aspects.

Her short existence had been scarred by loss and struggle; the energy she'd exerted ousting the English from her land would have been better spent living a young girl's dreams. At Marsali's age, Sarah had done nothing more strenuous than riding around Hyde Park.

Sarah.

Her betrayal should have hurt more than it did, but perhaps he was merely too numb to feel anything beyond the lingering aftermath of his anger. Or perhaps, unconsciously, he had half expected to lose her all along. Despite all the acclaim showered on him, Duncan had never moved easily within the prim parameters of British society. A Scottish marquess and cavalry general attracted a certain amount of positive attention, and while a well-bred young woman might harbor fantasies about a Highland barbarian, the reality of a marriage between them would soon override the romance.

Sooner or later, even if Duncan could have kept Sarah away from the castle, the subject of his past would have come up between them. A rumor would have reached her ear. If only secretly, she'd have wondered whether she had married a murderer, and Duncan couldn't have borne that.

In an odd way, losing her was a relief. He no longer had to fear she would find out who he really was.

Marsali laid the fishing pole carefully against the wall and picked up the dress Duncan had left outside the solar door. She'd forgotten to change her shoes too, and Edwina would explode if she caught her fishing in a pair of pearl-seeded slippers. Her lovely old boots with the comfortable holes were tucked under Duncan's desk.

Hell. She'd have to disturb the chieftain again, and from the sound of deep silence within the solar, he was engrossed in his writing and wouldn't appreciate the interruption.

She opened the door and crept inside, clutching her bucket. Her nerves were practically coiled into springs as she awaited a fierce scolding from Duncan. No one could shout like him.

Except that he wasn't behind the desk. Or at the window. A little disappointed that she'd missed an opportunity to watch him as he worked, she ducked under his desk for her boots. And straightened with a jolt of alarm at the sound of his voice only a few feet from her on the worn Turkey carpet.

"Damn the bastards," she heard him mutter. "They've surrounded our supplies. This is bad. Very bad."

Marsali froze, listening intently and rubbing her knee, which she had knocked against Duncan's chair. Who was he talking to in that terse angry voice? And *where* was he?

She crawled out from under the desk, astonishment widening her eyes as she spotted the chieftain sitting by himself on the floor by the window. A miniature country setting was spread before him: little wooden bridges, felt hills, trees, rivers of glazed silk, and tiny lead figures on horseback. She came up quietly behind him on all fours.

"I never knew you liked to play with dolls, my lord," she said over his shoulder. "What fun. May I play too?"

He glanced around, embarrassed to have been caught in his private game. "I had no idea you were here, Marsali."

She leaned up against him, studying the formation of soldiers on the floor. "Well, I didn't know you were here either, at least not until I heard you talking to your dolls."

"They are not dolls," he said in annoyance, brushing the feathers of her headdress from his nose. "They're toy soldiers, and I am reenacting a famous battle between the Scots Greys and the French cavalry."

She grinned in delight. "May I play with you?"

Duncan's scowl gave way to a slow cunning smile. "I am not 'playing.' Winning a battle is a serious business, and, clever as you are, I doubt you have a head for military tactics."

"Afraid you'll lose to a girl, eh?" she taunted, sinking down onto her knees beside him.

Duncan stared down at her, taken off guard by the tempting curve of her bottom as she stretched out full-length beside him. He could think of half a dozen other games he'd rather play with her on the floor. His gaze roved down her derrière to her silk-clad calves and ankles, crossed and kicked up in the air with complete disregard for the enticing view she offered of her creamy skin and lace-trimmed petticoats.

He swallowed with difficulty and clamped his hand around her ankles, forcing her feet back to the floor. Four days. For God's sake, he had the self-control to resist temptation for that long, didn't he?

"Did I kick you in the head, my lord?" she murmured, oblivious to the dark fantasies that held Duncan spellbound. "Sorry. It must be this damned gown. It makes me want to scratch in the most awkward places."

"Well, whatever you do, try not to swear and scratch when I present you to your future husband."

"Why not?" She glanced back over her shoulder. "He won't expect me never to scratch or swear once I'm his wife, will he?"

"Quite frankly, what you do after you're married is not my concern. Here." He nudged her away from him, the apparent rebuff covering the almost painful urge to press her down beneath him. "You'll be the French cavalry."

Marsali promptly sat up and began arranging her men in an intricate pattern on the carpet.

"What on earth are you doing?" he asked after a moment.

"I'm pulling the big ones in front to take care of the little ones."

Duncan hid a nasty smile, moving several tiny metal objects out from behind a miniature hill. "I can see that this is going to be the shortest battle in history. Your men are under heavy cannon fire."

"Now just a minute, my lord. You never told me you had a cannon hidden behind those hills."

Duncan slapped his hand to his cheek in exaggerated dismay. "Oh, dearie me. My aide-de-camp must have forgotten to mention that in the gilt-embossed invitations to tea he sent over this morning. I shall spank him senseless with my hankie."

Marsali rolled over onto her elbow, studying his sardonic face with a nod of understanding. "So it's to be that way between us, is it? Very well."

Duncan gave her an evil look and brought out a brigade of British infantry from behind the bridge; he was going to teach her a thing or two about the complexities of warfare.

While he was arranging a brilliantly unbeatable formation, Marsali reached across the carpet and palmed two of his strategically positioned cannons.

"You can't do that, Marsali," he said, scowling at her across the silk river that separated them. "You aren't allowed to steal cannons."

"Why not? There aren't any polite rules in a real battle."

Duncan eyed her with renewed interest, unwilling to admit she was right as he reached behind his back to produce another squadron of Scots Greys horsemen. "We're firing at you from the right. Your men are hopelessly outnumbered."

She threw him a challenging look, then stretched back across the carpet, analyzing the situation in absorbed silence before moving her men. "That isn't fair."

"No, no, no," Duncan whispered tauntingly in her ear, leaning over her. "Rush in and suffer heavy losses."

Marsali stiffened. The imposing weight of his body as it settled against hers was so distracting she completely lost her train of thought. Then the unprincipled devil put his arm around her shoulders. Her throat closed. Was he doing that on purpose so he could win the battle? If so, it was a very covert and potent weapon. How could she concentrate on their game when his physical presence dominated her mind?

"That is a marsh you are leading your men into," he continued in a softly wicked voice. "Your horses are sinking in the mud, sweetheart."

She blinked, her concentration jarred again as his hand drifted to the small of her back. "We're pulling ourselves out of the mud, my lord," she said in a stout if unsteady voice.

Duncan drew a deep breath, his fingertips flirting with the swell of her bottom. A shard of frustration shattered his focus. He still wanted her. A month of denying it had only intensified the dangerous attraction. Her unawakened sensuality stirred him even as he hated the selfishness that bred his desire for her.

"Marsali."

She didn't answer, still intent on the game. Innocence tempting sin. Fragility threatening power.

He closed his eyes. He was a heartbeat from pinning her small body down and suffering the consequences. His physical being ached with the need to touch her everywhere, to nuzzle the nape of her neck, to kiss her breasts, her belly. He imagined exploring the supple curves hidden under the layers of clothing, conquering her on a different battlefield altogether. He swallowed a groan at the thought.

"I'm across, my lord," she said in a tremulous whisper of triumph as she dragged the last of her men to safety.

When he didn't respond, she turned on her elbow to look up at him. He stared down into her baffled face with an unsmiling intensity that made her shiver as if a shadow had fallen over her.

"Get up," he said in a low uneven voice. He gripped her shoulders and raised her off the floor, an emotion Marsali did not understand tightening the planes of his face. "The game is over."

She didn't move, her translucent eyes riveted to his. He looked dark and dangerous, and she felt herself responding to the barely leashed charge of sexual energy that emanated from him in the pulsing silence. A delicious tension immobilized her muscles. For a month she had indulged in endless daydreams of another moment like this, the forbidden contact, the hardness, the warmth of his body against her.

"Get up," he said, a note of urgency deepening his voice. He loosened his hold on her, leaving his hands on her shoulders. "Get out of here."

"I want to play out this game, my lord."

His breathing deepened. He turned his face from hers as if he were going to ignore what she had said. Then without warning he lowered his head, his hands tightened around her shoulders again, and a guttural denial sounded deep in his throat as his mouth closed over hers.

"It isn't a game," he whispered, almost angrily, against her soft irresistible mouth.

She arched her body against his, whether in search of closer contact or to escape him, he neither knew nor cared. A dark curtain fell in his mind between self-discipline and desire. He tangled his battle-scarred hands in her hair, breathing in her fragrance, knocking over soldiers and cannons as he shifted his body to cover hers.

"I warned you," he said, his voice so harsh she almost did not recognize it.

Marsali wrapped her arms around his neck, offering herself to his rough hunger, reveling in it. He kissed her throat. His lips burned her skin. He kissed the swell of her breasts above her gown until she groaned with the sweet excitement that sang in her blood. She ran her hands over his shoulders, his back, feeling muscle and sinew hardening at her questing touch.

He lifted his head, his eyes searching hers with merciless desperation. For a moment she was frightened. What was he thinking, this man who had swept into her life like a thunderstorm? Who was she to challenge his power, to seek his love?

He slid his hands down her sides and lifted her against him, holding her so tightly that she could not tell the uneven rhythm of his breath from hers. "This is wrong." His voice was barely audible, its low notes lost in the tumult of her hair. "I'm going to hurt you, and then I would really never forgive myself. The women I take are never innocent. Not before or after."

She swallowed a cry of protest as his grip on her slackened. She wanted to comfort him but could not find the words as she grappled with her own confusion. "Why is it wrong, my lord? I'm not that innocent."

He raised himself away from her as if she were made of glass. Blood pounded in his temples as he regained control. "It's wrong because I am offering you as a prize to another man in only a few days, and a prize that is not worth protecting will not be valued by another. I have no right to touch you."

"I don't want to be a prize," she said in a mutinous whisper.

The appeal in her sea-mist eyes touched a chord deep in Duncan's heart. "But you are. You have inherited all your father's courage and compassion, and the man who wins you will be worthy. It isn't right that I defile what will belong to another."

"But I belong to myself." She frowned. "I always have.

Shouldn't it be up to me to decide whether you defile me or not?"

"I'll be gone in two months, Marsali. Back to the business of fighting real wars and setting up my Border estate. Save your virtue for the man who will stay with you."

She sat up, her frown deepening. "And you won't miss the clan at all? You've not come to care for us even a little?"

"Nobody wanted me to come back. Nobody will care if I leave."

"*I'll* care, my lord," she said passionately. "And the others care too, but they're too busy hating you to realize it."

"I don't think that makes sense, Marsali," he said after a long silence. "All I know is that I cannot stay here. This castle is a prison of dark memories I have no desire to resurrect."

He glanced up at the approaching echo of footsteps from the hall. "Get off the floor, lass. This looks improper."

She refused to move, looking hurt and angry and frustrated at her inability to make him care. When he held out his hand to help her rise, she pretended not to notice. The footsteps stopped outside the door.

"Damn it, Marsali," he said under his breath. Then he shrugged at her stubborn inertia, smoothed back his hair, and returned to his position beside her on the carpet. When the door opened, his dark face was dispassionate, revealing none of his own emotional turmoil as he righted the lead figures he had knocked over in his deep hunger for the silent, sulking girl who sat opposite him.

Edwina entered the room. If she was nonplussed by the sight of the merciless Marquess of Minorca engaged in mock warfare with the strange Highland girl on the carpet, if she sensed the tension that smoldered like the smoke of a hastily extinguished bonfire, she was too well bred and sensitive to comment on it.

"I thought you wanted to work alone, Duncan," she said in a tart voice. "The seamstresses are waiting for you, Marsali."

"We're busy reenacting the Battle of Brusage," Duncan murmured, lining up his toy horsemen to launch a charge against the main body of Marsali's troops. "Close ranks. Move forward. Sabers drawn."

Marsali looked up, indignant. "Just a minute. You're knocking over all my dolls."

"Doesn't matter." Duncan chuckled dryly. "Your men are either dead or captured. What do you think you're doing?"

"I'm bringing the dolls in the trench back to life."

"You can't do that," Duncan exclaimed, swinging his long legs over the carpet. "She can't do that, can she, Edwina?"

Edwina leaned back against the desk, her mouth thin with disapproval. "Not in a gold tulle gown. Marsali, get off that floor this instant and leave his lordship to his battle."

Marsali turned her gaze imploringly on Edwina. "But he's cheating. Help me, Edwina. He's cheating horribly."

Duncan was maneuvering his troops with demoniacal glee, sweeping forward to outflank Marsali's dwindling reserve of men, snapping them up like sweetmeats. "I'm not cheating. I don't need to. War is war, Marsali." He leveled a meaningful look on her. "Take a lesson, lass. You should have known not to let down your guard with the enemy breathing down your neck."

"I never realized you were the enemy," she said softly, unable to add more with Edwina listening closely to every word of the private exchange. "I suppose I'll be more careful in future."

"Well, it's too late for this battle," Duncan retorted. "It's turning into a rout. You've had it. I told you I was going to win."

Edwina pushed away from the desk, her sense of fairness provoked by Duncan's unaccountable display of aggression. "Bring out those men from behind the hill, Marsali," she instructed her, her expression intent; Edwina was the unmarried daughter of an army general herself and had played more than one mock battle with her father.

"Leave her alone," Duncan snapped.

"What men?" Marsali asked in puzzlement.

"The men under your skirts," Edwina said. "No, don't move them *that* way. Enemy encampment."

"Go away, Edwina," Duncan said with a scowl. "You weren't invited to play."

"I'm inviting her," Marsali said, motioning Edwina to her side. "She'll be my—what did you call it?—yes, my aide-de-camp."

"Look, Marsali," Edwina said, studying the floor, "you've got him outnumbered now. I think it's time to take out your guns. Advance your rear."

Duncan frowned across the carpet in fierce concentration. There was far more at stake than winning a game with Marsali than he cared to acknowledge, and being forced to play elbow to knee with her put him at an extreme disadvantage. Every time she stretched across the carpet he forgot the battle and remembered the exquisite pleasure of her soft body beneath his. Every time she worried her bottom lip with her teeth, he tortured himself with unspeakable fantasies about her soft red mouth. The poor bastard who married her had better be warned that his future wife was far more than the delicate creature she appeared to be.

For her part Marsali fought the remainder of the battle with a deadly resolve that took both Edwina and Duncan by surprise. The rudiments of warfare seemed relatively simple compared to the chieftain's behavior. She pressed her belly to the floor, suppressing a shiver. The need in his eyes, the naked sexuality had aroused the wildest feelings within her. For a few wonderful moments she would have done anything he asked.

All in all, it was a very unsettling situation, which Marsali could control less and less. Clearly the chieftain desired her, and he resented her for the fact. She concealed a grin as she observed him from the edge of her eye. He was really going to lose his temper when she refused to marry the man he chose for her after all the fuss with suitors and seamstresses.

They battled fiercely for another hour. Edwina stood on the sidelines, offering snippets of advice, but Marsali waged her own brilliant war campaign. In the end, Duncan swallowed his pride and quietly requested a cease-fire.

Marsali nodded in dignified agreement and rose stiffly to her feet, her bedraggled headdress leaning precariously over her left ear. "Well, my lord," she said with a pleased sigh, "I enjoyed myself. We'll have to play that game again some time. I've a feeling I might improve with practice."

Duncan couldn't bring himself to even pretend he was a gracious loser. He had underestimated both her intelligence and the depth of his affection for her. He got up and strode to his desk, plucking away the fishing bucket she had propped against the chair.

"I would like both of you to leave me alone now," he said in a restrained voice.

Marsali edged around his desk, watching him in concern. "It was only a game, my lord. Better luck next time."

Edwina waited for her at the door. "I don't think he's ever been beaten at soldiers before," she said in an undertone as she ushered Marsali outside.

He hadn't.

Duncan stared down at the disorder of his defeated troops on the carpet, shaking his head in bemusement. The girl had changed history. And she had won the only battle that haunted Duncan—the only battle he had come close to losing.

Cold terror washed over him. His instincts had proved true. Marsali had found the chink in his armor that so many of his enemies had sought. Her winsome charm was the most unbeatable strategy he had ever encountered.

The irony of his conflict was tearing him in half. He wanted to be the only man ever to touch her. At the same time he wanted to protect her from himself.

Because she was Andrew's daughter, he could not have her. And yet it was the qualities that she'd inherited from her father that had attracted Duncan from the start. He craved not only her sweet little body, but her warmth, her honesty, her wild passion for embracing life.

Friday could not come soon enough.

Friday had come too soon, and there was no reprieve from the chieftain's heartless plan in sight. Marsali walked swiftly through the soft white sand toward the familiar figure gathering shells along the shoreline. The ball was four short hours away, and she had escaped the castle in a panic.

Duncan had been shouting at her from the battlements.

Edwina had chased her across the drawbridge with a pair of curling tongs. Johnnie had met her on the moor with a vague promise about the clan coming to her rescue.

"Dinna fret, lass. The clan has the matter under control. Ye're not to worry about a thing tonight."

"You're not going to kill the chieftain, are you?" she asked in horror.

"We considered it, Marsali. We even got so far as to discuss what to do with his body, but then Owen and Lachlan came up with a better idea." Johnnie gave her a reassuring grin. "'Tis all taken care of. The lads won't let ye down."

She'd been too afraid to ask what "better idea" he was blathering about. If her fate depended on the clan's half-baked strategy, she was doomed.

"Uncle Colum!" She ran up behind him, splashing water all over his immaculate blue robe. "I've been trying to find you for weeks."

"Summer is always a hectic time for a wizard, Marsali. Nature's bounty is at her ripest, and I have to prepare for the dark months ahead."

"Your spell didn't work, Uncle Colum," she said bluntly. "Time is running out. If I don't get out of this mess the chieftain is cooking up, then I'll be forced to defy him openly, and no one will ever respect him again."

Colum tapped the cowrieshell against his ear. "Appearances can be deceiving. What has happened to your hair?"

"Lady Edwina tried to tighten the curls and tie them up with ribbons, and don't change the subject. The chieftain didn't go away, and his heart is still as hard as a cairn. Whatever spell you cast on him didn't work."

Colum slid his shell into the leather pouch at his waist, then began to stroll toward his shipwrecked home. "He's treated you well enough from what I hear."

"Oh, aye," she said indignantly, hurrying after him. "He orders me around morning, noon, and night. He tells me what to wear, what I may or may not drink, who I'm to marry. He's even confined me to the castle."

"I can see that, Marsali," the wizard said dryly, climbing over a huge rock that obstructed his way.

Marsali clambered after him, glancing up to see Eun

gliding down from the clifftops toward them. "Why are you being so obtuse about this, Uncle Colum? Why didn't your magic work?"

The wizard balanced his feet between two upthrust rocks and reached down to help Marsali make the climb. "Sometimes a spell needs time to work. It would appear the chieftain is not the total blackguard you believe him to be. Is he not throwing a ball in your honor?"

"It's more like he's throwing me out of the clan." Marsali froze in apprehension as Eun floated down toward her bare head. "He's trying to get rid of me, Uncle Colum. Can you believe he thinks *I'm* a troublemaker?"

"I wonder what could have given him that idea." He hopped down spryly onto the sand, leaving his niece stranded on the high rocks with the hawk perched on her head.

"Your magic never works, Uncle Colum!" she burst out in frustration. "I'm beginning to think you're an old fraud."

He glanced back at her with an enigmatic smile breaking across his face. "You're going to be late for your party, Marsali."

"Help me, Uncle Colum," she whispered. "I need your power to battle him."

He hesitated. Before he could answer, Fiona's frantic voice rose from the porthole of the wrecked ship behind him. Black smoke billowed out around her frightened young face.

"Help me, Dad! I was practicing conjuring flames from my magic stones and something went wrong! My crucible exploded when I added the consecrated wine!"

The wizard raised his eyes skyward. "Why me? Did Merlin have his magic constantly interrupted by these petty concerns? Did Solomon? How am I ever to work on immortality when so many mortal problems disturb my concentration? How am I to contemplate the wonders of the universe when I have to squander my energies putting out a FIRE?"

He turned in a swirl of blue robes and sand toward the burning cabin, where Fiona was running up and down the deck, frantically pitching buckets of saltwater into the clouds of dense black smoke.

A wave broke against the rocks where Marsali stood. "Please, Uncle Colum. Please."

He stopped. He gave her a pitiless look over his shoulder. "The power is within you, Marsali. All the magic you will ever need lies untapped inside your own mind. Use your strength of will. Help yourself."

Duncan had followed her, obviously afraid she would disappear and spoil his plans. She put her hand to her heart as she saw the dark rider thundering down the winding road that led to the castle. It wasn't fair. Despite everything, the sight of his powerful figure astride the heavy war horse still sent fierce chills down her spine. She could hardly catch a breath as he neared, his stone-cast face riveting and merciless.

He reined the horse to a halt within an inch of where she stood, a sprite defying a soldier. She looked up steadily into his eyes. Her courage faltered. For a heart-stopping second she shared the same sinking sense of defeat that enemy troops experienced when they saw the famous warrior across the battlefield.

This man would always win. Who was she to challenge his will?

"My God," he said softly. "Look at you. What have you been doing in that dress, lass? Running through a pigsty?"

Temper flashed in her eyes. Her fighting spirit flickered back to life. Her uncle was right. No Hay ever surrendered this easily. Hadn't she always managed to emerge from her trials unscathed?

Except that this time the chieftain was her foe, and her weak human heart was the weapon he used against her with consummate skill.

Duncan shook his head at her woeful appearance: the defiant little face, the half-curled windswept hair, the gold tulle gown sopping at the hem and caked with sand. "I'm trying to be patient, Marsali. Edwina has explained to me that you're very nervous about tonight and that I have been insensitive to your feelings. I want you to know that . . ."

She stared up at his face, not listening to a word he said. It was such a strong beautiful face. Her fingers ached to trace its angular symmetry, feature by feature. She loved his eyes the most, though, the fathomless blue of the loch at midnight. She loved it when a flicker of emotion showed.

"And no matter what—" He broke off abruptly. "Are you listening to me?"

"Aye," she lied, lowering her gaze.

"You're going to have to change before the ball," he said with a sigh. "And put your shoulders back, Marsali."

She slumped like an old crone with the burden of the world on her back.

He leaned across the pommel. "Hold out your—"

Her head snapped up. "It *is* out, my lord," she retorted, giving him an offended look before she stomped past his horse toward the dark brooding castle where her fate would be sealed before the day ended.

In a heartbeat he had wheeled his horse and blocked her way. Like a dark avenging angel, he plucked her up by the waist and settled her across his lap. She struggled, but he held her fast without straining a muscle. Her body fitted alarmingly into the haven of his, curves yielding to the hard contours. The blood in her veins hummed.

"Chin up, lass," he whispered in mock sympathy as he touched his heel to the horse's flank. "It will all be over by midnight."

Duncan rode back to the castle in bittersweet silence. This was the last time, thank God, he would hold the wee troublemaker in his arms. He inhaled the nostalgic perfume of sea air and heather that wafted from her hair. He savored the arousing warmth of her small body. He remembered the first day she had stood up to him and rendered him bare, as it were, to the world.

He realized grudgingly that she had been breaking down the barriers to expose his unsuspecting heart ever since.

He also realized, as the castle loomed into view, that Marsali's submissiveness made him suspicious. It was almost too much to believe that his plans for tonight would not blow up in his face.

"I am the chieftain, Marsali," he said in her ear, "and I'm warning you right now: It's either a husband or a nunnery. If you embarrass me tonight, you'll be embroidering Scripture on a sampler tomorrow."

She vaulted off his lap the moment they reached the barbican. Duncan watched her race across the drawbridge, hoping his apprehension would prove unfounded. Years of instinct in assessing his rivals' strengths and weaknesses warned him it would not.

Or perhaps it was only his own reluctance, his regret at losing her, that preyed on his mind. His body ached with the elusive imprint of her weight where he had held her. If she were anyone but Andrew's daughter, she would have been in his bed for the past month. He would have seduced her, taught her, made her his own.

A disturbingly familiar noise broke his worried reverie. He glanced up to see the drawbridge jerking in a slow grinding ascent. "Here!" he shouted in alarm. "What do you think you're doing? Open that damn drawbridge, Archie, or whoever the hell you are, and open it now! Marsali, if this is your doing, it is not amusing."

Effie appeared on the walkway above him, putting on her spectacles to give him an unsympathetic look. "Is that you, my lord?"

"Yes, it's me, you impertinent woman. Let me in!"

"Sorry, my lord," she bellowed. " 'Tis laundry day, and Cook's just ordered the wash hung up to dry. The castle is closed for the afternoon!"

Duncan almost fell off his horse. *"What?* What do you mean, it's laundry day? It can't be bloody laundry day because we are expecting visitors to the bloody ball! How are they supposed to get in?"

Effie shook her head as if pondering one of life's great mysteries. Then Marsali appeared beside her, staring down at Duncan with a malicious grin. "Is something wrong, my lord?"

"Open the damn drawbridge," he roared, jumping down into the dust, which only sent the chickens into a squawking frenzy.

The commotion lured Johnnie onto the walkway, followed shortly after by Owen, Lachlan, and a bevy of other curious clansmen. They watched Duncan with wary interest as if he were a lion in a coliseum. Finally Cook came onto the scene. The crowd parted respectfully to give her formidable girth room.

"This is all verra disruptive, my lord," she said, huffing for breath. "Here I was wi' my elbows buried in flour for yer ball tonight when I heard ye shouting and swearin', and us expectin' a castle full of guests."

"Guests?" Duncan repeated, his voice rising into another roar. "How the blazes can we admit guests with the drawbridge raised?"

Cook took his display of temper in stride. "And how can we admit guests, my lord, when our laundry is not properly washed and dried? What would these strangers think of us, I ask ye, if we greeted them like savages in our sweaty plaids?"

"She has a point," Lachlan said in support. "'Twould reflect poorly on wee Marsali if we smelled bad, my lord."

Duncan thought he was going to burst a major artery before he won this argument. "And when did this castle of slobs become a castle of snobs?" he demanded. "What am I to tell the visitors who are left standing outside after traveling for days to reach this godforsaken pile of rocks?"

"The castle gate is to open at eight o'clock," Cook answered in a voice that brooked no disagreement. "The visitors can make of that what they like."

Sabotage. Conspiracy. Duncan smelled its rank threat brewing in the air like a whiff of a London sewer. He was beside himself. He was being bested by the biggest bunch of fools in Christendom.

One by one the crowd of Highlanders melted away, until Marsali stood alone on the walkway like a bedraggled princess awaiting a prince who might never come.

She gave him a sly smile. "You might try to enter by the latrines, my lord," she suggested. "That is, if you can stand the smell."

Edwina suddenly appeared behind her. "What smell?"

"Edwina." Duncan released a long sigh of relief. "Thank God. Raise the damn drawbridge, would you? The idiots have locked me out of the castle."

Edwina frowned. She was wearing her nice Chinese dressing robe. Her wig was powdered and curled. "I can't raise the drawbridge, Duncan," she said after a long hesitation.

"Why the hell not?"

"Because I've just done my hair and it's laundry day, and Cook—"

Duncan's face reddened. "You . . ."

"—is pressing my best gown for the ball," Edwina concluded. "Rules are rules, Duncan. You of all people should understand the need to obey established authority. Anyway, I need to do something about Marsali's appearance. She wouldn't attract a ragpicker for a husband looking like that."

Chapter

14

Duncan had dressed to the teeth for the occasion, aware a display of authority was desperately needed to thwart the undercurrents of mutiny in the castle. A breacan and feilidh of blue-green tartan shot with gold swathed his powerful frame. The lower length of the plaid was pleated into a kilt, the upper part fastened to his shoulder with a bone pin. Beneath the coarse wool he wore a long white linen shirt with lace cuffs. Tartan stockings and buckled shoes completed the image of the deceptively proud chieftain.

The chieftain whose own clan would lock him out of his castle.

His clansmen behaved as though the drawbridge incident had never happened. As though he hadn't had to climb up the latrines and take a boiling hot bath with lye soap afterward. They tiptoed around his chair and took their places at the table as if he were an ogre who would eat them. Marsali's fate was foremost on their minds. He was surrounded by more moping faces and mournful sighs than had been at Queen Anne's funeral. Everyone seemed to think the poor wee lass was about to be sacrificed to some cannibalistic Celtic god instead of being offered in holy matrimony to a decent husband.

He glanced to his right at Marsali, a frown darkening his face. She didn't look unlike a sacrifice in her flowing ivory gown of Brussels lace, the dress that was to have been her wedding gown because she had ruined the gold tulle. She looked virginal. Untouched. A fragile rosebud waiting for a man's warmth to burst into bloom. She was achingly sweet for all the trouble she had caused him. She was, in fact, a portrait of submissive femininity, all a husband could possibly desire, and then some.

Until Lachlan leaned across the table and knocked a flagon of burgundy into her lap. Instead of complaining about her ruined dress, she giggled helplessly. Lachlan threw Duncan a terrified look and whipped off his blue bonnet to mop up the mess, dribbling wine all over his own damp but newly washed plaid in the process.

"She'll have to change," Edwina said in dismay, stylish herself in a rose satin gown with an embroidered stomacher. "This is a tragedy. She'll have to wear the yellow brocade, and it washes out her complexion in the candlelight."

Duncan's frown deepened. "Get upstairs and change, Marsali. Lachlan, for God's sake, don't put that dripping bonnet back on your head."

"The first of the suitors for the hand of Marsali Hay is here, my lord!" Johnnie yelled from the door.

A miserable silence met that untimely announcement. Cook almost dropped her platter of truffles on her way to the table. Heads turned in sly anticipation as a strange clunking sound echoed loudly from the hall.

"What the Devil?" Duncan sat forward, his hand sliding to the sword on his hip. A peculiar rotund shadow filled the doorway. Johnnie stepped back just in time to avoid being crushed by the herring barrel with hairy legs that burst into the hall.

Duncan bolted from his chair, his voice like a clap of thunder in the awestruck silence. "What in God's name is the meaning of this?"

The herring barrel sprouted a head and a pair of short bare arms. "I might ask ye the same thing, my lord," it said in sputtering indignation. "If *this* is an example of Mac-Elgin hospitality, to lure a man over mountain and moor only to strip him naked and—and—"

He dropped the barrel to reveal a plump backside plastered in peat and chicken feathers. Marsali covered her eyes with her hand but could not suppress a chuckle of delight. A few guffaws broke out here and there, only to die at the withering look the chieftain cast around the hall.

Duncan's gaze checked off the prime suspects one by one. Marsali, Johnnie, Lachlan, Owen, Donovan. None of the usual offenders were missing. But, by God, someone was going to pay.

"Who are you, sir?" he demanded, redirecting his attention to the indignant herring barrel.

"I am Dougal MacDougall of Glen Beag, my lord, here at yer own invitation and attacked by a band of your own clansmen."

"Is there anyone in this hall you can identify as your assailant, Dougal MacDougall of Glen Beag?"

Dougas hoisted the barrel back over his backside and waddled over to the table. His homely face furious, he examined each and every person present until his gaze stopped at Marsali, softening a little.

"I recognize no one here, my lord," he said stiffly.

"Perhaps a rival clan attacked you," Lachlan suggested.

Donovan gave his harp a discordant twang. "Aye, 'tis those damn MacKelburnes again. Always tryin' to stir up trouble."

Duncan narrowed his eyes, his long fingers tapping an impatient rhythm on the back of his chair. Rival gang, his big toe. He recognized a nasty MacElgin assault when he saw it, yet he couldn't very well admit that the "prize" he was trying to palm off was the leader of the ruffians who'd attacked the man. He glanced down at her in grudging respect. Her eyes glittered back at him with unholy humor.

"My men will scour the moor for the culprits and see they're brought to justice," he said quietly. "Describe your assailants to me."

Douglas looked mollified at the offer. Bumping his barrel against the table, he tried to reach the glass of wine Lachlan was holding out to him. "It was a woman, a skinny woman with spectacles, and her piglets."

From the corner of his eye Duncan watched Marsali cover

a grin behind her own goblet. "A woman . . . and her *pigs* did this to you?"

Dougal raised his quivering chin. "She wasna alone. There was a band of 'em." He clutched his barrel higher in a self-defensive stance. "I was overcome, outnumbered—"

"By a band of piglets?" Marsali asked, lowering her goblet.

Lachlan pursed his lips. "Perhaps he meant a band of women. They're meaner than pigs."

"He said there was only one woman," Owen said.

Marsali nodded. "Aye, in spectacles."

"Perhaps we misunderstood," Donovan said from the corner of the hall. "Perhaps he was attacked by a band of piglets wearing spectacles."

Marsali frowned. "Do pigs wear spectacles nowadays?"

"Aye, lass, they do," Owen said somberly. "Why, when I was in Inverness last year, I saw a dentist riding a horse that had false teeth."

"Incredible," Marsali murmured, shaking her head.

Dougal looked as though he would burst into tears. "'Twas a band of children, my lord! Filthy, evil wee monsters with bows and arrows aimed right at my vital organs. I had no choice but to surrender!"

"Dear God," Duncan said under his breath, putting his hand to the bridge of his nose. "Someone help me."

Marsali laid her small hand on his arm. "You have a headache, my lord?" she asked, all maidenly innocence and melting sweetness. "Shall I massage your temples? Brew some chamomile tea . . . sing you a lullaby?"

Duncan lowered his own hand and gave her a look of sheer evil that made her blood run cold. "This is the prize, Sir Dougal MacDougall," he said, gripping Marsali by the elbow and reeling her out of her chair. "Marsali Hay, daughter of the MacElgin tacksman, Andrew Hay, and descendant of King Olaf," he announced bluntly. "Do you still want to make a suit for her or not?"

"How can he resist when you offer me so delicately?" Marsali asked in an acidic whisper.

Dougal waddled up for a closer look, his barrel forcing Marsali back against her chair. While Duncan studied her in brooding appraisal as if from another man's position, he could only imagine the thoughts that must be running rampant through Dougal's mind.

Aye, he could see the nervous excitement on the fool's face, the prospect of winning this fey woman making him forget the humiliation he'd endured to get this far. With a few deft touches, Edwina had transformed her into a glowing angel of temptation. Her unruly auburn hair had been plaited into a glossy coronet that emphasized her piquant features. Roses bloomed in her cheeks. The white lace dress played up her deceptive daintiness, drawing the eye to every exquisite indentation.

"Aye," Dougal said hoarsely, swallowing hard. "I want her. Oh, God. I do."

Johnnie stomped over to the table, stepping between the herring barrel and the chieftain. "As lieutenant-in-arms of Clan MacElgin, I am allowed a vote on the council, and I object to the marriage between Marsali Hay and this man, my lord."

Lachlan lumbered to his big feet. "Aye, that goes for me too, my lord."

"And me," Marsali said heartily, rising from her chair.

Duncan gritted his teeth. By ancient law his council members could challenge whatever decisions he made, but who would have dreamed the morons could quote such a law, let alone possess the wherewithal to use it against him?

"Sit down, Marsali. Lachlan, you too. Dougal, you're dropping your barrel." Duncan's face remained as unreadable as stone as he stared down the table at Johnnie. "On what grounds do you object to this betrothal?"

Johnnie frowned. "Well, my lord, I recall your mentioning that Marsali needed a protector, and it seems to me that a man who canna defend himself against Ef—I mean, against a lone female, two pigs, and a few bairns is no goin' to be much of a protector. If ye take my point."

Unfortunately, Duncan did. He could no more hand Marsali over to this bumbling barrel than to a stranger. He inclined his head in a stiff nod of reluctant assent. "See that Dougal MacDougall of Glen Beag is given a good meal and decent clothes before he leaves the castle. *With an escort.*"

Amid thunderous applause, Dougal MacDougall of Glen Beag was rolled out of the hall. Duncan sank back down into his chair and sighed.

While he was reaching for his wine goblet, Effie sneaked in from a side door and crept to the table, darting him a sheepish smile.

Lachlan thwacked her on the back with his soggy bonnet, then winked at Marsali. "One down, lass. Only four to go."

Chapter

15

Sir Peadair Forbes, Laird of Inverdruich!" Johnnie announced from the doorway with a fleeting grin that did not escape the chieftain's notice.

Duncan rose uneasily from his chair to face the bedraggled young man who was helped to the table by a gray-haired attendant in a leather tunic and tartan trews. The young man appeared unable to even stand without assistance. He was in a very bad way. Shiny green-black strands of what looked like kelp hung from his kilt like beads. Wet sand dripped from his nose. When he saw Duncan's impressive figure before him, he whimpered fearfully and buried his face in his old attendant's shoulder.

"What is wrong with this man?" Duncan asked, afraid he already knew the answer.

The attendant shook his grizzled head. "I canna say for certain, my lord. He was so eager to get here to meet his future bride that he left our ship before I did. What happened to him between the ship and yer castle is a mystery."

"Then your ship was wrecked?" Duncan said hopefully, relieved that at least one calamity could not be blamed on his clan. Pray God let a shipwreck be the reason the man was whimpering and had seaweed hanging from his kilt.

The attendant shook his head again. "No-o-o. The ship wasna wrecked, my lord. We had fine sailin' weather all the way."

A sense of impending doom hovered over Duncan's relief like a cumulus cloud. "What exactly happened to him then?" he asked in a reluctant voice.

"Weel, my lord." The attendant carefully lowered the young man into a chair and walked around the table, motioning Duncan to incline his head. "It is a verra bizarre thing, my lord," he whispered in the chieftain's ear.

"How bizarre?" Duncan said, staring directly down at Marsali with a flame of accusation igniting in his eyes.

"I canna explain it, my lord. One moment he was a braw clever fellow eager to wed and bed this lovely wee girl, the next he was crawling about the beach swearin' that an old man in a blue dress had changed him into a lobster."

Duncan straightened abruptly. "A lobster. A *lobster?*"

"A lobster?" Marsali piped up in a hurt voice. "Well, damn my uncle's old hide. If he could do that to a stranger, why didn't he do it to the chieftain when I asked him?"

"Does he still think he's a lobster?" Duncan asked with a weary sigh.

"I dinna think so, my lord," the old man replied. "I dinna think Sir Peadair kens what he is anymore."

Johnnie came up to the table, his kilt swaying. "As lieutenant-in-arms of Clan MacElgin, I object to a marriage between—"

Duncan waved his hand in Johnnie's face to cut short the formality. "On what grounds?"

"Why, on the grounds that this suitor believes he's a lobster, my lord. It seems obvious enough. I dinna see the need to elaborate."

"He doesn't believe he's a lobster anymore," Duncan said in an undertone.

Marsali shook her head in concern. "But what if the urge to be a lobster comes upon him again, my lord?"

"She does have a point, Duncan," Edwina said, her face solemn beneath her wig. "Imagine the complications. As liberal-minded as I am, I do draw limits at marrying a man with claws."

Lachlan stood up. "I'm going to have to object too, my lord. The lass canna be married to a lobster. Where would they live?"

"Aye, and what would they eat?"

"What would their children look like?"

A resounding shout of agreement went up around the table.

And suitor number two was swiftly ousted from the hall.

Duncan gazed steadily at the disheveled man in a torn plaid who stood trembling before him. Twigs and leaves clung to the man's scabby elbows and knees. His pale frightened face sported a few fresh scratches. His head jerked at the slightest noise. His fingers twitched convulsively.

"Was it pigs?" Duncan asked tiredly.

The man blinked in bewilderment. "Pigs, my lord?"

"Were you a lobster?"

The man edged away from the table, clearly suspecting the chieftain was a lunatic who had lured him to the castle for evil purposes. "I—I d-dinna ken what ye're talkin' about."

"You were attacked, weren't you?"

"A-aye," the man said cautiously, taking a nervous step back. "I didna come to pay court lookin' like *this.*"

"Who—*what*—attacked you?" Duncan asked, ignoring the titters of amusement that had broken out around the table.

"'Twas a hawk, my lord. A big vicious creature with yellow eyes like a demon."

Duncan's gaze swept the length of the table and came to rest on the smallest figure, her head bent demurely downward.

"Don't look at me, my lord," she said without glancing up. "I haven't left your sight for hours, and besides, that bird has never obeyed me in his life."

Johnnie stepped up to the table. "As lieutenant-in-arms—"

Duncan dropped his head back on his chair and closed his eyes. "Get him out of here."

But suitor number three was already running for his life down the hall before the clansmen could rouse themselves, convinced he had escaped a fate worse than death.

Fiona took care of suitor number four. He never even reached the hall. It was the first time she had ever made a man-thing wilt in person. She leaned up against the castle wall, shaking with victory and a heady sense of power.

Actually, now that she thought about it, she wasn't sure whether the spell itself had worked (how did one ask for proof?) or whether the threat of it had sent the timid-faced wool merchant scurrying for his horse.

She only wished she could figure out exactly how she'd done it. Was it the Celtic incantation? The way she had waved her wand? If she knew, then she could counteract her papa's magic. Fiona was desperate to use her power to save her wee cousin from that black demon Duncan MacElgin's clutches.

Suitor number five was built like a burly old bear, muscles bulging from his muscles and shaggy brown hair covering every inch of him that wasn't wrapped in a pungent plaid. His black lustful eyes burned like coals above a bushy red-brown beard as dense as a forest. His whole smelly being exuded primordial instincts and animal motivation. He pounded across the stone floor, his primitive jaw outthrust with purpose.

He didn't bother to acknowledge the chieftain. This was a man who barreled his way through life using sheer bulk alone. He courted like a caveman.

Sweeping past the chieftain's chair, he proceeded to the other side of the table and plucked a speechless Effie from her seat. Holding her under the armpits so her feet dangled between his huge thighs, he shouted, "So this is the wee lassie up fer the takin'? Och, she's a scrawny bit o' nothing, ain't she? 'Tis a damn good thing ye're offerin' a big dowry wi' the scarecrow. I'll spend it all on fodder to fatten up the bag o' bones."

Then he yanked her against his chest in a bone-crushing hug. In the silence you could hear the vertebrae of her back popping one by one, and it was such an awful sound that even Duncan, accustomed to the casualties and broken limbs of battle, winced in sympathy.

The bear had plunked her down and was grinning broadly. Effie got a really angry look on her face and slowly pulled off her spectacles, handing them across the table to Marsali. The clansmen around her scrambled for safety, and just in time. Effie's fist flew up like a sledgehammer and hit the grinning Highlander right in the nose.

And knocked him out cold.

He toppled like a lightning-blasted oak. And that, of course, was the end of suitor number five.

Chapter

16

Well, so much for your ball, Fairy Godmother," Duncan said glumly, his voice barely carrying above the cheerful noise of celebration in the hall.

Edwina ducked as a dart went sailing over her head and thunked into Donovan's harp. "And so much for your matchmaking skills. Where did you find that pathetic group of men anyway, Duncan? The local gaol or lunatic asylum? It was an insult to the girl."

Duncan couldn't dredge up the energy to answer, dropping his head back against his chair. He felt like a kitchen rag must feel at the end of the day. Perhaps it was the claret he had downed to counteract the sour taste of defeat in his throat. He had underestimated the devious cunning his clansmen were capable of to prove their love and loyalty for their little princess.

Little witch, he thought, looking up from the table.

His burning gaze followed her energetic movements around the hall. It was almost midnight, and those clansmen not playing darts were dancing a celebratory reel, flaunting their victory over the chieftain's evil scheme. Marsali had pulled her plaits loose, and her flowing auburn hair shone like wine in the candlelight. She danced with joyful grace, the flush of victory replacing the rouge Edwina had dabbed earlier on her cheeks. Where did he go now to find a man worthy of her innocent mischief? Where in God's name was he to find a man with the strength and courage to take on not only her but his diabolical clan? It had been hard enough to come up with five suitable suitors.

His mind foundered for a strategy for the first time in years. He hated to admit it, but the clan's outrageous conduct had been justified. Not one of those five men had been worthy of even kissing her dainty foot.

He sank down lower into his chair, only to bolt upright as a teasing voice caressed his cheek. "Will you not dance with me, my lord?"

Marsali. He stared up suspiciously into her face. Let her laugh tonight. She'd pay the piper tomorrow.

"Are you angry with me?" she said.

His smile was droll. "No, Marsali. I can't imagine why you'd even ask. I enjoyed watching you make me look like a madman and mocking manhood in general."

"I had nothing to do with any of this," she said earnestly. She pulled him to his feet, a sunbeam that refused to be dominated by a shadow. "You need to relax, my lord."

"What am I going to do with you now?" he wondered out loud.

She smiled as if she were reassuring a child. "At least you tried, and no one can blame you because your plan didn't work. It's over now. That's all that matters."

Effie and Lachlan danced past them, knocking into Marsali on their way. Duncan caught her before he could stop himself, desire slamming like a fist into his chest at the tempting friction of her body against his. Without thinking, he moved his hands down her back before he forced himself to set her away. Defeat had lowered his defenses. He stared down in fascination at the alluring curve of her collarbone, at the finely wrought lace that flirted with the cleft of her breasts. His mouth went dry.

Marsali shook her head, misinterpreting the brooding darkness on his face. "Don't worry," she whispered, squeezing his arm. "Everyone will have forgotten about this in a few days. Our lives will soon return to normal. No one will make fun of you for very long."

He frowned down at the fine-boned fingers curled around

his massive forearm, imagining how it would feel to experience that soft touch on other parts of his traitorous male body. He set his jaw and willed the taunting image away. "Return to normal? Meaning it's back to the ambushes and arrests?" He gave her a cynical smile. "Do you think I'll give up this easily, lass?"

"I think you take life far too seriously," she said. She glanced out longingly at the dancers. "Can we not discuss this at a later time? Everyone else is having fun. It seems a shame to waste all the hard work put into the ball."

"Marsali." His voice somber, he tipped her flushed face up to his with his knuckle. "I'm running out of time. I've less than two months left to see you happy and the clan settled."

"You can't leave," she whispered. "We need you."

"Even if I didn't covet that Border dukedom with my entire being, I would still not stay here."

"But the clan is growing fond of you, in its own funny way."

"Are *you* fond of me?" he asked quietly, the question an exercise in self-torture that only made the ache of desiring her all the more acute. He couldn't live with the fact that he wanted the daughter of the man who had befriended him when he was an outcast, the man who had forgiven the darkest secrets of Duncan's soul. But he wanted her all the same. *He* wanted to be the man to initiate her into the pleasures of love play, to cradle her supple body in the aftermath.

"Of course I am," she replied in such a straightforward way that he couldn't help but smile. "Why the hell do you think I've gone along with this silly scheme to marry me off? It was only to please you, and all I can say is, thank God it ended so well."

"It hasn't ended yet, you little hoyden. You need a husband."

She grinned, sweeping up her wine-stained lace skirts in a flirtatious circle around her legs. "I'm dying to dance. Come on, my lord."

An unfamiliar emotion squeezed his heart. "I'm not much of a dancer. I . . ."

A sudden surge of energy resonated through the hall. The

raucous din of pipes, fiddles, and harps crashed to a discordant silence. Dancers froze in midair. Conversation hushed. The moment of sweet reconciliation between Duncan and Marsali dissipated as everyone strained to trace the source of the disturbance.

In the silence the determined tromping of at least a dozen intruders over the drawbridge vibrated in the summer night. His reaction instinctive, Duncan shoved Marsali toward the safety of the side passageway. She darted right back to his side.

"Get out of here." His hand was already at his sword. "Johnnie, why did the bloody watch not warn us we had visitors?"

Johnnie pushed Suisan, Cook's daughter, off his lap. Unoffended, she scrambled about on the floor to retrieve the broadsword and dirk he had discarded earlier. "The watch is dead drunk, my lord," he said. "They took to celebratin' the minute the last suitor left. Besides, the chickens didna squawk in warning."

"It must be the Sassenach soldiers from the fort," said a deep-voiced woman behind Duncan, and he glanced around in disbelief to see Cook sweep into the hall from the side door, wielding a meat cleaver and rolling pin. Her kitchen battalion followed, stout-hearted young scullery maids armed with the domestic artillery of soup ladles, skillets, and toasting irons.

"If it's British soldiers we have nothing to worry about," Duncan said brusquely. "They know who I am. They've probably only come to offer me their services as a professional courtesy, and we will *not* attack them." His gaze swung back to Marsali. "But if one of those suitors you reduced to quivering cowardice had an armed escort riding behind him, then we *are* in trouble."

It had been so long since Castle MacElgin had faced an invasion of anything more threatening than mice that the men had forgotten how to react. Valuable seconds were squandered as they argued over whether to hide behind the flowerpots or under the table, to flee to the dungeon or up the stairs. The clamor of men in the courtyard decided the matter: There wasn't time to run or hide.

Duncan cringed at their frantic efforts to arm themselves, plucking knives out of the fireplace, snatching pewter platters from the table to use as shields, darts from Donovan's harp. Cook and her kitchen helpers, positioned strategically around the hall, were obviously better prepared, and sober. Edwina had confiscated an ancient spear from the wall.

Duncan grabbed Marsali just as she pulled out her own pistol and propelled her back into Johnnie's arms. "Take her to the woods."

Marsali's eyes widened indignantly that she was to be excluded from all the excitement. "But I'm one of Cook's—"

"Protect her and Lady Edwina," Duncan told Johnnie curtly. "And make them put those weapons away."

Johnnie nodded, surprising Marsali with his wiry strength as he dragged her by the arm toward the side passageway. "I don't want to go!" she protested, knocking into Edwina in her struggles. "I want to stay and help the chieftain."

"The chieftain can take care of himself," Johnnie said impatiently, scowling as Edwina accidentally jabbed him in the side with her spear. "And I dinna want to go either, but it's that or . . ."

His voice died in the sudden hush that fell over the hall. The flagstones of the outer passageway rang with the approach of booted feet. A lot of feet. Marsali took advantage of Johnnie's distracted inattendance to break free and creep back to Duncan's side.

He flung out his arm and thrust her into the table, blocking her body like a shield as the footsteps stopped outside the door.

Chapter

17

He stared across the hall with his hand resting on his scabbard. The rigid set of his rugged features did not reveal that he was prepared to kill the first man to make a move toward the girl who stubbornly refused to leave his side. The girl who was probably going to cause a mass slaughter before the sun rose again over this stupid castle.

The heavy iron-studded doors burst open with such force that nearly all the candles on the table guttered and expired in dancing wisps of smoke. By a trick of light upon shadow, the remaining flames highlighted the tall brawny figure who posed with swaggering pride in the doorway. Young, roguishly handsome, with streaming blond locks and a red-gold plaid secured with a gaudy gold-lion broach, he swept a long assessing look around the hall.

And stopped dead on Marsali, breaking into a boyish whoop of delight.

Duncan heard her gasp in recognition. Then she started forward until he caught a handful of her lace skirts and yanked her back to his side. She threw him an irate frown over her shoulder, her lips pursing in a pout.

Somewhere in the castle a clock chimed midnight. The arrogant intruder snapped his fingers, and two fawning attendants bustled around him, brushing off his plaid, giving his flowing golden mane a few flicks of a bejeweled comb. The young man stepped through the doorway and paused, allowing his audience to absorb the full impact of his arrival. Moments later a dozen retainers swelled into the hall like a cloud bearing an Olympian deity, six on either side of his golden magnificence, kilts swaying above big knobby knees.

"What an entrance," Edwina said in admiration. "What timing."

"What a fool," Duncan said with a cynical scowl. "Who the hell is the clown?"

No one answered him.

No one, in fact, seemed to remember he existed.

Marsali was practically champing at the bit to fling her exuberant self at the charismatic arrival. His clansmen were gleefully fighting for the honor of being the first to greet the bold Highlander who stomped like a social conqueror into the hall, drained the glass of wine Effie handed him, threw out his musclebound arms, and shouted at the top of his voice with a lustful smirk.

"Someone give Jamie a candle and let him look at the lassie in the light! The wee brat had better be worth his journey here, or there'll be hell to pay!"

"Jamie!"

"Jamie MacFay, ye big stupid lout! Ye're looking bigger and more stupid than ever!"

"If we'd kenned ye were invited, we'd have met ye on the moor!"

"Aye, and left me wanderin' about bare-arsed in front of the woman I'm to wed," the popular blond newcomer joked back with a good-humored grin.

"Ye've lost touch, Jamie," one of the kitchen maids shouted from the post she'd abandoned. "Nowadays 'tis Marsali who leads the men on the moor."

"Aye?" Jamie said, staring with renewed interest at the dainty figure in lace who stood impatiently beside Duncan. "Well, that's another point in her favor."

Banging his goblet down on the table, he began to advance on Marsali like a lion who'd spotted its mate and would not be deterred. Duncan straightened, his hand tightening unconsciously on Marsali's skirt.

"A friend of yours?" he asked in a wry undertone.

"We've met several times, the last when I was eleven," she whispered, watching Jamie closely. "He and his father visited the castle while you were away at war. Jamie is heir to a chieftainship in his own right just like you were, my lord."

Jamie was prevented from reaching them by the numerous clansmen who darted forward to clap him on the back, by the women who flirted and begged him to dance, by his own retainers who intercepted him to polish one of the brass studs on his pigskin boots, to clear an overturned chair from his path.

"He looks too young to be heir to anything but his first pony," Duncan said in a disgruntled voice. "Where are his father's land holdings?"

"In Dunlaig," Marsali murmured, reaching up her hand unconsciously to smooth her tangled hair as Jamie approached her.

Duncan raised his eyebrow at the feminine gesture. Was she actually *preening* for the young peacock? He looked up slowly, squaring his shoulders, pleased to find that he stood at least three inches taller than the man who came to a swaggering halt before him.

"Jamie MacFay," he said in a neutral greeting that gave no hint to the irrational resentment simmering beneath its deep tones. "You're a long way from home, lad. Did you get lost?"

Jamie tore his gaze from Marsali and glanced up at Duncan as if noticing him for the first time. His cocksure grin slipped a notch at the gleam of hostility in the chieftain's cold blue eyes. He puffed out his chest and challenged Duncan's stern expression of established authority with a grin of reckless youth.

"Did Jamie get lost, he asks?" Jamie snorted, looking at Duncan as if he were a hermit who'd just stumbled into civilization after a fifty-year hibernation. "Was a MacFay born who couldna find his bearings in his sleep?"

Duncan granted him a cool smile. "But I don't recall sending you an invitation."

"An invitation?" Jamie clasped his hands to his heart in wounded disbelief. "And since when does a MacFay need an invitation to Castle MacElgin? Besides, I'm here on business."

"Business?"

"Aye." Jamie's gaze strayed back to Marsali's small expectant face. "I've come to claim my bride. We'll discuss the financial details later—after I do a bit of wooin'."

Jamie didn't bother to await the chieftain's response to his brash announcement. His self-confidence would not have accepted a rejection in any case. Before either Duncan or Marsali could react, he had grabbed her hand and ordered the entire hall to celebrate their betrothal.

Gay music erupted to accompany the wild cheers that followed a brief stunned silence. MacFay's retainers partnered themselves with the warm and willing MacElgin kitchen maids under the watchful eye of Cook. Duncan's lids narrowed as he watched Jamie whirl Marsali about the hall, all white lace and bewitching laughter at Jamie's primitive display of male possession.

"Well," Edwina said in a flat voice behind Duncan, "it looks like you've gotten your way after all. She likes him. He likes her. Why aren't you grinning and clapping in relief with the others?"

Duncan lowered himself into his chair, not bothering to reply. His dark gaze did not leave the dancers until he noticed Johnnie return to the table for his drinking horn. He snagged the lieutenant's arm.

"Why do you like him so much?"

"Who, Jamie, my lord? Why, he's a braw fine young fellow, son of the MacFay—"

"I know that."

"And he's a staunch Jacobite." Cook came to stand behind Duncan's chair like the queen mother. "Ye'd not catch any British soldiers carving up fields for roads in the MacFay holdings. The MacFays would fight to the death to protect their land."

"Jacobites," Duncan said. "And you approve of him too, Agnes?"

"I didna say that, my lord. He's a hothead, a malcontent."

Duncan glanced up at her in surprise. Even if the old battle-ax disliked him, she obviously harbored protective instincts for Marsali.

He turned his troubled gaze back to the dancers, sitting forward with a jolt of alarm.

The golden-haired man and the girl in white had vanished from his sight. Jamie MacFay had committed an act of sexual aggression right under his nose. It was insult beyond what he could bear.

He stood, his face like stone. "They've gone," he said in disbelief to no one in particular. "He's taken her without my permission."

Johnnie took another drink, chuckling wryly. "And how's he to be courtin' her in a room full of people? Leave 'em be alone an hour or two, my lord."

"An hour or two?" Duncan said grimly, pushing his chair back as his self-control threatened to erupt. "Leave them alone so that the arrogant lout can have his honeymoon before I've even agreed to a wedding?"

Edwina gave him a strange look. "They're neither of them children, Duncan. What harm can there be if they've decided to take an innocent walk around the castle or along the beach?"

"What harm could there be?" Duncan repeated. "I could write a damn encyclopedia of personal experience on the subject. Jamie doesn't strike me as the type to restrain his sexual impulses. And Marsali, well, she's like a wild strawberry more than ripe for the picking."

He strode toward the door, angrily sidestepping the pig sauntering in his path. The din of shuffling feet and boisterous conversation faded to a dull humming in his head. In a moment of careless fun, a clansman inadvertently sent a dart whizzing straight at Duncan's shoulder. He deflected it with the heel of his hand. The stinging pain drew blood but did not pierce the black fury that propelled him outside.

He didn't know what he would do when he found them. Never in the frenzy of battle, never when defeat hung over his head like an ax, had he permitted his emotions to rule his actions. Not since the raw days of adolescence had he allowed himself the luxury of acting on animal impulse.

It felt damned good to let go of his control. Aye, he

enjoyed the savage rush of feelings that flooded him like a red tide. It was enough that he had the right to decide Marsali's future, and he'd be damned if some hotheaded oaf with swaggering hips would deflower her under Duncan's nose. Like it or not—and, to his disgust, he was beginning to—he was the chieftain, and no one would lay a finger on Marsali without his permission.

Chapter

18

He found them alone in the castle garden, if you could call it that. Actually it was more like an overgrown witch's forest of herbs, dead flowers, and waist-high weeds. A pair of playful white kittens sprang out at him from behind a wheelbarrow. He scooped them up and set them down in a rusty bucket before closing in on the sound of soft uninhibited conversation. He was ready to murder Jamie with his bare hands.

"You've grown into a rare fine beauty," Jamie was saying in a low seductive voice that set Duncan's teeth on edge because he'd used that same tone himself often enough in the past, and with success.

"Well, I'm not bad," Marsali replied with the frankness that Duncan could only love. "I do wish I had more of a bosom, though. My brother Gavin keeps telling me I'm as flat as an oatcake. The chieftain is always scolding me to hold out my chest too."

Duncan frowned. Now that was a little *too* frank, and untrue. She had a beautiful little body. He adored her perfectly sculptured breasts. Besides, he didn't care for where the subject would inevitably lead; if he'd been in Jamie's place he would have exploited her naiveté to shameless advantage.

Which Jamie did.

"Come sit on my lap, sweeting," Jamie said, his voice coaxing. "I'll have a wee look for myself and prove yer brother a liar."

There was a long suspicious silence.

Duncan's face darkened as he was forced into the untenable position of either exposing his hiding place to interrupt the inevitable next step, or of allowing Marsali to expose herself to Jamie MacFay's sexual curiosity. He pushed aside the blackberry brambles to see what the situation warranted. A thorny tendril snapped back and hit him in the face as if to chastise him for interfering. He swallowed a curse and rubbed the droplet of blood that beaded on the end of his nose. This was the most ridiculous reconnaissance mission of his life.

"Oh, look, Jamie!" he heard Marsali exclaim. "They must have gotten out all by themselves. Aren't they the sweetest things you've ever seen? Would you like to hold them?"

Hold them? Would you like to *hold* them? Duncan's heart began to hammer so hard it roared like a tidal wave in his ears. Right then and there he decided he would throw Jamie in the dungeon for a few days to cool his overactive libido. Then he would send Marsali to the convent for some desperately needed moral guidance. The girl was as guileless as a—as a kitten.

"I've never seen a pair so white before," Jamie said with a chuckle. "Aye, and aren't they the softest things in the world?"

"Mind you don't squash them, Jamie. They're not used to being handled."

Duncan could not control himself for another second. To hell with letting true love take its course. To hell with minding his own business. He burst out of the brambles like an enraged bull, his bellow of outrage shattering the tranquil intimacy of the two figures seated on the bench of the rose bower.

"Good heavens!" Marsali cried, lifting her free hand to her throat. In the other she was holding a tiny scrap of wriggly white fluff across her lap. "You scared the life out of me, my lord."

"Aye, and the wee kittens," Jamie observed as the second white ball scampered down his leg and disappeared under the bench.

Duncan blinked. As the black haze receded from his brain, he was shamed by the innocent scene he had defiled with his dark imagination. "I thought . . . I heard . . ."

Marsali rose with an admonishing shake of her head. "I rescued those kittens from my brother's well, my lord. They aren't used to being handled, and thanks to your yelling like an ogre, they probably won't let anyone near them again. You really ought to control that temper."

"Don't raise your voice at me, Marsali. Get back inside."

She put her hands on her hips. "What for?"

"Because . . ." Duncan glanced over at Jamie, who had risen to stand next to Marsali, with his hand resting possessively around her waist. "Just go back into the hall, Marsali," he said again, his face closed to debate.

Jamie gave her a fond pat on the backside. "Run along then. We're going to talk man to man. To decide things."

"To decide what?" she asked, her face suspicious.

"Go away, Marsali," Duncan and Jamie said in unison.

She did, reluctantly. The two kittens dove after the train of white lace hemline that had come unraveled from her skirts. Duncan shook his head disparagingly until she had disappeared behind a wall.

Jamie chuckled and clapped Duncan on the shoulder, affecting a confidential demeanor. "Ye might have waited a little longer before ye interrupted us. Jamie was just warmin' up to a proper MacFay wooing."

"I heard." Duncan did not return the smile; he was thinking of Jamie's hand on her derrière and of his around Jamie's neck.

"Unfortunately, you weren't invited here tonight to woo her. In fact, you weren't invited here at all."

"But everybody likes me," Jamie said, smoothing back his flowing blond tresses. "Especially Marsali."

"Marsali is not the person you're going to have to please." Duncan leaned back against the trellis with his arms folded over his chest. "It's me."

Jamie's grin faded at the chieftain's look of cruel enjoyment. "I dinna like the sound of that, my lord."

"I don't give a tinker's damn what you like. I also don't like the fact that you have known her for years and have only now decided to court her. *After* learning she has an ample dowry."

Jamie's eyes flashed in indignation. "I'd have come for her before but her dad would never have had me. Always gave himself airs, he did. Anyway, I'd heard she was to be wed to someone else."

"Her betrothed was killed, along with her father and her brothers, in an uprising two years ago."

"Aye?" Jamie shook his head in sympathy. "Well, four more valiant deaths in the name of the Cause. Marsali has reason to be proud."

"You're missing the point," Duncan said impatiently. "They were unnecessary deaths. Marsali has reason to be sad and furious at the waste of life."

"But what else is a life for, my lord?" Jamie asked in genuine astonishment. "Would you not protect your castle if it were attacked by the Sassenachs?"

"Of course I would, but—" Duncan broke off in frustration. Why waste his breath explaining the fine points of military strategy to this empty-headed carpet knight? James Francis Edward Stewart would never usurp the Hanover king on the British throne. The Jacobite lairds were too scattered and poorly armed for a war with England.

"A man of your experience understands the glory of battle, my lord," Jamie said craftily.

"I understand the glory of peace," Duncan said with a frown.

"Peace?" Jamie scoffed. "They'll be no peace, what with England stuffin' its laws down our throats. One way or another, they're going to kill us. Ye suggest we should die without even a fight?"

"I suggest you should value the lives of your clansmen more."

Jamie looked uncomfortable, clearly not in agreement but afraid to argue with the chieftain. "I want to marry Marsali," he said sullenly, like a child being denied a sweet. "Ye've no reason to refuse me, not when ye're dangling her like a carrot to every man for miles."

Duncan controlled the urge to push his fist through Jamie's pouting face. "Does she want to marry you?"

"Why wouldn't she?" Jamie asked in surprise. "Dozens of women do."

"Oh, I don't know," Duncan said, a snide note creeping into his voice. "Perhaps her standards are higher than those dozens. Why do you want to marry her?"

Jamie hesitated, apparently more used to action than self-analysis. "Because she's Marsali, that's why. Because she isna like the others."

"Out of the mouths of babes," Duncan murmured with an ironic smile. The fool had captured the essence of her unique charm.

"Can I have her?" Jamie demanded bluntly.

Duncan straightened, releasing a breath. "That's to be decided in the hall before the clan."

"Well, everyone likes me," Jamie said with an arrogant grin. "What's to decide then?"

Duncan's smile was not encouraging. "The final decision is mine to make, Jamie. And I haven't decided if *I* like you yet."

As Jamie stomped off in a huff through the weeds, his kilt swaying around his knees, Duncan turned to the garden wall. "You can come out now, Marsali."

There was a silence, then the crackling of dry leaves as she crept out into the open with a sheepish smile. "I wasn't eavesdropping, my lord. I really wasn't."

"Of course not."

"I was trying to find the kittens again. Your bellowing frightened the wee things out of their wits."

Duncan stared down at her. There were leaves and a few feathers from her discarded tiara in her hair. The wine stain had blossomed into a crimson starburst on her gown. The hemline had unraveled another inch. She looked sweet, defenseless, and enchanting. Why wouldn't Jamie want to marry her?

"It looks like midnight came earlier than we expected, Cinderella."

"I'm sorry all your plans for marrying me off came to nothing," she said, scratching her nose.

He noticed that she held Jamie's pigskin leather glove in her hand. "A love token already?" he asked dryly.

"What? Oh, this. Jamie was letting the kittens hide in it. I'll have to give it back. You were spying on us, weren't you? You should be ashamed of yourself, a chieftain."

Ashamed, aye, he was that and more. Ashamed, jealous, confused by the ambivalence of his feelings for her. He lowered his voice. "You like him a lot, don't you?"

"Everyone likes Jamie, my lord."

"Yes, so everyone keeps telling me. But the question is, Does Marsali like Jamie?"

She crushed a leaf with the toe of her dirty pearl-seeded slipper. Her face was cautiously noncommittal. "Do you want me to like him?"

"It doesn't matter whether *I* like him, Marsali."

She lifted her head, looking puzzled. "But you told Jamie . . . It doesn't?"

"No. I'm not the one who's going to marry him. You are."

Her eyes widened. "Am I?"

The two kittens attacked his ankle, little claws drawing blood. "That hasn't been decided. I can't give him an answer until I know whether you like him enough to marry him or not."

She pondered his odd tone. Could the chieftain be jealous of Jamie? The thought brought a teasing smile to her lips. "Well, Jamie is very handsome, isn't he? He does have that long golden hair."

"He's a veritable Rapunzel. I tremble with envy."

He *was* jealous. Marsali couldn't believe it. "He has lots of money."

"Most of which he probably spends on combs and coiffures."

Marsali tried not to laugh. "He's a strong man, for all his vanity. Nothing like you, of course. But did you see the size of his shoulders?"

"God, I could squash him like a cockroach," Duncan said without thinking.

"When he was only a baby, he used to catch the boulders his father rolled down the hillside."

"That explains it. One of them must have rolled on his head."

She sighed deeply, plucking a feather from her headdress and letting it float to the ground. "He's going to be chieftain when his father dies."

"If he lives that long," Duncan said wryly. "At the rate he carries on he might not live past your honeymoon."

"At least he doesn't think he's a lobster," Marsali murmured when it seemed she had run out of other compliments to add to Jamie's character.

Duncan gently shook the kittens off his foot. His voice was gruff. "You seemed to like him well enough when you were sitting alone together on that bench."

Marsali smiled at the memory.

"He kissed me," she confessed softly.

Her mysterious smile was killing Duncan. The smile of a young girl infatuated with the man who wanted to marry her. Duncan wondered what the hell was wrong with him. It was perfectly normal for her to be attracted to Jamie. What was abnormal was *his* reaction, the resentment bordering on irrational rage. Wasn't this what he had wanted?

"From the silly look on your face, you must have liked him kissing you," he snapped before he could stop himself.

"I liked it well enough." She shook her head in confusion. "But something wasn't right."

A strange pain gripped Duncan's heart as he stared down into her face. A voice of logic in his head warned him to stop the conversation before it led to trouble. He told the voice to shut the hell up.

"What wasn't right, Marsali?"

She shrugged, pretending to stare down at the kittens chewing on her slippers. "It wasn't . . . well, it wasn't you."

Duncan stared at her as if he had been turned to granite. "What do you mean?"

"Never mind."

He took her chin in his hand and forced her small face to his. "Don't tell me never mind, lass. What are you saying?"

Her gaze clung to his, her eyes bright and uncertain. "He isn't you, my lord, that's all. When Jamie kissed me, I didn't feel the way you made me feel that night in the cave. I suppose it's just as well. I'd hate to spend my life with a man whose kisses left me that unbalanced."

There was a moment when Duncan should have said

something wise and discouraging to put emotional distance between them. He could have counseled her not to trust too much in her feelings. Marriage, he ought to say, should be built on a more substantial foundation. But the words refused to come. The shock of what she'd said had immobilized his mind. Her confession had sent a spear of longing straight to the center of his heart and ripped it wide open. His gaze drifted over her, touching her eyes, her tempting mouth, her body.

He let the silence lengthen.

"I'm expected to return to my regiment at the end of the summer," he said at last, as much to remind himself of the fact as her. "I would prefer to know you're taken care of before then. But if you're not, I will go anyway."

The hope that had blossomed in her heart wilted like a tender bud under a winter frost. She pulled away from him and leaned back against the rose trellis, its thorny, untended stems framing her face. "Jamie isn't you, my lord," she said with a faint catch in her voice. "But I think he'll do, after all."

Duncan did not move for twenty minutes after she ran out of the garden. If he'd moved a muscle, he would have caught her before she could escape. He would have finished the seduction Jamie had so clumsily initiated. She deserved finesse and infinite gentleness. His body and brain ached with the tension of desiring her and repressing it. In this untidy abandoned garden, she had been in her element. A bedraggled fairy princess who had bewitched and tamed the dragon in him. Her faith in him had challenged the raging beast of self-hatred in Duncan's soul but had not won a surrender. He could not imagine a man of his dark experience being entrusted with a girl like her.

Nor could he imagine entrusting her to anyone else. He suspected he could search the whole of Scotland and come short of a suitor who met his approval. He could have even killed Jamie MacFay and slept that same night with a smile on his face.

He isn't you, my lord.

Dear Christ, help me. How that innocent statement tempted him.

He gazed up at the castle as the raucous strains of off-key singing wafted into the garden sanctuary. Marsali was strong and resilient. She would forget him in a few months and settle down into whatever life he chose for her.

His own life was another matter. Happiness had evidently not been part of the master plan for him. Still, there were plenty of other battlefields to conquer. There were prizes to claim, accolades to add to his name, dozens of women to satisfy the physical. At least now he could forge ahead with the rest of his life, satisfied that he'd repaid the debts of the past to the best of his ability. At least now he would not fall in love with a woman he could not have.

The shadows from the torchlights in their tarnished iron sconces accentuated the harsh resolve on his face. The decision had been made. The determined glitter in Duncan's eyes gave no hint of the anguish that pitted his emotions against his better judgment. To look at the chieftain in all his ruthless hauteur you would never guess that he had a heart, let alone that it was silently breaking inside his massive chest.

Marsali would wed the MacFay.

The MacFay . . .

Duncan halted halfway down the passageway. An odd noise had interrupted the intensity of his thoughts. The husky tones of a man's voice and a woman's soft responsive laughter. Jamie and Marsali. He turned his head and stared down in horror to the shadowed corridor that led toward the turret staircase.

Two figures were entwined on the lower steps. Dear God, the uncouth swine was banging her on the stairs like a lowborn whore. Their soft moans of passion and intimate laughter drove into Duncan's mind like nails. He didn't stop to think. He reacted from a fury spawned by helpless frustration and possessive rage.

He had never experienced such jealousy. Not even as a boy when he had stood half naked and shivering, peering into other people's huts and gazing like a wolf at the warm nourishing food on their tables. Not even when he had watched the affectionate rough-play between the other fishermen and their sons on the beach, and the best he could coax out of Fergus was an angry cuff on the head or a curse.

The emotion ravished his control. It burned like black smoke in his system and curled into his gut until his stomach muscles clenched. It clouded his vision and swathed his ability to reason in a murky haze. Primal impulses drove him toward the stairs.

He had unsheathed his sword before he could stop the reflex. A horrifying thought flashed through his mind: He might not be Fergus's flesh and blood, but he had inherited the bastard's uncontrollable temper. He was going to murder Jamie MacFay. The trauma of it would haunt Marsali for the rest of her life, and Duncan didn't care.

He stood over them, as still and darkly ominous as a raven's wing. His voice fell into the sounds of their lovemaking like an ice floe. He jabbed the tip of his sword into the taut curve of Jamie's bare buttock.

"Pull down your kilt and defend yourself, MacFay. I'm not killing a man in that degrading position."

The prone figure beneath Jamie gasped and struggled to push him off. Jamie jerked his head around in outraged astonishment, his face slack with lust.

"Who the bloody hell—"

He gaped down at the sword tip that was pointing at his chest. His eyes black with anger, he pulled down his kilt and unfolded his burly frame to face Duncan. The woman sprawled out below him covertly straightened her brown fustian skirt and edged upward on her elbows into the concealing gloom of the stairwell. She looked terrified by the killing fury on the chieftain's face.

Duncan's gaze brushed over her trembling form in cold silence. Not Marsali, but the misguided clanswoman who had popped bare-breasted out of a barrel on his first night home. He felt a pang of disgust for her indiscretion, and sadness too, that her lack of self-worth reduced her to servicing a virtual stranger on the stairs. But more than anything he felt a sense of relief so acute his head reeled with it. It wasn't Marsali.

"You shame yourself and the clan," he told her in a voice of restrained admonishment that reduced her to tears. "Get yourself upstairs for the rest of the night." He set his teeth as she scrubbed in speechless gratitude at her tearful cheeks. "And don't tell anyone about this, lass."

She disappeared in a flash, her face averted in humiliation.

Jamie watched her scramble up the stairs, raising his thick blond brows in amusement as he glanced back at Duncan's face. From either sheer stupidity or bravado, he declined to comment on the sword that his host was holding unwaveringly to his chest. "She was followin' me around all night. I felt sorry—"

"Shut up."

Jamie scowled. "Now just a—"

The sword pricked through his plaid into the taut plane of his pectorals. Jamie wisely did as he was told.

Duncan's gaze flickered to the broadsword Jamie had left carelessly lying on the floor. "Only a boy would leave his back vulnerable and his weapon out of reach for a moment's pleasure."

"Since when does a MacFay need to watch his back in a friend's castle?" Jamie said in a belligerent voice.

"Since when does a friend dishonor a MacElgin clanswoman on the floor only moments after he has offered to love and protect another?"

Jamie smoothed back his long golden hair, his mouth turning down at the corners. "There's no harm in a man takin' his pleasure from a willing woman. Ye've done it often enough from what I hear."

"I've killed a few men too in my day, Jamie. Have you heard that?"

"Damn, I was drunk. I dinna even remember that woman's name."

Duncan's fingers squeezed the hilt of his sword, aching with inaction. "You didn't sound drunk when you took Marsali outside."

"I want Marsali Hay," Jamie said slowly, suddenly realizing where the conversation was headed. "Aye, I do. She wants me too."

Duncan ignored the unexpected pain those simple words invoked. "I doubt she'd want you if she'd caught you with your kilt rucked up to your shoulders."

"Hell, it isn't as if we're wed yet," Jamie retorted, his face reddening. "And if we were, it wouldna be the worst sin a man could commit." He glanced down at the sword still aimed at his furiously pounding heart. "Would ye murder Jamie for seekin' a bit of harmless fun in yer own home?"

A muscle contracted in Duncan's jaw. "If you hurt Marsali . . ."

The echo of approaching footsteps interrupted his response. Jamie licked his dry lips in relief as the chieftain resheathed his sword and glanced at the small figure rounding the corner. A flash of white lace, a woman's hesitant whisper.

"Are you lost then, Jamie? I warned you to walk with me, but would you listen? I know you drank an ungodly amount, but you've been over a half-hour in the privy . . ."

Marsali skidded to a halt, her innocent chatter dying into a puzzled silence at the sight of Duncan standing before her. She retreated a step at the brief glance of concern he allowed to flare in his eyes before all emotion faded from his face.

That look . . . She pressed her hand to her chest. That look, so replete with unspoken yearning, had caught her off guard and left her more confused than before. Surely she had misinterpreted it. Surely the naked desire in Duncan's eyes had not been directed at her.

She whipped her head around, amazed to discover Jamie at the bottom of the stairwell, watching her gaze up at the chieftain with her tattered feelings on her face. He frowned at the bright smile she forced to her lips.

"Jamie." Her voice sounded breathless and unnatural; the tension between the two men caught her in its crosscurrents. "So you *were* lost."

"Aye." He lowered his sullen gaze, looking hesitantly at Duncan before he reached down to the steps for his sword.

Marsali stared at him in puzzlement; he looked for all the world like a pouting schoolboy who'd just been scolded by his schoolmaster. And Duncan looked like—her gaze drifted slowly upward—he always looked: like a man. The powerful chieftain who could give her away on a silver platter to a stranger, and yet who could stare at her like a condemned man watching the last sunrise of his life.

"What happened between you?" she asked softly, glancing from one to the other.

Jamie raised his head. His faint smirk challenged Duncan to reveal the truth. And to his disgust, Duncan found he could not tell her. He'd cut off his left arm before subjecting her to that humiliation.

"Nothing happened." His face remote, forbidding further questions, he moved past her. "I gave Jamie a few words of advice on what happens to men who get drunk and wander about in the dark, that's all."

"Oh," she said, suppressing a faint shiver of reaction as their arms brushed by accident.

Her gaze followed Duncan as his tall dark figure disappeared into the tunnel of torchlit darkness. Her heart would have followed him too, but his rebuff of silence to her confession in the garden had barred that door. She had shocked him with what she'd said. Well, she'd shocked herself too; she hadn't realized her own feelings for him until the damning words were out of her mouth.

He isn't you, my lord.

Five simple words that revealed more of her dreams than she'd dared to acknowledge. She must be an utter fool, to yearn for a man who had hardened himself to all human emotion while she, in contrast, lived every second of her life on impulse and instinct, her hopeful heart begging to be broken.

Jamie slipped his arm around her waist. She tensed reflexively. "Arrogant bastard," he muttered, kissing her neck.

"Duncan?" She pushed away from him, her face puzzled. "You don't like the chieftain?"

"Does anyone?"

"You did have words with him, then?"

"Aye, we had words."

Her heart gave a little lurch. "Over me?"

"Not exactly." He plucked a feather from her hair and brushed it across the tip of her nose. "He's going to give ye to Jamie anyway. He knows I'm the one to take care of you. Feel these muscles, Marsali."

"What?" She pulled her head back as he flexed his biceps under her chin. "Don't be silly."

"Feel them." He took her hand and pressed it to the

bulging muscle. "Jamie is strong. Marsali is weak. We're a good match."

She frowned, swatting at his arm. "I don't love you, Jamie MacFay."

"Well, Jamie doesn't love you either, Marsali Hay," he said, unperturbed. "But I've admired ye ever since the day ye broke my brother's thumb wi' a hammer fer tryin' to ride yer pony."

She snorted. "What a memory to build a marriage on."

"There are others." He took her hand and led her back over to the stairs, pulling her down onto his lap. "We swam naked together in the loch when we were bairns. Your da liked Jamie a lot, as I recall."

"He thought you were a quarrelsome wee beast," she said dryly, leaning her head against his. Then: "Jamie, why did you and the chieftain have words?"

He hesitated, his brawny arms tightening around her waist as if he knew she'd flee when he admitted the truth. "Lass, what I'm going to confess will hurt ye deeply, but I'd not have the chieftain tell ye out of spite. He caught me wi' one of yer clanswomen."

"Caught you what?"

"You know."

"Caught you—" She stiffened in his arms as comprehension dawned. "You pig, Jamie MacFay. You incredible, disgusting pig. I wish I had that hammer right now."

She struggled to escape, but he held her fast, grinning in approval at her temper. "The way I see it, I'm winning ye by default, Marsali Hay. There's no other man wi' the stamina to handle ye."

"You're a disgusting beast, Jamie."

"Aye, but all that'll stop the day we take our vows. From what yer friends say, it's either me or a lifetime of spinsterhood in yer brother's cottage. And if I betrayed ye in body, 'tis nothing compared to the way you looked after the chieftain just a few minutes ago."

She wriggled to her feet. When she backed away, her hair fell streaming around her stricken face. "It's that obvious, is it?"

"To me it is." He rose and took her hands in his. "I need yer dowry, Marsali, and I've wanted ye for years. If we live a long life and raise a family, then so be it. But if we die together fighting against the Sassenachs, then that will be all right too. The point is that we're alike, you and I. The chieftain isna one of us, lass. He has no heart."

He sealed the odd betrothal with a gentle kiss. Marsali relented but did not respond. For all Jamie's rugged charm, it was Duncan's dark sardonic face that burned like a flame in her mind. She wished she could forget the look he had given her a few minutes ago, the raw pain of realization that he had failed, just for an instant, to hide.

Jamie nudged her. "Come on. Let's pretend to ask for his permission, and then we're away from here."

"Away?"

He started walking toward the hall. "My father's dying, lass. 'Twould be nice to have a wedding before a funeral, don't you think?"

She didn't answer. She trailed him as if in a trance. She couldn't envision marrying Jamie, or living in bleak Dunlaig on the eastern coast and leaving all she loved behind. She couldn't think of anything past the callousness of Duncan giving her away to a man he had caught rutting like an animal with another woman. She was disgusted at both him and Jamie.

She stopped in midstride. "I want to go to Virginia, Jamie."

"Virginia?" He swung around, almost knocking her against the wall with his elbows.

"It's my dream,"

He stared down at her, nodding slowly. "All right, lass, we'll go." He didn't know where the hell this Virginia was; probably somewhere near London. But he'd take her there because he was smitten enough with her to agree to anything and because she'd probably flatten his head with a hammer if he refused.

He paused outside the door to the great hall. "Do I look all right?"

"What?"

"Is my hair tangled?"

Marsali just stared at him. Aye, he was handsome, with the bold looks of an Apollo. The trouble was that his physical appeal was exceeded only by his vanity, and even when she was younger, she'd often thought that holding a conversation with Jamie was as fulfilling as talking to a tree.

"Your hair is lovely, Jamie," she said, moving past him.

He caught her arm. He gave her a knowing wink. "Wait, lass. Let Jamie go in first. So they won't be disappointed."

She shrugged, stepping away from the door, which Jamie opened with a flourish before striding into the hall. As expected, he stood basking in the adulation of the clansfolk who greeted him. His smile dazzled like the sun. He tossed his flowing locks and threw out his arms to let his minions admire him.

"Jamie is back!" he cried, allowing himself to be borne forward by the small crowd who rushed him. "And he's brought his betrothed!"

Chapter

19

Duncan's mouth curled into a cold feral smile as he watched them enter the hall. His hands gripped the arms of his chair as Jamie hovered possessively over Marsali, touching her shoulder, leading her by the hand as if he already owned her. A loud cheer went up as Jamie caught her hand and half-dragged her to the table. Donovan plucked a heart-stirring lover's lament on his harp.

Edwina sniffed, bringing her scented handkerchief to her eyes. "They're a lovely couple." She gave her nose a resounding blow. "To think I helped bring them together."

"He's a pig," Cook said behind Duncan's chair, and when he glanced up at her, she dropped her voice so only he could hear. "That was my niece on the stairwell."

Their eyes met in mutual accord; for the first time the two adversaries stood on the common ground of dislike for the MacFay. But as Duncan swept a critical gaze around him at the soppy faces of his clansmen gazing fondly at the young couple, it appeared that he and Agnes were in the minority. Even Edwina, the traitor, looked as if she were enjoying every minute of the budding romance.

Jamie MacFay, reckless Jacobite and hotblooded High-lander, had caught the clan's fairy princess in his palm. And they couldn't be happier.

Duncan sucked in his breath as a bolt of jealousy struck him with the physical impact of a kick to his solar plexus. He had been prepared to give Marsali away, but not to a man like this. Jamie sent him a arrogant smile, as if to say, 'Twill soon be me sitting in the chieftain's chair. I'm the one who'll enjoy Marsali's sweet body into the wee small hours. Her belly will swell with my seed. And when I die, men will weep at my grave and extol my bravery, while you remain forgotten . . . and unforgiven.

He passed his hand over his eyes as if to break the dark spell of his imagination. When he looked up again, Jamie and Marsali were standing at his side like a storybook prince and princess, awaiting his word of approval on their union. He detested the way Marsali eluded his eyes, her small hand clasped in Jamie's paw. He couldn't tell what she was thinking.

Despite the late hour, his entire clan had crowded into the hall. In the deep expectant silence, all one could hear were a few wistful sighs and the soft grunting of Effie's piglets as they lapped up spilled wine and leftovers under the table.

Johnnie cleared his throat, grinning in anticipation at Duncan. "We are gathered here tonight, my lord, to ask yer permission for Jamie MacFay to take to wife our own wee Marsali Hay—"

"For as long as we all shall live," Lachlan concluded, hurling his bonnet into the air with gleeful abandon.

Jamie smirked and elbowed Marsali in the side. She elbowed him right back, her gaze fixed fiercely on the floor. The bonnet landed in the remains of the platter of haggis on the table. Duncan felt Cook's beefy fingers squeeze his shoulder in either reassurance or warning. It didn't matter which. His mind was already made up.

He rose slowly from his chair. From the end of the table an overzealous clansman sent another dart whizzing toward his head. Cook deflected it with her rolling pin.

"You cannot ask for her yourself, MacFay?" he asked in an austere voice.

Jamie snickered, throwing out his chest with the confidence of a man aware he has at least a dozen swords to back up his bravado. "Jamie wants Marsali Hay," he said, tossing his head in recognition of the applause breaking out behind him. "He's takin' her too."

"Nobody is taking me," Marsali said, flashing Jamie an annoyed look. "I'm heeding my uncle's advice and relying on myself from now on. I'm going to Virginia."

"*We're* going to Virginia," Jamie corrected her. "We're ridin' there on our honeymoon."

"Really?" Duncan widened his eyes. "Why, I should like to see that, MacFay."

"Just keep your mouth shut, Jamie," Marsali advised him over her shoulder. "He's making you sound like an idiot."

Jamie gestured to one of his retainers, his voice worried. "Is he makin' Jamie sound like an idiot?"

Duncan's mouth stretched into a slow unfriendly grin.

The great doors banged open. "Not again," Duncan said with a frown as Effie breathlessly dragged a man and woman across the hall.

"Wait!" she shouted. "I've brought someone else to witness the betrothal!"

A disheveled-looking young man with dark hair and green eyes limped up to the table. He stopped to study Jamie and Marsali before looking up at the chieftain. A very pregnant woman followed, observing the same silent ritual. Duncan stared at them.

"I suppose I'll have to give my approval," the dark-haired man said with obvious reluctance. "It's time someone took her in hand."

"It's time she settled down with a man and bairns of her own," the pregnant woman added, looking Jamie up and down like a slab of beef. "Aye, he'll do. Big on brawn but short on brains. I'd hoped for better. At least he'll give her a home."

"Excuse me." Duncan leaned over the arm of his chair. "Who the hell might you be?"

"This is my brother Gavin and his wife, Bride," Marsali explained, smothering a yawn. "They have seven children—"

"Eight," Bride said, then patted her stomach. "With another in the oven. And by the way, Jamie, ye canna get to Virginia on a horse. It's across the ocean."

Duncan crooked his forefinger at Marsali to beckon her to

his chair. When she arrived, he put his arm around her shoulder and pulled her close. "Do you really want to marry this colossal idiot, lass?" he asked with deceptive gentleness.

Jamie frowned, overhearing this. Then he gestured to one of his retainers, whispering, "Is he tryin' to insult me?"

"Of course not, Jamie. Why would anyone insult you, lad?"

Jamie accepted this and forced his way into the family gathering. The air of romantic revelry was fading from the hall. The effects of the ale were wearing off. The fish-oil candles that had been relit began to sputter and smoke. Several clansmen had passed out under the table.

He banged his hand against the hilt of his broadsword. "Well, my lord. I've the family blessing. All I need is yours."

Duncan looked down his nose at Jamie. "No." He folded his arms over his chest, his loud voice carrying across the hall with the power of his dominant will. "As laird and chieftain of Clan MacElgin, I deny you the right to marry this woman, who is under my protection." He smiled with evil intent. "And by the way, Jamie, I've decided I don't like you at all."

Jamie's mouth dropped open. He stamped his big foot, and six retainers came running. "Did he just tell Jamie no?"

Everyone thought at first that the chieftain was joking. Uneasy sniggers punctuated the astonished silence. Marsali stared up at him as a strange undercurrent passed between them. What was he doing? His firmly chiseled mouth curved into a hard line of satisfaction. For weeks he had plotted to be rid of her, and now, when he could have easily done so, with a snap of his long elegant fingers, he had pulled her back into his power like one of his toy soldiers.

Suddenly she was furious at him. Not because he refused to let her marry Jamie, which she didn't really intend to do anyway. But because he enjoyed using his supremacy to play God in her life. Aye, he enjoyed making Jamie look like a nincompoop—which wasn't a difficult task, she had to admit—but it seemed that Duncan didn't want her for himself, and he didn't want anyone else to have her either. He just wanted to order her around.

Jamie jostled her into the table, his hands on his hips. "You can't do this." He pushed a plate of peas onto the floor and stomped on them like an irate child throwing a tantrum. "Yer entire clan stands behind me."

"Duncan," Edwina whispered uneasily, touching his elbow, "what has gotten into you?"

Duncan shook off her hand, not bothering to answer.

Johnnie picked a path through the squashed peas to address Duncan. "Jamie MacFay is a good man, my lord. Ye've no cause to refuse his suit." He lowered his voice, looking puzzled. "I thought ye liked him. He's a bit dense, but he's no as bad as the others."

Grunts of assent from the clan underscored Johnnie's opinion. Resentment was still running high toward Duncan for all the discipline he'd inflicted over the summer. By Highland standards his behavior seemed grossly unfair. Worst of all, he was actually making them work.

"Aye, and he hasna even stood the oath on the white stone yet," one clansman grumbled.

"He plays wi' dolls too."

"He's no right to be speakin' fer us all."

"The MacElgins and the MacFays have been friends for centuries."

Duncan's expression did not soften as the seeds of rebellion sprouted like barley shoots after a spring rain. Damn them. He wasn't about to defend an action he didn't wholly understand himself. His denial as chieftain should suffice. It was the first time he'd appreciated the power of his birthright.

Then suddenly Cook was at his side, harrumphing, the rolling pin tapping in agitation against the table. Duncan cringed reflexively. Johnnie retreated a step in self-defense.

"He speaks fer me," Cook said in a voice that dared anyone to defy her. "I'm castin' my vote against the MacFay."

"So am I," Edwina said, eyeing the rolling pin with respect.

Duncan's voice was droll. "I appreciate the support, but you're not a clansman, Edwina. You don't have the right to dissent."

"I'm wi' Cook," Lachlan said loudly, and Duncan didn't have a single doubt that the unspoken threat of starvation and Cook's wrath had swayed his vote.

One by one the clansmen threw in their support to Cook's side. Duncan stood in awe of the stout woman's influence.

"Thank you, Agnes," he murmured.

She nodded stiffly, a queen accepting her due. "Ye'll have a hell of a problem on yer hands now wi' Marsali," she warned him quietly.

Duncan's gaze drifted to the dainty figure in white lace who stood in Jamie's shadow. The two of them were whispering, standing too close together, plotting. His mouth tightened. He hadn't missed the look of pure fury on her face when he had turned Jamie down. Well, he could deal with her anger. At least he wouldn't lie awake tonight tortured by thoughts of MacFay's clumsy hands mauling her.

She glanced up as if sensing his gaze on her. Her eyes flashed like fire against the terse whiteness of her face. Did the damn girl not guess he was trying to spare her pain?

Suddenly Jamie left Marsali's side. His heavy blond eyebrows drawn into a scowl, he stalked up to Duncan and shoved him in the chest. Duncan did not move. He seemed to have not even felt the childish assault.

"Nobody tells Jamie no."

A collective gasp of anticipation went up around the hall. Even the piglets stopped their munching, snouts lifted to the chieftain's chair in trembling expectation.

Duncan smiled. It wasn't a nice smile, although Jamie was a little too dense to quite realize that. Encouraged by the chieftain's apparent passivity, he squared his palm to give Duncan another shove.

No one saw it coming, but to those standing beside the chieftain's chair, it looked like Duncan merely touched the heel of his hand to Jamie's sternum with the amount of energy he might have exerted to swat a fly. And sent him crashing backward down the hall, over chairs, squashed peas, into the arms of his astonished clansmen.

"This isn't the end of it, MacElgin," Jamie shouted from the doorway, his retainers brushing him off. "Ye're no the last court of law in the land! I'll appeal to a higher authority."

"What does he mean?" Edwina asked in an undertone of amusement. "Surely the big lout doesn't hope to take his case to the king?"

Duncan slowly shook his head.

"I'll go to the chief of yer clan," Jamie threatened as he backed away from the table. "Aye, I'll go above yer bloody head to the MacElgin *Mor*. We'll see who holds the power then." His retainers were dragging him away, wisely realizing they were outnumbered and in no position for a fight. But Jamie was livid, his pride insulted.

"Jamie wants ye, Marsali Hay!" he could be heard yelling down the hallway. "Aye, and he's havin' her too, MacElgin, ye bloody bastard!"

Chapter

20

In the subsequent furor over Jamie's dramatic leave-taking, the shouting, the clansmen jostling for a look, the candles extinguishing as the heavy doors were slammed, Duncan lost sight of Marsali.

Panic flared in his eyes at the thought that she might have gone running after Jamie. On instinct he shoved around his chair, stumbling over an indignant piglet. He brushed past a startled Edwina without even noticing her. Then from the corner of his eye he caught a beguiling flash of white lace vanishing through the side passage like a wisp of smoke. Fleeing the scene of her humiliation, but so far, thank God, she hadn't followed that fool MacFay.

He pushed back his chair and ran after her. By the time he reached the passage to the turret stairs, she was gone.

"Marsali!" he called in anxiety, taking the stairs three at a time to catch her.

There was soft scuffling of bare feet against stone. Then suddenly a shadow launched itself at him from the wall. He hurtled down half a dozen steps, regained his balance, and drew his sword. Just as his mind registered the fact that his assailant was a girl, a raven-haired creature with a poignantly familiar grin, she pitched a bucket of cold salty water into his face. "Take that," she said, her eyes flashing, and then she threw a handful of wet petals at his head.

"What the hell are you doing?" he yelled, throwing up his hands in self-defense.

She jumped back in alarm. "I'm protecting my puir wee cousin Marsali. Aye, I ken my magic's not as powerful as my papa's, but this ought to take care of you, my lord chieftain. Here!"

And then she waved a gnarled stick at his—God, there was water still streaming out of his eyes, but he could swear she was waving her wand at his—no, it couldn't be.

"And may it stay wilted until the next full moon," she whispered, squeezing around him to escape.

For a moment Duncan could not move, staring after the wild young witchling as she fled with her bucket clattering against the stairs. Recovering, he ran back up the rest of the stairs and burst out onto the turret walkway.

He had followed the wrong girl. Marsali was already riding her horse across the drawbridge. From the distance she looked like a white dove plunging into the grainy shadows of the northern gloaming. A wounded dove escaping the pain Duncan had caused her when he had only meant to protect.

He couldn't let her go, of course. Not with that bruised look in her eyes haunting him. Not with Jamie prowling the coast with his drunken retainers. Now he really did feel like Cinderella's wicked stepmother for the way he'd treated her. Why had he let Edwina talk him into the ludicrous ball in the first place? If he had interviewed her suitors privately to begin with . . .

He still wouldn't have found a single one worthy of her.

He ran back down the stairs and across the yard to the stables, ignoring Edwina's cries to wait.

He rode like a demon from the castle and found Marsali's horse abandoned on the cliffs above the wizard's ship-wrecked home. As he hurried down the wobbly gangplank, he caught a glimpse of Marsali's white lace gown fluttering like a flag of surrender from the yardarm. Or was it a trophy of triumph, flaunting her independence and anger in his face? Had Jamie left it to enjoy the last laugh?

Chills flashed all over his body. Had she run off with MacFay after all? Was he going to have to start some ridiculous clan feud to get her back? It was enough to make a grown man weep, the very thought of training his inept clansmen for warfare.

He could picture it now. Firing hard-boiled eggs from catapults. Cook leading her scullions on an assault against the MacFay fortress. Effie's piglets bringing up the rear to rescue one tiny girl who'd caused him more trouble than all the French forces combined. No, General MacElgin would not go to his glorious defeat on foreign soil. He would probably be killed by one of his own men while wrestling Marsali from MacFay's arms.

Suddenly he saw her angry elfin face watching him from the porthole, and he almost slipped off the gangplank with relief. If he was a master of military science, he was a mere apprentice in matters of the heart. She hadn't left with Jamie—but what was Duncan supposed to do with her now?

He burst into the cabin, and before he could blink an eye, Eun attacked him. The wizard wasn't there. Neither was the raven-haired girl who had waved her wand at him and kicked him in the shin.

"Help me! Damn it!" he said as Eun's wings beat against his face and needle-sharp talons nicked his neck. It was as gloomy as a cave in the cabin, only a single candle burning. The hawk had the advantage of good eyesight, and Duncan the disadvantage of losing his damn balance by stepping into a bucket, probably the same one whose watery contents that strange girl had hurled at him on the stairs.

"I'm having this bird stuffed and mounted in the hall if you don't call him off me, Marsali!"

From the bunk where she lay hidden under a pile of quilts, Marsali watched the chieftain with her eyes half closed like a cat's. Finally—and then only because she was afraid Eun would hurt himself attacking Duncan—she rose and gently caught the hawk in her hands.

He quieted instantly, then hopped onto her head to observe Duncan, his lids narrowed into slits. As Duncan swore behind her, she soothed the bird and loosely secured him to his driftwood perch, not bothering with his little velvet hood.

"You've been forbidden to leave the castle, Marsali." Duncan glowered at her as she flopped back down on the bunk, totally ignoring him. "My God, look at you, in your underwear and not at all ashamed of it. If you rode along the beach like that I wouldn't blame MacFay for thinking he had a right to abduct you."

She glared straight ahead. "Look at *you,* my lord. Criticizing me with a bucket on your foot. I hate those sort of fussy, scratchy dresses. I don't think I told you that. I hate you too. I didn't tell you *that* either."

He hobbled over to the bunk, trying to discreetly shake the bucket off his foot, and not to gawk like an adolescent at her practically naked body. "Pull the quilt up over yourself, Marsali."

She threw it at him.

"That's very clever, very childish," he said, swatting it away. "You look like a wanton in those silk underdrawers."

She turned her head stiffly to give him a tight smile. "And who bought me the drawers? I ask you."

"I only paid for the things," he retorted, lowering himself to sit beside her. "It wasn't my idea that you wear them. And if I had wanted you to wear them, it was under something else, which I was probably paying for too."

"Fine, then. I'll take them off."

"You will not." His face dark with terror that she would carry out the threat, he clasped her hips as she tried to wriggle out of her underwear. She arched her back in anger. She pushed against his strong hands to break his grasp.

"Stop it," she said through her teeth. "I wish you'd never come back here, my lord."

"So do I. Now hold still, Marsali. I'm stronger than you are, and you'll only hurt yourself. I need to talk to you, and it's difficult enough to hold a conversation with a woman in her underwear. Talking to you naked would be impossible. I understand that you're upset about tonight. It was very unpleasant, and it didn't turn out as I planned, but you and the clan have to share the responsibility. Along with your uncle, your cousin, and that bird over there."

"They're trying to protect me," she reminded him.

"Yes, and you make it a damned difficult job. Where is your uncle anyway?"

"He's off working a spell with Fiona somewhere."

She was still now, crossing her hands over her chest like a martyred saint. Duncan glanced down unwillingly from her face, her graceful curves an enticement beneath her thin ivory silk chemise. To complicate the situation, he had been imagining making love to her all night. In a variety of positions and settings. It was an amazing, if perplexing, phenomenon, the way his body routinely detached itself from his brain. Tonight the battle had reached fever pitch. The imminent threat of losing her to MacFay had roused possessive impulses in him that bordered on barbaric.

"The ball was not 'very unpleasant,' my lord," she said into the silence that had fallen. "It was a debacle. A disaster. My entire life is in ruins." A tiny frown furrowed her brow. "Who would want me now?" she said crossly.

"Any man with blood in his veins."

She sniffed. "I'm going to Virginia anyway."

"On Jamie's horse?"

She bit the bottom of her lip. "That isn't funny. You made him look like a fool."

"He is a fool." He touched her cold ashen cheek. Desire and duty tied his gut into a knot of aching frustration. "He wasn't the one to take care of you."

A tremor shot through her as he traced his thumb along her delicately carved cheekbone. "And who asked anyone to take care of me?"

"Look at me, lass."

"No."

"Do you really hate me?"

"Aye, I do. Besides, whenever I look into your eyes, my brain turns to porridge, and I always say things I regret afterward."

"I want to see you settled before I leave," he said quietly.

She rose up on her elbows and batted his hand away, upset because he'd mentioned leaving again, and she realized he really meant it. "You've played me like a puppet on a string," she whispered, emotion rising in her voice. "You've dangled me like a bone to a pack of dogs."

"They were dogs." He shook his head at the recollection. "Every last one of them, down to that fool MacFay."

"Marry this man, Marsali. No, I've changed my mind. Marry that one instead. Wear this on your head. Wear fancy underwear. Push out your chest, lass. Well, I don't need you, my lord." Her voice choked on the words. "I don't need anyone. Needing people makes you dependent on them, and the next thing you know, after you need them, they're gone, along with a huge chunk of your heart that never heals."

Her voice trailed off into a dry sob of self-contempt for revealing so much, and, too ashamed to await his reaction, she drew her knees into her chest and hid her face. Feelings that she had suppressed, of grief, of loss, of abandonment, surged and refused to be subdued.

Duncan stared at her. He ached to stroke her downbent head but didn't dare touch her again. He was distressed at the depth of pain that had spawned her outburst, at how immeasurably she had been wounded by the loss of those she loved. How much more unhappiness did she hide under the sunny warmth she presented to the world? And what had he done but hurt and humiliate her from the start?

Remorse deepened his voice. "I meant to find a man to protect you—no, not just to protect, but to cherish you and give you joy. I care for you too much to let you keep living your reckless life."

Slowly she lifted her head. Her sea-mist eyes looked dull in her piquant face. "I don't want to live anymore," she whispered without inflection.

"Don't say that." Her admission filled him with horror. He'd suspected as much from the start from her self-destructive behavior, but hearing the words made him want to shake and comfort her at the same time.

"You were my last hope," she said in a soft weary voice.

His face hardened. "I'm no one's hope, not unless you want an army trained or a citadel captured. The clan doesn't give a damn about me, and why should they?"

"You don't understand." She swallowed, the words barely audible. "I want you for myself."

For one insane moment, as their eyes met, he could think

of no reason to discourage her. His past, his future, did not exist. He wanted her with an urgency that defied logic. It took every ounce of his self-control to fight it. "I don't think you're quite yourself," he said when he recovered. "It was a foreign prince your father wanted, not an outcast."

She frowned at the resignation in his voice, forgetting her own misery. "Are you saying that the chieftain is not worthy of the tacksman's daughter?"

"Not this chieftain."

She sat up straighter. It was obviously a night for removing masks and revealing confidences. She had never seen Duncan like this, and his vulnerability disarmed her. "But why, my lord?"

Duncan stared past her, listening to the lulling wash of waves against the ship's hull. How did he untangle the shadowy twists of his thoughts to someone who was as light and uncomplicated as sunshine? "I'm just not for you," he said after a moment, rubbing tiredly at his temple. "Perhaps I'm not for anybody."

The anger in her heart began to melt; it wasn't in her nature to hold a grudge anyway, and she understood now that he was hurting inside even more than she'd guessed. "Are you still sad because Edwina's niece eloped with that man?" she said, touching his arm in sympathy.

Her delicate fingers brushed across his forearm, and a feeling of apprehension gripped him as if a butterfly had landed on a beast and did not sense its danger. Marsali, he realized, had never seen him as the others did. Perhaps she'd been too young to be swept along with the wave of public opinion. Or her father, bless his wise soul, had taught her to find her own truths. Whatever the reason, she viewed Duncan as proud and powerful, as strong and self-confident. The chieftain. The marquess. The military genius. She saw him the way he wished he could be.

It was the image he'd projected to the rest of the world. It was the image he had developed to protect himself from the painful memories that shadowed him of the dirty beaten boy who had survived abuse and a violent adolescence. But it was an image based on illusion, built on sand, crumbling grain by grain under his feet. One day, when it eroded, he would sink into a dungeon of self-despair.

"What am I to do with you now, lass?" he thought aloud, turning to look at her.

"Love me," she said, breaking into an appealing grin.

"Don't say that. Your father will rise from the grave."

"Love me." She twined her slender arms around his neck. Her small body sought the warm strength of his. "Love me," she whispered in his ear.

Her sweet breath stirred dangerous sensations along his nerve endings. A groan of denial caught in his throat. Her simple plea broke down the self-defensive composure of a lifetime. Duncan told himself he was going to push her away and walk out of this cabin.

A moment later he was pressing her down onto the bunk and kissing her into breathless silence. She tasted sweet like heather honey. She trusted him, and the eager yearning in her eyes filled him with ambivalence, with guilt and with a sexual hunger that shuddered down his neck into the base of his spine.

"Beg me to stop." His voice was a tortured groan against her mouth. "Lass, do you not understand what I want to do to you?"

His lips drifted down her delicate jawline to her throat, his teeth grazing her skin with a tender sensuality that sent a violent jolt of pleasure down to her toes. She could hear his voice, but the dark tones only dropped like stones and sank unheeded into the deep well of her dazed awareness. When his mouth sought the peak of her breast and laved it through her silk chemise, she gasped in shock that swiftly intensified to enjoyment.

"Tell me what you want to do, my lord," she whispered, shivering with pleasure.

He closed his eyes, pressing his face between the cleft of her breasts. "There are dark enough thoughts running through my mind without your encouraging them."

"Aye, but I like what you've done to me so far," she admitted with another reflexive shiver.

He ran his large hand down her hip and rubbed his palm against the mound of her womanhood, his voice rough with restraint. Feverish heat washed over his body. Just touching her there made him shake. "Well, there's this for a start. And then I would undress you, and kiss you everywhere."

"Everywhere?" she said with an underlying catch of laughter in her throat.

He had to smile; her sexual curiosity was more arousing than the wiles of all the courtesans he'd known combined. He empathized with MacFay's rage at being denied her. She was the sort of woman who, without even trying, fueled obsessions and started wars.

"Yes, everywhere. I'd kiss and touch you everywhere," he said hoarsely as his fingers brushed downward and sank into the slit of her drawers. Soft dewy flesh hidden beneath a tangled fleece of curls. Now it was his turn to shiver, temptation spinning its web tighter and tighter around his willpower. He was a pulsebeat from taking her and damning the consequences.

"Oh." Marsali arched instinctively into his hand, her eyes widening in surprise. She felt both curious and overwhelmed by her body's powerful response, not certain where it would lead. The raw passion in Duncan's unwavering stare disconcerted her. Confused, she buried her face in the sturdy musculature of his chest, breathing in his rich male scent, which mingled with the sweet pungence of the herbs hanging above and made her feel lightheaded. She liked the inescapable weight of his body against hers, the dominant strength that pinned her to the bunk, the gentle play of his fingers that sent pleasure streaking inside her.

Duncan clenched his jaw, consumed by a powerful commingling of affection and a lust that turned his mind molten. When she climaxed under his hand, her soft cries of pleasure absorbed by his shoulder, he thought his heart would burst with his own excitement. He imagined burying himself inside her, thrusting until his own need was relieved. His entire body ached with animal instinct, to mate, mark her, overpower.

"If you could read my mind now, Marsali," he said, gripping her to him, "you would know why I am bad for you."

She drew her head back from his shoulder, unaware of the violent impulses he was battling. She felt warm, sated and forgiving, savoring the closeness between them. She gazed off pensively into the distance, a smile playing on her lips.

"What are you thinking?" Duncan asked quietly.

She drew her gaze back to his face. "I was just thinking about the Old Testament story of Moses. He reminds me of you. Have you ever read the Bible, my lord?" she asked unexpectedly.

Duncan blinked. He couldn't have heard her correctly. "What?"

"The Bible. It shows how God seems to use the most imperfect people to achieve His ends. You were very bad before and now you have a chance to redeem yourself."

"Are you drunk, Marsali?"

"I can't imagine why you would think that."

"Because only someone very drunk would think that God sent me into this cabin to redeem myself when I'm a heartbeat from taking your innocence. That doesn't sound very biblical to me."

"I meant He sent you to the castle for a higher purpose." She sounded as perplexed as she had been pleased a moment ago. "I don't think we're talking about the same thing."

"Obviously," he said dryly. "I'm talking about sex, which is what men usually think about, although I'd have to say that after what just happened between us, it does seem a logical topic of conversation."

"Perhaps you ought to read the Bible," she whispered, staring into his eyes. "It would give you something else to think about."

He shook his head in bemused chagrin and pulled her back into his arms. She sighed, snuggling against his lap, never guessing the agony her innocent wriggling caused him, his selfish wee fairy. The gray-gold shadows of candlelight imparted a dreamlike glow to the cabin.

Contentment stole over him. Not sexual. Dear God. He was a seething cauldron of thwarted passion. No. It was a deeper satisfaction. Holding her. As if a cloud had lifted from his soul. Lust, its empty aftermath, he had experienced too many times. But never this . . . this strange combination of wrenching desire and heartwarming rightness.

"Where do we go from here?" he asked in a troubled voice.

She went very still, peering over his shoulder at the

porthole. Through the tangle of dismay and desire hazing his thoughts, Duncan could hear the hawk shifting nervously on his perch. If he could have abducted Marsali at that moment and gotten away with it, he would have done so.

Then she whispered in his ear. "I don't know where we're going to go from here, my lord, but I'll tell you one thing: It had better be a pretty fast journey. That's my uncle and cousin coming down the deck now."

Duncan's blood froze. "I thought you said they were off working their magic."

"They were," Marsali said with a little shiver of apprehension as the door crashed open. "But that's the trouble with magic. It either happens or it doesn't. You can't depend on it."

Chapter

21

Duncan had forgotten the bucket he'd managed to dislodge from his foot. As he sprang up from the bunk he stepped into it again, lost his equilibrium, swayed, and went crashing back down onto Marsali. She shouted before she could stop herself. When Colum and Fiona burst into the cabin, it was to see Duncan lying flat on his back with Marsali squashed beneath him, shouting and flailing her arms like a windmill.

Fiona jumped to the obvious conclusion and launched herself at Duncan's legs in a frenzy of outraged concern for her cousin. Between Fiona pounding her fists on his thighs and Marsali swatting his ears, Duncan thought he might be killed.

The wizard hadn't said a word. He just stood in the center of the floor with the strangest look on his face. Duncan could have sworn he saw a glint of satisfaction in those eyes.

"Move off me, my lord," Marsali whispered in a frantic voice. "This doesn't look very nice."

"Damn it, Marsali. I'm trying to move, but this girl is sitting on my legs, and either she gets off me, or I'm going to have to remove her by force, which is only going to upset your uncle more."

"Get off the chieftain's legs, Fiona." The words escaped

Marsali between pained little groans. "The chieftain is as heavy as a mountain, and you're not exactly helping matters."

Fiona reluctantly rolled off Duncan and scrambled up onto the bunk to cluck in sympathy over her cousin. "I can't believe he would behave like this, the brute. Thank goodness I worked a wilting spell on him earlier, or I suppose it might have been worse."

Duncan pushed himself into a standing position, bending briefly to yank the bucket off his foot. It flew across the cabin and clattered at Colum's feet. Marsali glanced from one man to another, covertly tugging the quilt over herself.

"Well," Colum said at last, lifting his hand in disdain to wave Marsali's wine-stained white gown under Duncan's nose. "Passion is one thing, my lord, but did you have to announce it to the world by undressing my niece on the deck?"

"I didn't undress her." Duncan shot Marsali a look fraught with frustration. "She undressed herself," he added, which, as a revelation, didn't do much to help.

Marsali nodded meekly. "It's true, Uncle Colum. I took off the gown because I was angry at him for telling me to wed and then not wed the MacFay."

"Jamie MacFay?" Fiona said, sitting up with a frown. "The chieftain was going to make you wed that big crude creature?" She gave her father a smug look. "Well, well. It doesn't appear that your wonderful love spell worked this time, Dad. I told you to let me help."

Marsali narrowed her eyes, sensing the undercurrent of conspiracy in the air. "What love spell?" she asked slowly. "Fiona, are you saying that Uncle Colum tried to match me up by magic to the MacFay?"

Colum glared a warning at Fiona from under his heavy white eyebrows. "No, she isn't," he said in a clipped voice. "Besides, it's not my behavior that is in question. I would like to know what you and the chieftain were doing on that bunk when I came in."

There was silence.

"Well . . ." Marsali swallowed and glanced over at Duncan, who was absolutely no help at all as he stood leaning against the bulkhead with his hand over his eyes. "To tell the truth, Uncle Colum, at the moment you arrived, we were discussing the Bible."

Duncan lowered his hand, staring in amused disbelief at her sitting half naked on the bunk and defending a basically indefensible situation.

"You were discussing the Bible?" Colum repeated in skeptical tones.

"Yes—actually, *I* was discussing the Bible. I was telling the chieftain that perhaps God intended to use him much like Moses."

"Moses?" Colum said in astonishment.

Marsali frowned. "Well, Moses lost his temper and committed murder, but God still ended up using him for glory." She paused. "God is good at doing things like that."

"You were shouting like a Viking warlord when I opened the door," Colum pointed out. "You were not reciting Scripture that I recall."

"That's true, Uncle Colum, but the chieftain had gotten his foot stuck in a bucket, and when he fell I felt like a brace of oxen had landed on my chest. You would have shouted too."

"*I* would have shouted," Fiona agreed.

Colum glanced down at the bucket, an array of unreadable emotions crossing his gaunt face. Slowly his gaze lifted to Duncan, calm and assessing. "I have tripped over that damn bucket many times myself," he said in an almost conversational tone. "It is a wonder I have not broken a leg before now."

Marsali studied him in suspicion. Only an idiot would have taken her story at face value, and her uncle was the shrewdest man she had ever met, intimidated by no one, not blinking an eye without first calculating the move. He was up to something, the crafty old codger, and intuition warned her she'd better get to the bottom of it.

Duncan, on the other hand, was only too glad to accept the wizard's pardon, undeserved though it might be. It had been the most peculiar and perplexing night of his life. "I am going back to the castle, Marsali," he announced, trying to salvage what was left of his power. "I want you to ride back with me. MacFay is undoubtedly still in the area."

Marsali hesitated. Part of her was not prepared to forgive

him for manipulating her; he had injured her pride. But another part, that unpredictable part that had responded to him only a few minutes ago, would have walked off the edge of the cliff with him if he'd asked her. Besides, even when they were fighting, she had more fun with him than anyone else in the world.

She stood up, raising her chin to a haughty angle. Duncan was impressed at how dignified she managed to appear with the quilt draped over her shoulders like a royal robe. "I'm not going back to the castle, my lord."

"Tomorrow then."

She shrugged. "I may not ever return to the castle after what happened there tonight."

Duncan could hardly make a scene, not with her uncle standing between them and that raven-haired girl just waiting for another excuse to launch an attack. He hadn't become a world-renowned general without recognizing when to beat a retreat. At least Marsali should be safe with her family for the night. He doubted Jamie had the intelligence to outwit the old wizard.

"Very well," he said tersely. "But the matter of your future is to be decided within the week, Marsali. One way or another. We haven't resolved a thing tonight."

The echo of Duncan's footsteps on the deck above resounded like an angry heartbeat in the deep silence of Colum's cabin. Marsali retrieved the white gown from her uncle's hand and donned it, looking expectantly from her uncle to Fiona, who had hung her head to hide her guilt-stricken face. When Marsali was dressed, she snatched her uncle's wand and slowly backed into the center of the room.

"All right. He's gone. It's just family now, and I know something is going on. What did Fiona mean by a love spell, Uncle Colum?"

Colum gave Fiona a vexed look, then knelt to pick up the bucket. "You are to leave this on deck from now on, Fiona. Not in the middle of the stairs where I will break my neck, mind you. Not by the door—"

"I'm going to hold your wand hostage, Uncle Colum." Marsali whirled back to the other girl, her eyes smoldering with anger. "And if you don't tell me, Fiona, I'm going to do something terrible to you."

"What kind of terrible?" Fiona whispered, squeezing herself back against the bunk, awash in wonderful dread.

Marsali felt the wand twitching between her fingers. "I don't know yet—the most terrible thing you can think of."

Fiona moistened her lips. "More terrible than what you did to Georgie last Samhain eve?"

"Aye." Marsali's voice sounded strangely husky to her own ears, and something was happening to her body as she held the wand; uncontrollable quivers of energy rippled through her. She stared down at her hands in awe: She could actually see the blood in her veins pulsing with power. The wand was alive in her hand, vibrating with vital spirit.

"Go to your cabin, Fiona," Colum said, his voice like the calm before a storm. "Marsali is not herself tonight."

Fiona scrambled off the bunk only to find Marsali blocking her way, an angry fairy on the warpath. "Dad," Fiona said with a catch in her voice, "I warned you not to interfere. L-look what's happening."

He looked, his gaze widening in approval.

As Marsali's temper had risen, so had the force of the waves battering the old ship. From the wand in her hand invisible sparks of energy and emotion burst to charge the air. As Colum moved slowly toward her, his long robes crackled with the electricity she had generated.

"Excellent," he said, nodding his head in a gesture of pride. "I always knew you had the gift. By the Goddess, I was right."

Marsali gazed down in disbelief at the wand, unable to speak. It was true; she could feel her entire body thrumming to some secret mystical rhythm. The very soles of her feet tingled with it. If the door had been open, she suspected she might have flown out above the stars. A sense of power embraced her, heady and dangerous.

She drew a breath. "I'm going to do something very, very terrible to you both if you don't tell me what is going on." She tapped the wand against her arm. *"Now."*

Fiona quivered like a feather. The wizard shrugged, acknowledging Marsali's power. "I cast a love spell to bind you to the chieftain for all eternity, Marsali," he said, his attitude unapologetic. "From what I witnessed tonight it was one of my more effective works of magic."

Fiona nodded eagerly, dying for every detail of the delicious secret to be revealed. "He used the hair entangled in your mother's cross. Yours and the chieftain's. It was the most powerful spell, Marsali. The Irrevocable Spell."

"You . . ." Marsali could not force the words from her throat. A red mist swirled before her eyes. Manipulated again, by magic. Betrayed by her own flesh and blood, by the two members of her family she trusted most, as peculiar as two members might be. Was there no way to escape the misguided attempts to control her life?

Colum was smiling in satisfaction, as still as a stone. Fiona darted past him and ducked behind the desk. Books, crucibles, and earthenware jars were starting to slide off shelves and hit the floor. Sprigs of herbs wafted in the air like stardust. The waves hit the ship's hull like cannonballs.

Marsali walked past her uncle with the wand clutched in her hand. Energy erupted from her like steam. To add to the confusion, Eun had broken free and was hopping back and forth from his perch to the bunk. When Marsali raised the wand into the air, the door flew open, and a gust of wind sent Colum staggering to his knees.

Bewildered by a power she could not control, Marsali ran out of the cabin.

When Eun followed her, the wizard understood that the bird would no longer obey him alone.

As Duncan watched on horseback from the cliff, he could not believe his eyes. Something very strange was going on in that cabin. There were colorful sparks of light flashing from behind the porthole. But the strangest thing was how the sea was perfectly calm except around the ship, where waves crested the hull as if driven by a gale-force fury. Clearly, this was not a normal family.

Then he saw Marsali come running out on deck in her white wedding gown; the infernal hawk was flying after her. As she reached the gangway, Duncan vaulted off his horse and rushed across the wind-tangled sea grasses to intercept her. This wasn't his idea of a safe evening spent at home.

They met on the path. Well, they almost met. Barely three feet from Marsali, Duncan walked into a gust of wind that flattened him to the cliffside like an invisible giant's fist. It knocked the breath from his chest. He could see Marsali through a veil of shimmering mist, her face as astonished as his by the supernatural phenomena.

"What the hell was that?" he asked hoarsely.

She edged past him, her voice a whisper in the wind. "I couldn't tell you, my lord. But I do know that I am very, very angry, and if you try to make me go back to the castle, something bad could happen to you. I could totally lose control of my power."

"I don't believe in spells and curses, Marsali," he shouted, stomping up behind her.

She turned; he slammed back two steps as if a current of lightning had shot through his body; aftershocks of discharged energy raced down his spine. "I don't believe in them either, at least not until tonight." She held out her wrist as Eun floated downward. "It would appear, however, that there exist certain powers in this world that thrive without our believing in them."

Her hair was blowing around her face in a soft enticing tangle; she looked both fragile and powerful, wild and ethereal, and he wanted to carry her back to the castle and to his bed more than anything he had ever wanted in his life. He wanted to be the one to master her wildness. He wanted to absorb her spirit into his.

He wanted to kiss her too. Damn it, he was *going* to kiss her. He reached out to grab her shoulders. Then he froze as the hawk on her wrist fluttered its short rounded wings in warning.

He decided he'd wait to kiss her after all.

"Come back to the castle with me, Marsali."

She was tempted, so tempted. Standing against the cliff in his chieftain's garb, he might have been made of magic himself. For all his dark arrogance, for all the sins he had committed, there was a core of goodness running through him, and that incongruous combination of shadow and light had stolen Marsali's heart.

"I'm not coming back," she yelled at him. Shaking her head, she backstepped another few inches up the path as the wind buffeted her body. "I'm still angry at you anyway. Don't try to stop me."

He glanced down, terrified they were going to be blown off the path onto the rocks below. He'd never felt such a fierce wind. "Marsali—"

"Don't even try to touch me," she warned him. "Nothing like this has ever happened to me before. I can't control it. I don't know what I might do next. I could end up killing us both."

Damn it. Every time he went to grab her, the wind forced him away. "Where will you go, lass?" he shouted. "Who will take care of you?"

"I'll take care of myself," she assured him. "I managed to do it before you came."

"Make this wind stop blowing, Marsali."

"I'm not sure how yet, my lord." She grinned suddenly, pushing her hair out of her face. "Besides, I like it. Aye, I like the power. Is this what you feel like when you sit in your chair and give orders?"

He didn't return her grin, fighting a panic born of fear and frustration. She could disappear, and he'd never see her again. MacFay could take her, and he wouldn't know until it was too late.

"Give me your hand, Marsali."

He tried to catch her as she darted higher up the path; it was a game to her now, wielding her power, but he himself was caught in the howling tail of the wind that rose in her wake. Salty foam and sand blew in his face, blinding him. When the air finally cleared, she was gone.

The sea grew calm. The wind died to a teasing whisper. If there was any consolation in the fact she had escaped him, it was only that MacFay would probably not be able to catch her either.

Cursing the helplessness that was intolerable to his nature, he stalked up the path to his horse. Where would she go? If this weird scene was magic, and he doubted it, what would happen between them now? Was she as powerful as she seemed? The thought was as intriguing as it was frightening.

Chapter

22

Duncan was roused from the depths of his dream by the sound of loud snorting in his ear.

He opened his eyes, wincing at the light that poured through the unshuttered window like a waterfall. A wet whiskery nose nuzzled his unshaven jaw.

He swallowed, afraid to look. After several moments he turned his head on the pillow. God help him. He wasn't alone.

It wasn't a wet nose. It was a porker's snout. He was sleeping with a pig.

"What the bloody hell!"

The raspy tenor of his roar sent blood pulsing into the constricted blood vessels of his brain. The brandy bottle that had nursed him to sleep rolled off his naked chest. As he bolted upright in his bed, Effie's girl piglet, Ailis, wearing a frilly maid's lace cap, scrambled under his legs for protection. The boy piglet, Alan, went off to sniff at the bottle that had fallen to the floor.

Duncan stared down at the twitching snout that poked between his feet, then he roared again. Ailis scrambled out from between the chieftain's legs in terror. Alan squeezed his plump belly to the floor. The twins hated it when people yelled.

The door burst open, Edwina and Effie bumping shoulders in a contest to see who could enter first. The room reeked of brandy fumes. The chieftain sat in the middle of his bed wearing nothing but his trousers and roaring like a wounded lion. Ailis cowered under the coverlet.

Edwina tutted under her breath. Effie whisked the bottle away from Alan's snout, her voice maternally reprimanding. "And you only a babbie," she said as she straightened. "The chieftain ought to be ashamed of himself for corrupting an innocent wee beastie."

Duncan groaned and lifted a pillow to his head. Her strident voice raked like a fingernail across raw nerve endings.

"This room smells like a distillery," Edwina said, her nose twitching in distaste. "I wouldn't dare light the fire for fear of an explosion."

Duncan lifted Ailis from the bed and deposited her on the floor, ignoring her squeals of protest. "Did Marsali come back this morning?" he asked in a voice that sounded like it came from the depths of a dry, dusty well.

"Marsali isn't coming back," Effie said cheerfully. "She's going to live on the moor with the men forever. Ye've offended her good and proper this time, my lord."

Edwina leaned up against the wall. "By the way, Major Darling is waiting for you downstairs, Duncan. He wants your official permission to raze—how did he put it?—'a few of the eyesore cottages and trees that stand in the way of his road.'"

"The bastard!" Effie exclaimed, standing in the doorway with a wriggling piglet hooked under each arm. "Ye're going to stop him, aren't ye, my lord? You willna let him destroy homes?"

Duncan frowned, lowering the pillow. He wasn't listening to them. He thought he heard Marsali's voice in the courtyard. He rose stiffly and went to the window, squinting his bloodshot eyes to make out the figures below. No. It was only a kitchen maid scolding Lachlan for stealing her fresh oatcakes.

He cursed under his breath. Well, they'd finally come full circle, he and Marsali. She was the little outlaw again, back on the moor with his clansmen, and he was a prisoner of his heritage and hating himself. He put his hand to his temples, massaging the tension that smoldered behind his eyes.

"You are going to stop them, aren't ye, my lord?" Effie asked, watching him closely.

He turned and gave her a blank look. "Stop who from what?" he said hoarsely. "And why does everyone make himself at home in my bedchamber?"

"Stop the British soldiers." Edwina frowned in disapproval. "You know, you really did make quite a mess of things last night. And Major Darling has been waiting over two hours for you to get up."

Duncan headed for the washstand and quaffed the contents of the water jug in one greedy swallow. He grimaced at his reflection in the mirror. He'd been hoping that last night hadn't really happened. Disjointed images flashed through his mind and made no more sense in the light of morning than they had in the wee gray hours.

Marsali, a maelstrom of unleashed emotion. Marsali, hurt and humiliated in the hall, flirting with MacFay. Raising the wind and the sea. Running away with that hawk. Fragile and furious, finally testing her wings.

She was gone. He could feel the castle slipping back under its spell of darkness, and he was slipping too, returning to the cold crypt of self-control. How the hell had he allowed it to happen?

He backed away from the mirror, staring morosely across the room. She held the upper hand now, and it didn't make him very happy. Still, while he'd never meant to hurt her, he couldn't let her run around openly defying him. He should never have let his emotions override his better judgment.

"I've never seen him like this before," Edwina told Effie in concern. "I hope to God he pulls himself together before he goes to London. No one would believe he was the 'Merciless Marquess of Minorca.'"

Duncan turned stiffly and walked to the door like one of his lead soldiers. "What did you say this captain's name was?"

Edwina and Effie shared worried glances. "He isn't a captain, Duncan," Edwina answered. "The man is a major, but no matter his rank, you can't greet him—"

"A major. Well, bring out the French brandy then. Find that ass Abercrombie while you're at it." He glanced down at himself with a frown. "What the hell happened to my shirt?"

"Ye threw it off the watchtower last night when the ghosts started to fight," Effie said, grinning in enjoyment. "Would ye like to borrow my plaid?"

Marsali was driving everyone mad by midmorning. Now that she'd discovered magic, she couldn't resist experimenting with her power. No cow, cairn, or clansman escaped her determined attempts at enchantment.

At first the clan sought her out in the moorland cave she claimed as her own, encouraging her efforts. She tried to change Donovan's calf into a bull, but the calf ran away.

She tried to grow hair on Lachlan's thinning scalp, and that didn't work.

She even tried to remove the birthmark on Owen's neck, and he swore she'd made it grow larger.

"Oh, well." Lachlan leaned back against a boulder outside the cave, rubbing the sore spot where she'd banged her uncle's wand repeatedly on his pate in an effort to sprout hair. "Ye've done yer best, lass. Perhaps what happened last night was a freak of nature."

Marsali frowned. "I wish that were true, Lachlan, but I'm afraid I'm cursed with my power, and if I were speaking to Fiona and my uncle, I'd ask for their advice on how to summon it at will."

"Do ye really have the power, Marsali?"

She lifted her shoulders in a wan shrug. "I suppose so. I mean, I raised the sea a bit, and there was a fair wind blowing. But I don't know that I'd care to do it every day. It takes something out of a body. You should have seen the chieftain when he tried to grab me on the cliffs. It was the first time I've ever seen him look frightened."

Marsali was quiet for a moment. She told herself it felt like heaven to be away from that dank, confining castle. No nasty chieftain to order her about, to criticize her clothes, her behavior, her beliefs. No one to scowl at her and tell her to put out her chest. What a relief to have escaped the dark spell of his power.

But the truth was that she felt miserable; she hadn't slept a wink, convincing herself all was well in her world. For one thing, her body had kept her awake, thrumming like a harp as the residue of last night's emotional storm faded away.

For another, Duncan's dark face haunted her every time she closed her eyes.

I care for you, lass.

He cared for her. She cared for him. You'd think it would be a simple enough situation. But the trouble was that the chieftain complicated everything with his twisted outlook on life.

He was hurting, and because of it he had hurt her too. Well, now they were both unhappy, and what did it prove?

"Put a spell on the chieftain, Marsali," someone suggested. "Make him go away fer good, lass."

"I tried to have Uncle Colum put a spell on him," she explained glumly. "That's what's gotten me into so much trouble in the first place. Magic is conspiring with my own human weaknesses to throw me into the man's arms."

Owen looked alarmed. "What do you mean, Marsali?"

She drew a stick figure of Duncan in the dirt with her wand, sighing wistfully. "Uncle Colum cast a spell to make the chieftain and I fall in love with each other, but only my half is working. The MacElgin is a horrible tangle of human emotion that even magic cannot touch."

Lachlan and Owen traded troubled looks as she sank down onto her knees, staring at the crude drawing of the chieftain. "But we thought ye wanted to marry Jamie MacFay," Lachlan said.

"Aye." Owen nodded in agreement. "Ye were angry as hell when the chieftain denied the betrothal last night."

Marsali sighed again, frustrated by her inability to make them understand. "But I didn't really want to marry Jamie, don't you see? I only pretended to because the chieftain wanted me to, and I was tired of obeying his orders and it . . . it just seemed easier than admitting I had true feelings for him, which of course I didn't realize until he looked at me like that in the hall after he caught Jamie with that woman. It was that look of his that did it."

Lachlan folded his wiry frame down onto the dirt, his bushy eyebrows drawn into a frown.

Owen made a fuss of picking bits of gorse from his plaid.

Neither man could make out a word of sense in anything she'd said, but they did understand that their Marsali was unhappy, and that somehow it was the chieftain's fault.

She rose, shaking her head. "There's nothing you can do to help. I've brought this all on myself, and now I've the burden to bear of knowing magic, which you would think would be a nice thing."

"Aye, a helpful thing," Owen murmured cautiously.

Lachlan nodded. "Ye would think so."

Marsali stood at the mouth of the cave, staring out across the moor at the castle. "Even magic couldn't make the chieftain fall in love with me, not that I wanted him to, mind you. But it just goes to prove that I was right: If something is meant to be, it will happen anyway. Magic or not."

A few minutes later, Marsali's young nephew came bursting into the cave to summon her. Her sister-in-law, Bride, had gone into hard labor. Gavin, as usual, was useless, and could Marsali lend a helping hand? Better yet, Bride wondered if Marsali could bring her magic and get the whole damned business over with fast.

Marsali had gone off like a martyr, carrying her wand and praying that she didn't end up changing Bride's baby into a goat. Clearly her life was no longer her own. Power carried grave responsibilities with it. No wonder Uncle Colum had taken to months of self-isolation in his secret hideaways.

Lachlan and Owen watched her leave in silence, not voicing their concern until she was riding across the moor into the woods.

"Dear, dear," Owen said, shaking his head in sympathy. "Puir lassie, to have fallen in love wi' the chieftain. What a wretched fate."

Lachlan scowled. "She's no in love wi' him, ye nitwit. 'Tis the MacFay the lass is pining for."

"The MacFay?" Owen blinked in surprise. "But she said—"

"Aye, and when does a woman ever speak the truth when

it comes to love? Anyway, the question is, are we going to help Marsali?"

"Help Marsali what?" a gruff voice demanded from the mouth of the cave.

Owen glanced up as Johnnie joined their circle, his weathered face tired and unsmiling. "We're tryin' to help Marsali win back the MacFay."

Johnnie brushed off the oatcake he'd found outside. "And why would she want to be winning the MacFay? He's a pig."

"She's in love wi' the pig," Lachlan explained morosely.

Johnnie's eyebrows shot up in surprise. "Aye? And I'd have sworn she loved the chieftain."

"P'rhaps she's in love wi' them both," Owen offered shyly.

Johnnie whistled through his teeth. "What a mess."

"Aye," Lachlan said. " 'Tis why I never fell in love, thanks be to the good Lord for tender mercies. Damn, I wish she could have fallen in love with the chieftain instead of Jamie."

Johnnie bit into the oatcake, crunching in agreement.

"The chieftain intends to leave us in a month," Lachlan continued, "and like it or not, our lives have changed for the better since his return."

"They have?" Owen asked, incredulous.

"Aye," Lachlan said. "For one thing, the bairns don't shoot me in the bum every time I run to the stables. And for another, no one has died from Cook's potage in almost two months."

"He loses his temper a lot though," Johnnie said. "Especially at Marsali. Where is the lass anyway? I have something important to discuss wi' her."

"She's off to the cottages," Lachlan answered.

Johnnie frowned, lowering his voice. "The Sassenachs are threatening to tear down more homes for their road, my ma's cottage, old Tynan's the tanner, and even Marsali's brother's place. The time has come for a show of strength."

Lachlan appeared to ponder this at length. "I dinna think strippin' them naked is going to stop them this time, Johnnie. There's too many of 'em for a start."

"That's what we need Marsali for," Johnnie said in a

tension-fraught undertone. "I'm thinkin' we make our move tonight. Marsali will know how to take care of it. She'll keep us safe from the Sassenachs."

Owen's eyes widened. "Perhaps we should let the chieftain handle this."

"The chieftain has other problems to worry about," Johnnie said with a sly grin. "Besides, it's time to prove to the man we're no the helpless idiots he thinks we are."

Chapter

23

I apologize again for leaving you waiting in the castle, Major Darling," Duncan said as he followed the stout, distinguished Englishman on horseback along the coastal road.

Actually, he hadn't left the man waiting at all. He'd completely forgotten Major Darling in his obsessive anxiety to reassure himself that Marsali had not run off with Jamie MacFay during the night. He scanned the cove for the hundredth time in an hour. Not a trace of the swaggering ass.

"I understand from the charming Lady Edwina that your Highlanders are proving to be a handful, MacElgin."

"Well . . ."

"Not that I mean to insult your heritage. It's just that I forget sometimes you're a native yourself." Major Darling gave rein to a raucous snort of laughter that sent a flock of sea gulls flying. "A chieftain—isn't that what they call you? By God, you'd look damn sweet in one of those skirts with those big hairy legs of yours."

Duncan pretended to smile. "My clan is very concerned that you're going to tear down their homes for your road, sir."

The major wheeled his horse around to face Duncan. "We're not in the business of tearing down homes, Mac-Elgin. But if a few abandoned huts or stones stand in our way, well, that's a different matter. The truth is we'd never disturb your Highlands at all if it weren't for your damned Jacobites trying to put that pretender on the throne."

"*My* Jacobites?" Duncan said, frowning.

"No one is questioning your loyalty, my lord," the major said, his ruddy face conciliatory. "If there were more sensible Scotsmen like you in the area to keep control, I wouldn't be here garrisoning this blasted fortress. I've nothing personal against your people."

"Some of those stones you want to knock down are sacred. The Scots believe they're even imbued with magical powers."

The major sighed. "You've always had my admiration, sir, and I don't mind admitting that we're both being wasted in these Highland wilds. Ah, well. Another month or so, and we'll be back on the battlefield where we belong. But don't worry. The surveyor told me this morning we won't need to knock down a single cottage. As for the mystical stones . . . I'll do my best."

"That's good of you," Duncan said. Relieved to have the problem solved, he wondered how long it would take him to run back to the castle for a spyglass. He had just noticed a sturdy little sloop anchored at the end of the cove. It could be Jamie, lying in wait. He should have taken care of him last night when he had the chance.

"Well, I'm back off to my fortress," the major said, oblivious to Duncan's lapse in attention. "Keep them under control, that's all I ask. I'd hate to arrest one of your relatives, but then orders are orders, and following them is what I'm paid for. I hear you're up for a cabinet position, by the way. Remember me, won't you, my lord."

His clansmen averted their faces as Duncan rode slowly across the castle yard toward the stable. No, there was no love lost between them. After the humiliation he had dealt their precious princess last night, the chieftain loomed in their minds as more the black demon than ever before. It didn't matter that his motive had been to protect Marsali. No one wanted to believe the best of him.

He heard them muttering behind his back. They were disappointed if they'd expected him to show any shame at his behavior.

"'Twasn't enough to break the wee lassie's heart last night. He had to entertain an English soldier wi' the old chieftain's best brandy this morning."

"Aye, and he's made an enemy of the MacFays too, after a hundred years of friendship."

"Puir Marsali. Moping out there all alone on the moor."

"He's scarit the wits out of her."

"Aye, he was born a mean bastard and will carry his meanness to the grave."

"'Tis a damn good thing he's leaving at summer's end. Walking away from kith and kin, clan and castle."

"And what would you expect from a man who abandoned his own child without a backward glance?"

Duncan stiffened in the saddle, aware that he was meant to overhear the complaining gossip. As silence fell, he could sense his clansmen waiting for him to react. He dismounted and strode toward the keep, his face betraying no emotion.

A child. His child. It was the second such reference to be slung at him since his return. Could it be true? Was one of the little bow-and-arrow monsters who terrorized the castle actually his offspring? The possibility inspired a confusing clash of curiosity and dread in his heart.

The unwanted child who had left behind another unwanted child. Pray God if there *had* been a child, its life had been happier than Duncan's own. At any rate it was time to find out the truth.

He walked straight to the castle kitchen and confronted Cook with the rumors that had plagued him since his return.

"There has always been truth between us, if nothing else," he said bluntly. "Did I leave a child behind, Agnes?"

She chased the kitchen maids outside before giving him an answer. A low fire burned in the hearth. Only Cook would dare tell him the truth to his face. In fact, after the previous evening's debacle, she was the only person in the castle who would willingly speak to the chieftain at all.

And Agnes, at her best, did not exactly exude the essence of motherly compassion toward anyone on earth.

"Aye, my lord, ye sired a wee lassie, and she must have died at birth because the doctor's wife had her buried before anyone clapped eyes on the bairn," she quietly explained while rolling out a pie crust on her scarred oak table.

Duncan stared into her sallow unsmiling face, seeing the cruel reality that he'd remained unaware of for fifteen years. "My father never told me that a child resulted from that union."

"And what would have been the point?" Cook shook her head. "All three of ye paid a price in the end. The doctor, who couldna have his own babies and found his neglected wife pregnant wi' yer love child. And her, well, he whisked the woman away the verra day the infant died. No one's heard of them since."

Duncan was silent, remembering how brash and sexually curious he had been at seventeen. And drunk. Aye, he'd awakened at dawn in the doctor's bed, uncertain exactly where he was or what he'd been doing when Cecelia had booted him out the window, tossing his trews in his face.

"'Tis done now," Cook said after a long silence, and it was as close to offering forgiveness as she could ever come. "The gossips have no right to be castin' stones."

Duncan did not know how to react, or how to feel. "I suppose I was hoping you'd reassure me it was only that. Gossip. Thank you for telling me the truth."

"I'm an honest woman if nothin' else."

He looked away, clearly uncomfortable by what she had revealed. "I am going to ride out to inspect the cottages to see what repairs will be needed before I leave." He turned to the door, his face careworn in the dim light. "Do you think Marsali will come back to the castle?"

"I canna say, my lord."

Cook wiped her hands on her apron and stared after him with a worried expression as he left the kitchen without another word.

The past haunted him, as if the present did not hold problems of its own. Should she have told him about the raid the clan was planning tonight on the British fortress? Should she have begged him to intervene? It probably didn't matter.

One way or another, whether the clan failed or not, Agnes feared there would be hell to pay in the end.

It was midafternoon when Duncan dismounted and walked slowly through the graveyard of the little hillside kirk. MacFay's ship, if that's what Duncan had spotted, had mysteriously disappeared before he could get a closer look.

And now, on top of worrying about Jamie MacFay, he had to face the tragic repercussions of yet another sin.

He stopped abruptly as the tiny white stone cross caught his eye. It stood alone on the hillside beneath the shadows of an old yew tree. For a moment he was tempted to turn back. What he didn't know couldn't hurt him. Aye, but he *did* know now. He drew a fierce breath. This was the deepest cut of all.

An emotion stronger than fear or even self-preservation compelled him forward. Part of himself lay forgotten in that sad little grave. Youth and innocence buried beneath the weight of adult transgressions.

The abandoned product of his adulterous affair with a lonely doctor's wife. The child he had fathered and never known existed till now. And all that marked her birth and death was a crude piece of stone and a sprig of dried heather that someone, perhaps Cook, had left in remembrance.

He knelt, his voice subdued as he smoothed his big hand over the unmarked cross. "How can I show you I'm sorry when you're not here but in heaven?"

A deep silence was his only answer.

Marsali slid down from her horse, her footsteps silent as she crept from tree to tree. Surely she was seeing things. That couldn't be the chieftain huddled over that wee grave. *Dhé*, was the big tyrant mourning then?

Intrigued, she edged as close to the circle of yews as she dared. His shoulders lifted in a deep sigh beneath his plaid but he didn't utter a sound. Truly he was suffering.

Compassion and the urge to console conspired to move her toward him. Then she heard Duncan start to talk, and intuition blocked the impulse. She pressed her face against the yew's bark, the anguished shame in his voice immobilizing her.

"No wonder they hate me," he said in a quiet voice to the tiny cross. "And of all the sins I've tried to undo, your death, my wee daughter, can never be forgiven."

Marsali caught a glimpse of his face, the angular planes softened by a remorse too deep for words. Stricken with sympathy, aching to ease his pain, she remembered the offhanded insult she herself had once thrown at him about abandoning his own child.

She hadn't dreamed at the time it was true. She had heard a rumor, that was all, and she'd used it in a fit of temper to hurt him. Guilt seared her heart as she realized how she had unwillingly added another stone to the burden of his pain.

Still, she didn't know how to reach him.

It was as if he were the castle under its dark spell of isolation, with its ghost and secrets; and she were the moor, her heart as open as his was locked away, her instincts as spontaneous as his were controlled. Making this observation, she began to back away, sadly wondering if the drawbridge of their differences could ever be crossed.

The bundle of herbs she'd gathered to take to Bride at the cottage scattered around her feet. There was nothing she could do to help the chieftain. All the magic in the world could not stem the flood of emotion that broke from his heart, begging to be healed.

Duncan rode straight for the cottages from the graveyard. If he could not protect the little girl laid to rest behind him, he could at least try to help his own people before he left. Not that he expected anyone to appreciate his efforts.

He stopped cold as he saw Marsali dismounting before a well-kept stone cottage in a hazel coppice. At the sight of her, a breath of sunshine and heather swept through the cobwebs of his sad reflections.

He slid off his horse. "What are you doing here?" he demanded, his gruff tone covering an unwelcome surge of emotion.

She turned slowly. Although his face did not betray his feelings, she could hear the tension in his voice. She couldn't tell him she knew he had just learned he'd lost a child.

"I'm going to my sister-in-law's childbed," she explained. "Bride is having a terrible time of this one. What a surprise to meet you here."

"I want to inspect the cottages." He studied her small animated face. Everything about her, from her bright mop of curls down to her dirty little feet, bespoke life and a freedom he suddenly craved for himself. "I'll come inside with you."

She looked taken aback. "But you're the chieftain, and ever since Gavin hurt his back, he and the rest of the family have been forced to live in the poor cots."

"I was born in the poor cots, lass," he reminded her, turning away from the well-trained stallion who would wait at edge of the coppice.

"But my sister has eight children."

"I was a fisherman's son before I became chieftain. I commanded the finest cavalry in the world. I imagine I can stand the sight of a few bairns for an hour."

Chapter

24

Marsali disappeared with the midwife behind the crude stone wall partition of her brother's cottage. Her abandonment left Duncan at the mercy of her eight unsupervised nieces and nephews, who ranged in age from two to twelve. They gathered around him in a circle of awestruck silence. He smiled uncertainly and backed toward the door.

The eldest boy pushed to the fore with a belligerent sneer. "My da said if we was bad, he'd send us to the castle for the chieftain to punish."

His twelve-year-old sister nodded in agreement. "He said ye'd boil us in a broth of blood, eat our wee bodies, and use our bones to pick yer teeth."

"Did he indeed?" Duncan asked dryly as Gavin of the gruesome stories himself limped through the doorway, his face flushed with embarrassment at what he'd overheard. Apparently the man had overheard enough of the conversation to make frantic hand signals at his offspring to stop.

Gavin set a bucket of freshly caught trout by the hearth and cleared his throat. "Children will exaggerate, my lord."

"Adults will too in my experience," Duncan retorted. "Anyway, now that you're here, Hay, I think I'll go outside and examine—"

"Oooh. Aaah." Gavin released a loud groan of agony.

238

Clutching his back, he sank down onto the oak settle by the fire. The children crowded around him with sympathetic faces, the little ones covering him with a plaid. The older ones brought him a pillow and pulled off his wet boots. The baby toddled over and patted his foot.

It was obviously an established ritual.

"Forgive me for not standing in your presence." Gavin paused to grimace dramatically. "The pain is that awful, my lord."

Duncan frowned. "Yes, I can see . . ."

He was distracted by the sudden moan that rose from behind the partition. Low and inhuman, it raised the fine hairs on his nape.

"Is everything all right in there, Marsali?" he asked, edging closer to the door.

"Everything is fine, my lord," she replied in an amused voice.

Bride moaned again.

Gavin groaned.

Duncan eyed the children. They eyed him back. "If you need me, Marsali, I'll be inspecting . . ."

Bride was moaning.

Gavin was groaning.

Duncan would have sworn they were competing in a contest of whose agony was greater. He pushed the door open, trying not to appear desperate to escape.

"Take the children with you, my lord," Marsali shouted as he sneaked his first step over the threshold.

He froze in midstep like an escaped convict caught by his warden. The children rushed him, with whoops of delight, clinging to his legs with astonishing enthusiasm, in light of his reputation for being a cannibal.

"'Tis good of ye, my lord," Gavin said in a weak voice from his chair. "They wear me out, if the truth be told."

Claire, the three-year-old, was unraveling a thread in Duncan's plaid. Her twin brother, Connor, was shooting spoonfuls of porridge into the air from the breakfast bowl he'd taken from the table.

"Wait a minute." Duncan carefully freed himself from the children and ducked behind the partition.

"Good afternoon, my lord," Bride said, giving him a

brave smile before another contraction caught her off guard, and she groaned, arching her back.

Then Gavin moaned.

Duncan took Marsali by the arm to draw her aside. He couldn't wait to get out of here. "It looks as if you've got everything under control. I'll ride back to the castle and send Effie here to watch the children."

Bride wasn't just groaning now. She was swearing like a fishwife. Duncan paled under his swarthy tan, stumbling over a stool.

"You can't leave now," Marsali said calmly. "She's very close."

"Close to what?" he whispered in alarm.

Bride squatted down in the corner. Duncan stepped back into the wall in bewilderment. Battles were one thing, delivering babies another. The mere thought of childbirth overwhelmed him. Women looked so fragile.

"What the hell am I supposed to do with eight children?" he wondered aloud.

"Well, don't swear at them, for one thing, and don't lose your temper. It scares people when you do—except for me, of course."

Duncan didn't move, a look of panic on his face.

"Take them outside. Let them play in the burn." Marsali hurried off to Bride's side, grasping her sister-in-law's shoulder in support. "Tell them a story, my lord," she said impatiently. "Do whatever you did to amuse yourself as a lad."

"Fine," he retorted. "I'll round them up and we'll go dropping mud pies down smoking chimneys for a start. If that gets boring, I'll take them down to the cove to drill holes in the fishing boats. Then we'll watch the boats sink from the caves while the men bail frantically and curse. After that, we'll steal a few goats and dress them in the tenant farmers' clothes hanging behind the cots to dry."

"That sounds lovely," she said without glancing up. "Just be sure that Amelia doesn't get too wet. She's had a nasty cough."

As he left, he heard them laughing behind his back, whispering about him in amused exasperation.

"And did ye see the look on his face when Bride squatted?" That was the midwife speaking. "I dinna care how strong and powerful a man is, they're all the same when it comes to practical matters."

"Hopeless," Bride agreed in a gasping voice.

Marsali giggled softly. "Well, I know he can handle a troop of horsemen. But eight bairns . . . I have grave doubts."

"This is awfully kind of you, my lord," Gavin murmured as Duncan stomped to the door, a gaggle of chattering children at his heels.

Duncan glanced down at the grinning faces. "How long will I have to watch them?"

"Bride usually doesn't take long." Gavin sat up, moaning faintly. "Probably another hour. Would you mind passing me that jug on the table, my lord? Yes, that's it, thanks. Oh, and the cheese beside it. The knife too, if it's not a bother. And a wee bit of honey—no, that's the wrong jar. Aye, there ye go."

Duncan put his hands on his hips. "Anything else?"

"Well, the Bible over there, since you were kind enough to ask. And if you could just open the shutters for a wee bittie more light."

Someone tugged on Duncan's trousers. "Gordie's gone, my lord."

It was the twelve-year-old girl named Dara. As Duncan stared down into her bright blue eyes, he realized with an unexpectedly sharp pang of regret that his own unknown daughter, had she lived, would have been even older. Had that unwanted baby experienced any love at all in her too-brief time on earth? Or had she, like Duncan, been despised from the moment of conception by the father who could not claim her?

He swallowed over the knot of repressed grief in his throat. "Gordie can't have gone far. I saw him not two seconds ago."

"Aye, my lord. That was before he fed yer horse an oatcake and rode it like hellfire over the hill."

Chapter

25

Duncan was exhausted. The battle of Brihuega hadn't taken this much out of him. Childbirth, children. He didn't have the stamina for it. A summer with Marsali had worn him down. War was beginning to look like fun in comparison.

He had chased down both horse and horse thief, herded up the remaining flock of children, and assembled them with military precision on the sunlight-dappled banks of the bubbling burn. They stared back at him, their faces openly challenging, promising more mischief.

"Well," he said, rubbing his hands. "Now the chieftain is going to show you how he *really* plays nursemaid. Military style."

Gemma gave a squeal of delight and pointed excitedly through the trees. "Look at that!"

Duncan glanced around in amazement at the tiny heather-thatched cottage. Sparks of colored light exploded from the chimney in a plume of grayish smoke. He half expected the roof to fly off. Then the water in the burn reversed direction. The children shrieked in delight, staring down at the current of churning wavelets.

"Oooh," Dara whispered in admiration. "Auntie Marsali must be working a spell."

Before Duncan could agree or disagree, the lusty cry of a newborn baby broke the silence, magic unto itself.

Leith snorted in disgust, kicking a stone. "Another baby. We'll never get to Virginia at this rate."

"Perhaps we could leave *you* behind," his older brother Keith suggested, giving him a punch in the shoulder.

Duncan grabbed both boys by the scruff of the neck. "There's to be no talking among the prisoners. The next one to break the rules knows the punishment."

Marsali trudged down the grassy incline to the burn. She could hear Duncan's deep rich voice rising above the water gurgling over stones and a joyful warmth washed over her, much like the satisfying sweetness of watching Bride nurse her newborn son. Her feelings for the chieftain threatened to resurface: the yearning, the anger, the fascination. What an emotional void he would create when he left.

How lovely, she thought. He's telling the children a story. Who would have believed the powerful chieftain capable of such tender behavior? And look at the children gathered round him, wide-eyed and unmoving, hanging on his every word. Why, it was a scene to bring tears to her eyes. She sniffed, deeply touched, moody and emotionally fragile.

"I'll tolerate no drunkenness among the ranks," the chieftain was announcing in a gruff voice. "Any soldier who disobeys will be lashed to the gun wheel and flogged with the cat."

Marsali gasped, halting in her tracks. He wasn't telling them a story—he was threatening them with corporal punishment! The children weren't standing voluntarily in that rigid circle—he had tied them to the tree with Bride's clothesline! Warping their wee innocent minds with the harsh images of army discipline.

Hiking up her skirts, she pelted down the incline. "And just what do you think you're doing, Duncan MacElgin? Who gave you permission to corrupt my nieces and nephews?"

Duncan turned his head, taking a moment to admire her shapely brown legs as she barreled toward him. "Would you like me to tie you up too?"

"No! Dinna stop the game, my lord," Gordie begged him, his young boy's voice breaking the spell.

"He'll be giving you nightmares for months," Marsali said angrily as she marched up to the tree to untie the children.

"But we like being tied up," Gemma said with a shy smile. "It's fun."

Duncan leaned back on his elbow, chuckling at Marsali's efforts to undo his knots. Her tangled curls covered her flushed face. The agitated rhythm of her breathing thrust her breasts out against her dress. God, he wanted her, and last night had only made it worse.

"What happens after we're flogged senseless, my lord?" Gordie demanded, shying away from Marsali in irritation. "What if we still haven't learned our lesson?"

"Well, depending on how much blood you've lost, and if you're still conscious . . ."

Marsali paled. "Don't you dare say another word, my lord."

"We might just leave you standing there a little longer to let the suffering soak in."

Marsali thrust her hand to her mouth, then recovered and began tugging at the knots in frustration; somehow, for all her struggling, she only managed to tie them all the tighter.

"It's all right, Auntie Marsali," Keith said in an undertone. "He took us prisoner."

"Aye," she said, "the barbarian, tying up helpless bairns."

"But we like it," Keith explained in a patient whisper. "It's only a game, after all."

Marsali dug her heels into the ground, her face turning purple with exertion as she grunted. "Aye . . . you'll be tied to this . . . damn . . . tree forever, by the look of . . . it."

Duncan rolled onto his back, remembering how sweet and ripe for seduction she had been last night in his arms. Then a startled "O-o-o-oh!" broke his train of thought, and he sat up to see Marsali come flying backward through the air. Before he could roll out of her path, she went tumbling over his shoulders.

His world went black, an explosion of delectable if conflicting sensations. Her skirts impeded his vision; the scent of her skin unleashed a sea of dangerous impulses in his blood. He grabbed her around the knees. She pounded on his back, laughing and cursing him for tying those damned knots in the first place. Obviously she had forgotten about the children.

He'd forgotten about them too. Then Marsali gave him a warning nudge. Sighing, he plunked her to the ground.

"My knots aren't meant to come undone," he said with a lazy smile. "That's the whole point. I keep what I take."

The children, not realizing he was waging an entirely different kind of tactical assault on their young aunt, attacked without warning. Gordie and the other boys jumped on his shoulders. The twins pounced on his feet. Wee Claire bombarded him with old acorns. Gemma tickled him.

"Shall we tie him up, Auntie Marsali?" Keith asked breathlessly, helping Dara to unravel the line from the tree.

Marsali backed away slowly, her heart heavy with poignant awareness as she watched Duncan gently wrestle the boisterous children, who pummeled and pounded him without mercy. It was almost impossible to reconcile this playful giant with the arbitrary chieftain who had only last night broken her heart.

"Tie him up," she said with forced cheerfulness, wishing that a simple rope were all that she needed to bind him to her.

Because she loved him.

Because she could not bear it if he left.

Chapter

26

Marsali could not believe she'd let the clan talk her into a midnight raid. The men had waylaid her as she was returning from Bride's cottage to the moor. Save us from the Sassenachs, lass, they had begged her. 'Tis time to take action, they'd insisted. She had ignored her instincts, not wanting to disappoint them, determined to take a stand to defend their homes.

Now she thought she might be sick to her stomach. Her nerves were tangled into knots of anxiety. It was one thing to order a Sassenach officer to strip naked on the moor on a breezy summer day. It was quite another to attack a stout British fortress teaming with fully dressed soldiers. In the middle of the night.

Especially when you were basically unarmed and commanding the sorrowful, untrained troops of Clan MacElgin. And you had no idea what the hell you were doing.

"Right." She released a terse breath and maneuvered her horse to the front lines. "Lachlan, you remember what you're supposed to do?"

"Aye, lass." He smothered a yawn. "I supervise the others in pushing the supply wagons off the cliffs."

"And all of you understand that there's to be no violence?"

The dozen or so heads nodded in agreement. Ailis and Alan snorted, rollicking among the herbage of the sparse garden that lay outside the fortress. Marsali could only pray that the crashing of waves against the cliffs would muffle their furtive movements.

"Right."

"You've already said that, Marsali," Effie reminded her quietly.

"I dinna see why ye're so edgy, lass," Owen added. "If we get caught, ye can always use yer magic to save us."

Marsali looked up at the dark bulky fortress. "Aye, and that's what's worrying me." She sniffed around her in displeasure. "Good heavens, Lachlan, what is that odor coming from your saddlebags?"

"It's me hard-boiled eggs, lass."

"I thought we'd agreed to bring no weapons."

"They're not for throwing, Marsali, they're for eating. I canna be pushing heavy weapons into the sea on an empty stomach."

She swallowed dryly, raising her hand to give the signal to disperse. "Right."

"Three times now," Effie murmured. "That's ill luck fer certain—I have a bad feeling about this. We should have asked the chieftain to help us."

"Mind your tongue and keep those damned pigs in line, Effie," Marsali said. "If the chieftain had wanted to help us, we wouldn't be here right now, would we?"

She slowly lowered her hand and slid to the ground, suppressing a shiver as her troops melted into the mist like ghosties. She had a bad feeling about this one too, but it couldn't be as bad as standing by while the English blew up homes and hills. Could it?

Marsali was never going to ignore a bad feeling again.

The attack had gone sour from the start.

Owen began the streak of rotten luck by running a cart over Johnnie's foot and breaking his big toe, which had caused such a row between them that the sentries on the watchtower had interrupted their dice game to investigate.

No sooner had the soldiers returned to their game than Lachlan crammed three hard-boiled eggs into his mouth, choked, and erupted into a coughing fit. At this point Marsali seriously thought about calling off the operation. But in the excitement of saving Lachlan's life, Effie's pigs—hating to hear anyone argue—had sauntered off for a midnight stroll.

Effie burst into hysterics. "Oh, my God. They've gone into the kitchens! Look, that's Alan's wee bonnet outside the door. The Sassenachs are going to eat my puir piggies. Oh, my God! Help me! Do something!"

"Pigs are meant to be eaten, Effie," Owen said, which of course wasn't the most comforting comment to make under the circumstances.

They were crouched, the five of them, under one of the tarps covering the supply wagons, which they'd rolled, one painstaking inch at a time, across the courtyard. The other clansmen were stationed at the gate and on the cliffs.

Johnnie lowered his spyglass, his weathered face grim. "We'll have to rescue them."

"Aye," Lachlan agreed. "The twins are a MacElgin tradition." He glanced up expectantly at Marsali. "Well, what shall we do, lass?"

She patted Effie absentmindedly on the back. "We'll need a diversion."

"I could go back to the castle and fetch Cook and the scullery maids for reinforcements," Owen suggested.

Marsali shook her head. "There isn't time. Ailis and Alan could end up as breakfast sausages before then—er, sorry, Effie."

"We could light a fire," Johnnie said, pointing toward the fortress. "Look at the pile of wood over there under that window."

Marsali bit her lip, wishing suddenly that she had asked for Duncan's help. But she hadn't, and he would have refused to intervene anyway, so the whole thing was neither here nor there, and as usual the responsibility had landed like a bomb in her lap.

"Right," she said, her small jaw tersely set. "Effie and I will chase down the twins while Johnnie and Owen light the fire. Lachlan, you'll stand guard outside the kitchen."

It was a simple plan. At this time of night it should have

worked, and it probably would have—except for the fact that Major Darling's personal quarters lay behind the window overlooking the woodpile. And an annoying case of heartburn had just gotten him out of bed.

Duncan stared down at the letters on his desk. One was a personal invitation from Prince Eugene of Savoy to inspect his Royal Horsemen. Another was from the British War Office, stating that the dukedom was definitely in the offing and a trip to London was strongly suggested. There was even one from Sarah, hinting that her marriage was a mistake. She missed Duncan. Was he ever coming back to England?

The long-awaited words wavered in the candlelight; they dared him to react.

He glanced up at the window, dark amusement playing across his face.

He wasn't thinking about wars, or horses, or duchies, or lost loves. He was thinking about *her*. Haunted by her. He had come to crave the peace and laughter he enjoyed only in her company. Yes, he actually looked forward to whatever trouble she had brewed up in her cauldron of good causes. That was the true magic of Marsali: her ability to turn the most mundane daily event into an adventure with her mischievous spirit. He had witnessed so much violence in his life that her sweetness was a balm to his soul.

He threw down his pen. Time was running out to make a decision about her future. It would have been unfair to keep her from Jamie MacFay if she'd really wanted to marry the fool.

And Duncan hadn't exactly helped matters by trying to seduce her last night. God, he could hear Andrew Hay cursing from his burial cairn. He could hear—

Footsteps. Soft, furtive, right outside his door.

He rose from the desk, hoping to see Marsali's bright face peeping around the door as it opened. If she asked to play "dolls" again, he wouldn't yell his head off. He would agree. He would enjoy the short time they had left together. Pray God they would come to a mutually satisfying decision about her future.

"Abercrombie."

Disappointment sharpened Duncan's voice as the man crept into the circle of candlelight. Like one of the castle rats, he usually only appeared at night, and then it was to scurry back and forth to his chamber on whatever covert missions of madness occupied his mind.

"What do you want?"

Abercrombie's eyes danced with glee. "They've been arrested, my lord."

"Who has been arrested?" Duncan asked as dread sank its talons into his composure. Because he knew. And Abercrombie knew he knew.

"The witch and her coven, my lord. Major Darling has taken them into custody."

"Where?" Duncan asked, wondering why the hell he hadn't made his life easier by clapping the bloody lot of them in the dungeon the first day he'd arrived.

"At the fortress, my lord," Abercrombie said excitedly. He trailed Duncan around the room. "They tried to set it on fire. The fortress. 'Twas almost an act of war. Can you imagine?"

"The fortress," Duncan repeated, his face white. He stared accusingly at the tall figure in a dressing gown who had just squeezed through the door behind Abercrombie. "Did you know anything about Marsali trying to torch the British barracks, Edwina?"

Edwina recoiled in horror, her rag curls quivering. "She didn't. Dear God."

"I tried to warn you, my lord," Abercrombie began. "I told you . . ."

He subsided into terrified silence as Duncan began to advance on him with his arm outstretched, his face a study in black fury.

"Dinna hit me, my lord. I had nothing to do with it. Dinna—"

Duncan reached over Abercrombie's cowering head to remove the scarlet coat and cockaded hat he'd slung on a medieval crest mounted on the wall. He would have to play the part of General MacElgin tonight to avert a charge of treason.

"I'll get your sword," Edwina said, "and I'm coming with you."

Duncan swung around, his hat shadowing the harsh planes of his face. "No. I can manage alone."

"I'm not coming for your sake, Duncan," Edwina said with a stern frown. "I'm helping Marsali. Someone has to protect her from you."

They were trapped.

British soldiers had backed them up against the high stone wall of the courtyard. Major Darling was yelling orders while he tucked his nightshirt into his hastily donned trousers. Effie's porkers were running loose in the confusion, giving shrill squeals of distress.

Johnnie threw out his arms to shield Marsali and Effie from the gunfire they expected to shatter the eerie spell of predawn silence. The soldiers inched cautiously closer.

"That's the end of us," Effie lamented in a loud whisper.

"Aye, and all fer yer pigs, which are goin' to end up getting eaten anyway," Owen couldn't resist complaining.

Marsali peered over Johnnie's shoulder, through the mist at the line of muskets leveled at her cornered battalion. "We can't just stand here and get shot," she said stoutly. "We have to do something."

"Get off my toe, Marsali." Johnnie grimaced as she crept around him. "And stay put so that if they shoot us, I'll be the one to go first."

"Be careful, men!" Major Darling shouted, looking more absurd than alarming with a bayonet protruding from his armpit. "They could be armed and dangerous."

"We aren't armed," Marsali shouted back. "Except for Lachlan's hard-boiled eggs, and those are for eating."

"Aye," Effie chimed in. "We aren't dangerous either."

"Except to ourselves," Johnnie muttered as he found himself staring down the barrel of a musket.

Suddenly a young soldier came pelting across the courtyard. "We've rounded up the rest of the enemy, sir. They were hiding on the cliffs—at least a hundred of 'em."

"Find the ringleader," Major Darling said in a terse voice.

"It was me," Johnnie announced, hobbling forward to bravely face the major. "I'm the man ye want."

"No, he isn't," Marsali said. She sidestepped Johnnie, her head held high. "I'm your man."

Effie shouldered a position between Marsali and Johnnie. "So am I."

"And the other two standing against the wall?" Major Darling asked in a dry voice.

Owen and Lachlan didn't answer. Marsali straightened to her full, unintimidating height. "You can let the others go. I'm the one who forced them to come here tonight."

The major stared down into her small defiant face. "By God," he said softly, "you're MacElgin's little clanswoman. I warned him what would happen if he didn't watch you. Do you know what the punishment will be for what you've done tonight?"

Marsali swallowed, the cruel implication in his eyes challenging her courage. "You can let the others go now," she repeated, feeling Effie snatch her hand for moral support.

"But I can't let them go." The major frowned, looking none too pleased himself at the realization. "In fact, none of you will ever be 'let go' again. As traitors to the Crown, you face a very unappealing fate."

Marsali could sense her four companions staring at her, waiting in hopeful silence for a solution. The first rays of sunrise had pierced the pewter clouds rolling across the sky. The air grew still. She glanced skyward and saw Eun circling above the distant cliffs. He was too far away to be of any help. Once again she was on her own.

She knew what she had to do.

"Stand back," she told Effie and Johnnie in a low voice.

Johnnie looked down at her in concern. "Be careful, lass," he whispered.

Effie gave her another reassuring squeeze before disengaging their hands. "Good luck, Marsali. You're the best friend I ever had."

She nodded stiffly. She took an enormous breath. She raised her gaze heavenward again. The trembling started in the soles of her feet. It worked its way upward to tickle her palms, coursing into her arms, her shoulders, her scalp, until the ends of her hair lifted. Static cracked from her fingertips.

Thunder growled in the distance. A gust of wind raced across the courtyard. A few of the soldiers backstepped in alarm.

"It's only another one of those blasted Highland storms," Major Darling said impatiently. "There's no reason—"

Whatever else he'd meant to say was lost as a bolt of lightning struck the ground between him and Marsali. A white-blue flash illuminated the grin of victory that spread across her face. Owen and Lachlan began hopping up and down like a pair of gleeful rabbits. Major Darling's mouth clacked open and shut in astonishment.

"You let us go now," Marsali told the major with arrogant dignity. "I made that lightning and I can make it happen again on your fat Sassenach head."

"Then do it," he said quietly.

Her smile faded. She couldn't "do it" again, at least not that fast. "Give me a minute," she said, casting a nervous glance back at her companions, who were huddled back together in a frightened ball.

She took a deep breath. She voiced a silent prayer. She turned back to the major, slowly raising her arms. Nothing happened. She tried again.

His smile stopped her cold.

"Arrest them," he said simply.

Duncan stared across the clutter of military maps and sketches on the major's desk and prayed he would wake up to find this was all a nightmare. His dukedom and cabinet position were going up in smoke before his eyes. His worst fear had been realized.

The major's voice, tinged with a frustration he could not suppress, droned on: ". . . arrested thirteen Scottish traitors in all, which included nine men, two extremely belligerent women, and two"—he glanced up at Duncan—"pigs, a male and female."

Duncan leaned across the desk, his face so fierce that Major Darling swallowed involuntarily. "I want them released."

"Released, my lord? But that's impossible. They were

caught red-handed trying to torch the fortress. The punishment for—"

Duncan rose from his chair, his broad shoulders blocking out the light of the single wall sconce. "I assume you value your position, Major," he said without inflection. "But they weren't trying to torch the fort. They were rescuing pigs."

Major Darling rose to his feet, uncertain which would kill him first: his heartburn or the intimidating Scotsman whose courage on the battlefield was said to border on insanity. He wished he could go back to bed and pretend the whole preposterous incident had never happened.

"I will pay personally for any damages incurred by my clansmen," Duncan said in a tired voice as he turned toward the door. "You have my word this will not happen again."

"I'll have to make a report."

Duncan pivoted, the lines of his face tightening in displeasure.

"I . . . I'll have to," Major Darling said defensively, pride demanding he at least win this point.

"You'll report that a handful of unarmed Highlanders slipped past your guard, Major? That the garrison under your guard was besieged by a pair of pigs?"

Major Darling sagged back against his desk. "Dear God." An unwilling laugh erupted from his chest. "I'll look like a bloody fool."

Duncan smiled reluctantly. "So will I."

"No one would believe it anyway."

"Probably not."

The major sobered. "Except that they destroyed the sovereign's property."

"The property will be replaced."

"There has been a strange ship sighted off the cove, my lord. French spies, perhaps."

Duncan frowned. Jamie's ship? Well, Jamie was a staunch Jacobite and a troublemaker to boot. That was all he needed to lead his clan into more danger. "If there is a ship, then investigate it. It had nothing to do with my clan."

"I ought to write that report."

Duncan's heart stopped. "Please—a personal favor."

The two men stared at each other across the desk, and

Thomas Darling marveled that MacElgin could be reduced to pleading when in reality he held the major's future in his very palm.

"It won't happen again." Duncan put on his black cockaded hat, his face suddenly cold. "I'll take care of her. You have my word."

Chapter

27

Duncan slammed the bedchamber door so hard that an ivory cherubim candlestick bounced off the nightstand. As it hit the stone floor, he dumped Marsali at his feet with a grunt of grim satisfaction.

She darted around him, pretending to investigate the damage. She was grateful for any distraction from his horrible temper, which had been preceded by his horrible silence during the endless ride back to the castle.

"Oh, dear," she said. "You've broken the angel's wing right off."

He stared down fiercely at her gracefully formed body, outlined by the damp muslin skirts that clung to her every curve. A downpour on the ride home had drenched them both to the teeth. Duncan had been so disgusted with her that he couldn't even shout.

At least not until they reached the castle courtyard, and she had the incredible brass to tell him, proudly, "I caused that rainstorm, you know. There wasn't a cloud in the sky until I made it happen."

He'd shouted at her then. And he'd dragged her by the waist across the courtyard and into the castle. Several clansmen had covered their ears to block out the shouting, especially when Marsali started to give as good as she was getting. But no one had dared intervene. Word of the crushing defeat at the fortress had broken the clan's feeble spirit. Even Cook couldn't bring herself to hit anyone until late that morning, and then it was only a half-hearted swipe with a slotted spoon.

"Take your clothes off, Marsali."

"Why?" She straightened, shivering, and lifted her hand to unbutton her bodice. She was hoping that all their shouting in the courtyard had taken the edge off his beastly temper. "Are we going to lie down together without our clothes on like we did in my uncle's cabin?"

Duncan closed his eyes, praying for control. By some aberration of human nature, her absurd innocence had managed to bypass his anger and arouse him, invoking flagrantly sexual images of fantasies he had tried all summer to suppress. And he definitely needed a woman. Self-denial might be a necessity during battle, but it wasn't a practice he enjoyed.

She tiptoed up behind him. "You're angry at me, aren't you?"

His shoulders stiffened when he spoke. "You risked your life and my name. Should I be angry at you?"

"Somebody had to stop them from pulling down our homes."

He was silent. He did not move. He did not trust himself to look at her.

I'm naked, my lord," she announced. "What are we going to do now?"

Against his better judgment Duncan turned to regard her, swallowing a groan. She stood nude before him in a puddle of rain-splattered muslin without an ounce of inhibition. Her lithe body blushed a becoming pink from the morning's excitement. Her small breasts peeked out from behind her waist-length tangle of dark red hair. Tiny, tantalizing, infuriating.

His mind turned to stone while the rest of his body literally pulsed with the most primitive of life's urges. "Dear God." He drew a breath. He calculated the distance to the bed. He was a bastard. He had always been a bastard.

"Come here, lass," he said quietly.

She did, like a lamb led to the slaughter.

He watched her, and hated himself.

"What . . ." she began, but the rest of the words fled her mind as he dragged her into his arms, inhaling her scent, capturing her in an inescapable vise.

She buckled at the knees. He caught her, easily supporting her weight. His mouth brushed her wet tangled hair. His warm breath was a whisper of sensation against her earlobe. Then he tipped her head back and kissed her with a soul-deep hunger that no other woman in the world could satisfy. He kissed her and damned the darkness in himself for doing so.

Marsali did not move. Her head swam. She had wanted this. She had waited for it all summer. His strength excited her. She grasped great handfuls of his damp linen shirt. His mouth devoured hers, tasting of passion and anguish. She drew a breath and stood on tiptoe to kiss him back with all the love and desire she had hidden in her heart. She kissed him with the irresistible power of innocence.

"God," he said in a broken voice, as if she had wounded him.

He thrust against her until he had backed her into the bedpost. He unbuttoned his shirt with an impatient tug and gathered her against his bare chest. A groan of bliss escaped him at the forbidden flesh-to-flesh contact. He pressed his forehead to hers and felt his body shake in a shock of anticipation.

"Marsali."

She stared into his eyes, drawn into the depths of dark inscrutable emotion. The barriers between them had fallen, and she was suddenly frightened at the power of their attraction to each other, feelings unfettered and given rein.

Her body felt swollen, aroused. She was aware of the sheer size of him, the hard shaft that pressed against her belly. He kissed her breasts. She gasped at the sweet, raw sensation. He traced his tongue across the sensitive tips until she closed her eyes and gripped his forearms, until her back arched and her hair fell in a tangle across her face.

"I wish I had never met you," he whispered roughly, running his large hands down the length of her spine. Then in the next tormented breath: "They could have killed you, lass, and I'd have lost my mind."

He dropped to his knees before her, his hands cradling her hips. Through the haze of black-red desire that clouded his mind, he prayed she would resist. But she was no match for his experience, and he could feel her responding, the telltale tremors that rocked her delicate frame as he traced his tongue across her belly. With a shudder of sexual arousal, he inhaled the private musk that rose like perfume from her skin. He could take her in a heartbeat.

"Make me stop." He raised his dark face to hers.

She shook her head. She touched her hand to his cheek, the black stubble that shadowed the hard contours of his jaw. "But I love you," she said, as if no other explanation were necessary. "Why should I want you to stop?"

He swallowed the warning that rose in his throat. His gaze hooded, his breathing uneven, he brought his hand down the back of her thigh, around to the delta of her womanhood. His fingers caressed the damp tangle of curls and brushed the distended tissue beneath.

"How lovely you are." His voice broke on a hoarse exhalation of breath. "Sweet," he said, closing his eyes to fight the surge of sexual excitement in his system.

Master. Conquer. Dominate. On the floor, in the bed, against the wall. Images of raw male aggression and female surrender flashed across his mind. Soft white skin yielding to his. Her delicate body sheathing him in its depths.

She was so small, every feature sculptured in fragile perfection, every curve a dainty enticement. He had never been as aware of his own size, his own power, before. He had never held a fairy in his hands.

She folded down onto her knees before him, placing her palm on his chest, feeling his heart hammering at her touch. "Duncan."

He opened his eyes, summoning the self-control of a lifetime to reject the melting sweetness she was ready to lay at his feet.

"No. Don't," he said, almost angrily, pushing her hand away. "Don't touch me. Get off the floor. I'll hurt you if this doesn't stop. You don't understand anything, Marsali.

You're willful and unworldly, and if you'd been shot down with those other imbeciles last night it would have been your own damned fault."

Her eyes blazed with emotion, puzzled and resentful. "At least I made an attempt to protect those homes. Which is more than I can say for our chieftain."

He gripped her wrists in his hand, his mouth tightening into a cynical line. "Those homes were not going to be touched, my dear. I had Major Darling's word on it, which won't be worth spit now."

"But why didn't you tell me?" she whispered, her face waxen in its frame of unruly curls.

"Because I talked to him only yesterday afternoon, and I never dreamed you'd do something so incredibly outlandish as attack a fortress. Do you realize the risk you took? This could well be the end of my reputation."

"Duncan, I'm sorry," she said in a raw whisper.

He swallowed hard. "I'm sorry too. For everything that's happened this summer. And for what I have to do." He released her hands. "I could have handled things more wisely. I let my feelings for your father interfere. Get up."

"Duncan."

He went rigid at the appeal in her voice.

He made to rise, but she caught his sleeve, holding him with all her strength. "I don't like the sound of that. What are you going to do?"

"Let go of my sleeve." He turned his face away. He couldn't bear to look at her, knowing she would never forgive him. "Put on some dry clothes, for God's sake, or we won't ever leave this room."

She stared at him, twining her fingers in his sleeve, baffled and hurt. "I love you, Duncan."

"Don't." Shadows stirred in the depths of his eyes. "Don't love me. I'm a born murderer, Marsali. You were right when you said that making war was my world. The others before you were right about me too."

She refused to accept the finality in his voice. He was hers. Her wounded warrior. She lifted his hand to her mouth and kissed his battle-scarred knuckles. "I don't care. Whatever you did happened years ago. I don't care what anyone has said about you."

Her unconditional acceptance should have been a balm to Duncan's heart; instead it stung like vinegar on unhealed hurts. She was naive. How could she possibly love him when he could not love himself?

"You should care what people say. You should listen well." His voice was fierce. He jerked his hand from hers, her gentle touch arousing needs that could never be fulfilled.

Her gaze met his, and he felt a stab of anguish at the unspoken question in her eyes. Had he murdered his parents? Was it possible? Could the darkest rumor be a reality?

"No," she said. She swallowed. She rocked back onto her bare heels. "No."

He stared down at his hands. "Yes," he said in a low emotionless voice.

She didn't move, searching his face in stunned silence. Then slowly she rose to her knees and awkwardly put her arms around his shoulders, trying to comfort him. His muscles stiffened in protest even as his heart ached with the human need to be held, forgiven, understood. He lifted his hand to touch her, seeking surcease from his pain, then stopped the impulse.

"I stabbed my father to death after I watched him kill my mother. They were fighting because she had fed me the last of the meat pie during supper. He always hated me. He always knew I wasn't his."

His voice was quiet. It was the first time since that night that he had admitted aloud what had happened. The memories flashed across his mind with sickening clarity. Staring up at the sooty ceiling to block out the ugly scene between Fergus and his mother, his sister huddled next to him in the loft, cringing at the sound of raised voices below. Then the hitting, the punches, the kicking, and finally a silence that was the most ominous sound of all.

He'd jumped to the uneven earthen floor and flung himself at Fergus; Duncan had been tall and strong for a boy his age. From the corner of his eye he glimpsed his mother lying across the hearth. Pale, unmoving, a knife wedged between her ribs. As delicate and helpless in death as she had been in life.

Duncan lost control. All the fear and helpless anger of his young lifetime erupted. He rammed his head into Fergus's chest, forcing him back against the ladder. He barely felt the wooden staff that struck his own face and shoulders, Fergus fighting back with drunken fury. He barely realized when the blows stopped, when Fergus fell forward and his own dirk protruded from Fergus's throat.

He stared into Marsali's stricken eyes.

"You're the only person besides my sister and your father to know the truth. Andrew never questioned me again after that first night. He believed me." Duncan's voice dropped to a raw whisper. "He never judged me. He believed me."

Tears misted Marsali's vision. "I believe you."

He averted his face. "Get up, Marsali. I have to pack. Get up before I convince even myself that I haven't a shred of decency in my soul."

"But I love you," she said in bewilderment. "No matter what you've done."

He rose without looking down, leaving her naked and as still as a glass figurine on the floor. Fragile. As if she would break if he touched her again. His chest tightened as he bent to lift the brass-bound chest at the foot of the bed into his arms. Ruining her would not be added to his long list of sins.

Marsali frowned, slowly rising to her feet.

His face unreadable, he took the chest to the wardrobe and began to methodically fill it with every last article of her clothing.

"Where are your things?" She glanced up from the chest with a suspicious frown. "Have you already packed? And where are you going, anyway?"

He leaned his shoulder against the wardrobe door, turning slowly to answer her. "The Isle of Inverothes. My sister's convent is located there."

"No." She stared, her face shocked and angry, as the words finally penetrated her mind. "To bloody hell with you, Duncan MacElgin. I'd rather go to gaol for treason."

A low cynical laugh escaped him. "You don't go to gaol for treason, little girl. First you're hanged, then cut down while you struggle to breathe so that the executioners can disembowel you. If they've done their job properly, you'll still be alive to experience the agony of having them roast your entrails—and chop you into little pieces to put on public display."

Her throat thickened with unshed tears of betrayal; she backed away from him, catching her heel in her own wet clothes.

"I'm not going," she said.

"You will go, lass. I'm taking you myself."

"Then I won't stay. Are you going to watch over me night and day? Do you really think a handful of nuns will be able to keep me there?"

"If you set one foot outside the convent, one tiny disobedient toe, your little army will be arrested and tried for treason. That's a promise."

His coldbloodedness turned her blood to ice. He meant it. The ruthless devil would betray the very people he'd been born to protect. "How could you?" she whispered, recoiling as if he were a monster.

He flinched inwardly at the disgust on her face. "I had no choice," he said. "Blame yourself if you must blame anyone. The price of your freedom was my promise to Major Darling that I would keep you out of his way until his road is finished."

She spun clumsily to avoid him, staring at the turret. Aye, she thought in mounting wrath, he had trapped her again. Duncan knew she would never hurt those she loved. He had used her own softness to manipulate her. He knew her too well.

She felt him come up behind her. Her body reacted with a traitorous rush of longing at his nearness, but it was squelched by the misery and confusion that swamped her.

"I'm doing what I believe is best, lass." He took her by the shoulders, turning her rigid body until she faced him. "Your dress is on the floor," he said quietly.

"Don't." She shied away from him, her delicate face hurt and defiant. "Don't touch me, Duncan. It makes it worse when you pretend to care."

"I do care, Marsali."

"Then stay here." She fought against tears, hating and loving him so much she thought her heart would crack in two. "You belong to us, my lord."

He shook his head. "There are too many ghosts in this castle. Do you not understand?"

"If you're going to send me away, the least you can do is stay to lead the clan. *Someone* has got to stop them from killing themselves."

"Not me."

She hardened herself to the brief spasm of anguish he had allowed to show on his face. "Then I don't understand. I cannot fathom what you say and do any more than I can the waters of the loch. All I know is that you have no loyalty or love inside you for your own. No wonder Edwina's niece left you."

Chapter

28

The mournful voices of her clansmen echoed in Marsali's ears as she trudged over the drawbridge to her fate. Even the chickens in the moat had fallen silent. Not a squawk or scratch to disturb the sad event. The skull and crossbones hung at half-mast from the parapets.

"Goodbye, lass. 'Tis a dark day for Clan MacElgin."

"'Tis a cruel end, Marsali."

"We'll never forget ye."

"Give the nuns hell, lassie."

Cook shook Marsali's hand. "Ye're no the first Scotswoman to learn the meaning of sacrifice, but ye're one of the best. I'm proud to have known you."

Effie stood in the barbican spouting tears like a faucet. "The twins and I will miss ye, Marsali," she said between loud emotional sniffles.

Marsali stared out across the moor, as stoic as a saint. Fiona and her uncle watched from the distant circle of standing stones. Colum's blue robes blended into the unbounded wash of summer sky, reminding Marsali of her own impending captivity. Despair swept over her.

"Fat-witted old wizard," she said under her breath. "Some help your magic has been."

Duncan's tall figure cast a shadow on her path. "The boat is waiting. Hurry up, Marsali."

Johnnie, Lachlan, and Owen were almost too upset to approach her. Then Johnnie snagged her hand.

"Nothing is forever, lass," he whispered gruffly. "If ye ken what I'm saying."

Unfortunately, she did. They planned to rescue her. But the well-meaning morons would probably only drown on the short sea voyage to the island. She didn't want that on her conscience.

"Stay and take care of the clan," she said bravely. "I'll manage somehow."

Then Duncan clamped his hand down on her shoulder. She flinched. Despite all that had happened, his touch still set off wonderful flurries of sensations. A bittersweet pang pierced her heart as she recalled the day not long ago when they had stood in this same spot. How wrong she had been about him.

"I should have let the drawbridge fall on your head, my lord."

"Perhaps you should have," Duncan replied, guiding her from the barbican with an inscrutable look. "But you didn't, lass."

"You haven't gotten this young woman pregnant, have you, Duncan?"

The blunt question dashed Duncan's hope for a heart-warming reunion. The woman who sat behind her desk could give him lessons in military composure. The angular but attractive face beneath the wimple exuded more disappointment than sisterly affection.

"That question irritates the hell out of me." He paused, still in his chair, distracted by the sound of Marsali swearing her head off outside the door. "Listen to that."

"Aye." Judith's voice was wry. "She swears like a soldier—I wonder where she could have learned that. And I've prayed so hard that you had changed."

Duncan bowed his head, in no mood to argue. What was the point? Judith, of all people, could never forget the things he'd done.

"I do hope you'll at least have the decency to provide for the child once it's born, Duncan," she said heavily. "We are a modest convent. True, we have wealthy benefactors—"

He surged out of his chair. "Marsali Hay is *not* pregnant, and I intend to keep it that way until she's married."

Judith straightened her shoulders, staring up at him in surprise. "I see. Then it seems I've been wrong about you after all."

He shrugged, staring out the window as five nuns struggled in breathless frustration to drag Marsali to her cell. The foul language peppering the sea air might have turned his sister's head, but Duncan knew Judith had heard far worse from her father growing up.

"I never thought to see you again," she said, her voice softer as the swearing outside faded away. "You've done very well by the world's standards."

He glanced at her. "Are you happy here?"

"Yes." She hesitated. "Content is a better word."

An uncomfortable pause fell. Sometimes, in rare moments of doubt, Judith still wondered why God had allowed it all to happen. Why He had let Fergus murder her mother. Why Duncan, in turn, had stabbed Fergus to death in a killing rage she had never dreamed her poor abused brother capable of.

"I could have tried to stop you," she said in a hushed voice. "I was as guilty as you for what happened that night." She stared across the room. "I wanted it to happen."

Duncan came up to her chair and placed his hands on her shoulders. "I don't condone what I did, but he deserved to die. Have you forgotten what he did to you?"

Tears came to her eyes. "No." She stared up into his troubled face, wishing she could smooth away the pain etched into its chiseled planes. "You were our only hero, our champion," she said softly. "What a burden you carry."

"All that blood, Judith." His voice was weary. "My life has been one extended battle after another. No one has ever guessed how the smell of death makes me sick to my stomach." He expelled a deep sigh. "I don't want to kill anymore."

"Then don't. No one can force you, can they?"

He didn't answer. How could she understand the worldly enticements, the lust for power that she had renounced for her serene isolation?

"They want me to take a place in the War Ministry," he said. "To use my knowledge to oversee other battles. If the Jacobite rebellions continue, I could be ordered to suppress my own people."

Judith's face brightened. "Unless you used your knowledge as a weapon for peace. From what I gather, your influence is considerable."

Her words lit a spark of hope in his heart. It was true. He had power, respect, the ear of the world's leaders. "Perhaps," he said thoughtfully.

She placed her hand on his. "Have you found no peace at all for yourself?"

"No. Except . . ."

The poignant face took form in his mind. He wanted to forget her. He wanted to sever the thread of tangled feelings that threatened to hold his heart.

For one wild whimsical summer she had dispelled the darkness. The mere memory of her flared like a candle flame and warmed him.

"Marsali," he said, not even aware he had spoken the name aloud.

Judith looked surprised. "The girl who was cursing like a little buccaneer outside?"

"Aye, that one." An unwilling smile crept across his face. "Good luck with her, Judith."

"I don't like that tone, Duncan. How long am I supposed to keep her here?"

"Until I find her a husband." He moved back to the window, suddenly self-conscious. "She's Andrew Hay's daughter."

"And?"

And I want her for myself. And I can't keep my murdering hands off her. And she's convinced she loves me.

He lifted his wide shoulders in a shrug. Her gaze was too perceptive. They had shared too much for secrets. "There's a young Jacobite Highlander named MacFay who didn't take kindly to my rejecting his suit. Marsali is not to be released to *anyone* until her future is settled."

"I suppose that is wise."

"Not to anyone, Judith. I wouldn't put it past MacFay to bribe or bully his way into your convent."

"A determined suitor. I've dealt with a few in my time. Your wee charge will be safe with us. Do you want to say goodbye to the girl?"

Duncan hesitated. The last look Marsali had flung him from the convent gate had burned with rage and resentment. "No. It would only make it worse."

"For you or for her?"

Before he could answer, a clap of thunder rumbled in the distance. "Oh, no," Judith said in dismay. "My seedlings will be washed away if it rains. There wasn't a cloud in the sky when I planted them this morning."

Duncan turned to the door, then paused as a twinge of guilt thwarted the impulse to escape. "There's something else you should know about Marsali."

Judith rose from her chair. "I don't like the sound of that, either. Or that sheepish grin on your face. Exactly what is wrong with the girl?"

"It's just that some people seem to think she's a witch."

"A witch."

"Silly, isn't it?" He backed into the door at the look of alarm on Judith's face. "Don't worry. She's a good witch, if you even believe in such things."

"Duncan . . ."

"I'll send money regularly for her upkeep," he said hastily, not giving her the chance to change her mind. "Remember, she's not to be released to anyone. Her life could depend upon it. The MacFays are an old-fashioned lawless clan."

Then he was gone.

Judith stood by the window, shaking her head in bemusement.

There were no answers.

Not even after a decade of contemplation and self-sacrifice. All she could conclude was that because of their tragic experience that night in the cottage, Duncan had given his life to violence and she had committed hers to helping women and children in similar situations.

More than once God had enabled her to save a young life.

There was healing in that, if not the answers she sought. But her brother's heart was still at war with the past. She wished devoutly to help him.

And now, after fifteen years with only an occasional letter sent from some foreign country, he had left this fey young creature on her doorstep. A witch, he'd said. A girl he obviously coveted for himself but respected too much to ruin. He had done the honorable thing.

Her prayers *had* worked. He'd learned to control his wildness. But Judith knew that God wasn't finished with her brother yet.

She bowed her head and clasped her hands, preparing to wage her own mode of battle. If Duncan had risen in the ranks of the world's military, Judith was herself quite practiced in the art of spiritual warfare. Her brother lived by power, she by faith; and, like Duncan, she would never admit defeat.

"I really didn't mean to make Sister Isobel faint dead away, Reverend Mother. I didn't think anyone could hear me when I dropped the washtub on my foot."

"The Lord is always listening, Marsali. Your language is inexcusable."

"I learned it from Duncan. I overheard him using it in the castle chapel."

"The chapel? My brother blasphemed—he used *those* words in a chapel?"

"You'd better sit down, Reverend Mother. You've gone all pale. Yes, it's true. He used worse words too, but I can't remember them. Don't worry, though, they'll probably come back to me during Mass."

"I really didn't mean to make the holy water come spurting up like that, Reverend Mother."

"Then why did you do it, Marsali? More to the point, *how* did you do it?"

"Well, I was experimenting with my powers, you see. And I'm getting much better at it. It was just bad luck that you happened to pass by when I made it rise."

"You're not to use those 'powers' again, Marsali. Whether anyone is passing by or not."

"I'll try, Reverend Mother."

"I really didn't mean to make it rain so hard this afternoon, Reverend Mother. I was only practicing to see if I could make a rainbow appear. They're such lovely things to look at."

"You ought to practice prayer and meditation, Marsali. Our patroness was not at all pleased to have to sail all the way back home in the storm you caused."

"I'll try harder next time. I really will."

"I'm starving to death, Reverend Mother. Pinch my wrist. Practically skin and bones."

"The next time I catch you trying to escape over the wall, Marsali, your punishment will be far worse than a one-day fast. Do you understand?"

"Yes, Reverend Mother."

"Go to your cell. You are to remain there until the calling bell. Well, what is it? Why do you stand there staring?"

"I just can't get over it, Reverend Mother. I'd never have guessed you had the strength to come climbing up that wall after me. It must run in the family."

Marsali had discovered a new talent. She could cast mist at will. In fact, the only good thing she could say about her captivity in the convent was that she'd been forced to concentrate on controlling her supernatural tendencies. Because she was always having to pay penances for breaking the convent rules, she had plenty of time to practice.

She had been weeding the garden for a week.

She pulled listlessly at a dandelion root and wondered if she had the power to conjure up people. She'd tried to make Duncan appear in the garden yesterday until her eyes crossed. Her anger at him had already begun to fade into a raw ache. How could he abandon her when he needed her so? It seemed obvious that they belonged together.

She flung the tattered yellow flower over her head. The damn fool could go off to another war and get himself killed

271

instead of spending his life with her. Still, if she practiced hard enough, perhaps magic and prayers could bring him back.

She peered through the chink in the high wall. No ships on the horizon. Hell, if there had been a ship coming to rescue her it would probably get lost in her mist and crash into a cliff.

"What are you looking for?" a curious female voice demanded behind her.

Marsali turned away from the wall with a sigh. One of the convent school prefects, a tall raven-haired girl named Hannah with an angular face and stormy blue eyes, came bounding across the garden toward her.

"Nothing."

"Pirates?" the girl, Hannah, asked hopefully, squinting at the chink for a look herself, only to draw away, shaking her head in disappointment. "Not a chance in hell. I'll never get ravished at this rate."

Marsali smiled in sympathy. According to convent gossip, the girl was an orphan and had lived here all her life. Someone had whispered that she was distantly related to the Reverend Mother, and because of this association she gave herself arrogant airs. She swore a lot, she had quite a temper, and for those traits alone, Marsali rather liked her.

"I'm waiting for the chieftain," she admitted, not understanding why she would confess such a thing to a girl she barely knew.

"The chieftain? Mother Judith's brother?" Hannah considered this, then gave Marsali a level look. "Well then, I hope you do know magic, because there hasn't been a decent man on this island for at least a hundred years."

"The weeds will not come out by themselves, Marsali," a wry voice remarked behind them.

Marsali sighed and automatically plucked a tender green plantling from the black soil.

"That was a bean sprout, not a weed." Reverend Mother Judith walked past them, tsking to herself. "Perhaps it's the mist. There is an unsettling influence in the air today."

"It's boredom," Hannah muttered under her breath.

"Aye," Marsali whispered in agreement. "Anybody would go mad wearing those hot scratchy habits, running to and fro to the chapel every time that bell was rung. Hell, it's because of the bell that I'm paying the penance of picking weeds today."

"What happened?" Hannah whispered.

"It was my turn to ring the matins. Well, I underestimated my strength and yanked the bell right off its old frayed rope. Before I knew it, I was sailing across the belfry." Marsali paused, wincing at the memory. "I smashed into a beam and sent the bell crashing down to the bottom of the tower."

That same bell, dented in many places, began to peal now for complines. Another afternoon was passing, and he hadn't come.

As Marsali lumbered to her feet, she cast a last yearning look to the mist-shrouded sea that stretched beyond the convent wall.

She hated him. She loved him. She missed him so much it hurt to even picture his face. Even now she couldn't believe he was cruel enough to abandon her. Even now her stubborn heart clung to the hope of goodness she had glimpsed in him.

Chapter

29

He was leaving the castle within the hour. Escaping at last.

He ought to be running down the haunted hallways, flaunting his freedom in front of the ghosts. Superficially, at least, his debts were discharged. He'd done his best. The heaviness would lift as soon as he fled the oppressive walls.

He picked up a toy soldier from the solar floor on his way to the door. A strained smile softened his face at the bittersweet memory of losing that battle to Marsali.

Oh, look, they're dolls. Can I play too, my lord?

"Silly girl," he mused aloud, gripping the lead figure in his palm. "They aren't dolls. I wasn't playing."

A curt knock sounded at the door. It was Edwina, looking overblown and uncomfortable in the red scarlet coat and plumed hat of her father's army uniform over her own riding habit. "The horses are ready. Good God. You're not playing with your toys again, are you, Duncan? I thought you wanted to be off just after dawn."

Duncan tossed the soldier down onto the desk.

"Aren't you even going to say goodbye to the clan?" Edwina asked in concern.

"What for?" Duncan frowned. "Where is Abercrombie anyway? He was supposed to hand over the accounts."

"Cook says he's run off to the British fortress to beg

asylum. By the way, I gave my coach to Marsali's nieces and nephews." She paused for effect, her face taut with disapproval. "It was the least I could do, since their beloved aunt was so cruelly torn from the bosom of the family."

"Don't start, Edwina. She got what she deserved."

Duncan brushed past her. He refused to glance back into the room where the phantom of poignant regret lingered in the stillness. His voice tense, he said, "Forget the fond farewells too. We'll be lucky if we don't cross the drawbridge without an arrow in the behind as a parting insult."

Predictably, he had to bellow to have the portcullis raised, the drawbridge lowered. He needn't have worried about the arrows, though. No one bothered to see him off. After all, it was still morning.

And he was no longer the chieftain.

He had handed the burden of responsibility to Johnnie the previous evening, although it was doubtful that Johnnie, half asleep at the time, even remembered the fact.

And now he was riding from his crumbling old castle for the last time. London beckoned, with its glittering ladies to fawn over him and lords to flatter. His dukedom awaited. He would return to a superficial world, which would welcome him as a hero.

He was finally free of rebellious little ragamuffins and insubordinate clansmen. He stared ahead to the sun-dappled hills, inhaling the perfume of fading heather and unfulfilled hopes.

He said a silent goodbye to his mother as he rode slowly past her grave in the churchyard. In the next breath he cursed Fergus aloud to hell for all eternity.

The heaviness hadn't lifted. By the time he reached the crag where Marsali had ambushed him, his heart felt as if it were entombed once more behind a stone that emotion would never penetrate again.

Yet, briefly, for one magical summer, a shaft of sunlight had broken through. Marsali, Johnnie, Lachlan, Owen. Even Effie and her piglets had carved out a place in his heart. And left it bleeding.

Edwina glanced up at the crag, her hand hovering above the pistol Marsali had given her as a farewell gift. "If they strip you naked when you enter, what do you suppose happens when you leave?" she asked worriedly.

"They probably roll a boulder or two down the road after—" His face attentive, Duncan swerved around in the saddle. "My God, do you see what I see?"

The thunder of hoofbeats down the hill heralded the approach of a single horseman—actually, a *horsewoman*. With the stamina of a Celtic warrior, Cook galloped straight toward them on Marsali's mare, waving a rolling pin over her head.

Effie followed on foot, blowing her hunting horn. The piglets trotted at her heels with their plump bellies swaying. A few seconds later Johnnie, Lachlan, and Owen climbed to the rise of the hill on their worn little ponies.

"They're going to kill us. I told you not to send Marsali away." Edwina backed her horse into a crevice of the crag. "Don't just sit there, Duncan. Defend us."

Duncan gave no indication he had heard. He was too intent on translating the look on Agnes's face as she drew her heaving horse alongside his. Fear, he would guess, and not vengeance, had sent her charging from the castle.

"What is it?" he asked in concern.

"My lord." She paused to catch her breath; her mobcap dangled from her ear. "The old MacFay is dead. Jamie's announced to anyone who'll listen that his first act as chieftain will be to rescue Marsali from the convent. He's threatened to cut down anyone who stands in his way. A Sassenach colonel who tried to question him was beaten senseless."

Duncan released his breath with a soft curse. He thought of his sister, of Marsali and the nuns, defenseless on their secluded island with only their innocent prayers to protect them. He envisioned Jamie and his decadent entourage defiling the sanctity of the little cloister. It was a crime he'd never thought even Jamie would dare.

"How do you know this, Agnes?"

"One of Jamie's cousins refused to join the attack and was banished from the clan. He rowed all the way here to warn ye and ask for refuge." Cook's eyes bored coldly into his. "Of course, he didna ken ye'd abdicated the chieftain-ship."

"They have a day's travel on ye already," Effie called down from the hill.

Duncan considered this in silence, calculating the distance to the convent from the castle versus that from the MacFay stronghold. Even with a day's disadvantage, the odds were that Jamie would reach the island at least several hours before him.

He glanced across the moor, thinking aloud. "It all depends on the weather."

The others had reached the crag, their faces uplifted in expectant silence. He turned to Edwina. "I can't let this happen. Not for a dukedom. Not for anything."

Edwina nodded in agreement. "I know that. Don't worry—I'll make up a delicious excuse in your defense for the prime minister."

"Anything but the truth," Duncan said, with a grim smile at the thought of what might be his final battle being fought to defend a nunnery.

And Marsali.

Duncan felt a rush of gratitude for his old friend as she touched her crop to her horse. "Edwina."

The Englishwoman drew back on the reins, her enormous pearl earrings glistening in the sunlight. "You want me to come with you?" she asked hopefully.

"No." Duncan grinned. "I want you to pull a few more strings and have the banns proclaimed for my wedding. Something tells me this is going to be a rushed ceremony. Go back to the castle first and have Martin ride to the fort to arrange an escort for you. I think Major Darling would jump at the chance to win your favor."

Edwina dug in her heels, eager to be of help. "I'll have Colum conjure up good traveling weather for us both," she called over her shoulder as she set off back across the moor at a canter.

Lachlan and Owen, having dismounted from their ponies, stared at each other in surprise. "Ye're getting married, my lord?" Owen asked the chieftain.

"Yes."

Lachlan frowned. "Before or after we rescue Marsali?"

"After. I can't get married in a convent, can I?"

"I dinna realize the chieftain had a sweetheart in the convent," Owen whispered.

Lachlan shrugged. "Perhaps she's made friends wi' Marsali. We'll have to rescue them both."

Johnnie shook his head. "Heaven knows what mischief Marsali has cooked up in that convent by now. I suspect Jamie is abducting her as much to defy ye, my lord, as to claim a bride."

Duncan beat down the panic that rose at the thought, threatening the cool logic he needed to rely on. "I'll need your help, Johnnie. I want you with me."

Johnnie nodded.

"Aye, we'll all be fightin' at yer side just like in the old days," Owen added, although he'd never used his sword to stab anything except a loaf of bread in his life.

Effie whipped off her apron and surrendered it to Cook. "The twins and I would like to enlist too, my lord."

Duncan swallowed. How absurd he should feel affection for his incorrigible clan. "Effie, I appreciate the offer, but I'd prefer having you and the pigs stay to protect the castle. Agnes, I'm leaving you in command. Johnnie, you and the men will ride with me to the cove. We're setting sail immediately."

Johnnie flashed him an approving grin. "Aye, my lord. Ye're the chieftain."

"So I am," Duncan said wryly. Then, spurring his heavy stallion toward the hill, he pulled off his hat and coat and tossed them over his shoulder into the tarn in recognition of the woman who had given him back his life.

He rode past the lonely memorial cairn on the moor where Andrew Hay had been buried. He didn't intend to stop; his entire being pulsed with an urgency to intercept Jamie before it was too late.

It was the white roses that caught his eye, placed on Andrew's grave in loving memory by a mourning clansman. The MacElgins were a loyal bunch of idiots, if nothing else.

He slowed his horse, urging the stallion up the hillside, its heavy body shuddering with impatience. War had been bred into its very blood, like the man it had carried through so many violent battles.

Duncan stared down at the simple cairn, gripping the reins in his gloved hands. A warm breeze teased the wilted petals of the white roses, carrying their scent into the air. It seemed hard to believe that Andrew's passionate spirit lay forever stilled under these stones.

"I'm sorry, Andrew," he said, swallowing hard as the horse shifted restlessly beneath him, eager to be gone. "All I can tell you is that I love her. I won't let anything hurt her, but I want her for my wife. I hope you will forgive me again."

The horse tossed its heavy head, snorting, pawing the ground. Duncan crossed himself and touched his spurs to his mount's flanks. As he rode back toward the road, he thought he heard a burst of disturbingly familiar laughter and a gruff voice that aroused an ache of nostalgic affection.

Aye, and it took you long enough, lad. What have you been waiting for?

Chapter

30

Fiona stared through the porthole at the four men who had launched out across the waves in a lobster boat. She couldn't believe it. The chieftain himself sat at the prow. Plying the oars with an effortless strength, he propelled the craft forward until she could barely see it against the horizon.

"It's the MacElgin, Dad," she said in astonishment. "Do you think he's heard about Jamie going after Marsali?"

Colum did not acknowledge the question. Hunched over a three-legged black cauldron in the corner of the cabin, he was lost in concentration. A tiny wooden boat that held four wax figures floated on the surface of the sea water he'd collected in the iron basin.

With painstaking care, he dropped the first of three pebbles into the water. Gently he blew against the boat, repeating a Celtic incantation.

"That looks like fun," Fiona said in his ear as she plopped down beside him. "What are you doing?"

He jumped in startlement. The pebbles in his hand hit the water with a loud splash. The tiny boat bobbed wildly in the ripples that washed across the cauldron. The four wax figures toppled against one another.

"By all the Gods in Gaeldom!" Colum shouted in exasperation. "Can't you see when I am working, Fiona? You've probably drowned the fools with your ill-timed interference."

"The fools—you mean, the chieftain and his clansmen?" She threw her thin arms around him in relief. "Oh, Dad. You *are* going to help Marsali. I knew you would."

He frowned in irritation. "Go outside and practice talking to trees, Fiona. Polish the silver pentacle. Find some pretty stones for your amulet collection. Project yourself into the Otherworld."

"But Dad—"

"Go now, Fiona. I haven't a moment to waste. If Jamie MacFay reaches the convent before the chieftain, there is no spell on earth that can save your cousin. She will end up marrying the simpleton, and he will get them both killed in some pointless rebellion."

The note of panic in his voice mobilized her. "Poor Marsali," she said, her face pale with distress as she rose to her feet.

Colum vented a sigh, reaching into the cauldron to steady the tiny boat. "Take Eun with you. Release him on the cliff."

"All right, Dad. No sacrifice is too great to help Marsali."

She crept past him to unhook the hawk preening his feathers on his driftwood perch. She didn't utter another word. Not even when Eun hopped onto her head and dug his taloned feet into her ears. Tears filled her eyes as she contemplated Marsali's fate. Imprisoned in a convent, unaware that Jamie MacFay, the pig, was on his way to abduct her. Why did her cousin always have all the excitement?

She stifled a sob. She brushed a tear from her nose. She was so upset she forgot about her father crouched on the floor. She even forgot about his Celtic cauldron until she tripped over it and sent its contents sloshing everywhere.

Duncan dropped the oars and grabbed Owen by the ankles as another wave slammed against the sidewale. The storm had erupted without warning as if stirred up by a mischievous sea deity. The lobster boat spun like a top and nosed into a trough.

Johnnie slammed into Lachlan, who slammed into Duncan, who clung to Owen's ankles as the craft threatened to capsize. It took all of Duncan's strength to fight the vortex twirling them in circles.

Strangely, the sun continued to shine through the deluge of heavy rain and unbridled waves. Duncan had never seen anything like it in his life. He could swear they were caught in the eye of a storm that hadn't struck anywhere else in the sea. Their own exclusive summer tempest.

"We're going to drown," Owen wailed to no one in particular as an oar sailed over his head into the turbulent waters.

A monstrous wave rose overhead and hit the boat like a block of green ice. A claw of salty water slapped Duncan in the face. Lachlan screamed and threw his arms around Duncan's neck, clinging like a limpet. Duncan fell on his face; his body ached with the shock of cold and the strain of holding on to Owen's ankles. In his profession he had always accepted the possibility of an early death. A violent death.

But not this. Not drowning in a lobster boat with one idiot choking him like an iron collar and another pulling his arm out of its socket. It reeked of indignity. It wasn't fair.

"God," he said into the roaring wind, "I always suspected You had a sense of humor. But don't let me die before I get Marsali to safety."

Then, just as mysteriously as it had erupted, the storm came to an end. The towering waves receded into playful whitecaps. The wind subsided to a sweet breeze. The boat righted itself like a leaf steadied by an invisible hand. Lachlan released his terrified stranglehold on Duncan's throat. Owen scrambled back over the thwarts.

"Thank God," Duncan said in a hoarse voice, pushing his wet tangled hair from his face.

He gazed across the water. The storm had blown them far enough along so that by now he should have been able to see the Island of Inverothes. Yet all he could make out was a mysterious body of mist rising from the sea where the convent should have been. Not a tree. Not a rock. Not a cliff.

Johnnie was bailing water from the boat with a rusty

bucket. "Well, my lord?" he asked anxiously. "What do we do now?"

Duncan rubbed his face as he stared in helpless silence at the nebulous shape on the sea. Was that the belltower rising from the mist, or an illusion of his own desperation? What the hell had happened to the island? They hadn't been blown that far off course.

He had built his military career on taking chances. He had gambled the fate of great nations on his intuition. He had never cared so much about the outcome.

I want Marsali Hay. I'm takin' her too, ye bloody bastard.

"Are ye all right, my lord?" Owen asked in concern.

Duncan raised his head as a dark graceful shape soared high above the misty contours, gliding on a thermal wind— a guidepost he could not misinterpret. "Eun," he said with a grim smile of gratitude. "The hawk is showing us where she is."

Judith stared at her brother in consternation through the heavy iron bars of the convent gate. Duncan had appeared so unexpectedly, springing up from the sea grasses and rock-strewn shore that encircled the cloister that she had crossed herself in alarm. She had been tossing out crumbs for the gulls.

Moments passed before she recognized the fierce dark face. MacElgin, the warrior. The man revered in the world she disclaimed. He looked like a total barbarian, banging at the gate with his sword drawn and his long black hair in a tangle down his back.

"What are you doing here?" she asked, recovering her composure. "You're soaking wet. Why are you brandishing that awful weapon?"

Duncan's dark gaze scoured the arcaded cloisters behind her. "Has Jamie MacFay been here yet?"

"I've no idea what you're talking about." She glanced past him in chagrin to the three other Highlanders dragging a boat ashore. "Duncan, who are these scruffy men? How dare you disturb our peace in this uncouth manner?"

His face grim, he shoved his sword back in his scabbard. "I want Marsali back. Bring her to me, and I'll be gone before anyone else sees me."

"You may visit at the end of the month for an hour with the other families," she said crisply. "Please leave before you upset the others. We have received a special dispensation for an Irish abbess and three lay sisters to join our order. I would not have them arrive to the sight of a man banging uncouthly at the gates with a sword."

Duncan gripped the bars, his voice husky with frustration. "I don't think you understand me. Jamie MacFay is on his way here to get Marsali. I'm taking her away before he hurts her or anyone else."

She leveled her unperturbed gaze on his. "I don't think *you* understand. I gave my word that Marsali would be protected until a husband is found for her, and I do not go back on my word. She is not leaving this cloister until then if it is in my power to prevent it."

Duncan curbed the impulse to grab her through the gate and steal her keys. "Listen to me. Jamie MacFay and his men don't give a damn about religious sentiment—"

"I've turned away ardent suitors before, and please watch your language. God will protect us."

"This is a personal attack on me, Judith. His men are liable to trample your nuns down like snowdrops. Where is Marsali?"

"Banished to the washroom until after breakfast as penance for breaking the convent bell, the convent loom, and for leaving a puddle of water on the cellar steps again, which nearly caused me to break my neck."

Duncan beat down the beginnings of a black panic. If he didn't whisk Marsali out of here in the next half hour, they'd end up sailing home in a dark misty sea in a battered lobster boat. If they waited until morning, they would undoubtedly run into Jamie, and blood would be shed on these quiet grounds. Blood that would be blamed on him, and rightly so.

The bell for complines rang to interrupt his thoughts. White-veiled nuns abandoned chores to scurry to chapel, drifting like wraiths through the convent's colonnades.

"Please," he said. "Unlock the gate and let me in. I'll take her while everyone is at prayer. I'll pay for whatever she broke. I'll build a new belltower, Judith. I swear to you, I will not defile the purity of your convent. I will not bring a weapon inside. Not a single drop of blood will be shed by my hand. On your mother's grave, I swear it. On my daughter's soul—"

Her startled look stopped him. "Daughter? What daughter is this?"

"I'll explain it later. Please. I'm giving you my word."

"And I've already given mine." Judith turned away in a graceful swirl of her long skirts, her face set and serene. "Now do not make me late for chapel, Duncan. Marsali is staying under my protection."

"Hell."

Duncan paced the outcrop of rocks, waves breaking against his booted feet. Only honor kept him from breaking his vow and behaving like one of the Viking invaders who had conquered this tiny island centuries ago. The nuns would faint dead away if he went tramping through the cloister looking for Marsali. Damn it, why did his sister have to be so much like him? Stubborn, iron-willed, determined to have her own way.

"Why don't you scale the wall and carry Marsali off?" Owen suggested, flung out flat on his back from exhaustion in the anchored lobster boat.

"Because I gave my word that I would not disrupt the convent."

"I canna see the problem." Lachlan clambered up on a rock to escape a wave. "All ye have to do is break yer word, my lord. No one will die."

"It's not as if anyone would be surprised," Johnnie added from the rock where he sat fiddling with his spyglass.

"Aye, my lord," Owen said in agreement. "Everyone knows ye're a bastard."

"Thank you for reminding me," Duncan said dryly. He cast a morose glance up at the convent, or what he could see of it in the mist. "Is there any sign of Jamie's ship yet?" he demanded, turning back to Johnnie.

"No. No sign, my lord."

Lachlan teased a crab with his toe.

Owen began to whistle.

Duncan blew out a sigh of frustration.

Owen interrupted his whistling long enough to indulge a

moment of passing curiosity. "Why do ye care if ye displease yer sister anyway? Forgivin' ye will only give her something else to pray about. 'Tis sinners like us that keep them busy."

Duncan didn't answer. How could he expect anyone to understand? Judith was the only person in the world who had witnessed him commit murder. How would he ever convince not just her, but himself, that violence was not the primary motivation of his soul?

All ye have to do is break yer word.

It's not as if anyone would be surprised.

He unbuckled his sword and let his belt and weapon fall to the wet sand beneath his feet. There had to be a way to get Marsali back without resorting to force. Damn it, he would not confirm his sister's worst convictions by another act of violence.

But violence is all you know, an inner voice mockingly reminded him. *Without your physical power, you are nothing.*

He stared at the locked gates, frustration slowly giving way to resolve. It was time to wage the ultimate battle from the bedrock of his being, to confront the black demon that had overshadowed him his entire life. It was time to challenge his own deepest beliefs about himself.

Chapter

31

Today was laundry day in the cloister.

Every convent inmate owned only two changes of clothing. One of these was worn an entire month before it could be washed and replaced with its alternate. As penance for breaking the loom, Marsali faced the arduous task of washing and hanging out a mountain of veils, habits, and stockings in the garden.

Laundry day.

She sighed. The unpleasant chore reminded her poignantly of the morning she had ambushed and undressed Duncan on the moor. She had believed in him from the moment he'd flattened his seven attackers and commanded the clan's attention. She had lost her heart over a laundry trough.

And I still believe in him, she thought sadly, dragging her heavy wicker basket to the wall. She believed in him even if he had abandoned her out of some misguided impulse for good.

"The laundry will never dry if you leave it sitting there all day," Sister Anne scolded from her bench, where she sat overseeing Marsali's efforts. "Why do you keep looking over that wall anyway?"

Marsali sighed again. "I like to look at the sea."

"Well, I dinna ken how ye can see even two feet in front of yer face." The elderly nun crossed herself, huddling into her mantle. "I've no seen such a mist in my life. 'Tis only by God's grace that the good sisters from the Irish abbey willna run aground in their wee boat." She paused to fix a suspicious look on Marsali. "If they make it here at all. 'Tisna natural, this mist, is it?"

"Um, no, Sister Anne." Guiltily lowering her gaze, Marsali turned back to the tedious ritual of hanging up laundry. Frankly, she was good at casting mist, but she hadn't quite figured out how to make it go away yet.

The heavy black habit she had just slung over the clothesline slowly plopped to the ground. She bent; the whiff of lye soap and wet wool so reminded her of Duncan's cloak that an aching lump rose in her throat.

As she straightened, she felt a tingle of excitement in her spine. It was strange. Suddenly she could sense his presence, the power of him, as if he were standing right in front of her. Perhaps her magic was working, after all.

She backed away from the clothesline in confusion, clutching the damp wool to her chest. A delicious tension gripped her, as if Duncan's dark gaze had actually reached out across the miles.

Sister Anne looked up, alarmed by the girl's strange behavior. She had been instructed by the Mother Superior to guard Marsali, but against what had never been made clear. "What is it?" she whispered, rising from the bench.

"It's . . . I'm . . ." Marsali frowned. How could she explain to someone like Sister Anne that the smell of wet wool made her imagine the chieftain's presence? "I think I'm having a vision."

Sister Anne stared at the veils hanging on the clothesline, her voice dropping in wonder. "A vision of Our Lady?"

"Not exactly, Sister Anne." Marsali hid a little smile and resumed her work, trying to ignore the pleasantly disturbing feeling that persisted.

She was so close that Duncan, on the other side of the wall, could barely restrain the urge to shout her name. He controlled the impulse out of concern that the frail old nun guarding Marsali would take a heart attack. It was a delicate dilemma.

"I'm hungry, my lord," Lachlan whispered loudly. "Can we climb over the wall yet?"

Duncan ignored him. All he could see through the chink in the crumbling stones were Marsali's small feet marching back and forth to the basket—and the fact that she kept dropping clean laundry in the dirt.

He heard her swear under her breath too, and the sound was music to his ears. Obviously an atmosphere of prayer and solitude hadn't penetrated deeply enough to damage her true nature.

He was starved for a glimpse of her. If it wouldn't scare that old nun to death, he'd scale the wall like a Viking warlord and carry off the hellion.

"I'm finished, Sister Anne," Marsali announced wearily, reaching down for the basket.

Duncan pressed his face to the wall. Anticipation quickened his pulse. If the chink were a little bigger, he could reach his hand through the mortar and grasp her hand. Of course she'd probably scream bloody murder if he did. But he needed to touch her.

The bells for vespers began to ring.

"Hurry. Hurry," Sister Anne urged, nudging Marsali onto the path. "The entire convent will be beseeching God with prayers that the abbess and her companions willna drown in this mist." She stopped to shake her head, her figure obscuring Duncan's view. "'Tis verra strange, unnatural, this mist. I dinna like it one bit."

The three clansmen crouched behind the jagged rocks, anxiously awaiting their chieftain's return. They were silent, except for the loud rumbling of Lachlan's stomach, and Owen biting his nails. Duncan had only been gone on his mysterious mission for about fifteen minutes, but to the nervous trio, it felt like an hour.

"I canna stand the suspense," Johnnie said at last. "What could have happened to him in there?"

Lachlan grunted. "Nothing too excitin'. 'Tis a nunnery, after all."

A broad shadow on top of the convent wall caught their

attention. They fell silent as Duncan dropped a heavy object between the rocks.

"All right, men, to the gatehouse. I have a plan for us to get Marsali without causing a commotion."

" 'Tis a laundry basket," Owen said, peering down at the rocks in disappointment. "What are we supposed to do with a load of women's clothes?"

"Which one of you idiots took my other stocking?" Duncan worked his thickly muscled left leg down into the cumbersome woolen skirts that hung about his feet. The sound of fabric rending followed. It was as dark as a grave in the small gatehouse above the convent gate, where the four men hid with their basket of stolen habits.

A damp stocking hit Duncan in the head. He grabbed it, but he couldn't fit the hose on farther than his shin. A telltale expanse of bulging calf protruded above the soggy wool.

"How did you manage to put your veil on, my lord?" Lachlan whispered in between the sound of Duncan cursing about his stockings and Johnnie complaining that his petticoats were going to give him a rash.

"You have to pin the blasted thing on."

"What about these strings that are hangin' down from it?"

"I haven't figured out what to do with them yet." A white linen wimple framed Duncan's scowling face. "I'll help you as soon as I finish getting Owen's habit on over his paunch."

"It's Johnnie's paunch, my lord," Johnnie informed him. "Owen is sulking in the corner because ye gave him the veil that Marsali dropped in the mud. By the way, ye've put these sleeves on upside down."

"Well, I'm not a damned lady's maid, am I? Owen, get over here. Give me the pins."

"Ouch, my lord! That's my delicate flesh ye're stabbin. *Ouch!*"

Duncan whirled around, muttering to himself as his feet became tangled in the unaccustomed layers of heavy material. "Let me unshutter this window so I can see what the hell I'm doing. It's a damn good thing I shaved this morning."

He gave the warped shutter a fierce tug, and it popped

open, dust motes dancing in the diffused gray light that filtered across his face. The three other men recoiled from him in mute horror.

"What is it?" Duncan snapped. He straightened, flicking back the drawstrings dangling around his chin. A shadowy white veil fluttered downward to accentuate the rugged angles of his jaw. "Well, what are you staring at? Do I have my wimple on backward?"

Johnnie recovered first, studying Duncan with a pained grimace. "It might be better if it were on backward, my lord. I dinna mean any disrespect, but ye're the ugliest woman I've ever seen in my life."

"Aye," Owen agreed, swallowing in distaste. "The ugliest, and the biggest too."

The gray light of gloaming had fallen by the time they managed to get dressed, and Duncan, who'd gotten a horrifying glimpse of himself in the window, thought that the darkest night couldn't hold enough shadows to disguise them. They were as homely as hell.

God, however, must have seen humor in the situation and decided to give him a hand.

Duncan had wandered off on a reconnaissance mission toward the kitchen quarters in search of Marsali. As he skulked about the back door, he was caught by a tiny energetic nun who almost dropped her ladle at the sight of him.

"Glory be to God!" she exclaimed, her ruddy cheeks like polished apples. "The Irish sisters are here, and this must be the abbess herself come to humble her soul by helping with supper." Beaming with delight, she dragged him into the hot cramped kitchen to introduce him to the two other nuns busy ladling soup into earthen bowls.

Now, in the refectory itself where meals were served, the nuns were not permitted to speak unless to utter a prayer or to read Scripture. But here in the kitchen, Sister Bridget and her helpers followed no such restriction. They chattered excitedly about how their prayers had been answered: that the Irish sisters had not gotten lost in this unusual mist, and how fortunate that the abbess herself had arrived to hear the devotional during supper.

And all Duncan could think as he listened in cynical silence to the happy chatter was how fortunate it was that the convent couldn't afford to burn many candles, and that no one had gotten a good look at his face yet because he suspected he was sprouting beard hairs by the second. God willing no one would look down at his legs.

"Here, let me help you carry that porringer, Sister Bridget," he said, hoping a falsetto Irish lilt would detract from the deep baritone of his normal voice. "You should be letting the schoolgirls do the heavy work." He moved around the table, grateful his veil fell forward to overshadow his jaw. "And where would the young misses be off to anyway? Employed in some beneficial pursuits, I pray?"

A smile brightened Sister Bridget's heavily lined face. "Why, of course, Reverend Mother Abbess. They're setting the table for supper and cleaning up the chapel. We had a wee accident there today, but the perpetrator is paying her penance—"

She broke off with a gasp of alarm as Duncan reached across the table to lift the heavy platter a nun had just removed from the oven. Duncan hesitated at her look of horror. Had she noticed his hairy forearms? His stubbled chin?

Or had she, like him, just noticed the poignant face that had appeared in the window, shock registering on its perfect little features?

Marsali. He grinned slowly, resisting the impulse to run outside as everything else around him faded to insignificance. She was safe, his naughty fairy. He'd found her, and he was never going to let her out of his sight again.

"No, Reverend Mother Abbess!" he heard Sister Bridget cry in warning, but her concerned voice barely dented his dazed relief at seeing Marsali. Finally, realizing he wasn't paying attention, the nun gave him a sharp whack on the back and shouted in his ear like a drill sergeant, "ARE YE DEAF? DINNA TOUCH THAT PLATTER!"

It was too late. He had already grasped the red-hot pewter handles in his bare hands. In fact, it took several moments before the searing pain reached his nerve endings, and then he threw the platter of baked fish on the floor; a curse rolled off his tongue before he could stop it.

"Hellfire and damnation!"

Sister Bridget dropped her ladle, whispering, "Reverend Mother!" in a shocked voice. "How could—"

"Hellfire and damnation is the price one pays for impulsive behavior and false pride," Duncan amended through gritted teeth, bending to retrieve the platter while a delayed reaction of burning pain sizzled up his palm into his fingertips. "I was so anxious to prove my humility that I foolishly ignored your warning. Scourge me with a whip, Sister, for my wicked conceit."

"Ah." The nun gave him a doubtful look, her face puckered in an effort to understand. "Well, very good, Reverend Mother. A little strongly put, but quite profound. False pride is a frequent sin among the sisters. However—"

A muffled snort of laughter drew her attention to the window where Marsali watched, her hand pressed to her mouth to muffle her irrepressible snorts of amusement.

Sister Bridget wagged an admonishing finger at the window. "Ye'll not be laughing so hard when ye have to pay another penance for laughing at the Reverend Mother's accident, Marsali Hay. Get ye to the refectory this instant, and dinna give me cause to scold ye again tonight." She turned apologetically to Duncan. "A new student, Reverend Mother, brimming over with human nature and all the willfulness in the world. She's the challenge of the convent."

"Perhaps I could have a word alone with the wee spitfire," Duncan suggested in a casual tone. "I might pray with the lass later tonight in private, offer her a few words of guidance."

Nodding gratefully as another nun handed her a clean ladle, Sister Bridget replied, "That's awfully good of ye. I'm sure Mother Judith would appreciate yer intervention, especially since she herself is spending the evening in the infirmary nursing several of the sisters who've come down with coughs. It's this mist, ye ken. I've never seen the likes of it. Thank God ye didna drown on your way here."

Humming a hymn under her breath, Sister Bridget returned to the task of ladling cabbage broth into bowls. Duncan bowed his head as he sailed past the three nuns to the door with his two platters of baked fish.

* * *

Marsali had disappeared by the time he got outside; he was furious at her, playing peekaboo with him when that hothead MacFay could come crashing like a boar into the convent at any second. Naturally she thought this was all a joke, or she was punishing him for leaving her here. He couldn't keep up this disguise forever. He didn't have the chest for it. The bodice of his habit was already bursting at the seams.

"Damn it," he muttered as he stared out into the eerie pearlescent mist that swathed the cloister. "Where the hell are you hiding?"

"Here, my lord."

Lachlan, Owen, and Johnnie fluttered out from behind the stone arches like a trio of clumsy bats.

"Grub, praise God," Lachlan said, reaching for the platter.

Duncan elbowed him away. "Wait until you're served at the table." He stared hard at the three pathetic faces hovering over the platter. "My God. If there's any praying to be done in this place, let it be for a total eclipse. You're the most sorrowful excuses for women I've ever seen in my life."

Johnnie snorted. "And look who's talkin', he with his shoulders as wide as a drawbridge."

"Owen, take that dirk out of your belt," Duncan said brusquely, handing the platter to Lachlan to yank the wimple down lower on his clansman's forehead. "Johnnie, I thought I told you to get rid of those boots. You're supposed to be a nun, not a bloody fisherman. Now behave yourselves and follow me to the refectory."

"Aye, my lord."

"What's a refectory, my lord?"

"It's a mess hall," Duncan replied, stomping past them in the black habit that barely came down to his knees. "Any man who swears, spits, or scratches himself at the table will answer to me afterward. We get Marsali, and we're gone. Is that understood?"

"Aye, my lord."

It sounded easy enough. Damn it, it should be easy. Hadn't he pulled off more daring rescues in his day, under more dangerous circumstances? Hadn't he negotiated the release of hostages, stormed an enemy citadel, captured entire armies? Except that this time he was motivated not by dreams of glory but by the two women in the world he loved and who, despite knowing his worst secret, loved him in return.

They were the ugliest women that Marsali had ever seen. In fact, her jubilation at hearing Duncan's voice from outside the refectory window had been superseded only by her shock at seeing his chiseled face framed in a white linen veil.

She was so eager to find out what he was doing in the convent that she bumped up against the lectern when he entered the refectory. Skim milk went splashing up all over his habit from the huge pitcher she was carrying to the table.

"Duncan." She knelt, rubbing milk off his skirts with her sleeve. "What are you—"

"Hush, child." He bent at the waist to half lift her from the floor, whispering from the edge of his veil, "Jamie's on his way here. I've come to take you away before there can be any fighting. Be ready to leave right after we eat. You'll have no time to change."

She wanted to touch him, to burrow against his broad chest like a child. Shivers of happy excitement streamed through her. "Why can't we leave right now, my lord?"

"Because Johnnie, Lachlan, and Owen won't have the strength to help me row home until I feed them. Anyway, we're sneaking away with as little fuss as possible."

"Where are you taking me?" Marsali whispered, daring to rest her hand on the powerful shoulder that shifted forward beneath his habit.

"With me." He nudged her chin upward with his thumb, aching to run his hands all over her tempting little body. He didn't even try to hide the longing that burned in his eyes as he looked at her.

"You took your time about it," she said irritably. "You were cruel to put me here."

"I wanted you safe, lass." He glanced down at her mouth. "I wanted you for myself but I couldn't admit it."

Her eyes clung to his, reflecting hope and uncertainty in the candlelight. "Do you really care about me, Duncan?"

"Would I be dressed like this if I didn't?" He allowed himself the dangerous indulgence of brushing his mouth across her hair. Pleasure teased his senses as he breathed in her scent. "Would I have let you turn my world upside down if I didn't care?" he asked in a voice hoarse with love and concern.

A dark form came fluttering up behind them. "Dear, dear. Not another accident," Sister Bridget exclaimed, shaking her head in woe at Marsali. "Ye know what the penance will be for soiling the abbess's skirts."

Marsali nodded dutifully, a wicked thrill coursing through her as Duncan squeezed her knee before they rose together to face the irate nun. "Yes, Sister Bridget."

Hell, Marsali thought happily, she'd agree to do a hundred penances standing on her head now that she knew her imprisonment was almost over. She grinned at Duncan over her shoulder. *With me. With me.* The words washed away all the weeks of doubt, of waiting, of aching. Her chieftain, her love. She had always seen the potential in him, the strength, the goodness. She'd always known in her secret heart that this moment would come—although, to be honest, she had never pictured Duncan admitting his feelings for her dressed in a nun's habit.

She caught a glimpse then of Johnnie, Lachlan, and Owen tramping to the table. Her own dear idiots who had gone to such drastic extremes to save her from Jamie MacFay. Of course, now that she was getting better at her magic, she could have probably saved herself from Jamie, and with half the bother. But men were so funny that way, needing to prove their power, to protect. Her heart tightened with tender affection.

How strange, how wonderful life could be, and yet not long ago, it was true what she had told Duncan in her uncle's cabin: She hadn't cared if she lived or died. She would always miss her father and brothers, her sweetheart Robert. She would always mourn them in a private corner of her heart. But somehow she sensed they approved of Duncan—indirectly it was their involvement in the rebellion that had brought him home. Suddenly she felt closer to her father than she had ever been before he died.

He was blessing this union from heaven. She sensed it so strongly that it was as if he were standing in the room. Andrew Hay had been Duncan's champion at a time when his other clansmen had shunned him. Had Papa known all along? Had he planted the seeds of self-worth and compassion in Duncan's embittered heart for a reason?

Her contemplation was broken as a nun rang the bell signaling the start of grace.

Duncan and his three "sisters" looked faint with hunger as they devoutly bowed their heads over the humble fare set before them. Marsali cast an anxious glance around the tables. She ought to be thanking God for the food, but in truth she was more grateful for the strict convent rule that said a nun may not raise her eyes from the table during a meal.

Duncan's beard was growing blacker before her eyes. Lachlan's wimple had slid back several inches to reveal his receding hairline. Owen was sneaking a crust of bread into his mouth. Johnnie was shaking a very manly, hairy-knuckled fist at him in warning under the table.

Grace ended; the four men practically dove into their seats, only to straighten in awkward embarrassment as they noticed that the other nuns had remained on their feet.

"You can't eat until after the lesson is read," Marsali whispered in sympathetic amusement as she placed the pitcher next to Duncan's plate.

Sister Bridget strode briskly past the low oak benches; she was so short one could barely see the top of her wimple behind the lectern. She had chosen to read a selection from the Book of Psalms. Psalm 119, announced Sister Bridget. It was a long psalm. At 176 verses it was, in fact, the most long-winded psalm in the psalter.

"Blessed are the undefiled in the way, who walk in the law of the Lord," Sister Bridget began, in a deafening voice that boomed across the room like musketfire.

Owen looked up at the tiny nun in astonishment.

"Amen," said Lachlan, then he reached for his spoon, only to drop it when Duncan slapped his wrist.

"Patience, Sister," Duncan murmured.

The psalm went on. Sister Bridget's voice climbed in passion; rumor in the cloister had it that she'd been quite the actress before God called her. Duncan eyed her in admiration; he could have used a pair of lungs like that on the battlefield.

On went the psalm.

And on.

Marsali went quietly about her duties, slicing warm brown bread, her eyes downcast except for the delicious glances she stole at Duncan. Her breath caught whenever she dared look into his face. His emotions were out in the open now. Desire, concern, possession: The wolfish gleam in his eyes marked her once and for all as his. Her body warmed under his scrutiny like a candle wick held to a flame. The nun's habit did nothing to dilute his potent masculinity.

He was all male, and no disguise in the world could hide it.

Time was passing in a torture of impatience for Duncan. His gaze shadowed every move she made, every graceful step, every tantalizing dainty turn. That plain convent dress emphasized her beguiling delicacy. He couldn't wait to play out this charade so he could have her to himself. His lids narrowed as he imagined in visceral detail how they would spend their first night alone. With every frustrating moment the ache to possess her intensified, to—

There was danger in the air.

The thought sliced unexpectedly like a sword thrust into his intensely pleasurable reverie. For a reckless moment he'd forgotten Jamie's fondness for violent behavior. But in a chilling flash of precognition he could picture Jamie and his amoral retainers bursting into the refectory. He could hear the shocked cries of the defenseless women, the prayers that would be drowned in the gusts of crude male laughter.

His hands tightened on the table. He would kill Jamie if he touched Marsali. He couldn't help it. Despite his promise to Judith, despite the fact that he was soul-sick with bloodshed himself, the primal male impulse to protect would overpower all his more civilized intentions. Aye, he'd kill Jamie, and enjoy it.

He had to get Marsali back to the boat before Jamie

arrived, even if it meant floating all night in that damned sea fog.

"At midnight I will rise to give thanks unto Thee because of Thy righteous judgments!" Sister Bridget shouted with such vigor that Lachlan, dozing on his feet, woke up and grabbed Duncan's arm in fright.

Midnight.

Duncan glanced at Marsali, then at the heavy doors of the refectory, measuring distance and obstacles to escape. Were Jamie and his retainers lying in wait outside? Had they hidden themselves in the alcoves of the cloister? Was there another way to the beach?

Slaughter. Abduction. In the ancient Highlanders' eyes, these were crimes that could easily be justified. He should never have forced his clansmen to disarm themselves. What good would their weapons do locked up in the gatehouse? Tension thrummed in his veins. Had Johnnie remembered his instructions to hide their boat?

I swear to you, Judith, I will not defile the purity of your convent. I will not raise a hand in violence. Not a single drop of blood will be shed by my hand. On our mother's grave, I swear it. On my daughter's soul—

Judith's startled face rose in his mind, the memory of it touching a disturbing chord. *Daughter? What daughter is this, Duncan?*

He looked up abruptly.

Marsali smiled at him, bewitching in the flickering gold shadows of the tallow candles on the table. Sister Bridget's voice boomed like a blunderbuss. The incompatible smells of damp wool, fish, and heated wax rose to his nostrils, making him long for a breath of sweet night air. Perhaps Jamie would lose his way in the mist. Perhaps he'd stay home to wash his hair.

"My soul fainteth for Thy salvation," bellowed Sister Bridget.

"Amen," Owen muttered. "My stomach fainteth for food."

Finally the psalm ended. Lachlan dumped the entire communal platter of baked fish onto his plate. Owen made so much noise quaffing his soup that a few nuns almost broke protocol by glancing at each other in disapproval.

Duncan ate his bread in anxious silence, wanting nothing more than to end the meal and escape. Each time Marsali leaned over him to refill his glass, he was reminded of her fragility. This was his fault. If he had not put her in such a vulnerable position in the first place . . .

"Where is she?" he demanded in a loud male voice that *did* lift several veiled heads around the table in alarm.

A moment of panic threatened to destroy his charade. He half rose from the bench, his heart drumming against his ribs as he scanned the room and realized Marsali had vanished. Then military training overtook his emotions. He shrugged apologetically and sat down, pulling his sleeves over his muscular forearms.

His voice an urgent whisper, he jabbed Johnnie in the side. "Where did she go?"

"I'm right here, my lord," she whispered, tugging on his skirt before Johnnie could answer.

Duncan glanced down in disbelief and saw Marsali's sweet face peeking out from under the table. He settled back on the bench, pretending to have risen to pass the pitcher across the table. The blood roaring in his head began to recede. Anxiety was a totally alien emotion to his nature.

"What on earth are you doing?" he whispered gruffly.

"I have to wash your feet," she explained with a sigh. "It's my penance for spilling milk on your habit."

A reluctant grin lit his face. "You're joking, lass."

"I am not. Now lift up your skirts and for heaven's sake, pull that veil over your face. Your jaw is looking like the Black Forest."

He glanced up, trying not to sigh in enjoyment as her small fingers pulled off his stocking, slid around his ankle, and gently massaged. The meal was ending. His men were snatching bites of food even as a pair of convent schoolgirls efficiently whisked the plates away.

One girl, who apparently did not obey rules any better than Marsali, lingered overlong at his side. He tried to ignore her. She was too curious, a troublemaker, he was sure. He hunched down deeper into his habit.

Finally, he worked up the nerve to look into her face. Surprise widened his eyes because for a puzzling instant he saw his own mother staring back at him. The girl gave a sharp gasp of astonished recognition; presumably one didn't expect the new abbess in the convent to boast shoulders as wide as a warship and a buccaneer's square bearded jaw.

Would she ruin everything?

Would she run to fetch Judith from the infirmary?

He clenched his pewter spoon, suspense ticking away between them as her gaze darted questioningly to Johnnie, then Lachlan, and Owen.

He couldn't read her expression. He could only see something bold and disturbingly familiar in the strong features of her face.

She smiled slowly, a shy but knowing smile, and the power of it slammed into his chest with unexpected force. Who the hell was she?

"Bless you, Reverend Mother Abbess," she murmured, then she began to back away from the table with an armful of dishes, leaving Duncan to puzzle over her in silence.

"You have the biggest feet I've ever seen," Marsali whispered under the table.

He frowned, distracted by her voice. "Who was that girl? Look, quickly, the one just going to the door."

Marsali twisted her agile body between the table and the bench to see. "Oh, her. That's only Hannah. She's one of the orphans who's been here forever."

"But she isn't a nun?"

"No, she isn't a nun. She's a prefect." Marsali's voice was thoughtful. "She's said to be related to your sister, which I suppose means she could be related to you. She swears like you sometimes."

Sister Bridget had returned to the lectern; she wasn't shouting again; now she was gesturing wildly with her arms for Owen and Lachlan to come to the makeshift stage.

"What is that woman trying to do?" Duncan asked in a wary undertone.

"It's time for the pantomime," Marsali whispered back. "She's just chosen Adam and Eve. We've been acting out the Book of Genesis. It's the only excitement we're allowed."

Owen and Lachlan had risen from the bench, bowing and

grinning like idiots to have been singled out for the honor of playing the original outcasts.

"Sit down," Duncan hissed. "We don't have time for a play."

Sister Bridget was waving her arms at Duncan like a windmill. He pretended not to notice. Marsali wriggled out from under the table to whisper in his ear.

"She wants you, my lord."

He looked alarmed. "She wants me for what?"

"She wants you to play God."

"God? She wants *me* to play God? What for?"

Marsali gave him a little encouraging push off the bench. "You're the only one in the convent with the beard for it."

Duncan lumbered to his feet, nodding to the nuns around the table, who politely motioned him forward. "I don't want to be God," he said in a peevish undertone. "I don't know *how* to be God."

"Listen, my lord, you were born for this part. In fact, it's what you do best. Giving orders. Frightening the hell out of people."

"I hate this, Marsali. There are probably twelve armed men waiting outside the door to abduct you while I prance around in a dress playing God." He flipped back his veil to glower at her. "How am I supposed to pantomime God anyway?"

The other nuns were beginning to look at them in earnest now. Sister Bridget frowned in admonishment at Marsali across the room. From the corner of his eye, Duncan noticed the girl named Hannah slipping back through the door.

He swore to himself. Judith would probably burst in at any second. He wanted to get the hell off this misty little island with Marsali. And now he was going to stand in front of a room full of women, nuns, pretending he was a woman pretending to be God.

Marsali nudged him again. "Just put a curse on the serpent."

"What serpent?"

"I think it's Sister Douglas. Yes, it's that chubby nun writhing around the lectern in spectacles."

"This is absurd."

"Put a curse on the ground too, and then you can toss Lachlan out of Eden. I assume Owen is taking Eve's part since he's shorter."

Duncan stomped toward the candlelit space cleared for the pantomime. "Don't forget to put enmity between their seed before you toss Lachlan out," Marsali whispered as he went. "Oh. There's a flaming sword at the end too. But never mind about the angels. You don't want to overact."

Duncan flailed his arms and made a menacing grandfatherly face. It was the best he could do, having never met God in person. He felt more confident when it came to the part about the flaming sword.

He feinted. He parried. He thrust his pewter spoon with one hand negligently poised on his hip. He even got a little carried away and jumped up on an unoccupied bench, kicking up his skirt to lunge across the table. Sword fighting, after all, was his forte. Disengage. Extend.

The nuns absorbed this dramatic display in utter silence, but Duncan thought he looked rather good, especially if one discounted the fact that he was wearing a linen headdress and a habit.

But had God Himself actually engaged in swordplay in the Garden of Eden?

Duncan couldn't remember much of the Bible, except the Twenty-third Psalm, which he read when a soldier lay dying on the battlefield, and then it was always with a sense of doubt and sadness that he could not bring himself to believe.

He executed a swift God-like riposte into the air. Damn, but it felt good to wield a sword again, power flowing through his veins as he jabbed at an imaginary enemy. MacFay. Yes, that was it. He was fighting MacFay.

He lowered his spoon with a swallowed curse, suddenly becoming aware of the shocked faces that watched him. Was he insane? Had he forgotten what the hell had brought him here?

Marsali, Owen, and Lachlan clapped politely as he jumped down off the bench. Only Johnnie showed any sense at all, standing by the door with a worried expression wrinkling his forehead.

"I thought I heard the gate, my lord," he explained softly as Duncan backed inch by inch toward him.

Duncan gave a terse nod. Sister Bridget studied him in open suspicion now. He shouldn't have been surprised. In his asinine display of derring-do, he had gotten his skirt hitched in his belt. The length of calf and thigh that bulged with muscle and gleamed with myriad white scars were a dead giveaway that he hadn't spent his life in spiritual pursuits.

The secret was out: The Irish abbess was a man.

Sister Bridget had caught on too, for she was stalking him in slow lethal silence.

He glanced at Johnnie. *"Now.* Douse the candles. We're getting Marsali out of here. Holy hell. That nun's got murder in her eyes."

Within thirty seconds the refectory lay in smoky darkness. A few schoolgirls screamed, more in anticipation than alarm, but to their credit the nuns did not break their silence. Duncan decided that they were frozen in terror. Not wasting another moment, he grabbed Marsali's hand and whisked her outside, down the long arcade, breaking into a run when the infirmary door opened and he glimpsed Judith standing before him with a horrified expression on her face.

"Wait," Marsali whispered, balking like mule behind him.

Duncan spun around, catching his feet in Lachlan's skirts. "We are not waiting, Marsali. I can't face my sister looking like this."

"Where's Owen?" Johnnie asked suddenly, his bulky form looming out of the dense mist.

"That's what we have to wait for," Marsali explained.

Lachlan untangled his skirts from Duncan's feet. "He was still in Eden the last time I looked."

"Eden?" A note of hysteria exploded in Duncan's voice. "What is the idiot doing in Eden? I thought I banished him."

Lachlan gave a sheepish shrug. "Ye banished me, my lord. Owen and I weren't sure whether he had to leave too, so he decided to stay while ye were doing that fancy sword dance."

The convent had never heard the creative flow of curse words that issued from Duncan's mouth. In fact, Marsali and his clansmen were still standing in a stupefied trance when Duncan returned with Owen a few moments later, Judith and Sister Bridget hot on their heels in angry pursuit.

They took refuge inside the small detached belltower, only to find that they had escaped one danger to face another. A far worse danger. The moment he stepped into the dark timber building, Duncan's nerves prickled down his back in belated warning.

MacFay and six of his retainers sprang out from behind the rickety wooden stairs to the tower. The scrape of half a dozen broadswords unsheathed in the silence reminded Duncan of his own sword locked up uselessly in the gatehouse. Unarmed. Outnumbered. Trapped. Dressed like a damn woman. Could it get any worse?

Still, he had the element of surprise on his side. In the dark he and his clansmen resembled the good sisters of the convent closely enough to seize the advantage.

Except that Owen tripped over a broom on the floor and went flying into Johnnie's arms, shouting "Hell's bells!" before anyone could shut him up. Which wasn't the sort of thing a nun would say under the circumstances.

"They're no bloody nuns," a MacFay clansman said in astonishment. "Look—that big one wi' the beard is the MacElgin himself."

Jamie pushed his way forward, his sword lifted, to confront Duncan. "Draw your weapon, MacElgin. I told ye I wasn't finished wi' ye in the castle."

Duncan raised the pewter spoon he was still clutching in his left hand. "En garde?" he said hopefully.

For a moment Jamie faltered, apparently not expecting the world-celebrated swordsman to counter his assault with a kitchen utensil.

"Defend yerself," Jamie said, thrusting the tip of his broadsword toward Duncan's chest.

Duncan raised his other arm, blocking the attack with a length of billowing black sleeve like a giant bat's wing. From the corner of his eye he noticed a slender figure sneaking up the stairs to the belfry. Marsali? Blast her. What the hell was she trying to do? Ringing the bell to summon the sisters to their defense? A damn lot of good it would do to have a bunch of screaming women in his way.

Jamie glanced uneasily from Duncan to the armed retainers who stood guard at the door. "Give him a weapon. Jamie will fight like a man."

A broadsword flew through the air and landed at Duncan's feet. He stared down at it in violent longing, his hand aching for the reassuring weight. "You're a wanted outlaw, Jamie," he said, the words calm and deliberate. "This is a convent, for the love of God. No Highland law will save you from being hunted down even if you kill me."

Contempt rippled across Jamie's features. His men-at-arms stirred in the shadows, sharing furtive looks as if asking why MacElgin would suffer this humiliation.

"He's a coward," Jamie said in amazement with a low nervous laugh, and when that drew no reaction, he flicked his sword across Duncan's face, flinging off his veil and wimple and raising a tiny trickle of blood down his cheek. "Look, I'm slicin' him to bloody ribbons, and he's lettin' me."

"Stop it, Jamie." Her voice trembling with fury, Marsali ran down the stairs toward him. "I'll go with you, but you have to promise to stop hurting people."

Duncan barely felt the hot sting of pain in his face as his own anger, frustration, and anxiety over Marsali trampled down the tender vow he had made. He had been born into violence. He didn't have the faith to rely on some intangible power that might or might not deign to help him.

"Get her into the boat." Jamie gave Marsali a cursory glance before returning his narrowed gaze to Duncan. "And watch yer backs. I'm smellin' a trick."

The first shaggy MacFay clansman took a tentative step toward Marsali; Duncan had the broadsword in his hand and he sent Jamie sprawling flat on the floor between Owen and Lachlan before anyone realized what had happened. In the blink of an eye he had become the barbaric warrior that the world revered and feared. The power he exuded was palpable. Johnnie grinned in relief.

Jamie's breath quickened as the sword pressed against his

Adam's apple. "Kill him," he said through his teeth. "Somebody kill the bastard. He's hurtin' Jamie."

No one moved.

Duncan stared down at MacFay in dispassionate silence; he was acutely conscious of the footsteps that had stopped outside the door, of Marsali's pale anxious face beside him. He was agonizingly conscious of every minute detail.

He felt his own clansmen watching him in concern, tension mounting in the confined quarters. His vision blurred. His mind turned inward, spiraling back in time.

As if he were standing at the end of a tunnel, he heard Jamie's voice, low with panic and resignation, asking, "Well, what are ye waitin' for, MacElgin? Murder me and be done wi' it."

Murder.

Murderer.

He's murdered his own mother and father.

She was stabbed twenty-seven times in the back.

Aye, slit his da's gullet, he did. The blood was everywhere. His old auntie didna stop screamin' for days.

Marsali watched Duncan in an agony of compassion, as did his three silent clansmen. For all his power and position of dominance, the vulnerability he exuded broke her heart. If he had not confessed to her that morning in the castle, she might not have understood the burden of guilt and horror that had tormented his soul since childhood. Everyone expected him to slit Jamie's throat. No one realized why he wavered.

His hand shook as it held the sword.

She felt powerless. There was no magical spell to reach into the dark place where he had retreated, reliving God only knew what nightmare. Worse, part of her wished he would kill Jamie and be done with it.

The MacFay clansmen waited in wary fascination for Duncan to make his move. It was a moment that would be talked about over Highland peat fires for decades to come, exaggerated until it reached epic proportions.

"Duncan." Marsali couldn't suppress the apprehension that quavered in her voice. Couldn't he hear the footsteps outside? Had Jamie positioned more armed men around the convent? How long would the rival clansmen stand in awe of the legendary warrior before realizing the MacElgin stood paralyzed by scenes from his own past?

With his sword positioned at his rival's throat, he held the power of life or death in his hand. But the decisive battle was being waged within himself.

The door opened slowly. Slow-moving swirls of mist and diffused light filtered over the strange tableau within the belltower. Duncan lifted his head. The movement looked forced and mechanical, like a statue coming to life against a backdrop of smoke. The look that passed between brother and sister pulsated with remembered pain.

"Judith," he said, shaking his head in denial.

Judith's horrified glance encompassed the unmoving man on the floor, the sword in Duncan's hand, the unkempt clansmen who crouched like ghouls in the pale light.

"What have you done, Duncan?" she whispered, her skin as white as the linen of her coif.

"Nothing." He stared down at Jamie, his face expressionless. "Get up, MacFay."

Marsali darted around Jamie to come to Duncan's side. His gaze still riveted on Jamie, he hooked his free arm around her waist and drew her against him.

"I told you to get up, MacFay," Duncan said wearily. "I'm beginning to have second thoughts about keeping my word."

Jamie slowly rose to his feet, his face humiliated as he met the shamed gazes of his retainers. "What the bloody hell is wrong wi' the lot of ye?" he howled in indignation. "There are five of you! He's the only one wi' a weapon, and ye made no move to stop him."

"He wasna' hurtin' ye, Jamie."

Jamie rounded on the man who'd dared to speak. "Who do ye serve, a man who's sold his soul to the Sassenachs, or Jamie?" The silence that met his demand for a show of loyalty further infuriated him. He stomped his foot. His voice rose in childish rage. "Who do ye serve, yer chieftain or the MacElgin? If ye serve me, then prove it now."

"This is a nunnery, Jamie."

"He didna hurt ye, lad."

He snatched up his sword, swinging it over his head in desperation as if he could rouse some primitive bloodlust in his kinsmen. "Who do ye serve?" he shouted, his hair tangling in his empurpled face.

Duncan gave a deep warning growl and pushed Marsali back into Johnnie, who caught her in a firm protective grasp.

One by one Jamie's men began to unbuckle their sword belts, tossing dirks, swords, and targes into a pile at Duncan's feet. The clatter of metal faded into the harsh stridor of Jamie's breathing.

"We're servin' the MacElgin," announced the short muscular MacFay lieutenant-at-arms known simply as Torc, which meant "boar" in Gaelic.

"Aye, the MacElgin!"

Jamie made a lunge at Duncan, only to be snagged like a spider in a web as four of his own kinsmen caught him by the arms. "What do you want us to do wi' him, my lord?" Torc asked.

Duncan hesitated. Part of him fiercely wished he had been allowed to fight Jamie and settle this thing between them man to man. There was, after all, a great measure of peace to be had knowing your enemy was dead. And now he had to face the consequences of following his damned conscience. Now he had to absorb a half-dozen MacFays into his own ragged clan.

He threw down the broadsword, raking Jamie with a coldly disgusted glance. "Your first act of fealty to me will be to take this man to the British fort and have him incarcerated for his crimes. Get him the hell out of my sight."

Jamie struggled against the arms confining him. "Ye are a black demon. And she's a witch!"

"Hush your stupid mouth, MacFay," Marsali burst out angrily. "Another word and I'll be killing you myself."

For a moment Jamie fell utterly still, like a puppet whose strings had been severed. Then he stared past Duncan to Marsali with a loud wail of immature desire underlaid with desperation. Compelled by curiosity, Duncan turned to gauge Marsali's reaction and felt an unwanted stab of jealous resentment at the flicker of compassion commingled with disdain in her eyes before she glanced away.

Jamie's men dragged him outside, darting apologetic looks at the two nuns who flanked the doorway in speechless bewilderment. Duncan felt suddenly drained, uncertain what his sudden reluctance to kill in self-defense meant in terms of his future. A man who had built his fame on fighting. Uncertain anymore of who or what he was.

Then Marsali broke away from Johnnie and burrowed up against him, her small warm body a promise of love and acceptance no matter how the rest of the world would view him. He caught her chin in his hand, tipping back her face, and kissed her in full view of the two nuns and his scruffy clansmen.

"Duncan," Marsali whispered, her eyes alight with mischief and joy, "the Reverend Mother is watching."

He sent Judith an amused glance. "So she is, but then I only promised her I wouldn't do any killing. I never mentioned anything about kissing."

Her mouth was warm and sweet, his kiss both rough and gentle. Ignoring his enrapt audience, he ran his hands down the delicate arch of his back and pulled her against him until she gasped for breath, breaking away with a dazed grin. He was afraid he would hurt her in his desperate anxiety to reassure himself they would never be apart again. This little brat meant the world to him.

Her soft laughter penetrated the moment of intense emotion.

He held her away at arm's distance, smiling despite himself. "You still find it amusing to kiss me, Marsali?"

"I can't help it, my lord. I keep thinking about the look on everyone's face when you were prancing about on the bench playing God."

Sister Bridget spoke from the doorway for the first time. "It was a little overplayed, all that thrusting about, although I have to admit he did manage to convey a certain sense of omnipotence."

"Thank you," Duncan said with a droll smile. His gaze moved to Judith, studying her face, searching for the key to self-forgiveness that had eluded him all these years. "I'm sorry for the disruption, but at least no blood was spilled."

"Except yours," Marsali said in soft concern, lifting her fingers to the dark red streak that would heal to scar his beloved face.

He caught her hand, gripping it in gratitude. "We'll be leaving your cloister now, Reverend Mother," he said quietly. "After we return the clothing we borrowed, of course."

"Of course," Judith said calmly, her gaze lowering from his fierce warrior's face to the fragile ethereal features of the woman he held like a lifeline. "But you, Marsali, you are supposed to take over for me in the infirmary tonight after chapel."

"No." The determination in Duncan's voice challenged her quiet authority. "We're leaving together."

Judith's expression did not change. "You've found her a suitable husband then. That's the only condition under which I will allow her to leave."

"I think so." Duncan did not speak for a moment, willing away the memory of the long-ago morning when Judith had left the castle for the convent. His father, the marquess, had offered to adopt the pale withdrawn girl as his own, but Judith had pleaded to be sent away, craving peace and solitude after a life of her father's abuse.

Duncan had been too drunk to even say goodbye. Until now he'd never even admitted to himself how he had missed her, depended on her.

"The man I've chosen loves Marsali very much," he said at last, "and although he is by no means a perfect choice, I'm afraid he'll have to do. Her friends have frightened everyone else away. At least he will protect her with his life."

"Does he love her?" Judith asked, amusement flickering across her stern features.

Duncan frowned. "Isn't that obvious?"

Owen nudged Lachlan in the ribs. "Who the devil is he talkin' about then?"

"I dinna ken," Lachlan answered in a baffled whisper. "Perhaps it's Johnnie."

"'Tisna me, ye half-wits," Johnnie said in annoyance. "It's himself, the chieftain."

"Ye dinna say," Owen said, sincerely astonished. "The chieftain and Marsali? I'd never have believed it. When did this happen?"

Lachlan shook his head. "I wondered why he was kissin' her."

Judith looked at Marsali. "And this match pleases you as well?"

Marsali grinned mischievously at Duncan, pretending to give the question serious thought.

He tightened his grip around her shoulders. "It had better please her because she doesn't have any choice in the matter. From now on she's doing what I tell her."

"I doubt it," Marsali said.

"So do I," Judith murmured.

"He could have saved everyone a load of trouble if he'd decided this a month ago," Marsali added. "Anyway, we'll all be leaving now."

Deo gratias," Judith said under her breath. "Thanks be to God."

There was a deep awkward silence. Duncan was dying to take off his habit and change back into his own shirt and trews. He couldn't even think about sharing his feelings with Marsali while wearing a dress. He couldn't keep his hands off her either. He couldn't resist touching and kissing her as a prelude to all the physical pleasure they would enjoy as man and wife. And he wished to ask his sister's forgiveness for everything he had done, and to reassure her that he had changed.

But these weren't the kinds of things a man could do or say in a convent belltower. So he had to content himself with a few well-chosen words and hope that they would convey the emotions he might never be allowed to express again.

"Judith," he began, "I want you to know—"

The tower erupted into an ear-deafening din as an unseen bell-ringer from above began to peal out the call for evening prayers. Duncan covered his ears reflexively; Marsali buried her head in his chest. Owen, Lachlan, and Johnnie gave vent to a few salty oaths, which, fortunately, due to the ungodly clanging, could not be heard by the Mother Superior and the convent headmistress.

Finally, just as the noise drove everyone to the door, and Duncan shouted, "Who is that numbskull in the belfry?"— the pealing came to an end.

Judith's voice rose with caustic emphasis in the throbbing silence. "That was your daughter, Duncan. And I am relieved to place the responsibility for her into your hands. Neither she nor your future wife show any sign of a religious vocation whatsoever."

Duncan looked as if the bell itself had hit him on the head. "My *daughter?* What daughter?"

Judith drew herself up. "We have named her Hannah Elizabeth. The doctor's wife gave her up when she was a bairn, and we have raised the girl the best we could. Unfortunately, she has your rather dominant nature, Duncan. She certainly does not have the makings of a nun."

Hannah came bounding down the stairs and hurled herself into Duncan's arms. As big as he was, the impact sent him staggering back into the courtyard. "Papa, I always knew you'd come!"

Stunned, Duncan put his arm out automatically to embrace her. His dazed expression was an amusing contrast to Hannah's exuberance. "Why didn't you tell me?" he asked Judith sharply. "Didn't you think I had a right to know?"

Judith lowered her gaze, unable to answer.

Marsali stood back to witness the poignant meeting with a wistful smile. "From the first time I broke up a fight between Hannah and the other girls," she whispered to Johnnie, "I felt a special bond between us. I just can't imagine it, all of us living together in the castle as a family."

"I canna imagine all of us fittin' into the boat," Johnnie retorted, shaking his head. "Oh, well. At least that queer mist is lifted."

Marsali glanced around in wonder. Nuns scurried toward the chapel, their veils wafting behind them like ghosts in the gloaming. What had made the mist disappear? There wasn't a shred of it to be seen.

Duncan held his daughter at arm's length, carefully, as if she too might disappear. "Did you know about her, Marsali?"

She turned, her heart lodging in her throat at the stark vulnerability in Duncan's voice. He stood between her and Hannah, his arm outstretched to encompass them both in his possessive grasp. He looked boyish and sinfully beautiful. The love brimming in his eyes was everything she'd ever dreamed of and more.

She flew to his side, grinning up into his face. "I always thought there was something a little familiar about her, my lord. And sometimes when I'd hear her swearing a blue streak in the dormitory, the image of you would cross my mind."

"But she didn't guess I was the chieftain's daughter," Hannah chimed in. "No offense, Papa, I always longed for this day, but I did expect you to dress a little more impressively."

Marsali leaned back comfortably against Duncan's broad ribcage. "Of course it makes perfect sense now. You do have his temper, Hannah. And his feet."

"She favors him a wee bit around the eyes too," Owen observed, joining the happy little trio.

Johnnie sauntered up to contribute his opinion. "Good thing she doesn't have his beard. Still, seein' the two of them standing there in those dresses, ye could take 'em for sisters."

Duncan swallowed a laugh. Joy was surging through him, so tender and unfamiliar that he was half afraid to trust it. It struck him with a sense of gratitude, as he looked at Hannah, taking in her young, hopeful face, that one good thing had come out of his misspent youth after all. He coughed to hide his emotions. Then he loosened his bodice with his free hand, his veil resting against his strong brown throat. "We'll change, and then we're getting out of here," he announced.

There were nuns, who were supposed to be in chapel, peeking at them from behind the broad colonnades. The convent schoolgirls had gathered in a giggling circle to see the scandalous excitement. Evening prayers had been forgotten; disorder spread through the cloister like an epidemic, and Judith was determined to restore peace to her cloister.

To add to the chaos, Owen had removed his veil to hold

the plums that Lachlan was picking from the convent's orchard, and Jamie could be heard yelling obscene threats to the men who dragged him down to the boat on the beach.

"You have to leave, Duncan," Judith said firmly. "Now. You may keep the habits. Quite frankly I shudder at the thought of you disrobing in public, but I insist you leave the cloister this very instant."

He smiled at her.

She almost smiled back.

"All right," he said. "We're going. I've got what I came for: a bride. Well, I've gotten more, actually. I've gotten a daughter into the bargain. Thank you for keeping the two of them safe."

Her lips compressed into a line, Judith gave him a faint nod and made a determined beeline for the chapel. Sister Bridget hurried after her but paused a few steps on the path to look back at Duncan.

A rueful smile flitted across her friendly face. "What a shame ye're not the abbess," she whispered with a chuckle. "I could've used a pair of shoulders like yours when putting up the henhouse."

Duncan grinned, white teeth flashing like a pirate's against his beard. "Don't give up hope yet, Sister Bridget. The abbess must be quite the athlete to row all the way from Ireland."

"Goodbye, Reverend Mother!" Marsali shouted from the convent gate, waving as the dark-robed figure ducked into the chapel, herding her charges in before her.

Hannah shook her head, her blue eyes mirthful. "Anyone would think she was glad to be rid of us."

Duncan gave them a gentle push through the gate, keeping a protective hand on each of their shoulders. "I can't imagine why," he teased them, and then he shook his head. Dear God, a wife like Marsali, and a daughter who had his temper. He had a feeling that all the battles he'd fought were scant preparation for the future.

They clambered down the sandy incline to the shore, splashing through tidal pools and cool sprays of surf. Jamie MacFay sat in the prow of his own fishing skiff, trussed up like a turkey with a gag stuck in his mouth. Someone had tied a bit of tattered plaid like a bow in his hair. Hues of silver mauve blended into the sky like watercolors. Starlight twinkled on the foamy waves.

"And we didn't spill a drop of blood," Duncan said with satisfaction as he helped Marsali into the boat. He sent a grateful glance of acknowledgment to his three clansmen. "In fact, it was the perfect military maneuver. My own troops couldn't have done better. I'm proud of you, men."

Owen, Lachlan, and Johnnie gaped at him in dumbfounded silence. They had no inkling how to respond. No one had ever praised them, for anything, in their miserable lives.

"It wasna completely perfect," Owen said humbly. "We did get our dresses wet, and I've ruined my stockings."

Lachlan settled down and onto the sailing thwart. "We probably should have helped Torc carry Jamie out of the belltower. As a courtesy, ye ken."

"Ye did a fine job though, my lord," Johnnie said with touching loyalty.

"Except for the part about playing God," Marsali remarked as she and Hannah squeezed down onto the damp floorboards at the bow, huddled together in preparation for the awful journey ahead.

Duncan gave the boat a powerful shove from the shoreline and jumped on board as Johnnie propelled them over the waves. The world looked placid and endlessly gray—until he looked down at Marsali and realized that because of her the familiar ache of loneliness and self-recrimination was slowly ebbing away from his awareness like the tide. A dozen incongruous emotions were attacking his composure all at once. He felt like laughing and hugging her and yelling at the top of his lungs that she was his woman.

He was beginning to view life with a touch of her delightfully skewed perspective.

He sat down heavily on the rowing thwart, pretending to scowl. "What was wrong with the way I played God?"

Marsali raised her brow as he hiked his habit up to his massive horseman's thighs. "I don't know. It was a little too theatrical for my taste. All that stabbing and twirling about on your toes."

Duncan's scowl deepened. "It's called thrusting and

parrying. It happens to be an art. Most people around the world consider me a master at it. There are poems—"

"That might be, my lord," Marsali argued mildly, "but I doubt if God would go around stabbing bits of boiled cabbage and hopping over soup bowls."

Hannah nodded in agreement. "It was a bit much, Papa."

"I liked it, my lord," Owen said, picking up a bucket. "It was the finest interpretation of God I've ever seen."

Johnnie handed Duncan the other oar. "You were so convincing that I half expected thunder to boom in the background when you held up that spoon to the sky."

Duncan was silent.

"In fact," Johnnie continued, "I've told the lads many times over, 'The chieftain reminds me of God.' Haven't I, lads?"

Owen frowned. "Actually, Johnnie, I think what ye used to say was, 'The chieftain acts like he's God.'"

Duncan shook his head. He didn't want to go from being their demon to a deity. Only Marsali had always seen him for what he was: a man with strengths and failings, a man who had struggled to overcome his past and who had made inevitable mistakes along the way. For all her inexperience, she possessed an emotional wisdom that would make her father proud.

The stars were slowly fading from the sky like distant candle flames extinguished in swirls of smoke. Something inside him was dying too, the old regrets crumbling to ashes as hope was reborn.

"How do we know which way to row?" Lachlan asked, gazing around in consternation.

"We'll follow the hawk," Duncan said, and everyone glanced up as the graceful bird rode an air current, gliding in lazy circles above the sea.

A few minutes later another tiny boat bobbed into view. Marsali and Hannah stopped bailing water with their buckets to watch. Three rather robust-looking nuns rowed vigorously past them while a fourth sat in the middle of their sturdy little craft, praying her heart out.

Marsali waved at them, shouting, "You must be the Irish abbess!"

"Yes, I am," the nun at the stern answered in surprise.

"We're looking for Our Lady of the Sea cloister, and we're lost."

"You're about an hour away," Duncan said, pointing with his oar. "Look, you can just see the tip of the belltower over there."

The little Irish boat hovered for a few moments in the water. The three nuns stared in complete silence at the four men dressed in habits who nodded and smiled politely.

"Thank you," the abbess said at last, snatching up her oar. "God bless you . . . sisters. I think."

Cramped. Cold. Wet. Miserable. Ravenous. The six intrepid voyagers were numb by the time dawn broke and found them approaching the misty coast of the cove. The rocks of the shore protruded from the water like the teeth of a predator waiting to devour the tiny boat.

Marsali groaned and threw down the oar she had taken over for Owen, falling forward in boneless exhaustion into Duncan's lap. "I'm dead."

Duncan grunted. He was too tired to keep her from sliding over his knees and hitting the floorboards with a wet thud. He stared down at her in sympathy. Every muscle in his body twitched in protest. His bones felt frozen, fused together in agony.

"We have to get married," he said weakly.

Marsali's eyes dropped with the weight of her gritty lids. "I'm too tired to be a bride . . ."

Her voice trailed off. In the cove, candlelight winked like a welcoming beacon from the leaded cabin windows of the wizard's shipwrecked sanctuary.

"We're home, Papa!" Hannah shrieked in excitement, crawling over the inert figures of Owen, Lachlan, Johnnie, and Marsali to wrest the oar from her father's rigid fingers.

Duncan grunted again. A more intelligent response was beyond him. Several yards away, Jamie's former retainers dragged their skiff ashore. The sight of the arrogant young Highlander gave Duncan a desperately needed shot of energy. His blue eyes burned with remembered anger.

"Little bastard," he said, grabbing the oar that lay across Marsali's chest.

She forced her eyes open, frowning up into his face. "What did you call me?"

"Not you. It's MacFay. I'd forgotten he has to be dealt with."

Owen moaned, regaining consciousness. Marsali exerted the last of her strength to struggle back onto the thwart.

"Home," she whispered, tears filling her eyes.

Duncan looked out at the waters, concentrating on rowing them in, closing his mind to the nostalgic affection on her face. Not in a hundred years would he call this inhospitable pile of rocks home. He fought an irrational urge to turn the boat around and set sail for anywhere but here.

Johnnie sat up, rubbing his eyes. "Look, my lord. The whole clan has turned out to welcome us back."

Duncan raised his skeptical gaze to the castle. "The first clansman who makes a comment about the way we're dressed is spending a week in the dungeon."

"It's not the clan." Marsali said, the fear in her voice penetrating his fatigue. "Those are redcoats on the cliff waiting for us. They're armed, by the look of it."

No one said anything. Duncan lowered the oar, scanning the cliffs with a still face. Like a fool, he'd forgotten his promise to keep Marsali hidden away. He'd forgotten that she and the men in the boat were practically marked outlaws whom even his rank and influence might not be able to protect.

He picked up the oar. His jaw set in tight lines, he slowly resumed rowing toward the cove. "I'll take care of this. Stay in the boat." He looked up briefly at the five expectant faces that watched him. "For God's sake, just behave yourselves this one time."

Chapter

32

God might not actually deign to indulge in a common sword fight, but Duncan decided He enjoyed a good joke. On him.

It was probably the most important negotiation in Duncan's memory. It had probably never mattered more that he make a formidable impression. After all, Marsali's life was at stake, and at least a hundred muskets followed his slow climb up the cliffside path.

And he was confronting his military inferiors in a dress. The situation called for full-scale bombastic male bravado.

He strode up directly to Major Darling, who did not immediately recognize the bearded man in a black dress as Europe's foremost military genius. And when he did recognize Duncan, his mouth dropped open and incoherent baby-bird noises sounded in his throat.

A tiny breeze fluttered across the clifftops. A buzz of speculative astonishment ran through the soldiers standing in readiness to shoot. From his peripheral vision, Duncan noticed Eun the hawk lighting on a nearby ledge as if to protect Marsali.

Duncan took Darling's arm to draw him aside. "I wish I could have let you in on this earlier, Darling. It wasn't that I didn't trust you."

The major blinked, lowering his voice to match Duncan's conspiratorial tone. "Let me in on what?"

"The secret mission to flush out the Jacobite leader. Surely you know about the British sentry who was severely beaten down the coast not a few days ago?"

"Of course I know, my lord. Why do you suppose I have my entire regiment blocking the cove?"

"Because you're a damned fine soldier, that's why," Duncan answered. "Because as long as you're in charge, no Jacobite traitor can carry out his subversive activities in safety."

"Well, it's true that I—"

"And because you are obviously a man of the highest integrity and dedication, Darling, I am going to take you into my confidence." Duncan paused, giving the major an inscrutable but measuring look. "You have wondered why I'm wearing a dress, haven't you?"

"No. Well, yes. Actually, it did cross my mind."

"Of course it crossed your mind, Darling. Nothing would get by that iron-trap brain of yours, would it?"

Major Darling's heart palpitated fiercely beneath his scarlet coat. This was the highlight of his career. Finally. Finally, he was to become privy to a genuine military genius's modus operandi. He who had dreamed of foreign bivouacs and battles that made history books, but who had been banished to this lonely Scottish coast to harass women and pigs.

"I can trust you, can't I, Darling?" Duncan said in a voice that hinted of intrigue and promotions.

"Count on it, my lord," the major said, his stout body trembling in anticipation.

"It was a secret mission."

"Ah."

"A mission ordained by the prime minister himself."

"Aaah. I thought so, my lord." He glanced meaningfully at Duncan's long black skirts. "What else could it have been?"

"That man trussed up like a turkey on the beach is your Jacobite leader. He attacked the colonel. It was a tricky operation, Darling. A dangerous one that called for complete secrecy and disguise."

"The dress." Darling nodded knowingly. "Brilliant, my lord. But what about the girl? You know, the ambush commander?"

"She's one of us."

"One of—a spy? My God. It was a ploy all along to flush out the traitor, wasn't it?" Darling stared at Duncan with renewed respect. "Why else would the Crown send a man of your stature here? I am speechless with admiration, my lord."

"Yes. Well, see that you remain so," Duncan retorted, thinking there'd be hell to pay if he had to explain this mess to the P.M. "And in the meanwhile, I can trust you to deal with the turkey—I mean, the traitor, can't I?"

"His fate is sealed, my lord." Darling glanced back along the cliff at the short familiar figure who was avidly observing them from behind the shelter of a line of armed soldiers. "But what should I do with him? Abercrombie, that is? He begged me to protect him from your clansmen."

Duncan narrowed his eyes, tempted to tell him to push the sour little steward off the cliff. "Send the idiot back to the Lowlands where he belongs. And make sure my privacy is protected from here on. That's an order, Major. I'm going on a honeymoon."

"Yes, my lord," Darling said, giving Duncan a grave salute and shaking his head in amazement. Secret missions. Spies. Nuns' habits. So this was how it was done.

Duncan glanced down at the boat, hiding a smile at the sight of Marsali watching him through Johnnie's spyglass. "Now, about that damned road, Major?"

"Road?" Darling looked dejected. "It's been canceled, my lord. The mountains are impenetrable. We'll be moving down the coast within the month."

Chapter

33

The entire clan came running out of the castle as soon as the ragged party appeared on the promontory road. A moth-eaten MacElgin standard was hoisted from the parapets. At first, as Duncan heard the cries of excitement across the barbican, he allowed himself the ludicrous fantasy of believing himself welcomed home the conquering hero.

Overwhelmed, he stopped in his tracks. He had waited for years for this tribute. His head held high, he began to move toward his kinsmen, resentment melting away with every step he took. He had rescued their princess. They liked him.

"It's quite a welcome." He squeezed Marsali's hand, drawing her to his side. "Look at that. Cook must have been too hard on them while I was gone. They're glad to see me. We'll have a banquet tonight to celebrate our betrothal. They'll enjoy that."

She gave him a coy smile. "Actually, my lord, I think it's me they're shouting for. They're calling my name."

"You? You. Oh. Of course."

Had he taken leave of his senses? Men, women, and children practically trampled him in a wild stampede across the drawbridge to reach the tiny woman standing in his shadow. The chickens in the moat fluttered and clucked raucously. No one even noticed him.

He stood unmoving, like a rock stack in a rush of incoming tide. The clan hefted Marsali in the air and bore her toward the keep. She gave him a helpless little wave as she disappeared over the drawbridge. Duncan folded his arms across his chest and watched her, a scowl settling on his face.

Johnnie tramped up behind him. "Home at last. I'm dying to get out of this dress."

"They don't even know I'm here." Duncan gave a self-deprecating laugh at his own immature sense of disappointment. "Well, what did I expect? A miracle? Hell, I don't care. They're always going to hate me."

Johnnie shook his grizzled head. "I think they're rather fond of ye, if ye want the truth."

"Fond of me." Duncan swept up his skirts, shooing a chicken out of the way. "God, that's a joke."

"Look at it this way, my lord: If they didna like ye, you'd be standin' in a shower of arrows by now. Being ignored means ye're part of the clan. It's the best ye can expect."

Duncan leaned against the doorjamb of Marsali's chamber, staring with longing at the dainty figure sprawled across the bed. She opened her eyes and gave him a lazy smile, the covers slipping down around her waist. His gaze moved over her body, possessive, dark with passion, claiming every beautiful inch of her as his own.

"You've shaved," she said softly as he reached her side. "And changed."

He set down the bottle of French brandy and two goblets he'd bought on the nightstand. "I've sent for the old priest. We'll be married in the morning. Can you possibly stay out of trouble that long, lass?"

She pushed up against the pillows. Her auburn hair tumbled in curls around the demure lace collar of her nightdress. "I'm too tired to get into any trouble tonight."

He sat down beside her, brushing her hair from her shoulder, tracing his forefinger along the edge of her ear. She trembled with pleasure. "I'm never too tired for this."

She stared up at him, her luminous eyes bold and

expectant in the half-light. He leaned into her and captured her face in his hands, his heart beating in hard painful strokes with hunger for her. His kiss was slow and deliberate, a torment of sensual self-control. He tangled his hand in the silky tumult of her hair and moved over her. The muscles in his neck knotted with the intensifying sexual tension in the air. He dragged a deep breath into his lungs.

"I love you," he whispered against her mouth. "I want to sleep with you tonight."

Marsali sagged back against the pillows with a deep sigh. Desire flooded her body, pooling in the secret places with an aching that bordered on pain. Her breasts tingled, awaiting Duncan's touch. The fragrance of sea air and male musk caught her senses spellbound.

"Marsali, why is there mist coming in through the windows?"

"I'm not responsible for every change in the weather, Duncan," she said, resenting the distraction; she'd been waiting all summer for him to seduce her. "Perhaps it's the ghosts. Cook said they were very active while we were gone." She pressed her palm to the hard wall of his chest. "Duncan," she whispered in a husky voice.

"There aren't any ghosts."

"Then why did I see one reaching under the bed for the chamberpot?"

He glanced down as he felt her hand sliding inside his shirt. With a dark smile, he unfastened the ribbons at her throat and brushed his callused palms over her soft white breasts. She quivered in response. His blood pulsed; he was burning to conquer, to bury himself in her sweetness. "I want to make love to you, lass," he said with a groan. "I worship you, Marsali Hay."

Pleasure danced along her nerve endings. She caught her breath as he dragged his mouth down her throat, teasing her with light playful love bites. His tongue flickered across her nipples. He lifted her against him, her fragile curves fitting to his hard torso. Marsali's bones melted, and anticipation sent tingles down her spine.

"I am a woman ready to be worshipped," she whispered with a smile.

He grinned, drawing back to the other side of the bed with an indrawn breath. "Tomorrow night."

Her smile vanished. She bolted upright, indignantly dismayed. Her aroused body pulsed with frustration. "What?"

"The bridal bed, lass. You're coming to it as pure as the proverbial dove."

"Hell's bells, Duncan," she said grumpily. "That isn't fair. I thought it was finally going to happen."

He stretched out alongside her, staring at the delicate swirls of mist that wafted across the room. His heart thundered with a fierce need that was tempered by the tenderness he felt for her. She relaxed, snuggling into him. Their bodies touched in tantalizing restraint, their breaths mingled in the sweet chill air. Duncan closed his eyes, desire burning in his blood like the fine brandy he had found in the cellar.

"Tomorrow will be perfect," he said after a silence. "You'll have the wedding celebration your papa always planned, if not the prince he thought you deserved."

"The chieftain isna going to like this, Donovan."

"Put the candle down on the nightstand, Suisan."

"Och, look at the pair of them, sleeping in each other's arms like bairns. Isn't that the sweetest sight?"

"Watch out, Effie. The twins are headin' straight for that bottle of brandy."

Marsali stirred, the familiar voices penetrating the depths of her dreamless sleep. Resentfully she opened her eyes and stared up at the row of the curious but kindly faces observing her from either side of the bed.

"Do you all mind?" she said in a testy whisper. She burrowed up against Duncan's big warm body as he slept like the dead, his leg thrown over her ankles. "I'm marrying this man in a few short hours. I don't want to be yawning through my wedding vows."

"I tried to warn them," Effie whispered, pulling the pigs away from the nightstand.

"It's the ghosts, Marsali," Donovan explained.

Owen nodded from the foot of the bed, fatigue etching dark circles under his eyes. "We canna sleep fer all the din they're makin' in the guardroom."

"It's been like this every night since ye were gone," Cook added. "We've even summoned the wizard to exorcise them, but he hasn't arrived yet."

Duncan made a noise in his throat halfway between a snore and a moan. Marsali patted him on the back. "The chieftain can't be expected to solve every little problem in the castle," she whispered. "Go back to sleep, all of you. And—"

She glanced up in alarm as a loud tinkling crash resounded through the castle. "What the devil was that?"

"The ghosts," Cook said succinctly. "Giorsal is throwing a chamberpot at Bhaltair again. It's the eve of the great battle when he was slain. Every year it's the same argument between them, her begging him not to go, and then for the next six months she keeps everyone up weeping and cursing Bhaltair from the battlements because he got killed, and she killed herself."

Duncan opened his eyes, slowly pushing up onto his elbows as he realized he had an audience. "What the hell are all these people—those pigs—doing in my room?"

"They've come about the ghosts," Marsali said, plumping up the pillows and in a more conversational mood now that she was awake.

Effie sat down on the edge of the bed, hauling Ailis onto her lap. "They're keeping me up, my lord."

"Well, you're keeping me up," Duncan said, "and I don't like it. Agnes, why have you let the situation get out of control?"

Cook settled down comfortably beside Effie. "I understood mine was only a temporary command, my lord. Anyway, even a chieftain has only so much control over the supernatural, and I didna presume to usurp your power, now that ye've returned again."

"I understand exactly how Giorsal feels," Marsali admitted quietly, turning to look at Duncan. "I don't want you to go to war again either. You've done your share of fighting."

He pulled her against his shoulder and kissed the top of her head. "Nothing is going to happen to me."

"My father said the same thing the day he joined the rebellion."

No one spoke for several moments, out of respect for the man they had all loved.

Then Owen crept to Duncan's side of the bed, lowering himself onto the mattress with a sheepish smile. "Have ye had a nice rest after all that rowing, my lord?"

"No. I haven't had a nice rest, Owen. How could I rest when everybody and their pig is sitting on my bed? This is an outrage. Go away."

Donovan squeezed down next to Owen. "But they'll keep this din up fer hours."

"I don't care," Duncan said. "This is my bed, and the entire castle is sitting on it. Get out. You ought to be ashamed of yourselves, and I don't want to hear any talk of ghosts again. It's only mice in the walls anyway."

There was a brief silence. Then one by one the intruders filed out of the misty chamber, muttering amongst themselves, the pigs trotting after.

"Have ye ever heard a mouse that cursed, Effie?"

"No, Donovan. I have not. I've never seen one that wore a dress either, or that could throw a chamberpot."

"The chieftain and I wore dresses once," Owen remarked with a reminiscent smile. "But then we weren't ghosts. We weren't even mice, fer that matter."

"Poor Giorsal. She'll lose her husband to battle all over again."

The door closed on their whispered lamentations.

Duncan and Marsali stared across the room, each pretending not to hear the dull thuds rising from the guardroom. The ghosts.

"You weren't very nice to them," Marsali whispered when silence came again.

"I thought I was very nice under the circumstances. That's another thing wrong with this castle. The entire clan thinks it has the right to sleep in my bed whenever it likes."

"Well, you are the chieftain."

He was quiet for a moment, studying her face. He could hear Owen and Lachlan shouting at each other from somewhere in the depths of the castle. The sound roused in him an unexpected sense of affection rather than his usual annoyance. Marsali, their love for her, was the thread that bound them all together.

And it was Marsali who, indirectly, had led him to Hannah, offering him another chance at redemption, for completion, and again that sense of coming full circle as if there had been a guiding hand of gentleness to lift him out of the chaos he had created. But only now had he stilled his inner struggling long enough to perceive it. Only now had he begun to awaken from the nightmare of his past.

At last he'd begun to fit the broken pieces of himself into a whole, and to his surprise, it didn't form such a terrible picture after all. That night in the cottage, the violence and unhappiness that had preceded it, had cast a taint over his entire life. He had brutally murdered the man who had killed his mother. For the first time he could begin to forgive the act and see that the tragedy stemmed not from any inherent evil in himself as much as from evil circumstances.

He slid off the bed, casting a long regretful look over Marsali's sleekly rounded curves, nestled temptingly in the untidy bedclothes. "I'll bring the locksmith back," he thought aloud, turning to the door. "I'm not having my honeymoon with a pair of pigs in the bed."

"Don't forget the ghosts," Marsali called after him, but he didn't hear her, and she wasn't surprised.

Ghosts probably fell into the category of domestic matters in the castle. As the chieftain's wife, it would be her duty to take care of them.

She waited until she heard Duncan's footsteps fading down the circular slabs of the staircase. Then she leaped out of bed and ran to the door, calling, "Effie? Effie, where are you? I need your help!"

Marsali felt deep empathy for Giorsal. Poor woman. Bad enough to have lost your husband to a pointless battle, but to keep reliving your last evening together? What a miserable fate.

"What is it, Marsali?" Effie whispered, stifling a yawn behind her fist.

Marsali grabbed Effie by the elbow, yanking her out of her stupor. "To the guardroom. The ghosts deserve peace, Effie. So does the chieftain, and we're going to help them find it."

Chapter

34

Duncan stared through the lancet window of the guard-room, a deep frown furrowing his forehead. "This is ridiculous," he announced as Johnnie finished buckling on his backplate and then began the task of attaching the breast-plate waist straps to Duncan's sides. "I can't believe I'm doing this."

"Well, it was your idea, my lord." Johnnie scratched his elbow, looking Duncan over with a critical eye. "What about the loin guard?"

"Leave my loins alone. I'm fighting ghosts, not a tourna-ment."

"What about the gauntlets then?"

"Yes, give me the gauntlets. I don't want the annoying ghosts, if there are such things, to notice me."

"Here's your helmet, my lord."

"No, Johnnie. Not that one. The pin is bent and the spring-catch is warped. Even if I could force it on over my head, I'd never get it off."

A few moments later, Duncan stood fully outfitted in a suit of rusty armor, a lethal mace held in his right hand. "Well, how do I look?"

Johnnie stepped back, shaking his grizzled head. "I

suppose some would say 'tis an improvement over the dress."

"Yes, well, this is what a man does for love, Johnnie."

"I wouldna know." Johnnie winced as Duncan wheeled and lurched across the room, creaking with every step. "Do ye need me for anything else, my lord?"

"No. Go back out onto the walkway. If the damned ghosts make an appearance, chase them back inside. I'm not having Bhaltair and Giorsal ruining my wedding night."

That said, Duncan lumbered over to the left side of the unlit fireplace, which he flanked along with another rusty suit of armor on the right. With any luck he would exorcise the damned ghosts and be back in bed with Marsali before dawn. The desire she stirred in him had driven him to these desperate measures.

He closed his eyes. He leaned his shoulders back against the fireplace, heaving a sigh into his helmet.

He was asleep before Johnnie left the room.

Doublet, leg pieces, skirt. By the time she and Effie got to the breastplate, Marsali could barely breathe.

"I can't imagine how they fought each other on horseback in these things," she whispered tiredly.

Effie frowned. "Or used the chamberpot. Ailis, Alan, stop sniffin' around that fireplace. Oh, look, Marsali, here's the helmet we couldna find. Bend yer head. I'll put it on."

"It's too loose, Effie."

"Be patient, Marsali. The pin's not put in yet. Alan, leave that suit of armor alone. My God, this pin is bent. Hold still. One good whack should force it in place."

"*Ow.* You've got my nose stuck in the visor. And tell the twins to stop snoring. If Bhaltair hears that, he'll suspect something is up."

"My pigs don't snore, Marsali. They snort." Effie stepped back with a nod of satisfaction. "There. When Bhaltair goes to put on his armor tonight, he'll have quite a surprise. Alan, Ailis, come on. We've been assigned sentry duty at the door."

Marsali straightened, her metal joints groaning, and took the first of several clunking steps toward the fireplace.

"Has that other coat of armor always been standing there, Effie?" she whispered, the words echoing hollowly inside her helmet.

Effie paused at the door with her pigs. "I think it has, Marsali. It looks different, though, doesn't it?"

"Aye. A knight in rusty armor. There's something very compelling about him."

"Look at the size of his breastplate, Marsali. They dinna make men like that nowadays, do they?"

"Except for the chieftain." Marsali sighed, missing Duncan, wondering if he'd appreciate the sacrifice she was making to ensure a peaceful wedding night. "He reminds me of the chieftain, Effie."

"That's daft, Marsali." Effie's voice grew fainter as she and the pigs wandered out into the hall. "He doesna look anything like the chieftain. Except for the size of him."

The sound of arguing roused Marsali from her restless catnap. She straightened abruptly and banged her head up against the mantle. A metallic echo resonated inside the helmet.

"Cease yer prattling, woman, and help me on wi' this doublet," an unfamiliar male voice demanded.

A coat of chain mail went flying through the air. "Put it on yerself, idiot! I'll no be a part of yer death."

Marsali raised her visor, watching the semitransparent figures of a woman in a yellow silk robe and a stocky figure in a leather tunic engaged in a passionate fight before the fireplace.

"Stop quarreling this instant, the pair of you!" she scolded in a sharp voice. "You ought to be ashamed of yourselves, squabbling into eternity. What a waste of the afterlife."

Bhaltair turned his head toward her in bewilderment.

Giorsal gave her a look of curious resentment. "And who, pray tell, are ye to be givin' me orders in my own castle?"

Marsali shoved off the wall to approach them, clanking and groaning rustily with every step. As she reached Bhaltair, her knee piece popped off and rattled to the floor.

"I'm the chieftain's bride. At least I will be in the morning if I don't pass out from exhaustion at the altar, and if you don't ruin my wedding night with your endless fighting."

Bhaltair looked her up and down. "She's no like the others, Giorsal," he said in an excited voice. "There's something different about her."

"Are ye a ghostie too?" Giorsal asked, trying to peer into Marsali's visor.

Bhaltair floated toward the fireplace. "Be careful, Giorsal. She might be the castle boggle who cursed us. She might be the reason why we've spent the last two centuries fightin'."

"I'm not a mischievous spirit," Marsali explained patiently. "I'm only a witch, a reluctant one at that, and I want to help you find your way back to the other side. It can't be much fun repeating the worst night of your lives for two hundred years."

Giorsal's transparent face grew tragic. "God bless her. She wants to help us."

"Don't go to war, Bhaltair," Marsali said. "You'll only get yourself cleaved in two with a battle-ax, Giorsal will jump to her death from the window, everyone will go mad hearing the piper's lament for the next six months, and I won't have a happy wedding night."

Bhaltair sat down on the edge of the hearthstone, hanging his head in dejection. "Giorsal, jumping out of the window over me? I never realized she cared that much."

"A battle-ax." Giorsal folded down beside him. "I told you, Bhaltair. I warned you."

Marsali said, "Yes, you must stop arguing, or I can't break the curse."

"She's a kindhearted lass," Giorsal said reflectively, glancing at Marsali. "Do you think we should tell her about the hidden treasure as a reward?"

Bhaltair frowned. "What hidden treasure?"

"The fortune that the old man hid before he went off to the last rebellion."

"Never mind the hidden treasure," Marsali said. "I'd rather have a proper wedding night. Now, the two of you hold hands and imagine a white light moving—"

She turned awkwardly, gasping in alarm, as the other suit of armor that had flanked the fireplace began to swear and creak to life. Giorsal stared in disbelief.

"Why, I'd recognize that swearing anywhere," Marsali exclaimed. "It's the chieftain. What in the world is he doing here?"

Duncan rattled up before her, his voice incredulous. "Is that you in there, Marsali?"

She grabbed his arm in excitement, their gauntlets clashing together like cymbals. "They're real, Duncan. Real ghosts, and they're right here. Help us undo the curse. Tell them who you are."

He lurched past her. "Talk to who, Marsali?"

She turned, banging up against his backplate. He had flipped up his visor, and skeptical amusement flickered in his dark blue eyes. Marsali stared at the vacant hearthstone in dismay. She had wanted to share the supernatural moment with him. Dare she hope that she'd finally broken the curse and the poor souls could rest?

At any rate, the ghosts had disappeared. And even though they hadn't even bothered to say goodbye, she decided not to hold it against them.

"You're pulling my head off! Are you laughing at me? Duncan, that *really* hurts."

"I can't believe you did this," he said, grunting. "Anybody with two eyes could have seen the pin was bent."

"I only meant to help you." Marsali's face turned peevish inside the helmet as he paused from trying to tug it off her head. "I think you're actually enjoying this."

"Get down on the floor, Marsali. Now put your head between my knees. Of course I'm not enjoying this. There are quite a few other things I would prefer to be doing in this position. Removing a rusty helmet isn't one of them."

Marsali lowered herself, one stiff-jointed leg at a time, before him. Then just as Duncan removed his own helmet to give the matter serious attention, she raised her head and looked at the door.

A telltale tingling crept up her nerve endings into the nape of her neck. "Oh, no," she gasped in dismay. "Not again."

Duncan glanced around the room. "Are the ghosts back?"

"Worse. Uncle Colum is coming. What are we going to do?"

"Hell." Duncan placed his hands on either side of her helmet, tugging with all his might. "Come on," he said through his teeth. "Get this damned thing off before he blames me again."

The door creaked open. The wizard slowly entered, bringing a *whoosh* of cool herb-scented air into the musty guardroom. Duncan jumped to his feet, dragging Marsali up alongside him.

"I am here to exorcise the spirits of Bhaltair and Giorsal from the castle," Colum announced with an impatient wave of his wand. "I assume that you two are the aforementioned spirits and are ready to receive the peaceful rewards of the afterlife?"

He stepped toward them, alternately sprinkling salt from a black satin pouch onto the floor and water from a crucible until he had formed a circle around them. He raised his wand of polished yew adorned with owl feathers.

"Actually, we're Duncan and Marsali," Duncan said after a long hesitation. "And this isn't what it looks like."

Colum went dead still, his sharp gaze moving from one animated suit of armor to the other.

"It's me, Uncle Colum." Marsali raised her gauntleted hand in a wan little wave. "My helmet is stuck, and Duncan was trying to get it off. That's why I was on the floor, and he was pulling my head."

Duncan forced a chuckle. "You probably thought we were up to no good. It probably reminded you of the night you found us on the beach, and I got my hair caught in Marsali's cross."

Colum did not move a muscle. He did not say a word.

Marsali gave a hollow-sounding laugh. "Wouldn't it be funny if there really were an ancient Celtic courtship ritual that included pulling at your lover's head as a sign of affection?"

"Ahem." Duncan smile's cracked under the wizard's basilisk scrutiny. "Well, I think I'd better see about fetching that locksmith now."

"Don't leave me here in this helmet, Duncan." Marsali's voice was a thin wail of misery. "Uncle Colum, help me."

Colum's voice was crisp with exasperation. "Marsali, I can draw down the moon. I can command the wind. I have even managed to confer invisibility on the random petitioner. But as long as you insist on getting yourself into these human entanglements, I am helpless to intervene."

Duncan went to pull her into his arms, but they were like two tortoises trying to embrace, their armor preventing intimacy. "There, there, Marsali. I'll take care of you."

The wizard swept past them, a tingling current of cool air in his wake. "I must say, my lord, that this isn't exactly what I had in mind the night I commended my niece to your care."

"It isn't what I had in mind either," Duncan said bleakly as he stared down at the suit of armor he had hoped to marry in the morning. "Wait here, Marsali. I'm going to fetch that locksmith."

"At least the ghosts are gone, my lord," she called after him, her spirits rallying.

He paused at the door, smiling despite himself. Trust her to put the problem into perspective. The ghosts, all of them, were gone, and he wished them peace.

Chapter

35

A poignant silence swelled within the tiny castle chapel, broken by the occasional sniffle of emotion from the clansmen standing witness in the pews. Marsali, in white lace, looked the picture of maidenly purity as she knelt with Duncan on a rush mat at the altar slab, their heads bent for the priest's blessing.

"Father Patrick looks a bit out of sorts," Johnnie commented under his breath.

"Aye," Cook whispered, "and wasn't the man pushed into the moat the last time he performed a wedding Mass in this chapel?"

" 'Twas an accident, as I recall," Johnnie murmured. "The bride was chasing after the groom and got the wrong man."

Effie wiped away a tear with her apron string. "Marsali makes a beautiful bride, bless her wee heart."

"Thank heaven that locksmith got here in time," Owen said behind them.

Lachlan shook his head. "She'd have had a hell of a time managin' to take Communion through that visor."

The priest had begun the Mass; he stumbled over the long-unspoken Latin phrases. After all, most of the clan's married men had either abducted their wives and said to hell with formality, or they had followed the ancient custom of handfasting and a hasty wedding on the bridal stone beside the loch.

Then, at last, the chieftain and wee Marsali Hay rose to exchange their vows. Duncan towered over her like a mountain; his deep voice resonated to the rafters where not long ago Abercrombie had hung his plucked chickens.

"I, Duncan James MacElgin, take thee, Marsali—" There was a catch of emotion in his voice; it was the most beautiful moment of his life, but he had to stop, distracted not so much by the sobs, the sighs, the nose-blowing, but by his own beloved Marsali, interrupting in wide-eyed surprise, "Duncan *James*. I never knew your middle name was *James*."

To which Owen added, "Aye, 'tis a fine name, James. I've five cousins and an uncle in Inverness named James."

"Dinna forget the exiled king in Rome," Johnnie said, which set off another surge of conversation in the pews.

It didn't matter. Nothing could mar Duncan's mood, and when the ceremony was over and he took Marsali in his arms, when her soft red mouth touched his in a kiss of eager acceptance, they were the only two people in the chapel, the castle, the world.

He swept her up in his arms, grinning at the good-natured cheers that assaulted him as he ran down the nave. "Where are we going?" Marsali shouted, snuggled comfortably and waving at Effie over his shoulder.

"Where do you think, lass?"

"They're following us, Duncan."

"I'm faster."

"They're not going to let us go that easily." She pressed her face to his chest as he plunged down a covert passageway, immersing them in inky darkness. Her nose twitched in approval at the smell of sandalwood and male musk on his plaid. "I hear them coming!"

Suddenly they were in his room; she gave a squeal of surprise as she landed smack in the middle of a vast four-poster bed, then heard a series of heavy *thunks* as not one but six iron crossbars fell into place across the door.

Fat beeswax candles, strategically placed around the chamber, imparted a warm seductive glow to Duncan's austere face as he strode toward her. A peat fire smoldered in the hearth. The sound of approaching footsteps and jovial voices faded into muted clamor.

"I put the locksmith to good use before he left," Duncan murmured, casually lifting his hand to unbuckle his ceremonial sword belt. "We're all alone. They can't get in."

She stood before him, her breathing suspended, as the last of her undergarments slithered to the stone floor. Entranced, Duncan drank in the vision of her naked vulnerability. The raw power of the passion she aroused in him devastated his composure.

Marsali swallowed. It was all she could do to restrain herself from jumping into his arms.

"Duncan," she whispered. "You remind me of a beggar standing at a banquet."

"Just let me look at you, lass." He came up before her, his gaze bold and possessive.

She bit her lip, her lashes demurely lifting to peep at him. "Do you have to look in such detail?"

"You're so lovely I could stare at you all night." He gave her a wolfish grin, tilting her shy face up to his. "Fortunately, I have other things in mind."

He kissed her, long and deep, until she swayed in his arms, and he walked them backward to the bed. Marsali floated on a cloud of happy anticipation. Her husband. The chieftain. She gripped his well-muscled forearms, laughing softly as he lowered her beneath him.

"Take off your clothes, Duncan," she teased as he forced her deeper into the bed. "Here. I'll help you with the broach. It's only fair that I should have a look at what I've married too."

He leaned back against the velvet quilt, vastly amused by her aggression. "As I recall, you had a good look that day you ambushed me."

"Aye." She tugged at his broach. "I'd never seen a man like you before."

He caught her small hands to his chest, his eyes studying her with unabashed enjoyment. "You'll never see another one again—'bare as a boulder'—whether he's like me or not."

He released her to unravel his rough-woven plaid and remove his long saffron shirt. His heart thundered like a war drum as she pressed her naked body to his, as uninhibited as a young animal, her eager innocence a powerful aphrodisiac.

The thought came again that he did not deserve her. Her delicate grace, her warmth, her humor.

"I've wanted you for so long, Marsali."

She smiled wistfully. "And all the time I was yours for the taking."

"Aye." He slipped into a low Scottish brogue, his blue eyes teasing. "I want ye, Marsali Hay. And I'm takin' ye now."

The blood bequeathed by generations of Celtic conquerors surged in his veins. His wife. His hand trembled as he touched her sweet uptilted face, the swordsman's hand that had commanded great armies, the hand that held the power to save or destroy. But now it wielded only a weapon of devastating gentleness.

True to his reputation, he was ruthless in his seduction of the woman he loved. He was a master at making war. And making love.

Every caress was a calculated assault on her senses, every kiss a direct blow, until her mind reeled, her muscles quivered under his tender mastery. Marsali felt more vulnerable, more powerful than she had in her whole life.

His callused fingertips found secret pulse points on her body she had not known could yield such pleasure. He traced the fragile curve of her collarbone, the peaks of her breasts, the contours of her hips. Her blood stirred, pounding through his veins in arousal. Her body arched, flooded with pleasure that pooled in the pit of her belly and spread outward like the ripples in a pond.

"So delicate," he murmured roughly. "So small. I feel like a beast. Ah, Marsali, I love you so much. I can't imagine my life without you."

She shivered as his fingers slipped between her thighs, at the sensations his touch evoked. She flexed against him, desire misting her mind.

The deep guttural tones of his voice rasped in the silence. "Now you will be mine. It was meant to be—sooner or later, I would have taken you as my own."

She smiled into his eyes, enticing, inviting. She ran her fingers down the flat plane of his stomach. Shock waves of sexual excitement rolled over him, and his muscles clenched in anticipation. She felt like wet silk in his hand.

"Tonight," she whispered, her smile fading, "the end of a sweet magical summer. I love you, Duncan."

He shook his head. "No endings for us, lass."

He moved over her, firelight burnishing the harsh beauty of his face. The muscles of his powerful shoulders and torso tightened as he bracketed her between his arms. His eyes burned like blue flames, branding her, touching her with fire. Marsali felt a shimmering heat ignite deep inside her. Body, heart, soul. She belonged to him.

His breathing quickened. Her response was driving him wild. He raised her bottom in his large hands, kissing her and murmuring soft words of reassurance against her mouth. He nudged her thighs apart, positioning himself above her.

"There," he whispered, passion roughing his voice. And slowly he penetrated her, filled her, stretched the delicate tissue until she tensed, then relaxed, until he began to move and her body pulsed, absorbing his size and power, and he possessed her.

The pressure, the pleasure, built and built. She clutched his arms, straining into him, soft cries breaking in her throat. "I love you," she whispered, her heart soaring. "I've loved you forever."

Their bodies melded in a wild joyous mating. The perfume of smoke, beeswax, and sea mist mingled with the musk of their lovemaking. Magic embraced them. Their souls touched, soaring to the stars.

From the deep within the castle rose the sounds of celebration. The wailing of bagpipes wafted into the darkened chambers from the great hall. A lament of losses suffered, a plea for hopes renewed. Grief and love, pain and triumph. The poignant refrain of the human heart echoing out over eternity. Ghosts of the past, dreams of the future.

In his young wife's arms, the chieftain was home. In her body, his restless yearning found a respite and renewal.

Duncan led the small procession on horseback to the forgotten house at the edge of the woods. It was the house where Duncan and Cecelia had made adulterous love so many years ago, where Cecelia and her doctor-husband had lived until the day of Hannah's birth. It was the last place in the world Duncan had planned to visit. He wished he'd brought Marsali along to counteract his grim mood.

"I don't see the point in this, Hannah," he said. "It's better to put the past behind us."

Hannah slid to the ground from her horse. "I just want to see where I was born. I want to know where my mother lived. Will you come inside with me, Papa?"

"No." Duncan's face was resolute. "I will not."

Johnnie dismounted beside her, his voice gentle. "Your papa has more of a stomach for bloodshed than for shame, lass. I'll go with ye."

Hannah looked up appealingly at her father, but he pretended to stare into the woods until she turned away. His heart felt heavy as she disappeared with Johnnie into the house. The reminder of his adolescent wildness embarrassed him. Still, out of it had come this beautiful girl, and he was astonished at the capacity of his love for her.

Still, love brought a fresh crop of concerns with it. Hannah was sweet, headstrong, and naive. She didn't see life with the cynical vision of experience. Somehow she had grown up untainted by her sad beginnings and abandonment. Duncan could only pray that one day she would find a strong man to protect her. She had been sheltered all her life in that convent, and her innocence made her vulnerable. She was also a little wild, as he had been. That worried him.

He drew a breath of relief as she emerged from the house, her angular face so fragile and yet like his. "Are you all right?" he said roughly.

"Yes, Papa." She remounted her horse. Her voice was wistful. "I wish I had known my mother. I wonder if she ever regretted giving me away."

Duncan didn't know what to say. He hadn't known Hannah's mother well. Hell, he'd only been seventeen at the time. He spurred his horse down the hill. He listened absently to Hannah and Johnnie talking quietly as they followed. Then when they reached the graveyard, he realized that he could no longer hear them.

"What are you doing?" he called over his shoulder.

"I just want to see my grave, Papa," she called back.

He wheeled his horse around. "Dear God, Hannah. Not the grave."

But Hannah was already running over the hill to the tiny stone cross that Johnnie had pointed out. Duncan dismounted and started after her, swearing under his breath. The girl had his stubborn ways, God help her.

"I reckon a body has a right to see his own resting place, my lord," Johnnie said behind him.

Duncan stiffened, not taking another step. He could see Hannah on her knees, studying the unmarked grave for a sign that she had meant something more to her mother than this crude anonymous memorial. The sight broke his heart. *Had* she meant anything to Cecelia?

"Her husband probably made her pretend you had died to preserve his pride," Duncan said reluctantly, aching to ease her hurt.

"Look, Papa," Hannah murmured, not hearing him. "Someone has put some heather on the grave. Dried heather."

Duncan stared down over her shoulder. There was a sprig of dried white heather on the grave, so delicate he knew it would crumble if he touched it. Was it the heather he'd noticed before?

"Cook probably left it," he said in a subdued voice.

"White heather doesna grow in these hills," Johnnie said, frowning.

"Then it was a clansman." Duncan didn't want his daughter to harbor any illusions that might cause her more pain. "Forget about the past, Hannah. You have friends and family who will take care of you now. What your mother did is unforgivable, and I was little better."

Hannah nodded and rose to face him. "Everyone deserves forgiveness, Papa," she said with a tender smile, "even you."

* * *

The moon lit their way back to the castle. Hannah didn't speak, reflecting on her past. She felt sorry for her mother and the disgrace she'd suffered. What kind of woman had she been like? Hannah's father had said Cecelia was clever and pretty, but he offered little insight beyond that. But then he was still a mystery to Hannah himself.

She stole a glimpse at his forbidding warrior's profile. She couldn't believe this powerful man was her papa. Had he really been the demon who had terrorized the castle in his youth? Hannah had heard the most amazing stories about his misdeeds. What a wicked bastard he must have been.

She grinned, wishing she had known him then. She suspected she'd inherited his wild streak, which Mother Judith had worked so tirelessly to tame. Hannah was afraid the woman had failed, and she didn't miss the convent at all. Coming to the castle made her feel as if she'd sprouted wings. She couldn't wait to test her freedom.

Her father helped her dismount when they reached the keep. He looked worried, and she knew he cared about her.

"You're sure you don't want to come with me and Marsali when we leave, lass?" he asked. "We're both of us happy to give you a home."

"Oh, Papa." Tears shone in her eyes. "This is my home."

"This?" He cast a dubious glance around the castle grounds. Johnnie had ambled off for a few rounds of golf in the moat. "This crumbling old pile of stones?"

She nodded shyly, but the feeling in her heart was bold and sure. She loved this moldering castle with every fiber of her being. She accepted her eccentric clansmen with an unconditional love and loyalty that they, in their childlike warmth, were only too glad to return. Cook had welcomed her openly like the long-lost child she truly was. Hannah felt a sense of belonging for the first time in her life.

She was convinced she had been brought back here for a purpose. She had visions of restoring the castle to its former glory. She had no idea how she would accomplish this miracle, but Mother Judith had taught her the power of faith.

Hannah had found her heart's home.

Epilogue

I can't believe I'm a duchess," Marsali confided as she peered into the oversized trunk at the foot of the bed. "I'd barely gotten used to being the chieftain's wife, and now we're going away."

Effie handed her a chemise. Marsali tossed it half-heartedly into the trunk. "Things won't be the same in the castle without you and the chieftain—I mean, the duke."

"Aye." Marsali sighed, curling her bare feet under her bottom. "He'll always be the chieftain to me too, Effie, and he's promised we'll come back every summer."

Effie polished her spectacles on one of Duncan's shirts. "What a shame, Marsali."

Marsali vented another sigh. Duncan was about to be appointed to the War Office, a cabinet position he swore he would dedicate to keeping peace, and there were rumors of a possible diplomatic post. "Well, in the scheme of things, Effie, I know that world peace is probably a wee bit more important than my personal life, but I'm glad he won't be going off to battle, even though it means we'll have to stay off and on in London, which everyone knows is a wicked city."

"I almost forgot," Effie said, putting her hand to her

mouth. "I just found out this morning that Ailis is expecting."

Marsali looked up with a grin. "More piglets, Effie. Well, congratulations. You'll have your hands full." She lowered her voice. "Don't tell anyone—it's supposed to be a secret—but I'm expecting too."

"That was fast," Effie said, grinning broadly.

"Well, Effie, don't tell the chieftain this either, but I'm working on another secret. If I can't convince him to move back to the castle by the time the baby is due, I'm going to bring the whole clan to live in our Border manor house. Won't he be surprised?"

"I'll say. By the way, is he still going to have Jamie hanged for treason?"

"Worse. They're cutting off his lovely golden hair." Marsali grinned ruefully. "It's a good thing for Jamie that the British soldier he beat up recovered with only a few bruises to show for it."

"But I thought the chieftain swore to kill Jamie if he ever set eyes on him again."

"Aye, he did. But Jamie begged his pardon on bended knee and promised never to trouble us again. Duncan's arranged for his release, but he isn't happy about it."

"Marsali!"

Effie glanced at the door. "That's the chieftain bellowing for you again."

"The duke," Marsali corrected her, springing up from the floor as the door burst open and Duncan, exuding impatience and male energy, entered the room.

"Aren't you packed yet?" He stared in dismay at the garments strewn all over the bed. "My God, what have you done to my clothes? Put your shoes on. Good morning, Effie. Did you both forget about the ceremony at the cove?"

"What ceremony?" Marsali asked, frowning as he began to rearrange the things she'd tossed willy-nilly into the trunk, including his uniform and lead soldiers.

"Those are verra nice dolls, my lord," Effie said politely.

"It's 'his grace' now." Marsali shook her head wistfully at the thought. "What ceremony are you talking about, your grace?"

Duncan closed the trunk, suppressing a smile. "The ceremony to name the temporary chieftainess. She's to be sworn in on the white stone in fifteen minutes."

"She?" Marsali and Effie said in unison, astonished.

Duncan picked up his black cockaded hat from the bed. "Yes, she. The only person in this damned castle who seems to command enough power to keep the clan under control. The woman most respected by my dunderhead kinsmen." He paused, bowing with a broad grin at Marsali. "Except, of course, for my extraordinary wife."

Marsali smiled at his warm expression. "But then who . . ."

He put on his hat, then tossed her a pair of shoes. "Cook. Now come along. We can't be late."

There wasn't a dry eye among the clan. Every last person—the men, women, and children gathered at the cove—shed at least one tear of sheer terror at the prospect of what lay ahead. The chieftainess had already threatened to make them take a bath once a month.

Cook looked resplendent in her tartan knife-pleated kilt and plaid, with her badger-skin sporran at her ample waist, her sturdy legs encased in white woolen hose and silver-buckled shoes. Her iron-gray hair blew in the breeze, topped by a bonnet with a sprig of rue, the MacElgin plant.

Marsali grinned as she watched Duncan step up to the white stone, washed smooth by the sea, to hand Cook the wand of office. The crowd gave a half-hearted cheer when, next, he presented her with the traditional sword, which she would wear next to her rolling pin. Agnes wasn't a woman to forget her humble origins. His deep voice rose in the silence, sending chills of pride down Marsali's spine as he began to recount Agnes's deeds of bravery and loyal service.

It was a ceremony that called for something special, a supernatural touch to make it a truly memorable event.

Marsali gazed up at the horizon, where the blue-green Scottish sea met blue sky. She raised her arms, feeling power surge through her. A strong wind sprang up, churning whitecaps on the waves that pounded majestically against the shore. Thunder belched in the heavens. A violet-gold glow backlit the clouds.

Duncan paused to glance down wryly at his wife. An ironic smile softened his austere face.

She gave him a happy grin, immensely pleased with herself. It was just the right touch of magic. Not too overdone.

From the deck of the shipwrecked frigate that sat at a lopsided angle below them, the wizard and his wayward daughter couldn't have agreed more.

"I wish I could do that," Fiona said with a sigh of envy.

"So do I," her father said, patting her hand. "But please don't try today. You just might sink the ship."

Fiona glanced up at the hawk riding an air current above the cove. "I wonder if Eun will follow her to London. Do you think she'll ever use her power again?"

"Only time will tell, Fiona."

"What a waste. I tried talking to the seals again, Papa, but I don't think they understood me. Could you show me how just one more time?"

Colum sighed in irritation. "Solving the problems of two troublesome girls is not how I planned to spend my twilight years, Fiona. At my age I should be studying immortality, or battling demons. I only have so much energy left."

The ceremony had ended. Duncan climbed down the staircase of stones to lift Marsali into the air, spinning her around and around until they collapsed together on the soft white sand. Their laughter blended melodiously into the wild music of the wind and the sea.

Fiona giggled, clasping her hands to her chest in delight.

There was even a ghost of a smile on the wizard's gaunt face as he returned to his cabin and to the spells he had yet to cast for the magical child Marsali and Duncan would soon bring into the world.